Retrograde Planet

David G. Gibson

First published in Great Britain

ISBN: 978-1-78003-829-2

Pen Press is an imprint of
Author Essentials
4 The Courtyard
South Street
Falmer
East Sussex
BN1 9PQ

A catalogue record of this book is available from the British Library

Cover design Jacqueline Abromeit

MONDAY

CHAPTER ONE

The restoration work was going well. The *Loch Tredwell* lay port side against the quay, gangways fore and aft. Her jib and three stepped masts thrust nakedly into a rare blue sky. Each mast supported a set of yards, the whole held in place by an array of standing rigging. Below a voluptuous figurehead, Cant and Dick had the camera ready on its tripod, atmos microphone clad in a wind muffler. In the morning sunshine everything looked perfect. Almost too perfect, Buerk thought.

Pacing between the forward gangway and a Portakabin, his portly frame bursting from his trademark leather gilet, Cant paused at his approach. 'Might have a problem, boss,' he said. 'Security guard's gone AWOL.'

Dick nudged open the door of the Portakabin to reveal an empty interior. T-shirt and tight-fitting jeans clung to his lanky figure. 'There's a full mug of tea on his desk and it's stone cold.'

Already running late, Buerk glanced at his watch. 'Must have forgotten about us and gone off on his rounds,' he said. The last thing he needed was this pair having to cool their heels for much longer. Dick had already started to wander off, and there was another reason for cracking on. 'Right, we'll have to start without him. Got held up by the deputy principal's office insisting I attend a meeting with him at two.'

Cant's lip curled. 'Won't be in your best interests if it comes from Hornblower.'

'That's putting it mildly, Genghis,' Buerk said. 'We'd best push on.'

While they had been talking Dick had wandered beyond the forward gangway. 'Is it just me,' he called, 'or should there be smoke coming from the stern like that?'

Alarmed, Buerk rounded the gangway blocking his view and spotted the thick pall of smoke billowing from the stern housing of the vessel. It was already drifting away downwind. 'Quick, Genghis,' he said. 'Call the fire brigade. Now.'

Out of the corner of his eye Buerk caught another movement. The smoke had initially screened an inflatable emerging from the starboard side of the vessel. With a roar from its outboard motor, it began to pick up speed as it cleared the smokescreen, bucking wildly downriver against the hard chop of the tidal flow. Two figures sat in the stern, the bow almost completely out of the water. One man crouched low over the tiller, his face turned away from them. Even in a sitting position, the man alongside towered over his companion. As they sped away, the hood of his fleece was whipped off by the wind-rush. Buerk caught a glimpse of buzz-cut, fair hair and the glint of gold from an earring. Then they were gone under the bridge and round a bend in the river.

Dick looked mystified. 'Where did they spring from?'

He didn't get an answer. Cant was busy talking rapidly into his mobile while Buerk was heading at a run towards the aft gangway.

'Where are you going, boss?' Dick called after him.

'Might still be somebody on board,' Buerk threw over his shoulder. 'Better make a quick check.'

'Maybe not a good idea, boss,' Cant bellowed. 'Fire brigade's on its way.'

Buerk was already at the top of the gangway. The smoke was coming from what had been the officers' quarters in the stern beneath the poop deck. As he reached the open doorway he caught a glimpse of a man lying motionless on his side. His face showed signs of a recent beating, but the real shock was the deep gash in the back of his neck. There was no obvious sign of life in the prone figure but Buerk thought he should at least try to drag him clear of the cabin, just in case.

He made a grab for the man's shoulders, still distracted by the wound in his neck. There seemed so little blood oozing from such a gash. A sudden whooshing roar jerked his head up. Inside the cabin, a wall of flames leapt into the air around the feet of the prone figure. He caught a faint whiff of paraffin. The noise and the heat from the flames made him take an involuntary step back. He caught his foot on a loose rope and found himself sitting on the deck clutching nothing but the man's jacket, which had come away in his hands. That was when he spotted the gas cylinder attached to a blowtorch. The flames were already licking around its base. Still clutching the jacket, he scrambled to his feet and made a dash for the gangway as though his life depended upon it (which it probably did).

He was halfway down the gangway when there was a loud explosion behind him. He felt a warm wind at his back, such as might have come from a desert storm. It seemed to pick him up and toss him down the gangway as though he were a rag doll. He landed with a dull thump on the quayside, his forehead taking the brunt of the fall. At some point he thought he heard the distant sound of a klaxon, but inside his head it had all gone terribly dark.

'Boss. You okay, boss?'

Seated on a packing case, Buerk was having a plaster applied over his left eye by two ambulance men. They finished checking him over and gave a parting nod of approval.

Cant's concerned features swam into focus. 'You look like shit, boss.'

'Flattery will get you nowhere, Genghis,' Buerk said. 'Apart from a faint roaring in my left ear, I'm just dandy.'

Under the bright floodlights, the sight of firefighters rolling up their hoses and carrying them down the aft gangway told him that somehow the fire had been contained. He gave a shiver of revulsion as he remembered. 'I saw a body in there,' he said.

'Take it easy, boss,' Cant said. 'There's a detective wants to have a word. DI Munro is the one in charge. Matter of fact, two female detectives seem to be running the investigation. They've spent the last half-hour with forensics and the crime scene boys inside the cabin – must have a strong constitution to face that prospect.'

Dick gave Buerk a sly nudge. 'Wait till you see the head honcho, boss,' he said. 'She's quite a looker.'

Buerk shot his sound man a jaundiced look. He'd heard the rumours around campus about Dick's amorous adventures. 'Get real, Moby. I'm the one who's had a bang on the head.'

Time passed. Remembering his appointment with Hornblower, Buerk was on the point of getting up to ask how much longer they were to be kept waiting when the small huddle on deck broke up, the corpse was conveyed on a stretcher down the gangway to the waiting van, and one of the detectives detached herself from the others and headed towards him. Long legs, athletic figure and red hair tied back from her face elicited more than one admiring glance from the retreating firefighters as she stepped off the gangway.

The effect on Buerk was enough to make him forget about his deputy principal. Guessing mid-thirties, he was already on his feet as she flashed her warrant card.

'Acting Detective Inspector Munro,' she said. 'You appear to have averted a major disaster.'

'Felt fairly major to me,' Buerk said, struggling to gather his wits as intelligent green eyes fixed him with a frank appraisal. He wanted to say something witty or smart like, *Is that 'acting' as in 'from central casting' or are you waiting, like me, for someone to decide if your face fits?*

Looking into those eyes, he decided the really smart thing was to say nothing. There was something about her, hard to define. A certain guarded quality in that face in which a spray of freckles around the nose showed through the lightly applied make-up. On the surface she looked in control, but underneath he thought she might have been touched by something that had left its mark.

'Sorry to keep you waiting.' Her apologetic smile flickered all too briefly. 'No pun intended, but the forensic team like to strike while the iron's hot.'

Buerk had been about to say he quite understood, only Cant, as usual, got in first. 'Whereas I suppose you think we've got all day?' he said.

The smile become a frown. 'Mind if we sit down?'

This time Buerk was faster off the mark. 'Be my guest.' He gestured for her to sit and joined her on the packing case. The others hovered nearby.

Buerk caught a whiff of a floral perfume. She wore a lightweight beige jacket over a green cotton blouse and slacks of a darker shade. In the late-morning sunshine her ponytail seemed to spill a trail of fire. He wondered what it would be like to touch it.

She looked at Buerk. 'I gather you tried to rescue the victim?'

Buerk ran a rueful hand through his hair. 'Fat lot of good it did him.'

'It was brave of you to try. You sure you're okay?'

'Yeah, fine.'

'Kinda fell down on the job though,' Dick said.

She shot Dick a look that caused his smirk to morph to a look of injured innocence. She turned back to Buerk.

'Did you recognise the victim?'

Buerk shook his head, which caused him to wince. 'I assume from the uniform it was the security guard we'd arranged to meet.'

Her reply was noncommittal. 'In the brief time you had, did you manage to see anything you thought might be significant?'

Buerk shivered. 'I noticed somebody'd had a go at rearranging his face, then I saw a hole in his neck and a trickle of blood. I figured it might be too late for him, but I thought I'd try to pull him clear.' He shrugged. 'The heat from the flames drove me back and I ended up with the poor sod's jacket. When I spotted the gas cylinder I figured it was about to blow any second and decided discretion was the better part of valour.'

A smile flickered briefly. 'Thanks to you we did recover the jacket and you did the smart thing, which probably saved your life,' she said. 'You'll appreciate there wasn't much left by the time we arrived on the scene, so anything you noticed, however inconsequential it might seem, could be a help to us.'

'On health and safety grounds alone that blowtorch and gas cylinder shouldn't have been left in the cabin, nor should a loose rope have been left lying around. They're fairly hot on that kind of thing here, so those items were out of place.'

'That's useful,' she said. 'Anything else?'

'There was that inflatable, of course,' Dick said. Hovering nearby, he was clearly trying to make amends for his earlier crassness.

She looked at him sharply. 'What inflatable?'

'Shot off downriver just after we became aware of the smoke coming from the stern,' Buerk said. 'Sounded like it had a powerful outboard motor. Couldn't say for certain it came from the *Loch Tredwell*, but quite a coincidence, don't you think?'

She digested the information. 'Potential witness at any rate. Did you happen to get a look at who was on board – the inflatable, I mean?'

Buerk frowned. 'There were two men aboard. The drifting smoke acted as a screen, initially obscuring them. One was crouched low in the stern so I couldn't see his face, but the other guy was big.' He raised his hand to indicate the man was taller than himself. 'Buzz-cut hair, gold earring. They were gone in a flash. The pair must have been heavyweights; the bow was really high in the water.'

'Big guy making his getaway had to be a troll,' Dick said.

This time DI Munro rose to her feet, gesturing for Buerk to do likewise. 'Can I have a word in private?'

'Sure.'

There was a distinct coolness in her tone as she first wagged an admonishing finger at Cant and Dick. 'Detective Sergeant Lennox will be coming to take statements from each of you,' she said. 'Don't either of you move from this spot until she says you're free to go. Do I make myself clear?'

'Perfectly,' Cant said.

'As crystal,' Dick added.

Buerk followed her in silence until they stood out of earshot of the others.

'You don't have your sorrows to seek with that pair,' she said bluntly.

8

'Look,' Buerk said, beginning to feel a trifle irked at the way his morning had panned out. 'Can we get something straight right from the start, so there's no misunderstanding?'

'Shoot.'

'I have to work with these guys...'

She looked him straight in the eye. 'The world can be a cruel place, Mr...'

'Buerk.'

The hard look wavered.

Buerk folded his arms, finding it easier now to get really annoyed. 'Asking questions is one thing. How are you at listening?'

Legs spread challengingly, her body language mirrored his own. 'Try me.'

'They're not bad lads. We came here to do a job and it's gone spectacularly pear-shaped. Since then, they've been cooling their heels waiting for you to get on with your job. I'd forgotten momentarily about the inflatable; Moby was just—'

Her eyebrows shot up. 'Moby?'

He shot her an irritated look. 'Dick... that's what we call—'

She held up her hands to stop him. 'Never mind,' she said. 'Tell me, what kind of outfit are you, Mr Buerk, or do you have a first name I could use?'

He shrugged. 'The name's Angus and we're part of the television unit at New Metropolitan University.'

She looked puzzled for a moment and then enlightenment dawned. 'Didn't it used to be King's University?'

'That's right,' he said. 'We merged with Queen's College to become the New Metropolitan.'

A fleeting smile lit her face. 'No kidding? King's is where I took my degree.' Then the smile faded as the police persona assumed its default position. 'So, you're an academic outfit?'

He shot her a defiant look. 'Why not just say "amateur"? That's what you're thinking, isn't it?'

The rueful shrug helped dissipate some of his annoyance. 'My boss, Chief Superintendent Douglas, would certainly think so. He has a thing about graduates, believe me.'

'Things have changed a lot in academia lately,' he said, suddenly feeling the need to create a favourable impression. 'Income generation is not only encouraged, it's essential – at least for those who are able. We're only here today because we've been commissioned by the city's director of cultural and recreational services to make a record of the restoration of the *Loch Tredwell*.'

'So, you and your motley crew go out into the big, bad world to earn a crust that helps keep your institution afloat. That's why the merger happened too: cutting out some of the dead wood. Right?'

His smile acknowledged her attempt to lighten the tone. 'Something like that, although some of the dead wood wouldn't necessarily agree with you. Think of themselves as more bookworm than woodworm.'

10

He was rewarded with another smile, again only fleeting. 'You did one thing of practical value,' she said. 'One of the items recovered from the scorched jacket was a business card.' She removed from her pocket a transparent evidence bag and read the name on the business card. '"River Dan's Video". Know anything about that?'

Buerk puffed out his cheeks and exhaled slowly. 'Dan St Clair has a small business in the industrial estate selling video production and editing equipment to outfits like ours. He has aspirations to climb the social ladder, but if you scratch the surface you'll find a barrow boy from the East End underneath.'

One eyebrow shot up. 'You don't approve?'

He shrugged. 'Dan's okay if you know how to take him. I'd describe him as a likeable rogue.'

She eyed him thoughtfully.

The bleeping of her mobile phone caused her to delve into her pocket. Making no effort to turn away from him she answered it, one hand raised in a gesture of apology. He took two paces away from her.

'Chief Superintendent.' Buerk noticed the way her shoulders slumped as she acknowledged the caller. As she made her report there were periodic outbursts of tinny static from her receiver which somehow conveyed the feeling that the caller was impatient with her responses. 'Yes, sir. A gruesome sight, but luckily part of his clothing was recovered from the scene and we've managed to ID the victim as Vinnie McGrath... No, sir, Goldfiever was from before. Apparently, he was currently working on the *Loch Tredwell* as a security guard. He may have disturbed intruders... No, sir, we have witnesses who saw an inflatable with an outboard motor leave the scene shortly after the fire was started, two occupants on board.'

She took two impatient steps away and then back again. 'No doubt about it, sir. Fire Chief McDonald confirmed it. He found evidence that an accelerant had been used, and then there was the presence of a blowtorch and gas cylinder... Well, sir, it would have been against health and safety rules to leave one on board during restoration work.' She threw a smile of acknowledgement at Buerk. 'Matter of fact, sir, I did check. They do have an excellent safety record to date.'

There was a loud blast from the fire tender leaving the scene and heading downriver. She put a finger in her other ear.

'Sorry, sir? Yes, forensics have just finished up at the locus.

'Well, you know Doc Mackie, sir. He did go so far as to say it bore the hallmarks of a professional... Hardly a leap in the dark, sir.' She half-turned away from Buerk before adding, 'The victim was beaten before being killed with a single stab wound between the first and second vertebrae, neatly done. Mackie thinks it had to be delivered by a competent and strong assailant.'

She glanced round at Buerk and discovered him chin in hand, a faint smile playing on his face as he appeared to drink in every word. 'A university film crew raised the alarm – they're apparently making a video record of the restoration project... we're taking statements from them now, sir.' Colouring slightly, she looked away to avoid

Buerk's eye. 'We haven't ruled anyone out at this stage, sir.' A wry smile in Buerk's direction. 'You might be surprised at how much they've given us, sir.'

There was a final burst of chatter and then, 'Very good, sir.' Switching off, she swung round to face Buerk, not wholly succeeding in concealing her annoyance.

'Is this where you tell me not to leave the country?' he asked.

'What? Oh...' She eyed him distractedly. 'Not without checking with me first. Now, where were we?'

'Vinnie McGrath,' he prompted.

'I thought you said you didn't recognise him?'

'Couldn't help overhearing.' Looking into those bewitching eyes he saw what he imagined were cogs in minute gear wheels whirring around; what should he be told, how much did he already know?

'McGrath was a low-life muscle for hire, much of it between the ears. He spent time lifting weights in Lynch's Gymnasium. Last I heard he was working as a bouncer in some casino; now he turns up here. What do you suppose is the connection with this River Dan's?'

'I can think of one possible link.'

'Which is?'

'Spider McVey.'

'Spider McVey?'

'He's an ex-boxer who—'

'I know who Spider is,' she interrupted forcefully. 'A promising flyweight with a wicked left hook until a fondness for even more wicked ladies ruined his prospects...'

'...And who now happens to work for Dan St Clair,' he said. 'So far as I know, Spider also works out at Lynch's Gym.'

'That's more like it, Angus,' she said. 'Now you're starting to think like a detective.'

He spread his hands wide. 'I ask you, just how far can a mere academic sink in one day?'

For just a fleeting moment there seemed to be a softening in her face, as if she'd forgotten herself. The resultant smile dazzled him. She took a card from her bag and tucked it into his shirt pocket. 'If you think of anything else that could be relevant, however insignificant, give me a call, any time. There's a good boy.'

'Very good, Detective Inspector Munro,' he said. He noted from the card her first name was Rowena. He wanted to say more, perhaps ask her for a date, dinner or even a cup of coffee, but his normally loquacious tongue felt stuck to the roof of his mouth. It did occur to him then that to earn another such dazzling smile, he might be prepared to endure considerable hardship.

CHAPTER TWO

Vera Goodnight reached across her mahogany desk and selected a cheroot from the cedar-wood box inlaid with silver. As her eye lingered on the box, her normally combative expression softened somewhat. The box had been a present from a recent admirer after a night of unbridled passion. She leaned back in her swivel chair as she recalled an image of a somewhat austere man. His name was Victor Parkes.

They had first met at an official dinner for an overseas delegation. As director of cultural and recreational services, she had been asked to talk to the delegation about her progressive ideas on staff development. Victor was there apparently as a consultant on the legal side of things. Someone had whispered in her ear that he was a very prominent QC in the city – quite a scalp. Some might have called him arrogant, others handsome but for a small scar under his left eye. To Vera the scar only made him more attractive. The moment he had kissed her hand as they were introduced, she had felt a frisson of anticipation run through her voluptuous body. There had been something about the way he had devoured her with his eyes.

Even now, a pink flush suffused her cheeks as she recalled how she had arranged to sit next to him at the official banquet in the city chambers amidst all those great paintings, the ornate stained-glass windows and the sparkling chandeliers. Over entrées she had contrived to accidentally brush his knee with her own, eliciting an immediate response. By the time dessert was served he had discovered that she was wearing nothing under her dress and her hand was on his manhood. A comfort break before the final round of speeches provided a heaven-sent opportunity for both of them to retreat to the ladies' (it being virtually an all-male affair), where matters were brought to a speedy and somewhat noisy conclusion.

She allowed herself a brief smile as she recalled that Victor would have a bit of explaining to do to his wife – by all accounts a right stuck-up bitch. There were some particularly nasty red weals on his buttocks which Vera had bestowed on him later in the hotel room as a prelude to a further bout of violent lovemaking. Most of the damage had been caused by a riding crop, a present from a previous admirer and currently lying on her desk. It bore a distinctly phallic handle carved from polished ivory while the business end was dressed in the softest chamois leather.

She had noticed some older scars on her lover's body, but when she had quizzed him about them he had merely shrugged and told her that pain was an old friend. On the most recent occasion, she had taken him to a private room in a casino where they had exceeded the bounds of convention. She was a bit hazy about the order of play but the strokes had certainly been memorable.

As she lit her cheroot and sent a rule-flouting cloud of blue-grey smoke spiralling towards the high, ornate ceiling, her expression resumed its customary hardness and she leaned forward in her chair to press the intercom button.

'Amanda, be a dear and get Piggy Halbert on the blower.'

'Right away, Ms Goodnight.' Safe from scrutiny, Amanda stuck her tongue out at the phone.

Vera was aware that Piggy was a self-made man who had come up the hard way. Apart from a rather dated fleet of fish and chip trailer outlets, he had had the good sense to acquire Customs House when the old dockside area was being demolished. Customs House was a fine two-story sandstone building situated close to the *Loch Tredwell*'s berth. Vera had plans to make both vessel and building the base for her proposed maritime museum, but Customs House was currently operating as a restaurant and Piggy had so far proved unwilling to sell.

Piggy's gravelly tones crackled on the line. 'Vera, always nice to hear from an influential dignitary. What can I do you for?'

She tried to sound casual. 'Just wondered if you've had the time to consider my offer for Customs House?'

Piggy chuckled hoarsely. 'I've always got the time to consider an offer, Vera, but I'm not sure I've got the inclination to accept.'

Vera swallowed hard. 'What seems to be the problem?'

'To be blunt, Vera, your offer's nowhere near high enough. You'd need to increase your bid before I'd even want to consider selling.'

'I thought we were close to agreeing a figure?' She tried for a light tone but inside she was raging. Only the day before she had been sure they were close to a deal.

'That was before I came up with the idea of converting Customs House into a disco.'

Fuck. Where the hell had that idea come from?

As if reading her thoughts Piggy began to explain: 'It's the creative muse in me, Vera. I can't help having ideas; I need to move on in my life. With that in mind I could let you have one or two mobile fast-food outlets at a knockdown price.'

'Gee, thanks for nothing, Piggy,' she said sourly. 'You realise I'd have to go back to my committee for their approval before I could increase my offer.'

Piggy's chuckle was unsympathetic. 'Well, Vera, if anyone can swing that committee, you can.'

She felt an attack of indigestion coming on. 'Easy for you to say. What on earth would you call a disco – "The Little Emperor"?'

Another rasping chuckle in her ear. 'Ouch, Vera. That tongue of yours is like a whip lash...'

Vera glared at the receiver. Had Piggy heard a rumour somewhere?

He was still droning on. 'You've got me all wrong, Vera. I'm no Napoleon. I was thinking more like "Funguys".'

'How appropriate, Piggy. You always had a knack for turning decay into something fruitful.'

'That's very poetic, Vera.'

'I'll be in touch.'

'Any time, Vera.'

She had scarcely replaced the receiver when Amanda buzzed. 'While you were on the line, I had a call from

Hunter's Quay. There's been some problem down there with the *Loch Tredwell*.'

Vera cursed silently and took a long drag on her cheroot. What now? The knowledge that the restoration project was dear to her heart seemed to make her underlings think that they could cop out of their own responsibilities altogether. 'Isn't there anyone down there who can deal with this?' she said irritably.

'The police won't let anyone aboard the vessel,' Amanda said cheerfully.

'The police?' The cheroot glowed an angry red. 'What the hell has happened?'

A deliberate pause. 'Seems there was an explosion aboard ship and then a fire broke out – or maybe it was the other way about. Nobody seems sure.'

'Oh, Jesus.' Vera viciously stubbed out the cheroot in the ashtray as if it might have been somehow complicit in the fire. Visions of her plan for the *Loch Tredwell* as the centrepiece of her new museum literally going up in smoke flashed before her eyes. Angrily she flapped her own smoke towards the open window and emptied her ashtray over the sill. Bad enough that Piggy was trying to hike up the price of Customs House. Now this.

Her worry was that she had already obtained substantial financial help for the restoration project from the Heritage Lottery Fund as well as from the city council and other development agencies. It might be difficult to go back and ask for more if the insurance didn't pay up.

'Was there... much damage?' Absently her right hand tightened around the riding crop.

'Could have been much worse, apparently.' Amanda sounded slightly disappointed. 'The TV crew from the university were down there to do some filming and spotted smoke coming from the ship. They promptly called the fire brigade, who managed to put the fire out before it spread.'

Vera stroked her cheek with the end of the riding crop. It might not be as bad as she feared. It would inevitably set the restoration back, but it might still be completed in time for the Tall Ships event next year.

'Wait a minute,' she said. 'We're paying for round-the-clock security. What happened to the guy who was on duty?'

Amanda suppressed a nervous giggle. 'Seems he's... missing.'

'Christ almighty.' Vera brought the riding crop down heavily on the desk, only to catch the ashtray a glancing blow and send a shower of fine ash over the front of her Armani blouse. Reflexively she brushed at it, leaving a fine smear of dirt. 'Shit.'

'There's more.' Amanda could barely conceal her glee.

Vera spoke through clenched teeth. 'Well, let's have it, girl.'

'They found a body after the fire was put out.'

'A body... as in dead?'

'Is there another kind?'

'Don't use that tone with me, my girl,' Vera snapped. 'Is it the missing security guard?'

'The police won't say.'

Of course. On top of all the fire and water damage, the plods would have to play silly buggers trampling all over the place in their size-elevens, hindering or even preventing the restoration work from progressing. None of this was going to make it any easier to convince the committee that making an increased offer for Customs House was a sensible use of scarce resources.

The indigestion was getting worse. She had a momentary panic attack. What if it was the first sign of an incipient heart attack? She got up and paced to the window, pausing briefly to glance down on the busy city square. No. This could not be allowed to happen. She returned resolutely to her desk.

'Amanda,' she said. 'Get me Chief Superintendent Douglas, *tout de suite*.'

'I'll check if he's still in his office,' Amanda said. 'He might have gone to lunch by now.'

'I don't care if he's shagging his pet goat,' Vera snapped. 'I want a word ASAP. Tell him I'm calling in a personal favour, and don't even think of sloping off yourself until you've tracked him down. Is that understood?'

'Yes, Ms Goodnight,' Amanda said. Disconnecting, she added, 'Absofuckinglutely, your highness.'

CHAPTER THREE

Buerk knocked and poked his head cautiously into the room, his smile taking an effort. 'You wanted to see me, deputy principal?'

Henry Thessinger Hornblower's face was florid and fleshy, twin furrows running from the corners of the nose to the edge of the mouth bestowing on him a hangdog expression. Fingering a black eyepatch (the result of stooping to smell a rose and scratching the cornea of his left eye on a stake), he turned a piratical scowl on the new arrival. 'Ah, there you are, Buerk,' he said. 'Glad you finally felt able to join us.'

'Apologies for being late, sir. Had a spot of bother while filming this morning.'

Hornblower harrumphed, making it clear he had not the slightest interest in Buerk's 'bother'. Truth to tell, he did not care for Buerk. For one thing, he knew him to be firmly in the principal's camp. Pre-merger, both had been members of King's University. For another, Buerk seemed to be constantly outshining Hornblower's own protégé, Fred Crawley, like himself a former member of Queen's College. Post-merger, Hornblower had lost out to Dr Truelove in the contest for principal. Now Buerk and Crawley were rivals for the post of head of television. With an internal promotion panel about to convene, Hornblower needed his own people in positions of authority if he was ever to supplant Truelove as principal.

'Care for a sherry?' He picked up a decanter and waved it airily at Buerk, as if he might prefer to use it as a club.

Buerk eyed the decanter dubiously. 'Perhaps a small one,' he said.

'I think you know the others here, what?'

Becoming aware for the first time of the presence of two other members of staff in the far corner of the room, Buerk felt his heart sink. They sat, glasses in hand, in easy chairs arranged around a low coffee table. Their huddle put him in mind of two alchemists caught in furtive discussion of the merits of some ancient recipe of transmutation.

Clearly, Hornblower disliked him intensely. Fred Crawley's bearded presence, Buerk sensed, was not a good sign, while the third member of the group, Lucretia Golightly, was yet another former member of Queen's. As the head of horticultural studies in that institution, she had been dubbed 'Motormouth' by fellow staff members because of the frequency and decibel level of her utterances in committee. Seeing her at close quarters for the first time, it took a moment to get over the green hair, swept up into a tight bun on the top of her head and seemingly woven there by two objects like knitting needles protruding from it. A severe, angular woman probably in her late thirties, she seemed at that precise moment to be regarding him in much the same way as his neighbour's dog might have eyed a pork chop. Whatever was being cooked up by this strange triumvirate, he had an uncomfortable feeling that in some shape or form he was on the menu.

'As I've been explaining to the others – damn...' In his agitation Hornblower managed to spill some sherry as he handed Buerk a glass. 'I'm trying to assemble a think tank in something of a hurry.'

'A sticky situation,' Buerk said, wiping the stem of his glass with a tissue he'd fished from his pocket.

'Quite,' Hornblower said, motioning him to join the group. 'As you all know, the principal is keen to diversify our activities and bring fresh income and prestige to the university.'

'A very laudable aim, if I may say so,' Lucretia said. She held her sherry glass poised at her lips, which Buerk noted were the same colour as her hair and fingernails.

'Hear, hear,' said Crawley.

'Having an aim is all well and good,' Hornblower said, 'but I'm absolutely determined that while I am acting principal' – he paused to ensure that they had all registered the significance of his last two words before continuing – 'we should mark the occasion by taking some initiative that will catapult this institution into the forefront of academic standing.'

'A considerable challenge.' Buerk grimaced at his first sip. Probably cooking sherry, he thought, cadged from the Queen of Puddings, as the students referred to the head of catering within the university.

Lucretia countered, green eyes flashing with missionary zeal. 'Not, I think, an insuperable one.'

Buerk cast his own eyes to the ceiling.

Hornblower glanced coldly at Buerk. 'I am about to invite Lucretia to explain the news, which she assures me singularly fits the bill of my... that's to say, *our* vision.'

Simpering coyly, Lucretia waved a sheet of paper in the air. 'Now, I know you're all going to find this a trifle strange.'

'Do try us, Lucretia,' Hornblower said.

'But not too far,' Buerk muttered under his breath.

'This is a print-out of an e-mail,' Lucretia said, 'of the type used by bird spotters and wardens up and down the country to make reports to the RSPB. It contains a comprehensive list of birds to be found in the UK. The idea is that the spotter ticks the species they have observed at a given locality and date, thus enabling the society to build up a comprehensive picture of present populations et cetera.'

Hornblower's mouth puckered like a carp's. 'Yes, I think we all get the picture,' he said evenly. 'What we don't see is where all this avian information is leading us.'

'This particular e-mail is from my brother Hilary.' Lucretia persisted. 'He looks after an internationally renowned bird sanctuary on the island of Papa Westray. It's one of the most remote islands in the Orkney archipelago. Over the summer months Hilary regularly sends me a copy of the return whenever he spots something of interest: the first puffin pair to nest or Arctic tern chicks to hatch, that sort of thing. *This* morning he spotted something much more significant – indeed I think it would not be too strong a claim to say "world-shattering".' She again waved the printout in the air as if the point should be immediately obvious to everyone.

Hornblower could contain himself no longer. 'What, for heaven's sake?'

Lucretia preened herself for a triumphant denouement. 'A great auk!'

Buerk used the stunned silence to surreptitiously empty his sherry into a potted yucca plant at his elbow, causing Crawley to almost choke on his. 'Forgive me for asking,' he said, 'but...'

Lucretia, however, was not to be robbed of her moment. 'Don't you see, um, acting principal?' she said. 'If we could be the first to obtain irrefutable proof that the great auk is again nesting in Papa Westray, we would have achieved all – perhaps more than – you dared hope for.'

Buerk tried again to intervene. 'I don't wish to throw a spanner in the works, but...'

This time Hornblower prevented him from having his say. 'Just how do you propose obtaining this... evidence?' he said.

Lucretia paused to direct a smile at Buerk (a rather worrying one from his perspective), the note of triumph giving her voice a husky tone. 'By leading Angus and his film crew on an expedition to gather video evidence of the historic sighting.'

'An excellent plan,' Crawley said.

From Crawley's undisguised glee, Buerk realised the plan was not for his benefit. Alarmed by the direction the conversation had taken, he finally blurted out his concern. 'Correct me if I'm wrong,' he said, 'but hasn't the great auk been considered extinct for about two hundred years?'

There was an ominous silence as the eyes of the others swung pendulum fashion from Buerk to Lucretia, waiting for the explosion.

Lucretia remained calm. 'Angus is quite right to be sceptical,' she said. 'Ornithologists have long believed that the last great auk in those northern isles perished in about 1813 before being stuffed and transferred to the British Science Museum. What was thought to be the last bird in the entire world was recorded in the arctic wastes around 1844.'

'But that only bears out what Buerk is saying,' Hornblower protested. The disappointment was evident in his voice. 'It hardly lends credence to your brother's claim.'

No shrinking violet, Lucretia withstood the challenge. 'Not necessarily,' she said. 'These are very remote islands and it's just possible that one or even two breeding pairs could have survived on an inaccessible cliff face.'

Despite her vigorous protest, Lucretia's case seemed to hang by a thread, but support for her cause again came from Crawley.

'I think Lucretia has a point,' he said smugly. 'Let's not forget about the takahe.'

'Now what the blue blazes are we talking about?' Hornblower demanded.

Lucretia seized the lifeline Crawley had offered her. 'It's a flightless bird from New Zealand,' she explained. 'All the experts said it was extinct until it was rediscovered in 1948.'

Crawley appeared to warm to the theme under Lucretia's encouraging gaze. 'There are other instances of birds thought to have been extinct which have turned up alive later,' he said. Reading from a list in his hand, he recited, 'There's the Bermuda petrel, only rediscovered in 1951, and let's not forget Worcester's buttonquail from the Philippines, previously known only from dead museum specimens.'

Hornblower stroked his chin dubiously. 'I see,' he said. Buerk was not at all sure that Hornblower did see, but he was clear that Crawley's assiduous research had an ulterior motive.

'In any case,' Lucretia continued defiantly, 'I have complete faith in Hilary's judgement. Of course it's possible to make a mistake, but in a case like this he'd be especially careful. I did try to confirm it with him this morning, but there was no reply when I telephoned. But look here.' She jabbed the bottom of the sheet of paper with her finger where Hilary had added the new discovery. 'He's even underlined it so that I couldn't possibly miss it.'

Buerk leaned over her shoulder to examine the underlined entry. '*Pinguinus impennis*,' he read aloud. 'Is that the Latin name for the great auk?'

'Bravo, Angus,' Lucretia said, flashing him a toothsome smile. 'We'll make an ornithologist of you yet.'

Hornblower began to pace up and down, desperately trying to weigh up the risks inherent in giving his blessing to such a project. He turned finally to glare at each of them in turn.

'I need to know how you each feel about the prospects of success,' he said.

This time, Buerk decided to get his oar in first. 'From a purely practical point of view,' he said, 'you shouldn't overlook the difficulties of weather and terrain for filming there. Add to that the fact that I'm lumbered with outdated equipment I was promised would be replaced when the much-postponed merger finally came into effect. All of that is predicated on the possibility that, by some miracle, the blessed bird does exist.'

Smug in the knowledge that it would not be his head on the block, Crawley had no wish to let his rival off the hook. 'Nothing ventured, nothing gained,' he said.

Sensing that Hornblower was wavering, Lucretia said quickly, 'My sentiments entirely, and think of the academic kudos if we get the proof.' Almost as an afterthought, she added slyly, 'Of course, acting principal, you'd probably have to endure the bulk of the acclaim and media attention on our successful return.'

In a suddenly-acquired self-effacing tone, Hornblower said, 'Naturally I don't give a fig for personal glory, but you may have an important point there, Lucretia: an academic feather in our cap, what?'

'We'll be tarred and feathered if she's wrong,' Buerk muttered darkly.

Hornblower shot him a look of alarm and came to an abrupt decision. 'No one apart from those immediately involved must know of this mission until we're certain of the outcome, one way or the other.'

Crawley directed a malicious sneer at Buerk. 'You'll have to swear that film crew of yours to secrecy,' he said. It was an open secret that Crawley had never hit it off with Cant and Dick.

'They can be dealt with on a need-to-know basis,' Hornblower said dismissively.

Buerk made a last-ditch attempt to introduce some sanity into the discussion. 'Shouldn't we at least contact the principal about this?' he asked.

'There's no need for that,' Hornblower snapped waspishly. 'If we're successful, he'll hear about it soon enough. If not, then the less said the better.'

'He'll be back in another three days,' Buerk protested.

Hornblower looked at Buerk as if he were a plague of aphids. 'Then that's exactly how long you've got to come back with the evidence,' he snapped. 'I need hardly remind you, Buerk, that there's the small matter of an internal promotion panel in the offing. A lack of *esprit de corps* on your record will hardly help your cause.'

'You can't afford to hang about,' Crawley offered helpfully. 'Word of this could easily get out.'

'I've taken the liberty of booking a flight first thing in the morning,' Lucretia said. She rose to place a placatory hand on Buerk's shoulder. 'Come on, Angus,' she murmured, 'think of this as an exciting adventure we're all in together, whatever comes of it.'

'That's the spirit,' Hornblower said. 'No time to lose.'

Fingering the plaster over his eye, Buerk caught the deputy principal's bleak smile, but it was the look in Lucretia's eye that troubled him most. Her smile had the slow, wet orifice-dilation of a giant squid that senses that a large mass of krill has just drifted into her ambit. When he had first noticed them, he had suspected complicity between Crawley and Lucretia. Now, it looked as if all three were in cahoots and he had little choice but to fall in with their scheme, however feather-brained it might seem.

CHAPTER FOUR

'Crawley, a word!' As Buerk and Lucretia left the meeting, Hornblower seized Buerk's rival by his arm and pulled him back inside, slamming the door closed behind him.

The deputy principal got straight to the point. 'This Golightly woman,' he began, 'do you think she's got anything substantial upstairs?'

Straightening his sleeve, Crawley shot his mentor a look of alarm as he conjured up an image of Lucretia's well-endowed bosom. He opted to stall for time. 'Upstairs?' he said.

'Yes, yes,' Hornblower snapped impatiently. 'Do you think the woman's right in the head with this great auk business?'

'Oh, that!' Crawley released a gasp of pent-up tension, relieved that his deputy principal was not after all developing an unhealthy sexual obsession with Lucretia. He had already heard some rather disquieting tales about Hornblower and the head of catering. 'Lucretia can be a trifle brusque in her dealings with colleagues,' he said. He had been on the receiving end of such brusqueness himself. 'In this case, however, her source of information is impeccable. Her brother is a renowned ornithologist; he's even been on television.'

Hornblower nodded, but the frown remained. 'Pity it had to be a relation who passed on this information,' he said. 'In my experience mental aberrations tend to run in families.' He fretted a moment longer, then came to a decision. 'All right. We need to stay on top of this situation every step of the way. You'll have to go with them.'

'Eh?' Crawley looked at Hornblower in sudden alarm. 'But... but isn't Papa Westray in the back of beyond? I've heard they're all savages up there and I've already made other plans. Besides, Buerk won't like it.'

'Then Buerk can lump it,' Hornblower said. He took two threatening steps towards his protégé. 'And since when could any plans of yours not be postponed for the greater good?'

His aggression caused Crawley to take an involuntary step backwards so that he caught the corner of the desk sharply with the back of his thigh.

Hornblower continued, blithely unaware. 'Tell him you're going to smooth his path by helping with the arrangements so that he can film in peace. He's bound to fall for that line. Creative parasites like Buerk always think they've been put on this world so that gophers like you can run after them.'

'Huh?' Crawley's jaw gaped as insult was added to injury.

'I'm speaking figuratively, of course,' Hornblower added quickly. 'Looking at it from Buerk's point of view.'

'I see,' Crawley said uncertainly.

Hornblower belatedly considered that a little buttering-up might not be a bad strategy. 'Yes, yes,' he said, 'you're really going undercover as my field operative... acting as a kind of double agent, if you will.'

'I am?' Crawley brightened visibly at this altogether more acceptable image.

'Yes, yes, but what you have to grasp here, Crawley, is that good doubles don't act their parts.'

Crawley blinked in puzzlement. 'They don't? I thought you said...'

Quoting from something he had read, Hornblower went on as though his minion had never interrupted him. 'They *live* them. They *are* them. Do I make myself clear?'

'Of course, sir. I see it now. I'll make the necessary flight alterations at once.'

'Good.' Hornblower treated him to a rare smile, finding the prospect of running his own mole rather appealing.

Buoyed up by his secret pact with the deputy principal, Crawley dropped in on Buerk to give him the good news. Buerk heard him out with growing impatience and incredulity.

'I don't get it,' he said. 'Isn't it enough that I'm being lumbered with Motormouth on this... this ornithological farce? Now you're tagging along as well. What's the big idea? You don't even like outside location work.'

Crawley squirmed under Buerk's onslaught, hopping from one foot to the other. 'It's in your own interests,' he insisted, his voice totally lacking in conviction.

Buerk shot him a look of hostility. 'Really? You don't mean in Hornblower's? Damned odd you only changed your plans after your little tête-à-tête with HT upstairs.'

Crawley desperately cast around for a convincing argument. 'All right,' he conceded. 'Hornblower thinks this business needs to be handled delicately. He... um, doesn't want Lucretia going off at half-cock, making false claims without some corroboration.'

'Well, there I agree with him,' Buerk admitted grudgingly, 'but what was wrong with just strangling the woman?'

Slanting sheets of rain were sweeping across monobloc paving in the small industrial estate as DI Munro pulled thoughtfully into the customer car park of River Dan's Video PLC. She parked her Volvo between Lennox's mud-spattered Polo and a shiny new top-of-the-range Mercedes. It had not been easy getting to her present position, she reflected. The law degree had given her a head start, fast-tracking her into the CID, but it had not protected her from the suspicion and resentment initially shown by some members of the elite squad, most of all by her own superior officer. It was for good reason that the other members of the squad called the chief superintendent (behind his back, of course) 'the Black Douglas'. He could never quite bring himself to call her by her first name: her sex and university degree twin obstacles to the easy familiarity of the boys' club that was the Serious Crime Squad.

It had taken a rather scary personal confrontation with a deranged man armed with a knife and holding a child hostage to earn her the spurs that had led to her present status. She had managed to talk the man into releasing the child unharmed, and then instinctively she had known he was going to attack her. As he had launched into a frenzied assault, she had managed to stay calm and call on her training in unarmed combat. The man was highly disturbed but no knife expert and in the end she managed to disarm and cuff him. The incident had given her acceptance within the squad, but it could still give her nightmares.

Chief Superintendent Douglas had taken pains to stress the temporary nature of her present promotion. She knew only too well that the sword he had grudgingly placed in her hands was double-edged. The chance to show what she could do might equally end prospects of permanent promotion, if she should fail.

Her lips parted in a smile when she recalled that she was following a lead that Angus Buerk had given her. She had been rather taken by his quirky sense of humour. He was quite good-looking too and if he was a shade overprotective of his crew, well, in view of her own experience, that wasn't such a bad thing, was it? Maybe that was what had prompted her to give him her card. The faint smile faded. Not that anything was likely to come of it. It never did in her line of work. The testosterone-fuelled men inside the squad were complete no-nos; their idea of a chat-up approach in a bar went something like: 'Hello, doll, you're with me tonight.' Dream on! On the other hand, the moment that any date from 'outside' discovered she was a member of the force, they seemed to melt away like snow in June (one of the hot days).

She was brought back to reality with a jolt as the passenger door opened, allowing the gale to drive in a blast of cold rain along with Detective Sergeant Mary Lennox, who had dived in from her car.

Slamming the door shut, Lennox smiled apologetically. 'Sorry for looking like a drowned rat, ma'am. It's absolutely chucking it down.'

Munro smiled a welcome at the dark-haired young woman wearing her trademark red beret. It had been Douglas's idea some time ago to foist the rookie detective on Munro rather than on one of the more experienced male officers. That way, his warped thinking went, he didn't spoil two units. After some initial misgivings, Munro had quickly warmed to the partnership and Lennox had quickly earned her promotion to DS. As well as an indomitable personality, she brought loads of common sense to her work and, as a former member of the uniformed branch, plenty of street credibility.

'Occupational hazard,' Munro said. 'Get anything interesting out of Mackie?'

Lennox brandished a manila folder. 'Nothing sensational,' she said. 'Essentially he's confirmed the murder weapon was a knife with a well-honed six-inch blade sharpened along both edges – reckons it could possibly be a switchblade. Typically these knives would have a long handle as well for both purchase and balance. He's also sticking with the notion that it was a professional hit based on the fact that it required prior knowledge and strength to push that knife in between the vertebrae, then be able to withdraw it again. Apparently it severed the spinal cord with the minimum of mess.'

Munro frowned. 'Wouldn't the fact that it needed a strong push work against the idea of a flick knife?'

Lennox smiled. 'Exactly what I asked Mackie, but apparently these things are fitted with a locking device against closure when the blade is fully extended. You've also got to disengage a safety catch before it'll spring into use.'

Munro grimaced. 'So essentially we're looking for a big-for-his-age Boy Scout who lifts weights and probably doesn't have much form since he's so efficient. That narrows the field down considerably.'

'Look on the bright side,' Lennox said. 'It appears to rule out Cubs and Brownies. Seriously, ma'am, these days switchblades are usually produced by small companies on a semi-custom basis. They're bought mainly by the military or by collectors in places where it still remains legal to own one.'

Munro gave her sergeant a sidelong glance. 'Thanks for that little nutmeg of consolation, Mary. It's almost certainly the illegally owned ones we're interested in, but it's as well to be thorough. For now, let's go and see how likeable a rogue this Dan St Clair really is.'

This time Lennox eyed her colleague curiously. 'Interesting way of putting it.'

'Hmmn.' Munro gazed fixedly out of the window. 'Came from an interesting source.'

They had to sprint into reception to avoid getting another soaking. Inside, Munro's eye took in the uncomfortable-looking chairs, the coin-operated coffee machine in the corner, the well-thumbed trade magazines in the rack and the handful of business cards and matchbooks piled beside an empty ashtray.

A dark-haired girl glanced up briefly from behind the reception desk before continuing with some repairs to chocolate-coloured nail varnish, the same shade already adorning her lips.

'Help you?' she asked without looking up.

'I'm Detective Inspector Munro. This is Detective Sergeant Lennox. We'd like a word with Mr St Clair regarding a murder inquiry we're presently conducting.'

This time the girl did lift her head and something in Munro's eye got her attention. 'If you'll take a seat,' she said, 'I'll let him know you're here.'

'Thank you.'

Within a couple of minutes a heavy-set, dark-jowled man appeared in the doorway smoothing down sleek black hair. Bright little eyes darted warily from one to the other. 'Detective Inspector Munro, Sergeant Lennox,' he said, extending to each in turn a limp hand from which dangled a heavy gold bracelet. A showy gold watch adorned the other wrist, perhaps as a counterweight, Munro thought. 'Please come into my office,' he said.

Munro smiled thinly. 'We'd like to ask you a few routine questions about an investigation we're conducting.'

Dan St Clair nodded gravely from a round face like a setting moon. About two stone overweight, Munro reckoned, and far too smug for his own good. She guessed he was in his mid-forties, but he might have been younger. Remembering Buerk's description of him, she thought she could easily buy the *rogue* half, but still needed convincing about the *likeable* part. As to exactly why she was thinking about Buerk now, she had no idea. This was strictly business, after all.

St Clair ushered them into upright chairs before settling into a more comfortable-looking one behind his king-size desk. Munro had a quiet smile about that.

'Can I offer you something? Tea... coffee... something a wee bit stronger, perhaps?'

'A coffee would be appreciated,' Munro said. She realised that she'd already skipped lunch, while dinner remained a remote prospect. Removing her wet coat, she gave it a shake before hanging it on a coat rack in the corner. Lennox followed suit. 'This *needn't* take too much of your time.'

St Clair pressed a button on his intercom. 'Letitia said you were conducting a murder inquiry,' he said. 'I sincerely hope it's nobody I know.'

'Does the name "Vinnie McGrath" mean anything to you?' Munro asked abruptly.

'Vinnie McGrath...' He broke off to speak into the intercom. 'Letitia, three coffees and some of those wee doughnuts, if you'd be so good.' He leaned back in his chair to gaze at the ceiling, rather spoiling the act by appearing to deliberate for too long. 'Can't say the name rings any bells. Is he a suspect?'

Munro shook her head slowly. 'He's the victim.'

For just a moment she thought she caught a look of alarm registering in St Clair's face.

'Got a knife through the back of his neck,' Lennox added, making a deliberately brutal gesture with her finger. 'Medical examiner reckoned it was the work of a professional assassin.'

St Clair started fingering his collar nervously. 'Sounds nasty!'

'Reason I ask,' Munro continued, 'I understand Vinnie McGrath was an acquaintance of one of your employees...' She made a show of checking her notebook. 'Mr McVey.'

St Clair's eyes narrowed. 'That's news to me, but Spider – that's to say Mr McVey – doesn't necessarily share all his thoughts with me; not that he gets too many of those, if you get my meaning.'

Munro's smile was glacial. 'I get your meaning all right, Mr St Clair. My information is that both Spider and Vinnie worked out at Lynch's Gymnasium down by the docks.'

'Frequented by boxers and sundry low-lives,' Lennox added.

'I imagine it's full of all kinds of headbangers, detective sergeant,' he said, 'but what does that tell us?'

Lennox leaned forward with a hint of steel in her voice. 'It at least allows the possibility that they had met.'

St Clair spread his hands as if keen to appear reasonable, the movement making the bracelet jangle on his wrist. 'All right. I concede the possibility that they knew each other.'

Munro shot Lennox a complicit smile which implied 'this one likes playing games and thinks he can outwit two dim female coppers'. She offered St Clair a different smile. 'I expect you know that Spider McVey got two-thirds of the way towards winning a Lonsdale Belt outright at flyweight?'

'He might have mentioned that,' St Clair said sourly, 'like a couple of hundred times.'

'By all accounts he has a good pair of hands.'

'Aye. Pity he can't keep them to himself out of the ring.'

Munro folded her arms across her body. 'That's a problem with many fly men, and not all of them are boxers,' she said. 'But maybe you weren't referring to Spider's fondness for the ladies. Maybe you were hinting that Spider is a tea leaf?'

St Clair looked at her in disbelief. 'No chance. He knows better than to try stealing anything from me.'

Lennox sat up as though she'd just had a bright idea. 'Maybe Vinnie and Spider were sparring partners?'

St Clair seemed to lose patience. 'You're barking up the wrong tree, the pair of you,' he said. 'They would never have sparred together. In the ring McGrath must have weighed in at around fourteen stone; matter of fact I thought he was putting on the beef when...'

Too late, he stopped in his tracks.

'...when you saw him last,' Munro finished the sentence for him. It was her turn to look smug. 'You know what, Mr St Clair? I think you've been telling us a load of porkies. You obviously know more about Vinnie than you've been letting on. Now, suppose we start again, unless you want to bring a truckload of grief down on yourself. What do you really know of McGrath's movements over the last few days?'

St Clair raised a hand in capitulation. 'Okay,' he said. 'Vinnie came looking for Spider late on Saturday afternoon. I had a dinner to attend but Spider was in finishing a rush job for me, dubbing some CDs from a video master. Maybe they stayed for a chat or maybe they went off somewhere together afterwards. They were up to something, that much was obvious, but I haven't a clue what it was and that's the God's honest truth.' He gave an apologetic shrug. 'I was only trying to protect Spider. I thought he might be in trouble.'

Munro looked him straight in the eye, deciding that he was probably on the level now. 'I suggest you stick to the truth from now on, Mr St Clair. Otherwise you might be the one in trouble. Understand?'

He nodded meekly. 'Aye, sure.'

They were interrupted by Letitia carrying in a tray with the coffee things. She served the coffee and, rather reluctantly, Munro thought, offered round a plate of small doughnuts. Munro accepted the coffee, but declined a doughnut with a shake of her head. Lennox showed no such scruples, eagerly sinking her teeth into one in a way that would not have disgraced a Doberman pinscher.

'What?' she said in answer to a look from Munro. 'I didn't have time for any lunch.'

'Just help yourself,' St Clair said, picking up a doughnut himself and tugging the plate from Letitia's grasp.

'Is Mr McVey available at the moment?' Munro asked.

'He's out doing cold calls,' St Clair said quickly.

Letitia made a small choking sound and almost dropped her empty tray. Recovering, she fled from the room, avoiding her employer's eye.

St Clair calmly selected a second doughnut between finger and thumb and, with exaggerated delicacy, popped it into his mouth. A mental rubber ball, Munro thought.

'Sure you won't try one of these, inspector?' he said, his mouth full of doughnut. 'They're absolutely scrumptious.'

'No, thanks.' Her voice had a righteous ring to it, but inside she was salivating at the prospect.

'Don't mind if I do,' Lennox said, reaching eagerly across his desk to take another one, much to the annoyance of both St Clair and Munro.

'Can you tell me when you expect him back in the office?' Munro asked.

St Clair swallowed the remains of the doughnut and waved his arm, bracelet jangling. 'Impossible to say. You see, detective inspector, you don't make appointments when you're cold calling. It's just like you turning up unannounced and demanding to speak to me – except my sales representatives can't insist.' He gave her a sly smile. 'In that respect you've an advantage over me.'

His fingers hovered over another doughnut. 'By the way, you never said if Spider was a suspect in your murder investigation.'

' "Suspect" is too strong a word,' Munro countered smoothly. 'At the moment he's the last known contact with McGrath and the sooner we can talk to him, the better it'll be for all concerned.' She got to her feet, put the coffee cup on the desk and took a card from her bag. 'Perhaps you could get him to ring me at this number – when he gets back from his cold calls, of course.'

Lennox gave a little ironic smile. 'Perhaps your secretary might raise him on his mobile,' she suggested helpfully.

St Clair leapt to his feet with surprising alacrity. 'I'll personally make sure Spider gets in touch, Detective Inspector Munro. Believe me, I'm as eager as you are to have this whole matter cleared up. It's not good for business to have members of the force hovering around, no matter how... um, presentable they are.'

'Thanks for being so... cooperative,' Munro said, face deadpan.

He hesitated in the doorway. 'You seem to know your boxing, inspector.'

Munro touched the side of her nose with a finger. 'You get in an awful lot of sparring practice in our line of work,' she said.

St Clair eyed her dubiously for a moment and then smiled ruefully. 'Aye, very good,' he said. Then, as they were leaving, he added almost to himself, 'Very good indeed.'

Outside, it had stopped raining. Munro thought the small industrial estate looked rinsed and refreshed as the emerging sun played over the beads of moisture on a row of dripping rowan trees. She paused to look at them. Her mother came from a small highland village and had once told her that a rowan tree had to be planted in the garden to ward off evil spirits. That was why she had been named after them. She supposed that it had turned out to be quite prophetic. Her role now was to guard others from evil.

'A bit of a chancer, don't you think, ma'am? Not too many St Clairs in the local directory. Wonder where that comes from?' Lennox eyed Munro warily as she failed to respond, apparently gazing vacantly into space. 'Ma'am?'

Munro snapped out of her reverie. 'Chancer he is, Mary,' she said. Buerk had got him to a T, she thought. She wondered briefly if he would ever pluck up the courage to ring her. Then, firmly dismissing such distracting thoughts from her mind, she added, 'Plenty of Sinclairs around. No law against changing one to St Clair to get noticed. Smart, really, when you think about it. With a stroke of the pen he's gone from sin to sainthood.'

Lennox chuckled, relieved that her boss appeared to be back on track.

'Fancy swinging by Jackie Lynch's gymnasium to see if we can pick up a few extra pointers?' Munro asked.

'Fine by me,' Lennox said. 'Someone there might have seen Vinnie.'

'Leave your car here. We'll pick it up on the way back to the station. Maybe by then St Clair will have debriefed Spider for us.'

Lennox gave her boss a sidelong glance. ' "Debriefing" might not be the most appropriate choice of word, ma'am.'

CHAPTER FIVE

Deep in thought, Dan St Clair watched Munro and Lennox drive off together. A sharp pair of cookies and no mistake, he mused, especially that Detective Inspector. She reminded him of a nun in the school he had attended when he was just plain Danny Sinclair. Sister Theresa had made it her business to thwart his budding entrepreneurial skills, especially when he wangled the job of running the tuck shop.

That pair would be coming back. They had seen to that by leaving the Polo belonging to the wee nippy sweetie of a sergeant. *Thought we'd just pop in while we're here and see if Spider's back from his cold calls,* he could imagine her saying. Hoping to catch him cold, more like. Yes, any way you looked at it, he'd do well to keep on the right side of DI Munro and her sidekick. Not bad-looking either, for a plod.

All his life Dan St Clair had tried to make it a rule to avoid confrontation with the law, tried not to cross the line. In this city, however – like anywhere else, he supposed – you had to earn a shilling in whatever way you could, did you not? Inevitably there had been times when he had teetered perilously close to that line. Certainly, bending the rules was a legitimate business ploy, but before you could go there you had to know not just the cards in your own hand, but those of as many of the other players as you could ascertain.

He moved resolutely back into his office, ignoring Letitia's quizzical look. Of course Spider wasn't out making cold calls. This was the last Monday in the month. He'd be at his desk in a corner of the showroom, trying to fiddle his expenses.

Reflexively, St Clair popped a doughnut into his mouth; he really would have to cut down on these, but now wasn't the time. Striding over to an inner door that led into the showroom, he threw it open violently. 'McVey!' Spattering the space with doughnut shrapnel, his voice boomed out: 'Get your arse in here on the double.'

A rake-thin figure emerged from behind a screened-off cubicle in a showroom full of video equipment – cameras, tripods, sound recording and editing gear – and slunk crab-like into the office. St Clair glared at his hapless employee, aware that Spider had been more than a sales representative to him. Few people welched on payments when his battle-scarred features called to collect. Even his legendary stupidity was useful in that no task was too bizarre for him to accept unquestioningly. But stupidity also had its drawbacks. Spider McVey may have once been a contender at flyweight, but he was no match for the heavyweight verbal onslaught St Clair now unleashed on his hapless employee.

'I have to tell you, old son, you're in hot water right up to your smelly armpits.'

'How so?' Spider's default setting of equal parts puzzlement and guilt registered on his face.

St Clair glared contemptuously at him. 'There was a detective inspector round here looking for you.'

'The law!' Spider shook his head as if to clear the fog that enveloped his brain in times of crisis. 'Look, if this is about me no' payin' the alimony...'

'It's far more serious than that,' St Clair cut in impatiently. Manipulating the facts for dramatic effect, he added, 'Your pal McGrath's been found with his throat cut.'

'Vinnie!' Spider reached a hand up to his throat. 'You mean – murdered?'

'Well,' St Clair sneered, 'I'd rule out a botched tracheotomy if I was you. Now, suppose you sit down there and tell me what the hell you and your pal were up to before I inform that nice detective inspector I found you hiding under a stone.'

Spider squirmed uneasily in the chair into which his employer had thrust him. 'See, Vinnie was doin' a spell in a casino as a night security guard,' he began nervously. 'He was keepin' an eye on an area barred to the general riffraff – special room fur high rollers, know whit ah mean?'

'I get the drift,' his boss growled. 'Go on.'

'Seems a hidden, movement-sensitive camera that covered the area had a video cassette inside the recorder. Vinnie noticed it had recorded a fair bit and got curious just when he heard somebody coming, so he pocketed the tape – meaning to put it back after he'd had a butcher's. Snag is he never got the chance. Seems there was a bit of a to-do over the missing tape, so Vinnie thought it best to move on. He's working over at Hunter's Quay now as a security guard for that sailing ship that's being restored, the *Loch Tredwell*.'

St Clair snorted dismissively. 'Somebody moved him on, more like.'

A look of horror came into Spider's face. 'You don't think that's why he was murdered, do you?'

St Clair eyed Spider warily. 'Depends what was on the video.'

'Right.' A slow smile crept over Spider's face. 'It is pretty hot merchandise, come to think of it.'

'You've had a look?'

Spider grinned. 'Vinnie came tae me for a playback. We only looked at a wee bit, but that wis enough. The tape was already lined up at a bit showin' explicit shenanigans between that high-profile QC Victor Parkes and some female – a right dog she wis.'

'A compromising video.' St Clair thought for a moment and then leaned closer. 'Tell me, old son, who was this enterprising employer of Vinnie's?'

Spider frowned. 'Far as ah remember, Vinnie said he worked on the somethin' Queen.'

'The *Melbourne Queen* – the floating casino berthed at Paddie's Quay?'

'That's it.'

St Clair leapt back as if stung. 'You're only talking about Ned Goldfiever's flagship casino.'

'Who he?'

St Clair shook his head in disbelief. 'If you didn't have your head buried in comics all the time you'd know Goldfiever's an Australian who's been muscling in on the gambling and entertainment scene. His organisation has a big fancy name, but it can't stop the rumours that it's all a front for extortion and money laundering.'

Spider turned noticeably paler. 'That's no' sae good, is it?'

St Clair leaned forward menacingly. 'That's as bad as it gets, old son.' He straightened up and clapped a hand to his forehead. 'Come to think of it, there's a case against him coming up at the High Court and, if I'm not mistaken, your man Parkes is prosecuting counsel.'

Even Spider made the connection. 'Bingo!'

St Clair's tone hardened. 'Aye, except this isn't a game. What happened to Vinnie is proof of that. Goldfiever will be needing that tape to put the squeeze on Parkes. You'll have to give it back.'

'How can ah?' Spider demanded indignantly. 'Yer just after telling me Vinnie's snuffed it, and...'

'Not to Vinnie, you eejit. To Goldfiever.'

'But...'

Ignoring the protest, St Clair had started to pace about the room with surprising speed for someone so overweight, fat legs swinging in wide arcs. 'I suppose,' he said, 'there would be no harm in making a copy. Obviously, Parkes is Goldfiever's target. Nothing to stop us making an independent approach to the other party.'

Spider frowned. 'Ah didnae say nothin' aboot a party.'

St Clair stopped pacing to glare at his employee. 'I'm talking about the female with Parkes.'

'Oh, right. The only snag is—'

'Time is of the essence here,' St Clair said. 'You'd have to do it straight away.'

'That's whit ah'm tryin' tae tell you,' Spider protested. 'Ah don't have the tape.'

'Who does?'

'Naebody. Vinnie hid it.'

St Clair sighed. This was like pulling teeth. 'Do you know where?'

'Maybe.'

'Come on, Spider. Either you do or you don't.'

Spider hesitated. 'Vinnie told me there was a wee secret ledge where he could hide it, inside the chain locker of the *Loch Tredwell*.'

St Clair shot his employee a look of complete incredulity. 'I'm afraid to ask,' he said finally, 'but there must be a reason for such a bizarre decision.'

Spider gave a shrug of his bony shoulders. 'I suppose,' he said, 'now that Vinnie wis working there, he thought it wisnae a bad hiding place. He could keep an eye on it without it bein' in his possession.'

St Clair threw his hands in the air. 'Whatever. The problem's solved. You can nip down there and retrieve it and then we're in business. Goldfiever might even offer a reward for its safe return.'

Spider eyed his boss glumly. 'Ah'll need a reason for bein' down at Hunter's Quay this time of night,' he said. 'Ah'd best nip down sharpish tae the gym first an' get ma training gear.'

St Clair waved a hand airily. 'I don't want to know how you do it; just get the tape back here ASAP.'

Typical, Spider thought to himself as he rose from the chair and made for the door.

'Oh, and one more thing.' As his employee paused in the doorway, St Clair stuck DI Munro's card in the top pocket of Spider's shirt. 'When you've done the business, I'd be grateful if you'd give that Detective Inspector Munro a call. She and her sidekick are too eager by half. I've got a hunch they feel they've got something to prove; I just don't want it to be at my expense. Just act dumb; that shouldn't be too hard.' He jabbed a stubby finger into Spider's lapel to underline his message. 'Am I getting through to you, old son?'

Spider swallowed hard. 'Aye. Loud and clear.' He was conscious that a long night stretched ahead of him.

Lynch's Gymnasium, run by the eponymous Jackie, was situated in a run-down part of the city, in an old converted warehouse which was about to fall prey to the developers. A derelict air hung over the building, exacerbated by the peeling paint on the windows and door and the malfunctioning neon sign that read LYN'S GAS, if you ignored the gaps caused by missing letters. At the entrance, Munro and Lennox paused long enough to breathe in the strange odours permeating the room: a heady mixture of stale sweat, plaster dust, broken dreams and perhaps something else, too vague for either of them to define. They counted about a dozen men and two young women working up a sweat: skipping, shadow boxing or working on the punch and speed bags.

Munro nudged Lennox and gestured towards the far end of the room, where a white-haired man was supervising a bout in the ring between what appeared to be an up-and-coming hopeful and a sparring partner who had clearly left his best years far behind him.

Wearing a faded blue tracksuit, Jackie Lynch had a face like crumpled paper and ears resembling cauliflower florets. Under bushy eyebrows his eyes were like willow leaves. They marginally widened in welcome as he recognised Munro. 'My, my, look what the cat's brought in,' he said.

Munro slid an arm around his shoulder by way of greeting. 'How are you, Jackie?' she asked. 'Looks like nothing much has changed around here since my last visit.'

'I'm still the same,' he said, giving her the once-over, 'but you've come on a bit. A proper sight for sore eyes, you are.'

She motioned mischievously towards the contest in the ring. 'Sore eyes are what you get from watching this rubbish, but I want you to meet a colleague, DS Mary Lennox. She's one of the good guys.'

'Pleased to meet you, Sergeant Lennox,' Lynch said. 'Any colleague of this lassie deserves my sympathy.'

'I think I know what you mean,' Lennox said, feeling the strength of the old man's handshake.

'This woman's dad was a copper and a good amateur boxer,' Lynch explained to Lennox. 'He voluntarily gave of his time to help me keep young lads off the street. She wasn't even out of her teens then, of course, but when some of the young tearaways tell me that all coppers are bent I tell them about Ena's dad. Excuse me a second.'

He broke off to bark furiously at his protégé in the ring. 'Come on, Benny. For Pete's sake tuck your chin in and push the left out. Jab, jab, jab. Show him who's in control.'

'Ena?' Lennox appeared to be studying the peeling plaster of the roof.

Munro stared evenly at her colleague until she had her full attention. 'You repeat that anywhere and you'll be back on the beat before your feet touch the ground. Clear?'

Lennox returned her stare, face deadpan. 'My lips are sealed, ma'am.'

Munro turned back to Lynch and explained briefly about the fire aboard the *Loch Tredwell* and Vinnie's murder.

Lynch took a moment to digest the information, his face grave. 'Sorry to hear that,' he said. 'You wouldn't wish that on anyone, although I can't say I'm totally surprised.'

'How so?'

Lynch shrugged. 'Vinnie always had a tendency to mix with the wrong sort.'

'Any of them show up here in the last few days?' Lennox asked casually.

His brow furrowed. 'Funny you should ask. There was a big guy in Saturday night, and again first thing this morning waiting for me to open up. Said he was looking for Vinnie. When I told him Vinnie was most likely working, he asked if he could wait. I told him it was a free country, but I got suspicious of the way he was hanging around the locker room and eventually I caught him fiddling with the padlock on Vinnie's locker.'

'Interesting,' Munro said. 'Another boxer, do you think, or just a friend?'

Lynch frowned. 'No, not a boxer. He didn't give off the right vibes. He was big all right but had too heavy a build, more like a weight lifter, if you know what I mean. Don't get me wrong, though, this guy had probably seen his share of fights, but likely they'd have been in dark alleys rather than a boxing ring. More likely as well to have been with knives than fists.'

'What makes you say that?'

Lynch shrugged. 'The scar on his face, of course. Also they're the weapon of choice among the back-alley cognoscenti.'

Munro exchanged a look with Lennox as the timekeeper rang the bell for the end of the round. 'You think maybe Vinnie was keeping something in his locker for the big man?' she asked Lynch.

Lynch kept her waiting as he put a bottle of water to his fighter's lips and held a basin for him to spit out the contents after rinsing his mouth. 'I got the impression that the big guy felt Vinnie maybe had something that wasn't his to keep.'

Munro nodded. 'Can you describe him for us?'

Lynch flapped a towel in his boxer's direction and frowned. 'He was well over six feet – six-six, or thereabouts – and mean-looking with it; you wouldn't want to meet him in the dark. Ice-cold stare, hair cut to the wood and there was a livid scar along the jawline – not the kind you get from cutting yourself shaving, if you get my meaning. Oh, and a gold earring in one ear.'

Munro's ears pricked up. 'Did he cause any trouble?' she asked.

'No. I told him the lockers were private property and, since Vinnie still hadn't shown up, I asked him to leave. He went with bad grace and said he'd be back, but I can tell you I was relieved to see the back of him. That guy looked

56

as if he would do in his own grandmother for a ha'penny watch.'

Munro bit her lip. 'I know I don't have a search warrant, Jackie, but do you think you could do me a favour and let me take a look in Vinnie's locker?'

The old trainer hesitated for a moment, draping the towel around his neck. 'I don't see why not,' he said. 'I mean, it's not as if Vinnie's going to object now, is he?' He fished a key from a chain around his neck. 'You want number twenty-nine.'

The locker rooms were off the main hall, next to the showers. After Lynch checked there was no one taking a shower they unlocked the door set in the middle row of identical grey metal lockers stacked against one wall. Both Munro and Lennox took an involuntary step backwards at the smell, but closer scrutiny revealed that the offensive odour came from nothing more sinister than a pair of worn leather boxing gloves, a sweaty singlet and a jock strap. There was nothing else in the locker.

Returning the key to Lynch with a head shake, Munro tried another tack. 'What about Vinnie's buddy, Spider McVey?' she asked. 'Has he been around lately?'

Lynch's papery face broke out in a rueful grin. 'Not your day, is it?' he said. 'You just missed him. Spider came tearing in here about ten minutes ago, got kitted out to do some road work and left without a word.'

'Any idea where?' Lennox asked, glancing at Munro.

Lynch nodded. 'Down where the *Loch Tredwell* is berthed. Goes there a lot, does Spider. Good jogging track alongside the river.' He chuckled quietly. 'Imagine. Spider interested in sailing ships.'

'Imagine!' Munro echoed, thinking that was exactly where his pal, Vinnie, had ended up dead. Curiouser and curiouser, she mused. 'Listen, Jackie,' she said, 'do you think we could arrange a time for you to come in and sit with an e-fit artist? We need to get a picture of this man with the scar. We'll send a car for you, of course.'

The bell sounded for the end of another round as Jackie said, 'No bother. Just make sure it's an unmarked one. I don't want anyone round here getting the wrong idea and thinking you've run me in.'

'Thanks, Jackie,' Munro said.

In the act of bending over his protégé with a water bottle Lynch suddenly reached over to grab Munro's arm, spilling water and leaving his boxer with his mouth open like a cuckoo in the nest. 'I've just remembered,' he said. 'The big guy with the scar; I knew there was something else about him I wanted to tell you.'

'What was it, Jackie?' she asked.

'His accent,' Lynch said. 'I'm absolutely positive he was an Aussie.'

'A compatriot of Goldfiever's,' Munro mused. 'Isn't that interesting?'

'Very,' Lennox said.

The action in the ring again drew Lynch like a magnet. They left to the sound of his voice ringing in their ears. 'Come on, Benny,' he yelled. 'Jab, jab, jab!'

CHAPTER SIX

Buerk buzzed his neighbour's doorbell and let himself in with her spare key. 'Anybody at home?' he called wearily.

'Just where the blue blazes did you think we'd be?'

Elvira's response was accompanied by a gruff bark and the scrabble of claws on a wood floor. There was just time to close the front door with his heel before her Rhodesian ridgeback reached him.

'I hope you're not tormenting Biltong out there.' Elvira's next salvo found Buerk pinned against the wall by the dog's front paws, his face being licked by a tongue like sandpaper. Extricating himself from the dog's attentions, he was aware of a sickly sweet smell coming from the living room before discovering his neighbour sitting awkwardly at her desk in front of a computer. Her left leg, immobilised in a plaster cast, was propped on a footstool. In an ashtray at her elbow rested a smouldering spliff.

Beyond the fact that she wrote a syndicated astrology column, Buerk knew little about Elvira, but from the way she spoke guardedly about her own affairs while subtly pumping him for information, he had a sneaking feeling she might be ex-MI5.

Until recently, he had spoken to her only on chance meetings on the landing (they shared the top floor of an apartment block), and then the topics had been confined mainly to the weather and Biltong (the latter rather difficult to ignore). Although Elvira initially appeared guarded, the dog took to him straight away, a source of as much amazement to Buerk as it clearly was to Elvira.

Two weeks ago he had met her hirpling with the aid of a pair of crutches (a cracked tibia resulting from a contretemps with what she described as a *Top Gear* nerd unable to control a supermarket trolley). Perhaps rashly, he had offered to run essential errands for her until her recovery.

'A good Samaritan!' she had mused. 'Truth is I can manage most of my needs via online shopping or by e-mail. Walking the dog, however, is temporarily beyond my earthly powers.'

With some misgivings, Buerk had accepted the implicit challenge in those eyes. It had taken a bit of luck to learn how to cope with the boisterous animal. Tonight, he reflected, would be the fourteenth night in a row that he had done so. Over that period Elvira had managed to winkle out of him most of his life story, while details of her personal life might as well have been locked in uncharted deep space where black holes lurked mysteriously. It occurred to him he had been thoroughly debriefed. Despite this, he felt comfortable in Elvira's company.

'In South Africa,' Elvira now informed him, 'ridgebacks were once used to hunt lions. Might explain why they can be a mite aloof with strangers, but we must never confuse this with aggression.'

'Dear me, that would never do,' he agreed. At that particular moment Biltong was attempting to burrow his nose into Buerk's groin, paying scant regard to aloofness.

'On the whole, probably not the best choice for inexperienced dog handlers,' she went on.

Taking the chair opposite, Buerk thought it a bit much she had chosen to mention this now, but was distracted from saying so as he watched her pick up the smouldering roach and puff it into life.

'Told my doctor I wanted to come off his painkillers,' she explained through the enveloping miasma.

'Alternative medicine,' he said drily.

Elvira had a small greenhouse on the roof terrace reached by an internal stairway. She had once told him she housed a telescope up there for empirical research on the heavens, but had never volunteered information on any specific flora that she might be cultivating. Now, a vision of rows of well-illuminated plants with stiff upright stems, divided serrated leaves and glandular hairs rose unbidden to his mind.

'The state of the country would drive anyone to drink, never mind the weed,' she said.

'Tell me about it.' Briefly enveloped in a haze of smoke, Buerk added, 'Seems to me the whole blessed country's developing an unhealthy obsession with hostile takeovers of one kind or another.'

She peered at him through a drifting smoke ring, shrewd eyes twinkling. 'I suspect you're referring to that Antipodean group, what's-its-name, that's been in the headlines.'

'SLIME.'

'I beg your pardon?'

'Southern Line International Media Edutainment.' He became animated as the name of an organisation with a highly dubious reputation and interests in the communications and entertainment field tripped distastefully from his tongue.

'That's the one,' she said. 'I have to admit it gave me a strange feeling of déjà vu when I heard on the radio this morning about their proposed merger with the Thistle Media Group.' She blew another smoke ring and watched it slowly rise, expand and fade. 'After all you've been through with your merger at the university.'

Buerk bristled. 'The only difference is that TMG will never buckle to outside pressure as our board did.'

She cupped her chin in one hand. 'Been talking to our broker, have we?'

Buerk grimaced. 'I wish! I did some work for them once; they're good people. For their sake, I hope they retain their independence.'

She shifted uncomfortably in her chair, prompting him to ask, 'How's the leg?'

'It's coming off tomorrow.'

He was half out of his seat. 'The leg?'

'The plaster,' she replied calmly.

Buerk heaved a sigh of relief. 'That's lucky. I have to be off filming on the morrow and couldn't have managed the usual walkies.'

Elvira cocked her head to one side. 'Going anywhere interesting?'

Buerk had to clear his throat before he could get the words out. 'Papa Westray, one of the more remote of the Orkney Isles.'

'What on earth would possess you to go there?'

'You might very well ask,' he said. Privately he was thinking this was something he was not ready to divulge, even to Elvira.

'I thought I just did,' she persisted.

He knew the drill. Stick as close to the truth as is feasible. 'One of the staff is keen I make a nature film,' he said. 'The deputy principal happens to think it's a good idea.'

She looked at him hard. 'A bit out of your comfort zone, I should have thought.'

'Very true, but needs must.'

She continued to hold his eye as she reached for the roach and said nothing until the tip again glowed red. 'You're a Virgo, aren't you, Angus?' Her voice had taken on a husky quality.

'Sorry?' For a brief second an image of Rowena Munro flashed before his eyes. Had she been talking to Elvira? No. Impossible. Then the penny dropped. 'Oh, you mean my zodiac sign?'

Elvira gazed at him from behind stray wisps of smoke. 'You should know, Angus, I haven't altogether given up on you. You simply need the right conjunction of circumstances to achieve that Damascene moment.'

'Easy for you to say,' he said. 'I seem to recall you telling me I was somewhat retarded... astrologically speaking, at any rate.'

'Quite right,' she said. 'According to my readings, your life does appear to be in some disarray.'

'Yes, well, you hardly need a crystal ball for that.'

Choosing to ignore his sarcasm, she continued: 'Of course, to some people the obvious remedy would be for you to get a grip and try to organise your life better, but, in a strange way, that might simply complicate matters.'

'That's what I keep telling anyone who'll listen.' He treated her to a wry smile. 'Not that anyone ever does, of course.'

Elvira sighed. 'You remember I explained to you, Angus, that your various situations were in transition, some of them big time, because your ruler, Mercury, happened to be retrograde?' She half-turned to make a few keystrokes on her computer. 'Until Thursday the twenty-seventh, to be precise.'

Buerk suddenly brightened. 'That's only three days away and it also happens to be the day of my interview. Is that a good sign? Excuse the pun.'

Elvira permitted herself a brief smile. 'Maybe. High time you began to focus your mind a bit more. You're one of life's drifters, you know – you need to become more proactive.'

While they had been talking Biltong had disappeared into the kitchen, and he now reappeared with the lead in his mouth.

Buerk sighed. 'Even Biltong seems to agree with you.' He rose, feeling slightly foolish at the sudden rush of optimism. He had never given much credence to astrological predictions; for him, at least, their promises never seemed to be fulfilled. He had enough problems dealing with the present. Strange, though, Elvira suddenly reminding him about Thursday like that. He shrugged. More than likely her readings of the cosmos were severely compromised by an overindulgence in the weed.

As he clipped on Biltong's lead, a shaft of evening sunlight slanting through her window illuminated Elvira in her chair while casting the rest of the room into comparative shadow. Dust motes danced in the shaft like a haphazard collision of electrons and for a moment he half-expected to see her beamed up from her chair into the heavens. And yet, even as he stood there, the light altered and the room darkened. That was the real problem, he thought. The metaphysical boundary between the darkness and the light kept shifting, most of the time too subtly for him to divine its meaning.

A brisk walk to the Black Bull would normally have taken Buerk about twenty minutes. He made it in half that time thanks to the pulling power of Biltong. Nose to the ground, perhaps he was in search of lion spoor? The moment Buerk reached his favourite watering hole he knew his troubles with the straining Biltong would be over.

On the first night of walkies with the brute, while desperately clutching his end of the lead he had been dragged along the streets, not to mention through two hedges (painful) and through a narrow gap between two wooden palings (a close shave), after a cat had been sighted. He had tried in vain to point out to the dog that his current quarry was not even feral, far less a lion, and ought to have been beneath his contempt. Where was all this aloofness that Elvira kept banging on about? The cat wisely found refuge in a tree. Biltong thereupon sat down on his haunches, clearly prepared to wait it out, until Buerk realised he was standing in the beer garden of the Black Bull.

It occurred to him that a stiff drink would not go amiss and he promptly ordered a restorative double of his favourite malt from a passing waiter. While he was waiting on his order a man fetching drinks from the bar almost stepped on Biltong and spilled some of his pint of stout on the paving. Biltong immediately lapped it up and looked up at Buerk, smacking his lips, the cat apparently forgotten. Buerk promptly ordered a half-pint for the animal from the same waiter, whose name tag indicated she was called Maisie.

Tonight, the weather being unpromising, he had opted for the bar and had just hooked Biltong's lead under the leg of his stool with a slip knot when Maisie again moved over to serve him.

'The usual, Angus?' she asked brightly.

He gave a preoccupied nod, his mind sifting over the events of the day and his impending and potentially disastrous mission to the Orkneys.

Maisie returned with his malt whisky and a half of stout for Biltong. She served the stout in a battered tinfoil baking tray of the kind the pub used to house their famous steak and kidney pies and which she now kept aside expressly for the purpose. Buerk watched as the dog greedily lapped up the stout and settled down beside the stool with a contented sigh. He knew from experience he now had about fifteen minutes' leisure while the dog slept off the drink. He permitted himself a wry smile, wondering if Elvira would approve of his reward-based training and socialisation technique.

He had scarcely taken an appreciative sip of his malt when his eye caught a news ribbon scrolling across the bottom of the screen of the muted TV set perched above the gantry. 'Be an angel, Maisie,' he called, 'and turn up the sound for a minute.'

As the sound came up the newsreader announced that a renewed hostile bid had been made for the Thistle Media Group by Southern Line International Media Edutainment. Buerk strained to catch the sound bite that followed from the chairperson of the Thistle Media Group, Sir Rankin Maltby. He frankly acknowledged in his measured tones that an increased offer had been made for TMG, but cheerfully and confidently predicted that it would suffer the same fate as the previous bid.

Buerk heaved a relieved sigh. 'That's something, at any rate,' he said.

Maisie shot him a quizzical look but, before he could satisfy her curiosity, she was called to attend to another customer.

Buerk's introspective mood was further deepened by thoughts of the impending internal promotions panel interview scheduled for Thursday afternoon. He was not an excessively ambitious man, but the merger had obliged him to apply for his own post of head of the educational television department. Buerk knew only too well that if

Deputy Principal Hornblower had his way he would lose out to Crawley; it was as simple as that.

While Biltong snored, Buerk became aware of a heavily breathing individual with a large poodle in tow who came to the bar for a quick gin and tonic. The poodle had been subjected to a recent cut whereby its hair had been shorn from its body, leaving a huge mane-like ruff around its shoulders. Thinking he had met a kindred spirit in the shape of a fellow dog-walker, Buerk gave him a friendly nod, but the newcomer merely grunted before retreating with his drink to a distant table.

As the whisky began to ease anxieties over his future, Buerk's thoughts began to turn to an altogether more pleasant subject in the shape of Acting Detective Inspector Munro, first name 'Rowena' according to the card she had stuck in his pocket. From a rather startling meeting earlier in the day, he recalled her mesmerising green eyes and wondered if perhaps she had been sending him a coded message. He decided to chance his arm. It was always a problem for Buerk, trying to read the signs women gave out. They could sometimes be as mysterious as the runes studied by the introverted scholars in the university's mediaeval history department. He considered Rowena Munro a particular case. In Elvira's terms, she might be considered as dark and mysterious as the rings of Saturn.

He had just stood up to take his mobile from his pocket when a curious throaty sound, half bark, half moan, escaped from Biltong's throat. Unlike his dog, Buerk had failed to notice the furtive gin and tonic disappearing through the swing doors, accompanied by the poodle with the leonine cut. Having just stirred from his slumbers, Biltong responded as would any sleepy-headed, half-cut ridgeback imagining he'd just glimpsed a lion disappearing out of the door. He gave chase.

Biltong was determined that nothing would frustrate his intent. Certainly not Buerk's belated and futile command calling him to heel. Nor the bar stool to which his lead was still attached, now being dragged behind him. Not even a table with which the flying stool collided, showering the laps of its two ancient occupants with spilt beer and dominoes.

After that, the swing doors presented no kind of opposition to the mindset of a dog with his dander up. He was out in the street, into his stride and off in full cry after the poodle, the stool bucking wildly in his wake. As Buerk belatedly reached the doors, he noted that it had started to rain.

Alarmed at the sudden uproar behind him, the poodle's owner quickly sized up the situation. He gathered up his pet and took to his heels. Biltong, dragging a slowly disintegrating bar stool, careered along behind. Bringing up the rear came a furiously cursing Buerk. He was only vaguely aware they were heading in the general direction of the river.

In a few bewildering moments, a sequence of events unfolded to bring matters to a climax. Alongside a new apartment block erected close to the old Customs House, the poodle and her master gained the sanctuary of their own protected entry. Seeing an opportunity to gain control over the disobedient mutt, Buerk made one last lung-bursting lunge for the trailing lead. The ridgeback, which had been steadily gaining on his target until defeat was cruelly snatched from the jaws of victory, slithered to a sudden and mystified halt. The inanimate stool blindly obeyed Newton's third law of motion. Still attached to the dog by the lead, it attempted to whip viciously through a 180-degree reaction only to smash itself to lignified shrapnel across the shins of a shadowy figure who had just rounded the corner running at full tilt towards them.

The blow felled the newcomer on the spot as effectively as a gaucho's bolas. Unable to stop himself in time, Buerk fell over the stationary dog and met the toppled figure in a bone-jarring collision that knocked the wind from him. At such close quarters he could not help but notice that his victim was wearing a ski mask.

He lay there, cursing his luck, dogs, and retrograde planets, in no particular order. He amazed himself with the range and colour of the stream of free-association invective his mind called forth to describe his lot. It was some time before he registered the fact that a third person had joined this tableau vivant. His first thought was that he must have suffered concussion and had started to hallucinate because he was certain Detective Inspector Rowena Munro was bending over him, those green eyes reflecting in equal parts amusement, irritation and concern.

'Angus Buerk,' he heard her say. 'Can it really be you, and in the wars again?'

Before Buerk's walkies with Biltong had come to such a dramatic end, DI Munro had dropped Lennox back at St Clair's now-deserted car park with instructions to go home and get some rest. Having watched her sergeant drive off, Munro decided on a hunch to take a detour that would take her past the riverside berth of the *Loch Tredwell*. She started backtracking along the new road down by the river, her mind busy with what Jackie Lynch had told her about both Spider and the mysterious giant who had been rather too interested in the lately-deceased Vinnie McGrath. Something about that description started to bother her, but she could not work out what, as other questions crowded it out.

For instance, had it really been pure coincidence that Buerk and his crew just happened upon the fire aboard the *Loch Tredwell* too late to save Vinnie McGrath? She knew that Chief Superintendent Douglas did not believe in coincidences because he'd told her so in unambiguous terms when she had reported in earlier in the evening. He had also suggested, none too gently, that finding Spider and getting the truth out of him was a condition on her being allowed to stay on the case. What a schmuck!

She was driving slowly along an avenue of saplings, past a new block of flats, and peering intently through the rain-slicked windscreen when she spotted two figures travelling fast in opposite directions. One figure, easily recognisable from the crab-like movements as Spider McVey, in a black tracksuit and ski mask, had just rounded the corner of the block of flats from the direction of the quayside berth of the *Loch Tredwell*; the other rain-bedraggled figure, head down (also vaguely familiar somehow), appeared to be pursuing a huge dog which had something odd attached to its lead. As the two opposing forces collided a mere dozen yards in front of her, she almost lost control of her car. Pulling to a halt directly alongside, she slid quickly from the driving seat as she also recognised the second figure.

'Angus Buerk,' she said. 'Can it really be you, and in the wars again?'

The incredulous voice of Detective Inspector Munro slowly penetrated Buerk's brain. He watched as she turned from him to tug the ski mask from his luckless victim. 'And Spider McVey, brought low by a technical knockout, delivered by our seemingly ever-available good citizen.'

Struggling slowly to his feet, Buerk tried to protest that felling Spider had been a complete accident, but Munro waved his protestations aside.

'You know, Buerk,' she said, 'I can't make up my mind whether you're causing me problems or trying to do my job for me.'

He was saved from having to reply by Spider struggling upright in his turn. He let out a groan and fingered a cut above his left eye which was already beginning to swell. 'Whit hit me?' he said.

'Afraid that was me,' Buerk said. 'Sorry. Spider.'

Recognising his unintentional assailant, Spider brightened visibly. 'Angus, whit brings you down here?'

DI Munro thought she would like the answer to that, too, but decided to defer satisfaction until a later time. 'All right, you two,' she said. 'Enough of the cosy chit-chat.' She turned first to Spider. 'Come on. I think you and I had better have a chat down at the station.'

'But ah huvnae done nothin,' he protested.

72

She looked at him doubtfully. It might just have been because he was badly shaken by the fall, but she had a feeling from his guilty expression he was covering up something. 'Into the car with you,' she said. 'We can have someone take a look at that eye while we're at it.'

Without further protest Spider allowed himself to be ushered into her car.

She returned to face Buerk. 'Are you okay to walk your dog home?'

'Sure,' he said. 'Apart from being soaked, I'm fine. Oh, and the dog belongs to a neighbour, who recently broke her ankle.' He waved a hand in a vague gesture. 'I was just doing her a favour.'

She eyed him for a long moment, her lower lip trembling until she managed to regain control. 'You and I must have a chat real soon,' she said, 'but right now I have a more pressing engagement with Spider.'

'Fine with me.'

Having been thus dismissed, Buerk recovered the lead of a strangely docile Biltong and started to make his weary way homewards. There was, however, a smile on his face. After all, he now had a date, of sorts, with the rather dishy Rowena Munro.

CHAPTER SEVEN

Harvey Watt date-stamped the books of the last customer in what had been a long queue at the counter and thought it would be a welcome relief when the new bar-coded self-check system was introduced at the end of the month. It would save him a chore but would most likely cost him a member of staff. So what? If they replaced them with cardboard cut-outs, no one would be able to tell the difference. Zombies, the lot of them. Two years in the position of head of the branch and he was bored out of his skull. He needed a bit of excitement in his life.

He turned to check the clock on the wall behind him. 'Ladies and gentlemen,' he announced, 'the library will be closing in five minutes.'

A handsome young man with short-cropped blond hair, he had the kind of physique that signalled frequent visits to the gymnasium. His 'healthy' skin tone perhaps owed more to visits to tanning beds than to expensive holidays abroad (not that he didn't wish for those). Perhaps his only blemishes were a slight downturn of the mouth and a look in his eye that suggested his tastes might run a little more on the wild side than those with which most of his readers would feel comfortable. One or two of his older female readers had already been shocked by an occasional glimpse of a metal stud which pierced his tongue.

His practised eye took stock of the situation presently before him. A couple of down-and-outs looked up from their newspapers and shifted uneasily under his scrutiny. He knew, full well, that they came in to get out of the cold rather than with any intent to glean information. He smiled cynically at one of his regulars, who had glanced at him anxiously from the true crime section while feverishly trying to decide which selections would stimulate her otherwise mundane existence.

He moved into the reference room and his smile quickly faded. A familiar face looked up at him with what he considered to be studied insolence. He estimated the man to be in his late thirties. He had strong hands and thick hair tied back in a ponytail. Watt knew the man's name was John McManus. His expensive-looking leather jacket was draped round his chair. Under his tight-fitting shirt, his body muscles rippled. A large art book was open on the table in front of him.

Watt cast an appraising eye over the man's physique. Being a shallow thinker, he assumed because of his build and weather-beaten features that the man was some kind of labourer. Being also an intellectual snob, it was a constant source of annoyance to him that the fellow was always to be found poring over his expensive art books. To Watt, it was fairly obvious what he was after; he knew the sort only too well. Several times he had slipped into the reference room after the man had gone just to check that the books were all accounted for and that none of the illustrated pages were missing.

'Lights-out time, folks,' he announced, this time with considerably more firmness. 'The library is closing now.'

Under Watt's continued scrutiny, McManus shrugged, closed the book he had been studying and calmly replaced it in its correct place on the shelf. As he did so, Watt leaned across the table and saw that he had made several sketches of the nudes he had been poring over – excellent copies, he grudgingly conceded. He was sorely tempted to go over and tear them up before publicly consigning them to the bin, but some inner counsel advised him against such a rash course of action. Instead, he watched in surly silence as McManus pocketed the sketches and drifted past with a casual, 'Good night.'

Watt grunted and followed McManus into the main body of the library just as a leather-clad motorcyclist breezed through the swing doors. Still wearing a crash helmet with the visor down, the figure brushed brusquely past McManus.

'Easy, pal,' McManus said in a good-natured tone. 'Where's the fire?'

Even with the visor down McManus could feel the hostility in the glare directed back at him. He was saved from further possible grief when Watt's assistant, Jacqueline, rushed over to head off the newcomer clad in expensive blue leathers. 'I'm very sorry,' she said. 'We're just clos...'

The words died on her lips as the figure raised the visor and Jacqueline found herself staring into the unnaturally bright eyes and flushed cheeks of her ultimate superior, Vera Goodnight.

Ignoring the nonplussed assistant, Vera glanced sharply at Watt, motioned him towards the staffroom door set behind the counter, and marched inside.

Watt swiftly set Jacqueline to rounding up the stragglers and followed Vera into the staffroom. Having removed her helmet, she was fussing with her short hair in front of the mirror fixed above the sink. 'Get rid of them,' she snapped.

'They're just going,' he said soothingly. 'I've already called time twice.'

She swung round abruptly. 'I want them out. NOW!'

'Jacqueline has to come in for her coat and scarf,' he said.

Vera glanced scornfully at the items, removed them from the peg and thrust them into his arms. 'I don't want that moon-faced cow coming in here,' she said with a snarl. 'Tell her her house is on fire and her mother's trapped in the john. Just get her out of here.'

Watt suppressed a nervous giggle. 'Absolutely.' At the door he hesitated. 'Everything all right?'

'Everything's far from all right,' she said curtly. 'Somebody has to pay for the day from hell I've had. I've chosen you.'

Feeling slightly giddy, he protested mildly: 'But I haven't done anything.'

She fingered the zip-tag at the neck of her figure-hugging leathers and smiled archly. 'Oh, but we're about to change all that, are we not?' The zip started to slide down slowly until it was obvious she was wearing nothing underneath.

He fled into the main body of the library fighting an attack of nervous hysteria. Reaching for the master switch, he put out all the lights save the one at the door. 'Ladies and gentlemen,' he called, 'I must ask you all to leave now.'

Seeing Watt clutching her outdoor clothes, Jacqueline came towards him, concern showing on her pale face. 'Is something the matter?' she asked.

He pulled a face. 'Just something that her majesty wants me to attend to straight away.'

Jacqueline clucked her tongue sympathetically. 'She's in one of her moods again, isn't she?' Vera's fits of temper were well known among the staff.

Watt suppressed a titter. 'You could say that.'

'Then you go ahead,' she offered. 'I'll see the stragglers beat a hasty retreat.'

This time a manic giggle did escape from his lips. 'Ms Goodnight insists that everyone leave the premises, including staff,' he said. 'Anyway, it's high time you had an early night for once. I know your mum worries about you.'

She flashed him a grateful smile. 'That's very thoughtful of you, Harvey. You know I don't mind helping out – I could make you both a cup of tea while you have your chat?' She reached up to flick an imaginary speck from his shirt. 'I wouldn't get in your way.'

The truth of the matter was that she was in no hurry to get back to her mother's incessant complaints and ever-increasing demands. She wanted to say that she could offer him a lot more than he had ever dreamed possible, but, as always, she kept those kinds of thoughts to herself.

'That's sweet of you, Jacqueline, but best not antagonise her further.' He offered her a smile and handed over her coat and scarf. 'This doesn't need to tie up both of us.' He had to suppress another giggle as the prospect of a threesome leapt graphically into his imagination. 'Now, off you go and I'll lock up after you.'

Before she could protest further, he ushered her almost brusquely out of the door along with the remaining stragglers. He locked and bolted the door, shut down the computer system and flicked off the remaining lights. Striding back into the staffroom, he stepped over the leather jacket on the floor. 'Really, Vera,' he said, 'you have to learn to control your impulses. That kind of behaviour could land you in hot...'

He stopped dead in his tracks. Vera was leaning back against the table, stark naked, each hand cupping one gibbous breast.

'You don't know the meaning of "hot",' she said, 'but I'll soon knock some sense into you.'

This time he could no longer suppress his giggle. 'What are you going to use: your handbag?'

She responded with a curious, throaty laugh that hinted at amusement and irritation in equal measure and more than a frisson of sexual tension. 'No,' she said. 'What I had in mind was this.' She produced a silver-topped riding crop from behind her back. 'Now, on your knees, boy,' she commanded. 'You've kept me waiting rather longer than was wise.'

Sitting in her car, Jacqueline watched the shadows behind the curtained window of the staffroom dance in confusing patterns. She did not know exactly what was going on in there; she was not even sure she wanted to know. She only knew that, for the moment at least, it was severely detrimental to her own ambitions, and that she was powerless to intervene.

CHAPTER EIGHT

Fifteen minutes after his collision with Buerk, Spider was sitting in an interview room at the local nick, an ice pack on his bruised eye and a mug of tea on the table in front of him. Apart from his mobile, also on the table, a small key, which Munro readily accepted fitted the locker room at Lynch's Gymnasium, was all the personal property he had on him. He was currently being required to answer Munro's questions, albeit grudgingly, for the benefit of the tape.

Q: Why had you decided to go running along the river path close by the berth of the *Loch Tredwell*?

A: Ah often go there. It's a good four miles there and back.

Q: It hadn't been your intention to go on board the *Loch Tredwell* for any reason?

What might have been a guilty look was covered up by a groan and a show of adjusting the ice pack.

A: Definitely not. Anyway, how wis ah supposed tae know that there had been a fire? Ah kin tell you that wis a shock tae ma system.

Q: It wasn't the sight of a policeman on guard that made you run?

A: It reminded me that's where Vinnie had bought it an' that's why ah legged it. Ah wis pure shocked, so ah wis.

Q: Why the ski mask? You were a long way from the slopes.

A: Aye, very good, inspector. Actually ah often wear the ski mask rolled up, keeps ma heid warm.

Q: On this occasion it was pulled down over your face. You were hoping to avoid being recognised, right?

A: It wis dark. Who wis gonnae see me?

Q: When did you last see Vinnie McGrath?

A: Ages ago.

Q: Can you be more specific?

A: Two days ago at the gym.

Q: What did you talk about?

A slight hesitation requiring a reapplication of the ice pack.

A: We were there for sparring practice, no' tae huv a chat.

Munro brought her hands down hard on the table. 'Don't give me that crap, Spider. You never sparred together; Vinnie was too big for you.'

This time Spider removed the ice pack from his eye to glare at her. 'Vinnie might have been a big man, but he wis rubbish when it came to technology.'

Imperceptibly she straightened in her chair. 'But that's your area of expertise,' she said calmly. 'That's why Vinnie came to you. He needed your technical help with something.'

At that precise point, Chief Inspector Douglas, who had been watching the interview from behind a one-way glass screen, entered the room, turning a cynical smile first on Spider and then on Munro. Spider responded by reapplying the ice pack as though trying to hide behind it. Munro knew from experience that that look meant trouble.

'DI Munro, a word.'

She followed him into the corridor and turned to face him. His face, heavy and fleshy at the best of times, was now flushed, and the two deep furrows running from the edge of the mouth to the corners of his nose gave him the look of a bloodhound. A sleuth of the old school with a deep mistrust of fast-tracked academics and the new technologies. Even his deep-set eyes reminded her of a lugubrious canine tracker. But there was something else in those eyes, some kind of missionary zeal that made them gleam. She had no idea what it was, but it made her heart sink.

'I rather think Spider McVey has been leading you a merry dance, Inspector Munro,' he said.

'I'm sorry to hear that, sir. In what way?'

His brow darkened. 'You haven't got him to mention Buerk once – you know, that fellow academic of yours who just chanced on Vinnie McGrath's body this morning. When he just happened to turn up for a second time at the scene of a crime to meet the other suspect, surely even you can see there has to be a connection between them. Maybe you think this sort of thing is all in a day's work for an academic. Well, let's face it, they haven't got a hell of a lot else to do.'

She glared at Douglas, arms folded, wondering how much more of this she'd have to swallow. One or two heads had started poking out of the CID room into the corridor to see who was on the receiving end this time.

'With respect, sir, I was just about to explore such a connection through...'

Douglas held up a hand to silence her before continuing his harangue. 'McVey might very well have passed something to Buerk when they so conveniently collided. Pity you didn't ask *him* to turn out his pockets. Now maybe, just maybe, you might feel you should start digging a little deeper into Buerk's activities. If you ask me, Spider is a mere fly in the ointment.'

She wanted to point out the image presented something of a mixed metaphor, but there were more important issues to discuss. In the end he wouldn't allow her to mention any of them.

'Mark my words, inspector. Your man Buerk's involved in this somehow. You want to stick to him like glue until you've figured out what his game is. And I'll tell you something else...' His voice began to rise, the veins in his neck standing out like knots. 'I'll lay you odds he'll lead you straight to that muck-peddling villain Goldfiever. Now, why don't you pull the finger out and give us a result? This business has set back the restoration work on the *Loch Tredwell*, and none of us wants that to happen, do we?'

'No, sir.'

As he turned on his heel and strode back to his office, slamming the door behind him, she leaned back against the wall and puffed out her cheeks, exhaling slowly. Douglas

84

had never shown the slightest interest in the restoration of the *Loch Tredwell*. Vera Goodnight had to be the one jerking his strings. Not for the first time she wondered what kind of hold Vera had on Douglas.

More worrying for Buerk was this alleged link to Goldfiever. Presiding over a growing empire of dubious activities, Goldfiever had long been regarded as public enemy number one by her superior officer, but this leap in the dark linking Buerk with Goldfiever was not good. If the Black Douglas had Angus Buerk anywhere in the frame with Goldfiever, it was going to take some persuasive evidence to get Buerk out from under. Beyond female instinct, however, did she have a single shred of evidence that he was as innocent as he had appeared?

Buerk's first task on returning home was to return a weary Biltong to Elvira and explain, in as little detail as possible, the cause of his late return. He had barely had time for a shower and change of clothes when someone rang his doorbell. Thinking it might be Elvira with some revised predictions of doom, he was astonished to discover Munro standing on the doorstep. The sight of her gave him an immediate lift. 'Don't you have a home of your own to go to?' he asked.

'At least you can still talk,' she countered. 'The way your mouth was hanging open there, I was afraid you'd lost the power of speech. In any case, my governor thinks having a home to go to is an outmoded notion. It seriously interferes with getting the job done.'

'You'd better come in,' he said. He beamed as he ushered her inside.

Her smile was apologetic. 'I'm afraid this isn't a social call. I have some official questions for you.'

'Pity,' he said. 'At least let me offer you a drink. God knows I need one.'

'That makes two of us,' she said. 'A glass of red would probably do the trick.'

Buerk retrieved a bottle from a wine rack and poured two glasses, leaving her a moment to admire the spacious living room dominated by floor-to-ceiling bookshelves along two walls.

'Yarra Ridge Merlot,' he said, placing a glass in her hand. 'Been saving it for a special occasion.'

She took a sip and nodded approvingly. 'Good choice.'

'You eaten yet?'

She shook her head ruefully. 'That's still on my to-do list.'

'Mine too. I was just about to rustle up some linguine with clams. Care to join me?'

She looked startled. 'You cook?'

'Doesn't everyone?'

She shook her head. 'Not me. I do toast and coffee. After that it's either microwaving ready meals or takeaway.'

'Well, you can't be good at everything.'

She eyed him curiously. 'You're not trying a snow job on me, are you?'

He grinned. 'Absolutely not. You can even grill me while I cook, if you'll pardon the pun.'

The offer reminded her she'd scarcely eaten all day. 'All right, you're on.'

'Make yourself at home,' he said. 'It'll take me ten minutes... fifteen tops.'

He disappeared into the kitchen, leaving her to examine the contents of the room. On a coffee table was the programme for a recent production of *Don Giovanni*. She couldn't think when she had last been to an opera. Probably *Carmen*. Amidst the impressive collection of books, she noticed a number of DVDs.

As she sipped the wine, the idea suddenly leapt unbidden into her brain. Videos provided a legitimate connection between Spider and Buerk through St Clair's business. Buerk himself had been the first to suggest a connection between Spider and Vinnie McGrath. If Vinnie had previously worked for Goldfiever, then that linked Buerk, however tenuously, with the underworld king of media sleaze. Could the Black Douglas be on to something?

God, where was she going with this? Maybe she was beginning to unravel. Buerk's camera crew looked shifty enough, but could he really be involved in anything sleazy? Fanciful as it might be, she found the Black Douglas's insinuations more than vaguely disturbing... but she was getting way too far ahead of herself. If the labels were anything to go by, Buerk's taste in DVDs did not seem to extend beyond some recent mainstream films – mainly thrillers, she noted. She moved on. An altogether different section of books then caught her interest. She called out in surprise, 'You read poetry?'

'In the bath mostly,' his detached voice came from the kitchen. 'Anything from Baudelaire to Burns.' She followed the voice to its source. He turned briefly to grin at her. 'Afraid I haven't got any further than the B's.'

The small table was already set for two, complete with candle. Pasta simmered in one saucepan while he busied himself with the sauce in another. It gave her an opportunity to look at him critically for the first time. Here he was cooking a meal for her. He was clearly intelligent, good-humoured and not bad-looking either. She felt a rush of anger towards Douglas course through her, not just for the way he treated her but for the way he'd accused Buerk of being implicated on the flimsiest of evidence.

'One way and another,' she said, 'it's not been your day.'

He gave a quick shake of the head. 'You can say that again. Elvira thinks I just need a Damascene moment to achieve self-fulfilment.'

'Elvira?'

'Lady next door. Does horoscopes. Biltong's owner.'

'Oh, the dog. Um. I know I shouldn't ask, but... Biltong?'

'He's a Rhodesian ridgeback. Biltong's a kind of cured meat somewhat similar to beef jerky that originated in South Africa. It evolved from the dried meats – beef, springbok, even shark and ostrich fillets – carried by the Voortrekkers who needed durable food on the Great Trek from the Cape Colony.'

She stared at him for a moment. 'Goodness. You are a fount of knowledge.'

'Not me. Elvira.'

'To be honest, I'm more interested in what happened to you this evening.'

'Oh, that.' He waved a hand dismissively and gestured at the food. 'This is about ready; might as well talk while we eat.'

'Suits me,' she said, taking the seat he pulled out for her.

Heaping steaming pasta on to two plates, he poured a generous helping of sauce over each and garnished it with a sprinkle of basil from a pot on the window ledge (hand-torn, she noticed). When he placed one helping in front of her, the aroma of the rich sauce had her salivating at once. Unbidden, she picked up a fork and started eating.

'This is wonderful,' she said, her mouth full. 'What's all in here?'

He cupped his chin in his hand and watched her eat. 'Just garlic, chillies, tomatoes and onions blended with the clams. It's hunger that gives it the edge.' He brandished the opened bottle. 'Care for a top-up?'

She put a hand over her glass. 'Better not, and I'm still waiting to hear your story, so don't think you're off the hook.'

Between mouthfuls, he launched into an explanation of his bizarre evening. Eating steadily, she listened attentively, occasionally stopping him to seek clarification. He told the story with wry amusement, without sparing himself. If he was lying about his innocent involvement in the shambles that had led to Spider being felled, he was extremely convincing about it.

When he'd finished, she eyed him across her empty plate. 'Did you know that until recently, Vinnie McGrath was working for Ned Goldfiever at his casino?'

He looked at her sharply. 'That scumbag!'

Her eyebrows shot up. 'You know Goldfiever?'

'Never met him,' he said bluntly, 'nor do I care to. I just want him to keep his thieving hands off the Thistle Media Group. They're good guys there and I don't like the idea of a sleazebag like him taking them over. Besides,' he added ruefully, 'I've had enough of mergers.'

She looked at him in astonishment. He'd used the 'sleaze' word that had been on her own lips. She decided to let that fly stick to the wall.

He put on some coffee and suggested they move back into the lounge. She elected to take the single armchair, leaving him the sofa.

'We're still holding Spider down at the nick,' she said casually.

He looked at her sharply. 'What on earth for?'

'I'm convinced he knows more about Vinnie than he's admitting,' she said. 'I'm letting him cool his heels for a while. He may well be implicated in something that led to Vinnie's death.'

Genuine astonishment registered on his face. 'You're kidding. Spider... a mastermind? Surely that's a contradiction in terms?'

She fought to maintain her stern expression. 'Hardly that, but you obviously know him, Angus. How does he strike you?'

He got up to serve the coffee before settling back in the sofa. 'Spider seems remarkably resilient despite constantly getting stick from St Clair. He's in and out of our place on a regular basis; say about once a week.'

'Doing what exactly?'

He puffed out his cheeks. 'Delivering blank master tapes and discs, drumming up custom for new equipment – I've had a new digital camera lined up with him for ages. We chat about new developments, he invites us to exhibitions, cadges the odd coffee between calls, that kind of thing.'

She leaned forward in the chair. 'What about finished productions?'

He shook his head more emphatically this time. 'He's a supplier, not an end user. Besides, what would Spider do with educational and training videos?'

She hesitated. 'You never produce anything' – she appeared to search for the right words – 'less politically correct?'

He stared at her for a moment, then gave a quiet chuckle. 'Well, I know that Cant and Dick sometimes do wedding homers on the QT. Crawley would certainly disapprove, but I can't see that whetting Spider's appetite.' His eyes narrowed a fraction. 'Somehow I don't think that's quite what you had in mind.'

She shrugged evasively. 'Crawley?'

'My rival for head of department.' He shook his head in response to her questioning look. 'I can't stand the prat, but I'd doubt Crawley would get involved in anything remotely questionable.'

'But making videos is your forte,' she said.

He leaned back in the sofa, a faint smile playing on his face. 'I wondered where this was all leading. You think I'm involved in something shady – but you can't mean with someone like Goldfiever?'

She eyed him carefully as she put down her cup. 'My governor certainly does,' she said. 'And you have to admit the circumstantial evidence fits. There is a chain in place, however tenuous: producer... middle-man... distributor, and plenty of muscle to back it up.'

'If you don't mind me saying so,' he said calmly, 'that's just a bit too tenuous. You're the one who's thinking like an academic now. Good grief, the mind boggles at the thought of directing Cant and Dick in the making of a skin flick. For one thing, we'd never be able to persuade Dick to stay on our side of the camera. Nor does your theory explain why Vinnie was killed.'

Her eyes flashed challengingly. 'He did leave Goldfiever's employment under a cloud; there has to be a reason for that. Maybe you've got a better theory?'

He took a moment to gather his thoughts.

'For starters,' he said, 'I don't think you really believe any of this circumstantial crap.'

'Interesting point,' she said noncommittally. 'Go on.'

'I've heard St Clair whisper in an indiscreet moment that he sold Goldfiever some sophisticated video equipment aboard his floating casino.'

'The *Melbourne Queen*?'

'That's the one.'

'Surely it's standard practice these days to have surveillance cameras fitted on business premises?'

'I know cameras are everywhere in a casino, but what was being hinted at were hidden cameras in special rooms for high rollers and their, um... *guests*.'

She took a moment to digest this information. 'Are you hinting at blackmail?'

His shoulders came up in a silent suggestion that it was a possibility.

'My governor regards Goldfiever as public enemy number one,' she said. 'Proving he was into blackmail would certainly earn a few brownie points. Again, blackmail could easily lead to murder, and proving that could put Goldfiever out of circulation for a long time.'

His eyes locked disconcertingly with hers. 'Maybe Vinnie stumbled on some of that "special" video material?'

That had to be it, she thought. She knew Vinnie had been beaten and possibly threatened with torture (hence the blowtorch) before being killed, but they hadn't released that information. Whoever had done it had obviously wanted information from Vinnie. According to McDonald, the fire chief, the blaze had been started to cover up Vinnie's murder, but it had been done clumsily, perhaps prematurely. Maybe they had been disturbed before getting the information they were after and then panicked when Buerk's crew arrived?

She shot to her feet. 'Angus, you're a genius. I rather think I need another chat with Spider first thing in the morning.'

'Then you don't have to go right now?'

She smiled at his obvious disappointment. 'Sorry. I do need to get some sleep. You know, you'd be all right, if you didn't have this irritating habit of popping up at the wrong time on my patch. My governor doesn't like coincidences.'

'He's giving you a hard time, isn't he?' He stood up a mere three steps away from her.

'Nothing I can't handle.' She shifted uncomfortably under his gaze.

Two steps away. 'Tough guy, huh?'

One step. 'You better believe it.'

Reluctantly, she stayed him with an outstretched hand.

'Angus... Chief Superintendent Douglas still regards you as a suspect.'

'I know,' he said quietly. 'The important thing is that you don't.'

There was an answering smile on her lips. 'You know, you probably saved my life with that meal tonight,' she said. 'I really ought to return the favour sometime.'

'Any time,' he heard himself say.

After she had gone, a small voice started nagging at the back of his mind; it was probably something important, but he was on such a high his mind couldn't focus on what it was.

TUESDAY

Chapter Nine

After spending a restless night in the cell, Spider was brought back to the interview room. Worrying about how St Clair was going to react to the news of his failed mission, he gazed at DI Munro with stony-faced sullenness. His damaged eye had closed completely now and his shins hurt where the stool had smashed against them. 'Ah'm sayin' nothing more,' he mumbled, 'until ah've spoken tae ma brief.'

She took a deep breath and let the air out slowly. 'Okay, Spider,' she said. 'If that's what you want, but I wouldn't have thought you were cut out for the life of a Trappist monk.'

'Eh?'

She shrugged her shoulders resignedly. 'They never open their mouths either, except of course to eat their porridge. On the other hand, they do spend rather a long time in a cell. You should know you're looking at anything from five to ten years for being an accessory to murder.'

'Aw now, jist hold on a minute,' he spluttered. 'Ah didnae top anyone, especially no' Vinnie.'

Of course you didn't, she thought. You're just the sprat I need to catch a rather large and nasty mackerel and – who knows? – maybe even a great white shark.

She sat down on the edge of the table, her voice conversational. 'It doesn't have to be like this, you know.'

She glanced pointedly at the recorder and for the first time he noticed the tape was not running. 'There might be another way,' she said, 'if you fill me in about Goldfiever's videotape scam.'

A look of astonishment registered in his one good eye. 'Who told you about that?'

She shrugged. 'I can't possibly tell you that, but ask yourself: who stands to gain by making you the scapegoat?'

'You mean St Clair?'

She remained impassively mute as he fought an internal struggle with himself.

'This is strictly off the record, right?'

'Absolutely.'

There was a real sense of grievance in his voice now. 'He wis the one that wanted me tae copy the tape in the first place,' he said. 'An' ah wis the mug that had tae get the tape from the *Loch Tredwell*. That's where Vinnie hid it, you see. On a wee ledge in the chain locker behind the bowsprit. But ah never reached it. When ah saw the state o' that ship, the police tape blockin' off the gangways, an' that copper on duty, ah cleared off in a right stew. It brought Vinnie's death right back tae me. Ah wisnae thinkin' straight. That's how come ah ran full-tilt into Angus Buerk.'

She leaned across the table towards him, being careful to hide her triumph. 'A perfectly understandable reaction,' she said. 'Maybe it's time to get your own back, strike a blow for Vinnie. What do you think?'

Spider took a moment to process her question. 'Aye, too right. Vinnie wis ma mate, know whit ah mean?'

Odd, she thought, that Buerk had planted the idea about the tape in her head. Then again, she thought, feeling a warm glow spreading within her, that was not the only thought he had planted in her head last night.

'All right,' she said, briskly. 'We've wasted enough time on this piddling business. Let's see if we can't work something out between us.'

A sly look came over him. 'Whit's in it for me?'

'We're after bigger fish,' she said brusquely. 'Help us catch them, we lose all interest in small fry like you.'

'You don't mean' – his voice dropped to a whisper – 'Goldfiever?'

Munro's face remained deadpan. She hesitated for a fraction of a second before adding, 'Can't say Angus Buerk's off the hook, though.'

Spider's parchment face creased even further. 'Whit's Angus got tae do wi' this?'

'He's involved in this too, isn't he?' She did not move a muscle as she waited.

'Naw, naw, you've got that all wrong, inspector. Angus is a straight-up guy. He hasn't got a Scooby about any of this. It wis that stupid, blasted dog o' his that got in the way.'

'That a fact?' she said. Things were just getting better and better.

Back in the squad room she found DS Lennox had brought in Jackie Lynch and sat him down with a composite computer artist using the EvoFIT procedure developed by Stirling and the University of Central Lancashire. When they had finished, Lynch was satisfied they had an almost exact likeness of the scar-faced man he had seen loitering by Vinnie McGrath's locker at his gym. Beneath buzz-cut blond hair, his sinister Neanderthal looks, complete with receding forehead and prominent brow ridges, gazed impassively out at them from cold staring eyes. A single gold earring and a scar running down his left cheek to his lip were prominent features.

Lennox invited her boss to inspect the finished product. 'There's a face even a mother would be pushed to love,' the sergeant said.

' "A cold fish" is how my mother would have described him.' Munro pointed at where the scar reached his mouth. 'Look, he's even got the mark on his lip where the hook went in.'

They drew a blank with a trawl through the HOLMES 2 system, but when Munro suggested a search on the Interpol computer files they struck gold. A wanted criminal by the name of Goren Nordmann, aka Eaglehawk (apparently on account of his ability to strike before his target could react). His mugshot was virtually identical to the EvoFIT composite. It also had a red tag against his name. With a long record of quick-tempered and threatening behaviour with a knife (check), he was also wanted for questioning by the Australian police in connection with a fatal stabbing in Melbourne (check). He had been employed as a bouncer in a casino that was part of an entertainment complex on the banks of the Yarra River. The major shareholder in this casino in Melbourne and its sister casino in Freemantle, Western Australia, at the time was none other than Ned Goldfiever (bingo).

'What on earth is an eaglehawk?' Munro asked.

Lennox smiled. 'Had to look that up,' she said. 'Apparently it's another name for the wedge-tailed eagle, largest bird of prey in Australia.'

'Well done, Mary,' Munro said. 'Looks like you might have found Goldfiever's hitman.' It crossed her mind that she should have Buerk take a look at the mugshot, but not necessarily here at the police station.

'Fuck.'

Buerk gave vent to the expletive as he realised he had slept in. He had a plane to catch in less than an hour. He called a cab, unwilling to take the hit from the extortionate car park charges. While awaiting its arrival he checked his e-mail. One message stood out.

Angus,

Had an interesting chat with Spider this morning. He seems to feel you're an honourable sort, can't think why.

I've got some free time owing which will allow me to do some shopping. Why not drop round to my place tonight around seven and I'll cook us something. I hope you appreciate the magnitude of the offer.

Rowena

p.s. I leave dessert to your imagination.

He noted her address was on the Crow Road in the West End. Even as he took in the letter's contents, his mind went from rapture to dejection in the blink of an eye. On account of his trip to Papa Westray, he would have to cancel the dinner date. Forgetting to mention the trip was what had been nagging at him the previous night after she had gone. Fuck!

His mood got worse when he heard the news on the cab's radio. The lead story announced a dramatic change of heart by the Thistle Media Group towards the proposed merger with SLIME.

TMG's normally outgoing chairperson, Sir Rankin Maltby, appeared strangely reluctant to elaborate on his apparent volte-face, restricting himself to a few vague references to altered circumstances connected with the bid which required a serious reconsideration of his position. Stuck for some explanation of what those circumstances might be, the station had even vainly tried to contact Sir Rankin's daughter, who worked as a presenter on his channel, but she was apparently off sailing somewhere in Scotland and could not be contacted.

Ned Goldfiever was much more upbeat about the prospects of the merger going ahead and hinted at a key role for TMG in his rapidly expanding media organisation. Fuck!

This latest development in the takeover battle depressed Buerk. Although the matter did not concern him in any tangible way, he had begun to identify with the company's stand and now experienced something of a let-down from the inexplicable turn of events.

In the taxi he pulled out his phone, but Munro failed to answer her mobile or her personal office number. Eventually the internal switchboard patched him through to Sergeant Lennox.

'Inspector Munro's not available at the moment,' she said guardedly. 'May I take a message? I'll make sure she gets it the moment she returns to her desk.'

After a moment's hesitation he gave his name.

'Sorry, Mr Buerk,' she said, recognition of his name allowing her to drop the formality. 'She's out shopping at the moment for a rather historic dinner she is planning for this evening.'

'Why historic?' he asked. Something about her switch to a light, bantering tone made him feel vaguely uneasy.

'Because it will be the first time she's prepared a meal with her own fair hands,' DS Lennox said. 'It appears you are to be the only guest and I think I can reasonably say without betraying any confidences that she's quite excited about it. Very likely she has switched off her mobile so that nothing could deflect her from that express purpose.'

He groaned aloud. 'I was afraid of that. My reason for calling was to tell her something urgent has come up and I really have to ask for a rain check.'

There was a long pause at the other end of the line. 'May I ask if this urgent matter is going to take you out of town?' Lennox asked.

'To one of the more remote islands of the Orkney archipelago,' he said.

There was another long silence, during which he heard the intake of the sergeant's breath. 'That may not be far enough, Mr Buerk.'

'That bad, huh?'

'I could be seriously underestimating the situation here.'

'I'm afraid it really is unavoidable,' he insisted lamely. 'I'm going to be filming up there for two days. It's a ukase from the deputy principal.'

'A what?'

'An arbitrary command, as from the tsar of all the Russias.'

'I'd appeal to a higher authority if I were you.'

'You're enjoying this, aren't you?'

'So far,' came the muted reply. 'However, I still have to relay your message. Around here they sometimes shoot the messenger, in case they've become tainted by contact.'

'There is no higher authority,' he said. 'The principal is out of the country. His deputy is, de facto, acting principal.'

He heard an ominous sigh. 'I was really thinking of some form of deity here. Anything else you'd like to get off your chest? We always tell a condemned man that confession is good for the soul.'

'No,' he said, his heart sinking. 'That's about it.' Under the circumstances he deemed it wise to make no specific reference to the reason for his trip.

Lennox's parting, 'Good luck,' sounded more like a death sentence.

Having reached the airport he had to run to the check-in counter where his colleagues were waiting with varying degrees of welcome. Fuck!

The flight to Kirkwall on the Orkney mainland proved turbulent but uneventful save for Crawley spending the entire journey studying the inside of a sick bag. Lucretia had impressed on everyone the need for speed and secrecy.

They were engaged in a race against time, she explained, with a place in history as the ultimate prize.

Before his eventful walk with Biltong, Buerk had done some internet checking on their supposed quarry. The great auk, he discovered, had been about the size of a goose. It had laid a single egg on exposed sea-cliffs and resembled a huge flightless razorbill, another penguin-like bird, save for a large patch of white between bill and eye. It reinforced his view that Hornblower had good reason to hedge his bets. There was absolutely nothing he could find about the great auk to suggest it was anything other than extinct. It seemed boatloads of men from St Kilda and the Orkneys through Iceland all the way to Newfoundland, owing no allegiance to ideas of species conservation, had hunted to oblivion both bird and egg in their quest for sources of food.

As they took their seats on the first leg of their journey to Kirkwall, he challenged Lucretia about it. She shook her head resolutely. 'Some of the very communities that hunted the auk have also vanished,' she said. 'Every location you've cited is extremely remote and the nesting sites inaccessible.'

'Apparently not inaccessible enough,' he said bluntly.

She remained obdurate. 'I'm sorry, Angus. I simply can't go against my instincts on this one. Hilary would know how significant such a claim would be to the wider ornithological community and he clearly entrusted me with the message.'

Buerk remained thoughtfully silent. Her argument carried the ring of personal conviction, but it could also be interpreted as the emotional response of a woman who appeared to be living on the edge of her nerves. Her brother simply had to be mistaken. All the objective evidence was against it. What bothered him in all this was that Hilary above all people ought to have known that. What the hell was his game?

As if reading his thoughts she became more agitated. 'If only we could speak directly to Hilary,' she said. 'He could confirm the sighting at once.' Then another thought seemed to occur to her and she reached out a hand to grab his arm. 'You don't suppose he might have had an accident, do you? He still hasn't responded to my calls despite several attempts to reach him. I've been obliged to e-mail him about our travelling arrangements.'

Buerk gently prised his arm from her grasp, but relented enough to try to reassure her. 'The sooner we get there, the sooner this mystery will be cleared up,' he reasoned. 'If Hilary really believes he's discovered a great auk, he might well be guarding the site around the clock.'

She seized on his words, her eyes shining with gratitude. 'Yes, of course, that's it. That's exactly the kind of thing Hilary would do.' She squeezed his arm again. 'Thank you, Angus, for being so supportive.'

St Clair looked more worried than Janice had ever seen him when she brought in his early morning coffee.

'Has Spider called in yet?' It was the third time since she'd appeared for work that he had asked.

She shook her head. 'He's not answering his mobile either.'

As she left, St Clair passed a hand wearily over his face and pushed away the plate of chocolate biscuits. Things had all looked so promising last night, but Spider's continued absence was a concern.

He looked up hopefully as Janice again appeared in the doorway. The shock on her face told him the news was not good.

'You're not going to believe this,' she said. 'It seems that Spider spent the night in the clink.'

CHAPTER TEN

Drinking coffee in the open-plan lounge of the terminal building at Kirkwall, while waiting for their onward flight to Papa Westray to be called, Buerk ran a long list of problems through his restless mind. Foremost among them was failing to contact Rowena Munro. It bothered him that he had been unable to apologise in person, to make sure she understood he had no choice in the matter of standing her up. He was fairly sure that DS Lennox would pass his message on to her, but he doubted it would carry the same degree of sincerity or conviction he might have given it in person. There had been more than a hint of cynicism in the sergeant's tone when he had spoken to her. He had tried again to reach Rowena on her mobile but, again, there had been no reply. Not a good sign.

His next problem was Crawley. Despite his present incapacity, he was fast becoming a tiresome nuisance in the way he kept dogging Buerk's footsteps. On at least two occasions since their departure, even a visit to the toilet had failed to shake him off. Buerk shot a sidelong glance at the hunched figure sitting next to him. His colleague had a pair of binoculars slung round his neck and God knew what in that bulky rucksack strapped to his back. It had not escaped Buerk's notice that not once since they had left the city had Crawley allowed that out of his sight. The only consolation, judging from his sickly pallor, was that his shadow appeared to be enjoying the experience even less than he was himself.

Next on his list was the perpetual problem of Cant and Dick. He was fond of the pair of scallywags but they were always a liability on any production of this nature, let alone one with the additional hazards of dangerous cliffs and running seas. Nor had it altogether escaped his notice that they were presently at the bar sampling with obvious enthusiasm the product of the local distillery. He had to concede that he had himself bought a half-bottle. If this trip proved to be half as disastrous as he feared, it might come in handy as a form of consolation.

Following Buerk's gaze, Crawley was quick to heap coals on the fire. 'Those two look set to give us a right showing-up,' he said. 'I can't understand how they could make such fools of themselves.'

In his present mood, Buerk's voice dripped with sarcasm. 'I suppose that's never likely to happen to you, Fred, is it?'

'Not bally likely,' Crawley said. Obviously taking his words as a compliment, he added, 'I've vowed to stay clear of the hard stuff ever since a drop too much one Christmas knocked me silly.'

'Hmmn. I wonder how you could tell.'

'Well, I was slurring my words and...' Crawley's explanation halted as the penny belatedly dropped. 'Oh, I get it,' he sneered. 'Another of your sick jokes.' He suddenly clapped a hand to his mouth and made a bolt for the toilets as autosuggestion kicked in.

Buerk's final problem concerned Lucretia. The nearer they got to their destination, the more excited and anxious she became; she had already confessed to him that her doctor had prescribed sleeping pills to help her through her current crisis. From Buerk's point of view, these emotions seemed to have been transferred into a kind of physical dependence on him. She seemed to have developed a disconcerting need to touch him for reassurance – innocently enough at first, but once or twice on the journey, he had caught her looking at him in a way that made the hairs on the back of his neck stand on end. He gave an involuntary shudder. This whole business was beginning to get the better of him.

Mercifully, as he mentally checked off the various threats to his sanity, he heard their flight being called over the public address system. Climbing slowly to his feet, he saw Lucretia bearing down on him from the direction of the magazine racks. Crawley at once emerged from the toilet to resume his watching brief. Out of the corner of his eye Buerk spotted Cant and Dick weaving their way towards him. Great. They had not even reached their destination yet and already he was becoming paranoid.

Following the flight courier onto the tarmac, they had their first sight of the narrow-bodied aircraft that would take them on the final leg of their journey. It had a maximum capacity of seven passengers plus the pilot, allowing them to sit in pairs with outer elbows brushing against the fuselage.

Crawley baulked at the sight of the aircraft. 'My God,' he wailed. 'We'll never make it in that heap.'

Swaying unsteadily on his feet, Dick nudged Cant to announce in a stage whisper, 'Hasn't Creepy turned a funny colour?'

'Right enough,' Cant agreed, 'he doesn't look a well man.'

Having seen the equipment stowed in the tail section, Buerk clambered into the tiny passenger compartment to occupy the first seat behind the pilot. He was immediately joined by Lucretia, who had ruthlessly elbowed the others aside to make sure of the seat beside him. Cant and Dick stumbled on behind them, leaving Crawley to drag his reluctant body aboard in the rear, his rucksack clutched protectively against his stomach.

Already feeling wretched from the first leg of the journey, Crawley gradually became conscious of something digging into his ribs. It took a moment for him to register the presence in the adjoining seat of a rather forbidding, bespectacled woman swaddled in waterproofs. She was reading the current issue of *Bird Watching* and carried about her person a plethora of equipment including camera, binoculars and rucksack. It was the metal-framed rucksack on her lap that was the source of Crawley's current discomfort, and he glared pointedly at the offending article until she was obliged to take notice. Reluctantly placing it under the seat in front of her, she sniffed at him distastefully until she noticed, as he followed suit, that his rucksack was an identical model.

'Snap!' she said. Her voice was a piping treble that would have done credit to an oystercatcher. She perked visibly in her seat. 'I rather fancy you might be after the same thing as me,' she said archly.

Crawley glared at her, for the first time noticing the nervous tic in her left eye. In spite of his condition, alarm bells began to ring in his head. Suspicion and hostility vied with each other to gain the upper hand. 'I beg your pardon?'

'A fellow twitcher, if I'm not mistaken,' she said confidently.

Catching what might have been construed as a wink, Crawley bridled. 'Speak for yourself, madam,' he said. 'I most certainly am nothing of the kind.'

The tic became more pronounced as the first doubts crept into her expression. 'You're going to Papay like me, aren't you?'

'I may be going to Papay,' he countered waspishly, 'but I assure you, madam, I'm not in the least like you.'

She glared accusingly at his binoculars as if to implicate them in her betrayal. 'Then you don't intend visiting the tern sanctuary on North Hill?'

Unsure what she was talking about, Crawley leaned towards her with all the authority he could muster, causing her to cringe at the smell from his breath. 'Madam,' he said. 'What I intend to visit is my affair, but the only sanctuary I seek is to escape from your infernal questions and get off this sardine tin in one piece.'

'My mistake, I'm sure.' She sniffed and withdrew behind her magazine and a frozen wall of silence.

The small plane taxied onto the runway and began to gather speed, causing Crawley to let out a low moan and reach for the sick bag. Lucretia felt obliged to clutch

Buerk's arm for reassurance as they lifted off the ground and effortlessly gained height. At cruising height, a vista soon unfolded below them of an aquamarine sea dotted with tiny emerald-green islands, each surrounded by a fringe of pristine, white sands.

As a pretext for breaking free, Buerk pulled an Ordnance Survey map from his bag and made a great show of studying their island destination. There was not a great deal to it. The island was about four miles long by one and a half at its widest point; a single main road ran along most of its spine. A smaller island, known as the Holm, lay off its eastern shore. It was also on this side and to the north where the cliffs rose out of the sea.

Some time later, dropping down through the low cloud ceiling, the pilot had started landing procedures before anyone detected the nature of the airstrip beneath them. Inevitably, Crawley was the first to raise the alarm. 'My God,' he wailed, 'we're making a forced landing in a field.'

His companion emerged from her self-imposed isolation long enough to glare contemptuously at him. 'This is the airfield at Papay,' she scoffed.

Crawley gave a whimper of relief, but the next second, having spotted a flock of sheep scattering before their final approach, he prematurely released his seat belt and made an involuntary grab at his astonished travelling companion. Moments later, he was catapulted forward into their collective belongings, ending up, as the plane came to a halt, jammed between her legs and the seat in front, his head neatly pillowed on her lap.

Some of that lady's natural reserve finally snapped, doubtless aided by a festering resentment at Crawley's earlier rebuff. In any event, she suddenly shot to her feet and almost trampled him underfoot in her haste to extricate herself from his embrace. Before he could react, she had snatched up one of the rucksacks that had become entangled and pushed past him off the plane. A moment later, she was whisked away by a waiting car, leaving the rest of them standing by a clearly deserted terminal.

Lucretia wailed to the heavens. 'Where is Hilary? Surely he should have read my e-mail asking him to meet us?'

They were still waiting as the plane lifted off again into the mist, heading for the neighbouring island of Westray. Watching it go, Buerk felt that somehow his last remaining lifeline to the outside world had been severed. As if to reinforce this feeling of isolation the terminal building itself now appeared to be closing down, the second of the two daily flights having come and gone. The helpful part-time employee pointed them in the direction of Hilary's cottage along an intersecting road before he too left on his bicycle and was promptly swallowed up in a smirr of rain.

There was nothing for it but to start walking in the drizzle. At least, Buerk thought glumly, it was mostly downhill past the small hotel complex that doubled as shop and hostel, past the tiny school and towards the old pier. His sombre mood did not last long, however, as the well-maintained and recently extended cottage came into view lying behind some dunes. Its setting, close to a beach of white shell-sand that sloped gently to the clear turquoise waters of the bay, took his breath away. Even the rain relented at their approach and the sun emerged from between the clouds in broken shafts of light. One of these fell on the whitewashed cottage, causing it to gleam in the reflected light.

Offshore stood the Holm, a seemingly low-lying skerry, still crowned by a slowly dispersing mass of cloud which caused a dark shadow to move over its length. A trim, white yacht lying off its southern tip was picked out by another shaft of light, which illuminated its single mast devoid of sail. As it rode at anchor, it looked to Buerk like a picture postcard setting.

They found the door unlocked but no sign of Hilary inside. The first room they entered was the kitchen. The table bore the scattered remains of a recent meal. A chair had been overturned and, in one corner, Buerk crunched underfoot some shattered fragments of glass and plastic strewn on the floor. A moment later he found the source. Both a computer and a printer had been swept onto the floor from a worktop and smashed on the flagstones.

A wail from Lucretia signalled her discovery that the telephone receiver had received similar treatment.

'Explains the lack of response to phone or e-mails,' Buerk said grimly.

A bicycle lay abandoned where it had fallen in the narrow hallway that led to an annexe, equally deserted. Together, they checked the two bedrooms and the bathroom without further mishap. The final room they examined came as a surprise to Buerk. It was a small but well-equipped darkroom.

'Hilary contributes articles to ornithological magazines,' Lucretia explained. 'He often illustrates them with photographs of birds which he develops himself.'

Buerk curtly dispatched her inside. 'Take a look for anything recent that might show a great auk.'

'Good idea, Angus,' she said.

'Looks like the birds have flown the nest,' Dick said on his return to the kitchen.

'Maybe he's showing a party where the nesting site is located,' Crawley said.

'Bang goes our exclusive if he is,' Buerk said.

Crawley looked at him with a preoccupied air as the others continued to examine the mess.

Cant gestured at some empty beer bottles he had discovered in a corner. Two more of the same brand stood on the table. 'Looks more like the party was right here,' he said. He picked up a bottle to examine the label more closely. 'Dogbolter,' he read. 'That's a new one on me.'

'Just our luck to get here too late to try it,' Dick said.

Lucretia returned from her search of the darkroom, shaking her head at Buerk's look of enquiry. She saw Dick draining a bottle of its last few drops in growing alarm. 'I don't like the look of this,' she said. 'Hilary never touched alcohol.'

Buerk picked up a hairbrush from the worktop with long blond hairs caught in the bristles. 'I very much doubt these belonged to Hilary,' he said.

Lucretia bit her lip. 'Looks like he's been entertaining a female guest,' she said.

'Maybe she's been entertaining him,' Cant said, winking at Dick.

'Explains everything,' Dick agreed with a vacuous grin.

'It explains nothing,' Lucretia snapped, snatching the brush from Buerk's grasp.

Sensing the mounting tension in the room, Buerk decided it might not be a bad idea to keep everyone occupied. He looked up from the table where he had cleared a space to spread out the map. 'All right, listen up, all of you,' he said. 'If this expedition is not to degenerate into utter farce, we need to get our act together.'

He rounded first on Lucretia, who looked as if she was about to unravel. 'On the face of it,' he said, 'your brother's had a rather different kind of bird on his mind these past few days, and that, coupled with the empty beer bottles, doesn't augur well for his credibility.'

Lucretia opened her mouth to protest but thought better of it when she saw the look on Buerk's face.

'Let's assume for the moment there is a grain of truth in his story,' he said. 'Without any supporting information, I need you to point out the most likely nesting site for the auk.'

'Of course, Angus,' she said, with unaccustomed humility. 'The last sighting was recorded at Fowl Craig, here.' She pointed to the spot on the map where the cliffs were indicated. 'That's still our best bet.'

Buerk gave a terse nod. 'Then that's where we'll head, so let's all start gearing up.'

'There is one other place he might go,' Lucretia added with an apologetic smile, 'especially if he had a visitor on tow.'

'Which is?' Buerk asked.

'The hide on Hyndgreenie Loch.' She pointed out its central location on the map, close to a Bronze Age burial site. 'It's a sheltered position from which to view part of the bird sanctuary.'

He glanced up at her sharply. 'But not a likely spot to sight an auk?'

Lucretia swallowed hard and her reply was almost inaudible. 'No.'

Buerk continued to study the map, thinking furiously. On the fairly reasonable assumption that the great auk story would not stand up to scrutiny, he badly needed an alternative scenario to protect himself from complete ridicule on their return. 'All right,' he said, tracing the route on the map. 'We'll take in Hyndgreenie Loch first, as it's on the way. Then we'll take the long way round to Fowl Craig by way of Mull Head. We have to hug the coastline all the way to avoid straying into the bird reserve.'

He rounded on Cant and Dick. 'Come on, you two, don't just stand there gawping. Get the gear together and let's get on with it. I want to get some location shots in the can while the light's still good and the rain holds off.'

Cant snapped off a mock salute. 'Whatever you say, boss.'

Dick amiably aped his colleague. 'Your wish is our command.'

Buerk turned to scan the room, suddenly aware that someone was missing. 'Where's Crawley?'

'Probably throwing up in the john,' Cant suggested.

'Funny,' Dick said. 'Wouldn't have thought he had anything left to throw up.'

CHAPTER ELEVEN

A white-faced Spider sidled hesitantly into St Clair's office, closely followed by Letitia. A look of deep anxiety was etched across the ex-boxer's battle-scarred features as he caught sight of his employer's expression. He felt that a streak of bad luck had dogged him ever since Vinnie McGrath had approached him to play a section of the stolen video and then confided in him where he intended to hide it. When Detective Inspector Munro had offered him an unexpected lifeline, he had hoped that bad luck streak was about to end.

There was, of course, something required of him in exchange for Munro's magnanimous gesture, but to Spider it seemed a ridiculously small price to pay, especially since it coincided (give or take the odd detail) with his employer's own wishes. All he had to do was return the tape, when he recovered it from the small recess in the chain locker, to its rightful owner aboard the *Melbourne Queen*. He had been assured that after midday, there would no longer be coppers on duty at either gangway. By the time he again jogged to the crime scene, the way would be clear for him to do the necessary. Of course there was still the small matter of making a duplicate for St Clair. After that, it was out of his hands.

Clearly, DI Munro felt it was worth going to all this trouble, to say nothing of the risk to her own career, for the sake of catching the big fish behind the operation: in this case the great white shark himself, Ned Goldfiever. There was to be no mention of Spider's own role in the drama to anyone, least of all his employer. Munro had been clear on that. She had not been quite so clear, however, about what would happen to Spider's employer if he did keep a copy. His scrambled brain tried to recall her exact wording but, for the moment, it escaped him. Then again, before he could discharge his obligation in this new and uneasy alliance, he still had to convince his employer that he was himself free from compromise after his recent overnight experience in jail.

'What happened?' St Clair demanded to know. 'Letitia told me you were in the nick. For pity's sake, tell me they didn't find the video on you.'

Spider had been coached to keep his account as brief and truthful as possible. 'Naw when ah got down there, the place wis in chaos. The *Loch Tredwell* had been set on fire in an attempt to cover up Vinnie's murder. The gangways were taped aff and there were polis everywhere. That's when ah got lifted.'

'The tape?'

'It wis never in danger. The fire wis at the other end o' the ship.'

St Clair's brow darkened. 'You're telling me it's still where Vinnie left it?'

'Exactly,' Spider said. 'Ah kin have another try the day. Ah heard them say forensics were finishin' up this morning. Someone further up the food chain is puttin' pressure on them tae allow the restoration work tae get movin' again.'

St Clair shot him a suspicious look. 'How come they held you overnight?'

Spider shrugged. 'Ah think that female detective kept me in for spite, but she hud nothin' on me and hud tae let me go.'

Spider prayed that his voice carried sufficient conviction. Although St Clair continued to eye him suspiciously, the possibility of still salvaging something from this fiasco seemed to overrule his natural scepticism. So long as it had not been discovered by the police, Goldfiever would still want his video back.

From the moment they had arrived at Hilary's cottage, Crawley had become increasingly agitated, making frequent, furtive time checks against his watch. He desperately needed to find a place where he could be alone. It was time to send his first transmission to his deputy principal. He knew Hornblower would be anxiously awaiting his first report and, as he knew to his cost, Hornblower did not like to be kept waiting. First, he had to give the others the slip and set up his equipment.

The opportunity presented itself sooner than he could have anticipated. As Buerk began organising the crew in preparation for some location filming, Crawley saw his chance. He snatched up his rucksack and scurried quickly into the bathroom, where, settling on the toilet seat, he began to unfasten the buckles of the rucksack. He allowed himself a brief moment of self-congratulation at having skilfully managed to conceal the fact that he had brought his laptop and modem on the trip. The fact that Hilary's computer had been mysteriously smashed merely underlined his own far-sightedness.

He had been vaguely conscious that the rucksack had seemed somehow lighter since alighting from the plane, but he had initially put that down to the euphoria of setting foot on terra firma after the hateful flight. Now, as his fumbling fingers finally exposed the unfamiliar contents, such feeble-minded reasoning was exposed to the harsh light of reality.

'Aaa... rgh!' A strangled cry escaped his lips before he quickly clamped a hand over his mouth to avoid drawing any unwelcome attention to his predicament.

The laptop was gone!

In its place he hauled out a notebook, half its pages already covered with detailed notes of bird movements written in a spidery hand. After the notebook came a pocket reference book on birds, an Ordnance Survey map covering the island, a compass and a foil-wrapped packet of Marmite sandwiches. The smell from the last made his stomach knot, but mercifully it was now completely empty.

He sat rigid with tension, the knuckles of one hand crammed into his mouth, and tried to force the panic to subside. What the hell was going on? He had carefully double-checked everything before the transfer at Kirkwall.

It was then he remembered his fellow passenger on the onward flight to Papay, whom he had been obliged to put firmly in her place. He had already noted that her rucksack was identical to his own. Then he remembered the fumbling confusion as they'd got off the plane. That was it: she must have picked up the wrong bag. Stupid cow.

A banging on the door jolted him out of his musing. He recognised Buerk's voice. 'You all right in there, Fred? We're all ready to head out.'

Crawley removed his fist from his mouth. He needed time to think. 'Why don't you go ahead?' he called out. 'I'll catch you up.' He had tried to make his tone sound nonchalant but was afraid that it had come out a bit too quickly.

There was a long silence before Buerk replied. 'All right. I'll leave the map. If you miss us at Hyndgreenie Loch, we'll be heading for Mull Head on the far side of the reserve. Don't be all day, and remember to take the long way round to avoid trespassing on the reserve.'

Buerk turned away thoughtfully. For someone who had stuck to him like glue throughout the day, it was totally out of character for Crawley to suddenly want to hang back. Not for the first time that day, he wondered what was going on inside that twisted mind.

In late-afternoon sunshine, Lucretia led the way over the stile towards the hide at Hyndgreenie Loch. Despite her obvious misgivings about the recent discoveries at the cottage, she tried to keep upbeat about their chances of finding Hilary and his unknown companions. From time to time her eyes darted in Buerk's direction as if drawing comfort from his proximity.

Buerk strode along, hands thrust deep in his pockets, oblivious of her presence, let alone her thoughts. He whistled tunelessly, partly to convey what he hoped was an optimistic note and partly to avoid the need for talking while his mind tried to come up with a survival strategy for himself and his crew. Not having a great deal of faith in the great auk's resurrection, he had decided to cover himself by gathering material for a more general, if less sensational documentary on bird life on the island. That way at least there would be less chance of aggravation from penny-pinching auditors to whom he seemed increasingly accountable. It did not help to dwell on the fact that it was harebrained schemes like the present one that helped to justify their existence.

Behind him Cant and Dick trudged along, quietly discussing the odds of catching Hilary 'in flagrante' with his mysterious new playmate. The combination of hangover and the weight of the outdated equipment they were carrying kept their enthusiasm within acceptable bounds.

Situated on the edge of the reserve, the hide was a wooden shack of fairly sound construction complete with its own toilet. The building afforded protection from wind and rain to visitors wishing to observe at some length the array of birdlife on and around the small loch through the observation window provided.

To Lucretia's profound disappointment they found the shack empty. Buerk immediately announced that, since they had come this far, they might as well take some footage around the hide. While Cant and Dick set up the camera on its tripod, Buerk asked Lucretia about the sanctuary, as much to distract her from dwelling on Hilary's continued absence as out of any genuine interest.

Responding mechanically to his promptings, she explained that the reserve occupying most of the headland, known as North Hill, contained the largest Arctic tern colony in north-west Europe and was internationally famous in its own right. On the other hand, she conceded at once that as a site for the great auk it was a complete non-starter. Only the sea cliffs at Fowl Craig could possibly provide that.

Buerk plausibly explained that the location still constituted valuable background material, and so they began to record the terns gracefully wheeling and swooping around the hide while under constant harassment from a number of predatory skuas.

Having overseen the completion of this task to his satisfaction, Buerk gave instructions to Cant and Dick to pack up and prepare to move around the headland to the cliffs on the north-east side of the island. Briefly scanning the horizon, he could see no sign of Crawley. Returning to the hide, he became aware of a curious expression on Lucretia's face.

'What's up?' he asked.

She glanced up from studying a notebook on a ledge by the window. 'Take a look at this,' she said. There was an unaccustomed calmness in her voice.

Crossing to the window, he saw she was clutching a log book in which visitors were invited to write comments. She pointed to the latest entry, dated two days previously. It was written in a spidery scrawl which he managed to decipher only after some prompting from Lucretia.

'*Knap of Howar landing,*' he read. '*Great Auk in danger?*'

'What does it mean?' she asked.

He shook his head. 'What's the Knap of Howar?'

She made vague circles with her hands. 'It's a ruined settlement of some archaeological significance,' she said. 'I believe it's supposed to be the earliest known standing house in northern Europe, dating back some five thousand years.'

'Could this be Hilary's writing?' he asked.

She shook her head. 'I'd guess it was a woman's hand,' she said, 'and by the looks of it probably written by someone in a tearing hurry.'

He frowned. 'Could this... Knap of Howar be a possible nesting site for the great auk?'

She gave an emphatic shake of the head. 'Absolutely not. It's virtually at sea level there. If the auk exists anywhere it will be on the cliffs on the other side of the island.'

He noted an element of doubt about the auk had crept into her thinking, but, before he could say anything, they were interrupted by Cant none-too-gently pushing open the door.

'Ready when you are, boss,' he said. Suddenly his large frame stiffened. 'Hang on a minute. What's that on the floor behind you?' He pointed towards something in a corner of the hide.

Buerk turned and saw something glint in the shaft of sunlight streaming through the open door. 'Looks like a camera lens,' he said.

'Not just a lens but the whole caboodle.' Grunting with the effort, Cant bent his heavy frame to retrieve it from under the table, the lens still slotted intact into its camera housing. He gave a low whistle. 'Expensive baby, this,' he said, caressing it lovingly. 'Single-lens reflex, telephoto lens; not exactly what you'd call the disposable type, and hardly any dust on it either.'

As they all crowded round to examine it, Cant sprang the hinged compartment on the back of the camera giving access to the film compartment. 'Correction, boss. Not the whole caboodle. Looks like somebody's already removed the film,' he said.

Buerk shot him an incredulous look. 'Then just tossed the camera away as if it had no importance?'

Dick looked at him as if he had taken leave of his senses. 'Come on, boss,' he said. 'Get real. No film could be worth more than this camera!'

'It might...' Lucretia's voice made a curious throaty sound which caused the others to stare at her. '...if the film happened to contain snapshots of the great auk.'

CHAPTER TWELVE

A light rain greeted Watt and Vera as they left the pub in Byres Road, fortified by two pints of lager and two gin and tonics respectively. It was a pub frequented by students and no one in the lunchtime crowd had paid any attention to them as they had sat quietly in a corner. She was again clad in her leathers and he in a worn leather jacket and jeans. He staggered slightly as they emerged onto the pavement and clutched Vera's arm for support. The alcohol had helped to dull the pain and stiffness he felt on the lower half of his body, particularly his buttocks. His companion, by contrast, was relatively unmarked by their torrid session in the library the previous night.

By a curious coincidence they both lived on the outskirts of the city, within a few miles of each other: Vera in a desirable suburb to the north of the city, Watt in a considerably less fashionable housing estate two miles further west. It being Watt's afternoon off, Vera offered to give him a lift home during the extended lunch break she had awarded herself. She never failed to derive a thrill from the power unleashed between her legs when she opened the throttle of her motorbike with its 1200 cc flat twin four-stroke engine. That feeling was accentuated by having Watt's lithe body huddled tightly against her back, his arms around her waist. Nor could she help pondering on the unlikely alliance that had formed between them in such a short time.

They had first met at an official reception for leisure and recreation staff for whom she had a civic responsibility. In the stiffly formal setting, he had stood out from the crowd in his moleskin trousers and open-necked shirt which afforded intriguing glimpses of a heavy metal chain around his neck. As she worked the room, she became aware of him and his immediate response despite the fact there was no shortage of other women around him. One person in particular, she observed, doted on his every word: a mousey creature in a dated Laura Ashley frock. She would later discover this was his assistant librarian, Jacqueline something-or-other.

Vera had bided her time until her own duties had been fulfilled and the throng began to thin. She then dispatched his shadow, Jacqueline, who was completely in awe of her presence, to fetch them drinks. She quickly discovered that Watt's predilections meshed with her own and, before the bemused Jacqueline could return with the drinks, she and Watt had left the reception.

Now, on the final stretch of the journey to his home, Vera suddenly braked and turned into a side road. She drew level with a dilapidated trailer set up as a fast-food stall close to a DIY store. Such food outlets were still to be found near the sprawling housing estates on the outer reaches of the city. This particular one was painted a garish green and yellow.

Watt pushed up the visor of Vera's spare helmet. 'What's up?' he said.

She motioned towards the trailer, smoke belching from its bent aluminium chimney. 'I fancy a bite to eat,' she said over her shoulder. 'Didn't have time for breakfast and all that shagging last night has given me an appetite.'

He chuckled in her ear. 'It's just left me shagged out.'

Her face broke into a grin as she cut the engine. 'Clearly, the inner man needs some sustenance,' she said. 'What you need is a black pudding supper.' She swung round to give him a hefty nudge in the ribs with her elbow. 'That'll put you back on your feet in no time.'

'Be a change from spending half the night on my knees,' he muttered, gingerly sliding off the narrow pillion seat. He waited as she propped the bike up on its stand, and gave a feigned sniff of disapproval. 'In any case I don't know how you can eat black puddings; you never know what rubbish they put in them. I'll stick to fish if you don't mind.'

'That's just horse manure put about by vegetarian wankers,' she said. 'Your fish is probably radioactive from all the nuclear effluent in the sea.'

He put a hand on her shoulder as they reached the van. 'Then you'll see me coming in the dark.'

Vera grinned. 'Now, there's an idea worth pursuing. Far as I'm concerned, nothing gives me the urge faster than a good pudding supper. The very thought of it makes me salivate.'

The van proclaimed in large white letters that this was the Chapatti Tatti. Vera knew that there was the odd independent operator working in the city but one major player dominated the business. The man behind it was her old adversary, Piggy Halbert. Ever since he had mentioned the idea of converting Customs House into a disco, she'd had the feeling that he was simply stringing her along to see how high she was prepared to bid. The thought fired a resentment building inside her. The fire aboard the *Loch Tredwell* had further stoked the flames. Piggy ran a chain of vans known as the Fat Friars, complete with a monk's-head logo. Spotting the independent outlet had given Vera an idea of how she might exact some revenge on Piggy.

Still wearing their crash helmets, they approached the counter. Judging from the tantalising aromas of oriental spices, the Chapatti Tatti appeared to offer more exotic alternatives along with the more traditional fare. Two boys, obviously at least second-generation Scots-Asians, grinned expectantly at them from inside the van. The older of the two leaned his elbows on the counter and said in a thick accent, 'Vijay an' Sachin Kumar at your service. Whit can ah get youse?'

Vera nudged up her visor cautiously with a gloved hand. 'A pudding supper for me and a fish supper for my mate.'

Vijay smiled apologetically. 'Sorry, ah don't huv any puddins left. Ah kin gie you sausage an' chips, pakora an' chips, tandoori chicken an' chips, an' fish an' chips. Ah kin even gie you fried Mars bars an' chips, or just chips wi' curry sauce.'

Vera stared at him with feigned displeasure. 'No puddings,' she said. 'That's a bloody disgrace.'

The boy looked crestfallen. 'Ah kin only apologise,' he said. 'It wis ma brother, Sachin, here that picked up the order today. He obviously didnae huv his heid screwed on right.'

The slightly built Sachin gave them an embarrassed grin as his more worldly brother eyed Vera speculatively.

'Tell you what,' he said. 'Since you're obviously disappointed and we value your custom, I'll make youse a special deal. I'll offer you sausage an' chips at half price. Whit dae you say?'

Watt gave Vera a nudge of encouragement. 'It's a bargain,' he whispered in her ear. 'I'd take it if I were you. After two gin and tonics I wouldn't know the difference.'

'You might not,' Vera said tartly, 'but I would.' Addressing Vijay, she said sternly, 'I'm sorry, but I can't accept your offer. I'll have to take my custom to the nearest Fat Friar. They always have enormous black puddings.'

'But their chips are rubbish,' Vijay protested. 'You're much better aff wi' us. Ah promise the next time ah see youse ah'll huv black puddins in stock. That's a cast-iron promise fae Vijay.'

'*If* there is a next time.' Vera was improvising as she went now. 'We heard a rumour that the Fat Friar boss is planning to turn you over for muscling in on his territory.'

Vijay darted a worried look at his brother before replying. 'You're kiddin', right?'

Vera looked to Watt for confirmation. He duly nodded vigorously. 'Straight up,' he said.

'We wouldn't kid about a thing like that,' Vera added. 'Only the other day an independent in another estate was set on fire.'

'Ah thought that wis an accident,' Vijay protested. 'The council already want tae close us doon on health and safety grounds.'

'An accident's what the police would have you believe,' Vera said with a knowing look.

Vijay gave his chin a worried scratch. 'Thanks for the warning, pal. Here...' He hastily scooped a generous helping of chips into a bag and handed them to her. 'Huv these on the hoose.'

'That's more like it,' Vera said. She turned away as Watt collected and paid for his fish supper.

He ran to catch up with her. 'Here, Vera,' he said. 'That stuff about the Fat Friar: was any of that true?'

Vera winked at him, tossed a chip into the air and caught it in her mouth. 'Of course not,' she said. 'That fire was an accident but it could easily have been arson. I know the owner of the Fat Friar chain. He's a wee fat grasping bastard who needs to be cut down to size. Speaking from personal experience, there's never any love lost between him and any potential rival.'

Watt looked genuinely shocked. 'Even so,' he said, 'it probably wasn't wise to say as much. You obviously put the frighteners on Vijay and Sachin back there, and who knows what they might do on the strength of your claim?'

Vera munched on her chips. 'You mean like get a spot of retaliation in first?'

Watt paused with a piece of fish halfway to his mouth. 'Yeah, something like that.'

Vera rammed two more greasy chips into her mouth and pretended to give his suggestion some thought. 'That's quite an interesting idea you've come up with, Harvey,' she said. 'Might even shake Piggy out of his complacency.'

'It could even drive his customers away.' Watt stopped in his tracks as he caught the expression of Vera's face. 'Wait a minute,' he said. Feeling a jolt of excitement shoot through him, he took hold of her shoulder. 'You're way ahead of me here. You're trying to start something, aren't you?'

Reaching her bike, Vera crammed a final fistful of chips into her mouth, screwed up the wrapping paper into a ball and tossed it carelessly onto the waste ground. 'Who, me?' She tried for a look of injured innocence, but with her mouth full of half-masticated potato she did not quite pull it off. 'I was merely commenting on a hypothetical situation.' She swallowed the chip bolus and put on the glove she had temporarily removed to eat her chips. Jabbing a finger at Watt, she added, 'Don't think for one minute I'm willing to forego that black pudding.'

Watt dropped his wrapping paper into the wastebasket provided and climbed onto the pillion behind her. 'You've just eaten a free bag of chips,' he protested.

The light of battle already gleamed in her eye. 'It's the principle of the thing,' she said. 'We've also got a message to deliver from Vijay and Sachin.'

He pulled her round by the shoulder to look her in the eye. 'To whom?'

'To the nearest Fat Friar outlet, of course. There's usually one stood by the bus terminus on the other side of this estate.'

He eyed her suspiciously. 'What sort of message did you have in mind?'

Vera started the engine and grinned mischievously. 'Maybe more of a lesson than a message.'

Watt shook his head grimly. 'You really mean to make a nuisance of yourself, don't you?'

She squeezed his knee hard. 'Now, don't go getting all melodramatic on me,' she said. 'This was your idea, remember. Now, be a good boy and hang on. We haven't got all day and there's a couple of items I want to pick up first.'

Smiling to herself, she pulled down her visor and let in the clutch.

'What the hell have I let myself in for?' Watt yelled above the roar of the engine.

Her reply was carried off by the wind-rush before it could reach him.

Crawley waited until the last heavy footstep receded from the slabbed courtyard before emerging from the bathroom to pace the kitchen floor, grinding further shards of plastic and broken glass from the smashed computer into the still-unswept flags. His mind was completely absorbed by the problem of how to retrieve his laptop. He was so deep in thought that he did not hear the knock at the door. It was only when the kitchen window was rattled hard that he suddenly jerked round.

He could hardly believe his luck when he saw the face painted against the window. A bespectacled face with a nervous tic winked agitatedly at him. It was his erstwhile travelling companion frantically gesticulating with – wonder of wonders – his rucksack. As he raced to open the door to her, however, it soon became clear that she was on no errand of mercy.

As he flung open the door to her, she immediately launched into the offensive. 'Young man,' she said, 'having been obliged to make extensive enquiries as to your whereabouts, I have finally tracked you down to demand the return of my property. In exchange, I give you back your belongings. Placing the most generous interpretation on events, I can only assume you switched the bags in error, rather than out of any malicious intent.'

Her verbal assault caught him on the back foot. 'You're saying I switched the bags...'

His protest stuttered as she forcefully thrust the rucksack against his body. The hard edge of the laptop at the bottom caught him low in the abdomen, causing his eyes to mist. The resultant intake of breath was enough to loosen his dentures. He sucked at the air like a gaffed fish.

'Let me athure you, madam, there ithn't the thlightest chance of me intenthionally parting with the contenth of my rucksack.'

She held up a restraining hand. 'Save your protestations of innocence, please. When I extended the hand of friendship, you chose to pretend, doubtless for your own amusement, that you hadn't the slightest interest in birds.'

Crawley managed to restore his dentures to their rightful place. 'I don't,' he said.

She closed her eyes in a way that suggested her worst opinion of him now had been confirmed and further argument was pointless. 'I simply ask that you return my property intact. Some of my books are irreplaceable. I warn you if anything has happened to them...' She left the threat hanging in the air.

Deciding to humour her, Crawley treated her to his most fawning smile. 'Believe me, I'm as upset as you appear to be,' he said. 'I have your belongings right here. Please, come in for just a moment?'

She glanced over his shoulder through the open doorway, where her piercing gaze took in the chaotic state of the kitchen before locking on the empty Dogbolter bottles on the table. 'I most certainly will do no such thing,' she snapped. 'I can assure you, people know where I am. If anything were to happen to me, enquiries would be launched.'

Almost beside himself, Crawley wrung his hands in sheer vexation. What was the matter with the damn woman? How could she possibly imagine for a single moment he had the slightest interest in her? 'Madam,' he said, 'nothing could be further from my intention.'

Alas, he had set her off again. 'I don't know what comes over young people these days,' she ranted. 'No sense of responsibility; dereliction of duty on any pretext.' She again glanced pointedly in the direction of the table. 'To enjoy a celebratory glass is one thing, but to drink yourself silly and swan off with your cronies, abandoning your post like your predecessor, is quite another.'

Crawley ran a hand through his hair in sheer exasperation. 'Who's swanning off?' He clutched the doorpost, as much for restraint as for support, as something in her tirade finally triggered a connection in his bemused brain. 'Wait a minute,' he said. 'What predecessor?'

'The young man who was warden here before you, of course.'

In his excitement, Crawley began to stammer, unable to get the words out fast enough.

'W-what about him, for G-God's sake?'

Surprised by his sudden interest, the woman drew herself up self-importantly. 'Naturally I didn't see this personally,' she explained. 'Another guest staying at the hotel saw him go off with three companions. Apparently they were all the worse for drink. It seems both the warden and the girl had to be supported by the others.'

Crawley could hardly contain himself. 'Did this guest happen to see where they went?'

Something about Crawley's abrupt change in tone threw her on the defensive. She sniffed. 'Not that it's any business of mine, nor am I in the habit of exchanging idle gossip. I did, however, wish to contact the warden, and the hotel guest was on the point of returning to Westray by boat.'

'Yes, yes, never mind all that,' Crawley said impatiently. 'What did this guest see?'

She eyed him coldly, clearly torn between a reluctance to help him and the desire to prove her superior knowledge. In the end vanity won the day. 'Two of them were so out of control they had to be half-carried by their companions down to the beach in the South Wick,' she said. Her voice dropped to a scandalised whisper. 'They were obviously celebrating something or other. Then they got into a dinghy and rowed out to a yacht moored in the bay.'

Unbelievable. Fireworks were exploding inside Crawley's head. Anxious to be rid of her, he said, 'Just stay right where you are.' Quickly retrieving her rucksack, he thrust it into her outstretched hands. 'There you are,' he said brusquely. 'You've got what you came for. I needn't detain you a moment longer.'

The woman stood abashed, one eye winking furiously at him. 'I was hoping for a conducted tour of the sanctuary,' she protested. 'Aren't you at least going to explain?'

'I don't have to explain anything,' he snapped, all pretence at civility gone. 'I'm neither the warden nor his replacement. Besides, you were right. This is none of your business.'

She took a step back under the vehemence of his attack, her tic working overtime. 'There's no need to take that attitude with me, young man. You can be sure I'll be writing a letter of complaint to the RSPB. I can honestly say I've never met such rudeness or ingratitude in all my life.'

'Write to any Tom, Dick or Harry you like,' he said waspishly. 'Maybe you should try getting out more often.' Treating her to a leering wink, he slammed the door in her face.

Alone again, he almost cheered with relief and excitement. It only took a quick check of the rucksack. Everything was intact; he was back on schedule again... almost. Glancing at his watch, he realised that Buerk and the others had been gone for the best part of an hour. This long an absence was bound to have caused comment, but he had the perfect riposte. He decided that there was no time now to send his first dispatch to Hornblower; he might even be missing something important outside.

Glancing swiftly around the sitting room, he spotted some deep shelving carrying a double row of books and magazines. He quickly quarried a hiding place for the laptop and rearranged the books in front of it. Satisfied that it was completely hidden from the casual observer, he set off to alert the others to the news that Hilary had been seen going sailing with his drunken friends. The only possible conclusion was that they were celebrating the sighting of the great auk.

They would all have to afford him some respect now, he reflected triumphantly. Buerk with his supercilious put-downs, that uppity two-faced Golightly harridan and those two half-wits Cant and Dick, who had never accorded him the respect his position merited. Well, now he would show them all that he could deliver the goods while they blundered about in the dark. All information was power, he had read somewhere, and boy was he in a powerful position now!

CHAPTER THIRTEEN

Following Lucretia's directions, Buerk and his crew carefully skirted the edge of the maritime heath to avoid the vast hoard of nesting sites in the sanctuary. A few parent birds rose in squealing protest at their approach and, even at a distance, an air of brooding menace seemed to hang over the reserve. As they reached Mull Head they drew to a halt, even Cant and Dick silenced by the awesome grandeur of the place.

Primaeval slabs of rock thrust acutely out of the sea like a gigantic slipway, only a green algal slime able to hold fast to surfaces scoured smooth by wind and water. In some places, monstrous storms had plucked huge slabs from the surface and used them to grind the exposed coastline in an unrelenting war of attrition. Further along, the angle of the coastline changed abruptly, rising steeply to form the towering wall of rock that was Fowl Craig.

As Cant and Dick again set up the equipment, Buerk walked ahead with Lucretia, climbing the steep and narrow path towards the crag. Nesting fulmars hissed and spat on them as they picked their way up the rock-strewn pathway. When it eventually levelled out, Lucretia stopped him at a point she judged to be above the position of the last recorded nesting site of the great auk. As they peered over the vertiginous cliff edge, the acrid stench of guano invaded their nostrils, their ears assailed by a cacophony of screeching and piping from thousands of seabirds around them.

Below, perched on precarious ledges, a variety of birds – guillemots, puffins, razorbills, shags and cormorants – had somehow managed to find nesting sites. Still more circled watchfully overhead while others placidly rode the waves or fished in the productive waters, choosing to ignore them altogether.

Buerk risked another peek over the rim. Far below the brooding wall of rock, alive with its avian inhabitants, snarling crests of white water laid perpetual siege to its foundations. The repetitive boom of a venting blowhole reverberated up the tortured crag like cracks of thunder.

The brief reconnaissance was enough to confirm Buerk's worst fears. Backing away from the edge and the unsettling force of the updraught in his face, he said, 'We've got a major problem.'

'What now, Angus?'

'We can get some establishing shots from down there, where the boys are setting up,' he explained. 'There's simply no way we can train a camera over this cliff. The only way to get close to anything on these ledges is from the seaward side.'

Lucretia looked crestfallen. 'It's those very ledges that are our best chance of seeing the auk,' she wailed.

Buerk scanned the waters below until his eye came to rest on a fishing boat. It pitched and rolled in the swell close to the cliff, its sole visible occupant busy hauling up a line of crab or lobster pots. 'Then we'll just have to see about hiring a boat,' he said resolutely.

Lucretia's eyes began to fill with moisture. 'I hope you don't mind me saying this, Angus. A quality I greatly admire in you is your determination never to be defeated by any challenge, no matter how seemingly insuperable the odds.'

He looked at her in astonishment, privately wondering if the anxiety over Hilary had finally pushed her, metaphorically, over the edge. He was not altogether sure he was comfortable with the way she was looking at him. 'Good of you to say so, Lucretia,' he said uneasily. Turning abruptly on his heel, he threw over his shoulder, 'We'd best join the others.'

Buerk threw himself into the challenge of filming on the exposed coastline. With the wind plucking at his clothing, he began to feel the adrenaline flowing as he picked out the shots he wanted. Despite the absence of the star attraction, this was still a stimulating place to be filming. He briefly chivvied Dick about the excessive wind noise until Dick solved the problem by fitting an extra muffler over the head of the effects microphone.

For the best part of an hour, Buerk alternately coaxed and nagged Cant into producing some spectacular footage of a wide range of seabirds. Cant obliged by catching shots of them perched on precarious ledges, skimming over the water, diving under the waves to catch fish or performing acrobatic feats in mid-air. Warming to his task, the stocky camera operator poetically caught a fulmar lazily planning on the updraught above the cliff edge and, more dramatically, tracked an Arctic skua as it tenaciously pursued a tern through a series of twists and turns. The sequence ended with the tern being forced to release its catch of sand-eels from its blood-red beak, allowing the skua to swoop down and snatch the fish in mid-air with an acrobatic flourish.

The first set of batteries was beginning to run low when Lucretia raised the alarm. At first Buerk could see nothing amiss as he turned to follow her pointing finger. Then he spotted an all-too-familiar figure staggering towards them from the middle of the bird sanctuary. He leaned forward to tap Cant on the shoulder and gesticulate towards the approaching figure. Cant swung the camera, quickly checked his focus and started to record a long steady zoom-in.

'My God,' Dick hissed. 'It's Creepy.'

Buerk nudged Cant aside to peer into his viewfinder. It relayed the evolving drama more effectively than his eyesight could yet manage. The screen was filled with Crawley's panic-stricken features, eyes out like organ stops, clothes torn and muddied.

Awestruck at the spectacle unfolding before his eyes, Cant whispered, 'Looks as if he's stirred up a hornet's nest.'

Eyes widening in disbelief, Dick corrected him. 'You mean terns' nests.'

'Whatever,' Cant said distractedly. 'The silly bee's certainly stung them into a right frenzy.'

Crawley did not know quite how it had happened. Eager to impress Buerk and the rest of the film crew with his newly acquired knowledge, he had realised that he had wasted more time than they were likely to spend at Hyndgreenie Loch. His best bet, he had reasoned, was to go straight on to their ultimate destination at Mull Head. He was vaguely aware that Buerk had given him some spiel about taking the long way round. That, he was certain, had been simply to impress Lucretia and assert his authority. No, with news such as this, there was no time for delay. Armed with the dubious logic that the shortest distance between two points was a straight line, he had set off at the double across the maritime heath that provided the unique environment in Papay for breeding Arctic terns.

What he had not realised, however, was that nowhere else in Europe was there a larger concentration of nesting Arctic terns than on the reserve on North Hill. There were around six thousand breeding pairs in the sanctuary, to say nothing of great skuas, numerous gulls, and a variety of waders such as redshank, curlew, dunlin and oystercatcher. In addition, around one hundred pairs of marauding Arctic skuas constantly harried the adult terns and preyed on their eggs and young. One factor that both Arctic tern and Arctic skua have in common is that parent birds become extremely aggressive in defence of the young, with human intruders not exempt from this treatment.

Before he had trespassed more than a hundred yards into the reserve, the buoyancy with which he had set out had left his step. He had become quite leaden-footed in amazement at the commotion around him. The sky above him visibly darkened as thousands of birds took to the air squawking in protest at this unaccustomed intrusion into their domain. He blundered on, narrowly avoiding standing on eggs and young chicks in nests that were nothing more than shallow scrapes lined with grass. The din grew to a deafening chorus.

By the time he harboured serious doubts about his safety, it was too late. He had reached the point of no return. He cursed his own folly under his breath. This was what came of slavishly following orders, he told himself bitterly. The dark thought occurred to him that if Hornblower could only experience what he was having to go through to keep him abreast of developments, he might be a damn sight more appreciative of Crawley's efforts than he had been to date.

He stopped to glance around himself apprehensively. The air was so thick with mobbing birds that it had become difficult to see where he was going. It was as if night had fallen prematurely. Taking a deep breath, he hurled his imprecations at those he held responsible for his plight (not that any of them could hear). 'Damn you, Lucretia, for your harebrained schemes,' he bellowed. 'Damn you, Buerk, for failing to warn me, and double damn you, Hornblower, for dropping me in it.'

He stood, rooted to the spot in wretched indecision, and felt the wind tug and jostle him, a sudden flurry of rain seeding the gusts like soft, cold shrapnel. Some of the birds most immediately threatened began to make low swoops over his head until, eventually, he was struck on the forehead. He reached up and felt blood seeping from the wound. He broke into a run, but only succeeded in trampling on a few nests, causing even further furore. Now the attacks became more concerted. Another skua drew blood from his ear.

Scared and nauseous from the stench of the creatures, he cast desperately about himself, his breath coming in wheezing gulps. The sky seemed full of the speed-blurred bodies of his assailants. Now the attacks became more concerted as lifelong enemies in skua and tern joined forces against a common foe. Yet another skua drew blood, causing him to yelp in pain and hold up an arm protectively. No longer looking where he was going, he stumbled into a patch of blanket bog where sodden peat began to drag at his footsteps.

He knew nothing of the plants that might otherwise have warned him he was straying onto dangerous ground. The great rafts of spongy sphagnum moss, the orange-yellow flowers of the bog-asphodel, or the silky-white tufts of cotton-grass meant nothing to him. He was clear enough, however, about the solid object which finally tripped him up, plunging him headlong into the mire.

The brief glimpse he had been afforded before measuring his length sent a fearful shiver through his body. His first reaction was to struggle to his feet and keep on running, but something made him turn back. Had he really seen a corpse or was this just another part of a dreadful nightmare?

The stench of the feathered horde had already made him gag, but with the screeching wall of noise pressing in on him on all sides, he doggedly crawled on all fours to take a closer look. As he neared the motionless figure a skua started from almost under his nose, something nasty dripping from its sharp beak. It gave a shriek and with a flapping of wings lifted skywards.

The object that had tripped him up was the body of a woman, or at least what was left of it. He let out a sudden whimper of fright. Her mouth was crammed full of the accumulated debris of the heath, her eyes had gone from the sockets and her nose had been savagely gashed, but it hadn't been the birds that had killed her. As he nervously leaned closer, he spotted the long haft of a knife protruding from the back of her neck.

He opened his mouth to scream and realised he had lost his dentures during his fall. A frantic search on all fours finally led to their discovery by a nest on a raised patch of cross-leaved heath. With half an eye on the corpse and distracted by the frenzied birds circling overhead, he seized an egg in error and tried to force it into his mouth. Belatedly realising his mistake, he scrabbled desperately in the mire, recovered his teeth and spat out shell fragments embedded in a yellow, gooey mess.

He staggered to his feet; his breath came in great sobbing gulps. The air seemed filled with the bodies of birds whirling in a blur of white and brown feathers. Completely lost, he felt fear, frustration and rage build inexorably within him until, lungs bursting with the effort, he bellowed at the feathered throng, 'This is all your bloody fault, Hornblower. I'd like to see how you'd manage.'

Miraculously, the press of whirling bodies momentarily lifted and, through the gap that opened, he spied the familiar figures of Buerk and his camera crew. Previously regarded with such odium, the sight of them now before his wildly staring eyes filled him with the greatest joy. They appeared to be carved from stone as they collectively stared in his direction, monolithic signposts to his deliverance.

With the last remnants of energy in his body he flung himself towards them, no longer able even to call out. Perspiration, mixed with the blood and mud, coursed into his eyes. He ran blindly across the final stretch of heath, still hotly pursued by a host of vengeful birds. He reached the smooth sandstone of the steeply shelving rocks before he was fully conscious of it. One skua, bolder than the rest, bore down sharply, forcing him to duck his head to avoid one more painful thrust from its beak.

He suddenly found himself rushing past the astonished group. Too late, he heard a warning shout from Buerk, but found himself unable to stop. His legs, tried beyond endurance on the boggy heath, had turned to jelly. His feet, coated in sodden peat, vainly scrabbled for a grip on the weather-burnished surface.

He might have plunged to his death if he had not lost his footing altogether. Half-sitting, half-lying, his momentum still carried him over the edge where he began to slide none-too-gracefully over the dipping strata, as though in a personalised flume. Swooping erratically down one great slab of polished rock after another in a series of breathtaking and bone-jarring cascades, he finally came to a halt on a broad ledge just above the water's edge.

Some twenty feet above him, the astonished group peered down at him. It was obvious to all that he was lucky to be alive, but Crawley was in no mood to appreciate such relative good fortune. Lying flat on his back, feeling the world spinning uncontrollably around him and with every bone in his body aching, he began to direct an endless stream of invective against his deputy principal.

Gazing down dispassionately on Crawley's motionless form, Cant shook his head in disbelief. 'You have to admit it, Moby,' he said, 'Crawley's a right fall guy if I ever saw one.'

Dick stood quietly at the edge beside him, visibly shaken by what he had witnessed. 'What do you suppose he could have done to get those birds so riled up?'

'He trespassed on their breeding grounds, that's what,' Lucretia said. Shock and helplessness had made her angry. 'Are you lot just going to stand there gawping? We need to get help.'

Buerk saw no option but to take matters into his own hands. 'There's no time for that,' he said. 'I think I can get down there all right, but I'd need a rope to get back up.'

'There's thirty feet of cable back at the cottage,' Cant said helpfully. 'Moby could be back with it in a jiffy.'

'Then what are we waiting for?' Buerk demanded, trying to exude a confidence he didn't entirely feel.

'On my way.' Dick flung the words over his shoulder, already loping away around the edge of the sanctuary.

CHAPTER FOURTEEN

It had started to rain in earnest by the time Vera drew her motorcycle to a halt on the crest of a hill overlooking another part of the housing estate. Below them, drab apartment blocks emerged from pockets of mist as if struggling to escape the clutches of their bleak environment, a proverbial desert with broken windows. A few vapour-shrouded lights on in windows and in the streets below only seemed to accentuate the pervading gloom.

She pointed towards another fried food outlet, a thin plume of grey smoke issuing from a squat, aluminium funnel, further polluting the atmosphere. This one was parked on a stretch of waste ground close to a bus terminal and had a more permanent look about it. A garish logo of a friar's head (denomination unclear but sporting a beaming moon face) was painted on the side.

It was now late afternoon (Vera's digression having taking longer than intended after the black pudding had worked its predicted magic). A small string of people were waiting in line for an early evening meal. The two of them coasted down to park on the waste ground, perhaps rashly close to the burnt-out shell of what had probably been a stolen car. Nearby, in what local planners might euphemistically have called 'green space', two children and a mangy dog paused from playing with a ball to watch their arrival.

Showing unaccustomed reticence, Vera said, 'We'll wait until the queue thins out a bit. No point taking on half the population on our first sortie.'

Watt made no protest. Unsure of just how far Vera intended to go, he was experiencing a touch of the jitters. Dismounting, he warily eyed the baseball bat in his hands. It was one of two she had commandeered from a local sports hall within her jurisdiction. He'd had them strapped to his back on the short journey here.

He raised his visor to peer at the slowly dwindling queue. A young woman he guessed to be still in her teens stood at the counter waiting to be served, a toddler with a comforter in its mouth straddling her hip. Behind her, an older woman with a plastic shopping bag engaged her in conversation.

As he watched, he became aware of someone tugging at his jacket. It was the older of the two urchins who had been playing with the dog. The boy was about eight going on eighteen; the girl was probably a year younger.

'Are youse aliens?' the boy asked. His old-young face betrayed not a flicker of emotion. His younger companion stared at them, eyes like saucers.

Watt closed his visor and grinned. 'You better believe it,' he said.

The boy motioned towards the baseball bat. 'Dis yer stick no' light up?'

'Only when I swing into action.'

'We'll watch yer space bike for a quid while ye get yer chips,' the budding entrepreneur offered.

Watt bent closer. 'Do a good job and I'll make it a quid each.' He made to reach into his pocket, but Vera shook her head.

'Rule is,' she said, 'payment after the job gets done.'

'Deal,' the boy said. He promptly spat on one grubby hand and offered it to Watt, who took it in his, grateful he was still wearing his gloves.

Having agreed on the parking fee, they started down the hill, tucking the baseball bats inside the front of their jackets. Joining the back of the queue, they had some time to observe the operation. An attractive dark-haired young woman worked in tandem with an older man who flashed a set of nicotine-stained teeth at his customers while maintaining a line of inane banter.

As the last woman in front of them gave her order for a hamburger with cheese and a pudding supper, the female assistant pushed in front of the man to empty a fresh basket of chipped potatoes into the hot fat. Vera sighed because it meant a longer wait.

'Come oan, Sadie,' the man said. 'Let the dug see the rabbit.'

Sadie grinned and moved out of his way. 'Sorry, Vincent,' she said. 'You should've got in while ye had the chance.'

'Story of ma life,' Vincent said. He winked at the woman waiting for her order and gave his colleague a suggestive nudge.

'Dirty old man,' Sadie said.

'They're aw the same, hen,' the customer said.

'Less of the "old", if ye don't mind.' Vincent turned to play to his audience. 'Ye jist can't get a decent class o' help these days.'

During these exchanges, Watt had become aware of a soft footfall behind him. Risking a furtive glance over his shoulder, he felt his pulse rate surge. Despite the newcomer having the collar of his leather jacket turned up against the light rain, there were enough of his features visible to cause Watt some disquiet. The ponytail was the clincher. He was certain it was the man, McManus, who constantly plagued his library for its collection of art books. The one good thing was that he appeared not to have recognised Watt. Watt tried to draw this to Vera's attention but, eager to signal her own intent, she impatiently shrugged off his hand.

She began in what she hoped was a threatening snarl. 'You really need to keep your eyes open, pal.'

Vincent chuckled and mopped his brow with the edge of his apron. 'Ah know,' he said. 'Otherwise ah'll no' see. Am ah right or am ah right?'

'No, straight up.' Vera was a little more forceful this time. She was becoming thoroughly miffed by this clown behind the counter, and it had not escaped her notice that his colleague appeared to be developing an unwelcome interest in Watt, who, irritatingly, kept tugging at her sleeve. 'Me and my mate here have just come from the Chapatti Tatti van.'

'That was your first mistake,' Vincent said.

'What?'

Vincent flashed his yellow teeth at her. 'You went for an obviously inferior product, didn't ye?'

Vera allowed the baseball bat to slide from under her jacket. 'Look, pal,' she said, 'I'm trying to do you a favour here. There are two Asian boys planning to discourage your customers.'

At last Vincent seemed to be taking her seriously as he deftly removed cooked chips from the hot fat with a wire ladle and lobbed them into a serving hatch. 'Just how do they propose doing that?' he demanded.

'We heard them saying something about taking over your pitch.' Watt belatedly attempted to adopt the supportive role Vera was expecting of him. He had become distracted, first by McManus's surprise appearance and now by the girl behind the counter, Sadie. She had chosen that moment to feign a yawn which involved stretching her arms in a way that pulled her thin overall tight across her ample chest.

'The boss has been expecting trouble like this for some time,' Vincent said. He stroked his stubbled chin. 'There's no' room for us and these independents, that's fur sure.'

Watt nudged up his visor to grin at Sadie. 'Reckon the warning is worth a pudding supper,' he said.

Vincent gave a mirthless chuckle, his hands busy patting a portion of chips together with a black pudding before wrapping them in greaseproof paper. 'Nice try, son,' he said, 'but the boss organises his own protection. Cannae afford tae pay fur it twice.'

Vera turned to give Watt the nod. 'Well, he can't say we didn't warn him,' she said. 'If anyone deserves a doing it's this smart-fucking-alec.'

Watt allowed his bat to slide from under his jacket, and he and Vera brandished their baseball bats menacingly just as the customer ahead of them turned her head and spotted them.

'They're carrying weapons,' she called in alarm. She reached up to collect her order but, before she could reach it, Vera struck her a blow behind her knees which sent her staggering sideways against the van. In the same instant, Watt turned to viciously stab his bat into the stomach of McManus behind him. The blow caught him completely by surprise, knocking the wind from him, but as he doubled over he made a grab at the bat.

'Bastard,' he hissed. 'You're going to regret that.'

Watt seemed to be losing the wrestling match for his bat when Vera stepped in and felled McManus with a blow to the back of his head. McManus slumped to the ground.

'Leave that guy alone,' Vincent yelled from behind the counter.

Released from a momentary paralysis and perhaps trying to make amends for his earlier dithering, Watt ran to the counter and whacked Vincent on the side of the head with a roundhouse blow that sent him slumping across the counter. 'Tell Piggy that's just a warning of what's to come from the Chapatti Tatti boys,' he yelled.

To prevent further damage, Sadie tried to bring the shutter down but only succeeded in crashing it against the back of Vincent's neck just as he started to struggle upright.

Her voice hoarse with bloodlust, Vera yelled into the gap below the shutter. 'If you come back here, don't expect your van to survive a second visit.' She made a grab for the uncollected order still on the counter and turned on her heel, heading back up the hill. Watt followed close behind, leaping gleefully over McManus's body, which was now beginning to show faint signs of recovery.

Vincent clutched his face, blood oozing from a cut on the eyebrow. 'Cowardly bastards,' he yelled defiantly. 'You lot huv had your chips. Come back here an' ah'll gie you your heid in yer hauns tae play wi'.'

'Save yer breath, Vincent,' Sadie said. 'They've gone. When we get back to the depot I'm gonnae ask Piggy for a sawn-off shotgun. If they show up again I'll personally shoot the fucking goolies aff the pair of them.'

Still operating at the heightened speed of an adrenaline-fired rush, Vera tucked her ill-gotten gains inside her jacket and began to laugh. As she started the bike, she could feel her heart thumping in her chest.

Watt pulled off a glove and flicked a pound coin to each of the urchins who had witnessed the carnage below in open-mouthed silence. As he let out a whoop of pent-up emotion, they fled from the spot, the dog yapping in their wake.

'Was that a gas or what?' Vera demanded of him.

He mounted the narrow pillion and slapped her on the shoulder. 'Positively orgasmic.'

'Save that for later,' she yelled over the revving engine. 'That rumble has got me feeling randy again.'

'Don't get your hopes up too high,' he said. 'I've got a preschool reading group to contend with first thing in the morning.'

Vera turned to meet his eye and they both began to giggle uncontrollably. They were still laughing as they roared off into the rain and gathering gloom.

Buerk strapped the spent battery belt round his waist and was about to ease himself down onto the first slab when he felt Lucretia take hold of his arm. 'You can't go down there, Angus,' she protested. 'It's far too dangerous.'

A low moan from Crawley alerted him to a new danger. Crawley lay motionless on a rock that was only inches above the water now, the tide on the flow. His precarious landing place would soon be submerged.

'Time isn't on our side,' Buerk warned her. 'If we don't make a move he could drown.'

Lucretia saw his point at once and reluctantly released him from her grasp. 'Please be careful,' she whispered.

He began to slither down the same rock slabs that had so recently witnessed Crawley's precipitate passage. As Buerk made his way down carefully, Cant finished plugging in the reserve battery belt, casually swung the camera round to bring him into focus and pressed the record button.

By the time Dick returned with the cable, Buerk had reached the slab of rock on which Crawley lay moaning. 'Take it easy, Fred,' he said soothingly. 'We'll soon have you out of here.'

As he leaned over to check for broken bones, Crawley made a sudden grab at his sleeve, the move almost jerking Buerk off his feet on the treacherous surface. 'Buerk,' he whispered feverishly. 'It was ghastly, just ghastly!'

'I can imagine.' Buerk clucked sympathetically. 'It certainly didn't look like a picnic with all those birds on your tail.'

The grip on his sleeve tightened, Crawley's whole body convulsing at the memory. 'You don't understand,' he persisted. 'I don't mean the birds. I mean that dead body.'

Deciding that his colleague had probably suffered mild concussion as a result of the fall, Buerk tried to reassure him. 'No need to worry about that now, Fred. You're bound to get the odd dead animal on a reserve like this.'

By now Crawley's grip felt like a tourniquet. 'I'm not talking about animals,' he hissed. 'I'm talking about a human being.' The vehemence in his voice startled Buerk. 'I tell you, if you'd seen that woman lying there with her empty eye sockets an inch from your face and a bloody great knife sticking out of her neck, you wouldn't find it so easy to be so damn smug.' He gave another involuntary shiver. 'And those birds, they were all over her... like vultures.'

The graphic detail forced Buerk to take Crawley seriously. 'Are you saying you saw a woman's body in the sanctuary?' he asked. 'Is that what was stirring up those birds?'

Crawley nodded, not trusting himself to speak further on the subject.

'All right, first things first,' Buerk said. 'Let's see about getting you out of here. Do you think you can stand up? Careful, it's treacherous underfoot. Mind you don't have us both in the drink.'

As he was helped to rise gingerly to his feet, Crawley immediately winced and began hopping rather precariously on the slippery surface. 'My ankle,' he gasped. 'I think it's broken.'

Buerk shook his head, steadying his colleague with an outstretched hand. 'It's probably just a sprain,' he said, 'but we'd better not risk any further damage.' He glanced up at the route they had to negotiate and said to Crawley with a confidence he did not entirely feel, 'Right, then. We'll just have to play piggyback.'

At Buerk's signal, Cant sent the cable snaking down towards him, and at the second attempt he caught it. With the cable attached to the broad, leather battery belt strapped to his waist, he slung Crawley over his shoulder in a fireman's lift and allowed Cant and Dick to reel them both slowly up the incline, bracing himself against the slabs with his feet, both hands clutching the cable tightly.

Drenched in perspiration and with his arm muscles shrieking in protest, Buerk finally made it to the top, where he released Crawley before himself collapsing in a heap. He scarcely registered the kiss Lucretia impetuously planted on his cheek before she turned to minister to Crawley. He was completely unaware that the camera had caught the entire episode. Eyes closed in fatigue and relief, it took him some time before he registered the bulky presence at his elbow.

'I think you should hear what Crawley has to say, boss,' Cant said, nodding to where Lucretia and Crawley were clearly becoming embroiled in a heated exchange.

Buerk accepted Cant's proffered hand to help him to his feet and followed him to where Crawley lay dejectedly, his head propped against a rocky outcrop. Lucretia was busy strapping up his ankle, using her scarf as a makeshift bandage. Visibly squirming under Lucretia's none-too-tender ministrations, Crawley seemed on the verge of having a complete nervous breakdown, a noticeable tremor in his voice.

'What I'm trying to tell you,' he was saying, 'is that the reason I rushed over here was to tell you the news about Hilary.'

'What news?' Lucretia demanded, violently tightening the improvised bandage and threatening to wreak further damage. 'Why didn't you say something before this?'

'Take it easy,' Buerk said, prising her steely grip from Crawley's ankle. 'He's hardly had time to say anything before now.'

Turning back to Crawley, he went on patiently. 'All right, Fred, you'd better tell us the whole story from the beginning.'

Crawley's eyes darted nervously back in Lucretia's direction as she continued to loom threateningly over him. 'Well,' he said finally, 'you remember that twitcher woman who got on the plane with us at Kirkwall...'

It was getting late as Hornblower sat alone in his office. From time to time he would glance forlornly at the screen of his desktop computer, vainly waiting for the first prearranged e-mail report from Crawley. He hated these things at the best of times, but now...

Nothing!

He was becoming restive. As the minutes ticked away beyond the appointed hour, he began to glance distractedly at the book on plant disorders he had borrowed from the library. He had already turned automatically to the section that dealt with roses. That had done nothing to help his mood, since his roses seemed to be suffering from a fair number of the afflictions mentioned.

The rose-hip wine he kept for medicinal purposes and small emergencies only seemed to make matters worse. He had availed himself of a drop or two during his lonely vigil and it now lay heavily on his stomach on top of the toad-in-the-hole he had unwisely eaten in the refectory. He knew hindsight to be something of an exact science but, he told himself, he really ought to have known better. Dining there had never been an enriching experience for him. A bit like relying on Crawley.

Still nothing!

For well over an hour now he had been expecting the little bleep he detested (it always made him start guiltily) telling him he'd got mail. He returned to his book to take his mind off the growing feeling of irritation that always seemed to accompany his dealings with Crawley. The section on fungal infestations lay open before him.

Symptoms: Distinct black or dark brown spots on leaves which soon turn yellow and fall prematurely. Of course, he was all too familiar with such symptoms, but the thought occurred to him that Crawley appeared more of a black spot in his life with every passing minute. It was becoming clear that his chosen method of maintaining contact was doomed to premature failure.

Danger period: Most serious from May/June onwards. Of course it happened to be late May now and this delay was becoming most serious. If Crawley could but know it, the danger period for him was imminent.

Treatment: Spray with appropriate fungicide. Rake up and burn diseased leaves. Apply foliar feed and take good general care. The silence was deafening. He could have heard a diseased leaf fall in the deserted building. That cretin Crawley had better take good care, he thought bitterly, drumming his fingers on the open page. It was just possible that enough of his faults could be raked up to justify burning him at the stake.

When it became clear even to a man of his dogged persistence that there was going to be no message that evening, Hornblower slammed the book closed and levered himself unsteadily to his feet. With a look that was part reproach, part disappointment, but mostly pure vexation, he logged out of the e-mail server and switched off his computer. He'd never really trusted these things and events had just shown that his judgement was not at fault.

Now he would be obliged to wait until morning to find out whether his gamble had come off. One thing was certain. If Crawley valued his hide, let alone his position at the university, he had better not fail to contact him a second time.

CHAPTER FIFTEEN

It took an hour to get back to Hilary's cottage. First, Buerk had to verify Crawley's story about the corpse in the bird sanctuary. To that end, he and Cant set off at once to retrace their colleague's steps. Their combined presence made a more daunting prospect for the birds and although sprays of Arctic terns again rose in protest at their approach, they maintained a more respectful distance from which to vent their disapproval.

They found the body located in the boggy section of the reserve, exactly as Crawley had described it despite the disturbed state of his mind. Coming across his second corpse in two days, Buerk was a little more composed in confronting it and, after his encounters with DI Munro, a little more curious. He found it difficult to put an accurate figure on the age of the unfortunate woman, but her callused hands and broken fingernails suggested someone who frequently worked out of doors. The design and make of her clothes, from the torn cagoule to the worn cord trousers, owed more to a desire to blend with the terrain and be protected from the elements than to being a sop to the latest fashionable style. He was satisfied that this was not Crawley's twitcher friend.

The empty eye sockets and damage the birds had done to the face clearly disturbed Cant, who steadfastly kept his distance.

Under the circumstances, Buerk felt justified in carrying out a quick search of her pockets while scrupulously avoiding any contact with the knife whose long haft projected from the back of the neck. It did not escape his notice that its position was exactly where the hole in Vinnie McGrath's neck had been. That had to be important, he thought.

He found it puzzling that the woman carried no personal effects whatsoever. Perhaps someone had deliberately removed them to make identification more difficult? As he had leaned over her, he had caught the faintest hint of a scent, something floral but too vague to identify.

Having verified Crawley's story, he improvised a marker using his handkerchief tied to the tripod that Cant, forewarned by Crawley's horrific experience, had brought with him to ward off possible attacks from the birds.

Satisfied that he had observed everything that could reasonably be expected of them, he and Cant made a strategic withdrawal. The grilling he had received from DI Munro at the last crime scene was still fresh in his mind but, for Buerk, there were also more recent, more pleasurable memories stirring within him. Not for the first time he felt a pang of regret that she was now far from his sight.

Once they had joined the others, Cant and Dick fashioned a cradle seat from the two battery belts in which to carry Crawley, while Lucretia and Buerk followed on behind, laden with the rest of the equipment.

Back inside Hilary's cottage, Buerk started a peat fire in the small parlour at Lucretia's request while she made Crawley comfortable in an armchair and provided a stool on which to rest his injured ankle. After a more prolonged examination, she confirmed Buerk's earlier diagnosis that no bones were broken. Preferring to play safe, she ordered complete rest for the invalid. For his part, Crawley seemed determined to milk this unexpected treatment for all it was worth. He had already voiced a particular desire to be seated close to the bookshelves by the fire. That way, he argued, he would not have to trouble anyone if he wished to find some reading material.

Since there was no police presence on the island, Buerk made a call from his mobile phone to police headquarters in mainland Orkney to report the body found on the maritime heath. It took him some time to convince the officer on duty that it was not a hoax call. He had to go in painstaking detail over who he was and what his colleague had been doing without the warden's permission in the middle of the bird sanctuary. He knew that explaining Hilary was himself missing was a mistake, but somehow it came out. It was certainly a further mistake to suggest that unless Hilary was a transvestite, it had not been his body that Crawley had stumbled upon on the heath.

After a subdued meal, he decided he needed some fresh air. Wishing to be on his own, he slipped quickly from the cottage before anyone could protest. He need not have worried since Lucretia was again fussing around Crawley, while Cant and Dick were sharing some of the whisky they had brought with them.

The utter stillness of the island impressed itself upon him as he skirted the white sands of the South Wick, noting that the fishing boat he had seen earlier standing off Fowl Craig was now tied up against the old pier. Swinging away from the shoreline, he made his way up the hill on the tarmac road deep in thought. Despite Crawley's ramblings, Buerk did not believe Hilary had gone off on a celebratory spree. It was wholly out of character with how Lucretia had so far described him. So what the hell was going on?

The plaintive notes of a curlew circling high above the salt marsh gradually intruded on his musings. Somehow they struck his ear as dark forebodings of some unspecified peril.

As he reached the neat low terrace of cottages comprising the hotel, youth hostel and shop complex run by the Island Community Cooperative, he noticed a small group of young men standing idly gossiping, their conversation seeming remarkably lively. He paused at the shop to buy a few items and briefly engaged the friendly shopkeeper in conversation.

By the time he left, the gathering of young men was breaking up but the lad who had been pointed out to him by the shopkeeper was still there. A big ruddy-complexioned young man, he was in the act of waving off a friend on a motorcycle with a defective silencer. Once the bike had roared away into the gloaming, Buerk's target leaned back against a wall, appearing in no hurry to leave. Buerk had already noticed that his drink was wrapped in a brown paper bag and guessed that the glow on his cheeks was not entirely due to the weather.

He moved forward to greet him. 'Mr Patterson?'

The lad turned at his approach, a surprised smile on his face. 'Aye, Lachie Patterson. That's me.'

167

'I hope you don't mind,' Buerk said. 'I understand you're the skipper of the fishing boat down at the old pier.'

'Aye.' A note of pride crept into his voice. 'The *Mallimack*'s my boat, all right.'

Buerk introduced himself. 'I'm making a documentary film for New Metropolitan University in Glasgow about the seabirds nesting on Papay and I need to get close to the cliffs off Fowl Craig. I was wondering if you'd allow me to charter your boat for a couple of hours sometime tomorrow.'

A secretive smile played at the corners of Lachie's mouth. 'So you're the Glasgow boys, are you?' he said. 'I saw you on the cliffs the day. You want to be careful up there.'

Buerk nodded. 'That's why we need a boat,' he said. 'Do you think you could help us out?'

Lachie smiled agreeably. 'I don't see why not,' he said. 'Anything for a change. Once I'm finished laying out my crab pots, ken, I could easily take you to Fowl Craig – say about eleven, when the tide's high and we can get in as close as is sensible.'

Buerk glanced around, checking that they were on their own. 'That's great,' he said, fishing from his pocket the half-bottle of Highland Park he had kept for emergencies. 'This calls for a celebration.'

Lachie's eyes lit up. 'Oh, my,' he said. 'You boys believe in doing things in style.' Buerk watched him savour the malt and make a gesture towards the inside pocket of his jacket. 'A definite improvement on my electric soup here.'

'There's quite a selection of birds on the cliffs,' Buerk said innocently.

Becoming noticeably more outgoing as the whisky took effect, Lachie asked, 'Did you have any particular species in mind, Angus?'

Buerk chuckled softly. 'How about the great auk?'

Lachie slapped his thigh and roared with laughter. 'Oh, my. You're a caution, Angus, and no mistake. You're only about two hundred years too late for yon chiel.'

Buerk spread his hands, palms uppermost, and smiled apologetically. 'I'd have asked the warden, but he seems to have vanished. I don't suppose you've seen him around?'

Lachie shook his head. 'I sometimes catch sight of him on North Hill where you were the day, ken, but he keeps pretty much to himself except when he has visitors. I expect he'll turn up before long.'

'I'm sure you're right,' Buerk said. Privately he hoped it wouldn't be in the same condition as the mystery woman in the torn cagoule who'd also been found on North Hill. 'Anyway, I'll see you at eleven tomorrow, down at the old pier in the South Wick?'

Lachie nodded amiably. 'I look forward to it, Angus.'

They shook hands and went off in separate directions, Lachie with the whisky bottle tucked into his jacket pocket, which he insisted was all the payment required for chartering his services.

Piggy Halbert swept a hand over his bald pate and stretched his small, thick-set frame in his swivel chair as his secretary knocked and entered with a cup of tea and two plain biscuits. She was already dressed in her coat and hat, ready to leave. When she placed the cup on the desk in front of him, his small porcine eyes began to glitter as they moved from the biscuits nestling in the saucer to lock with her own. It was those eyes, curiously pink-tinged and set narrowly apart above a snub nose, that had earned him his soubriquet. Curiously enough, he had never objected to it; it always seemed to put any adversary at a disadvantage. He even seemed to derive a certain satisfaction from being so addressed.

'What's happened to the yum-yums, Ruby?' he asked.

Ruby heaved a long-suffering sigh and pointed to a diet sheet with which his wife had supplied her and which she had pinned to the wall above his desk. 'You know perfectly well, Mr Halbert,' she said, 'that doughnuts in any shape or form are not on this list.'

'Well, they're still on mine,' he said. He took a sip of his tea and grimaced.

She returned his stare unflinchingly. 'Sugar's not on the list either.'

Piggy scowled. 'What in hell is the world coming to?' he said. 'A man can't even get any loyalty from his own staff.'

He had been in a bad mood ever since Vince Henderson had called to report the tea-time events concerning one of his fried-food outlets.

Piggy had already been thinking that the Fat Friar fleet of trailers had had its day. With his proposed venture into the exotic world of disco bars, he liked to think of himself as being upwardly mobile. Nevertheless, he was still more than a little vexed at the news that someone had the temerity to threaten part of his empire, to say nothing of causing alarm and actual bodily harm to two of his employees; this latter activity he liked to think was his exclusive preserve.

After Henderson had relayed the gist of the attack, Piggy had growled, 'Right, two can play at that game. If they want to play rough, they can have it rough. I'll put Rob Roy in to ride shotgun.'

A renowned hard man, Rob Roy McGregor owed his nickname to his erstwhile profession as a petty thief rather than to any romantic association with his Highland namesake. Vince Henderson clearly saw the value in having Rob Roy along as protection against any future trouble, but, in the confined space of the van, he envisaged a potential logistical problem. 'There's no' enough room tae swing a cat in that van as it is,' he protested. 'How the hell is Rob Roy gonnae fit in wi' Sadie an' me?'

Piggy already had the solution. 'Considering your injuries,' he said, 'you'll be needing to take a few days' sick leave. Naturally, since I'll be paying the big man, I'll have to deduct it from your wages.'

'Whit aboot Sadie?' Henderson switched to his second reservation: an awareness of Rob Roy's somewhat dubious reputation with women.

'She's old enough to take care of herself.' Piggy opted not to elaborate on the source of his information but relied on his tone of voice to brook no further protest.

Henderson had heaved a resigned sigh. 'Piggy,' he said, 'you're a prince.'

Now Piggy eyed his secretary with a new resolve. 'To hell with the diet, Ruby. I want yum-yums back on the menu as of tomorrow. Is that clear?'

Ruby sniffed. 'You're the boss.'

'Good,' he said. 'Now, tell me who owns the Chapatti Tatti fast-food van.'

Ruby looked blankly at him. 'Never heard of it,' she said. 'Sounds like an Indian outfit to me.'

'Maybe so,' he said irritably, 'but I want to know why two daft cowboys think they can threaten one of my vans and get away with it.'

Ruby's brow furrowed. 'Whatever do you mean?'

He told her about the attack on Henderson's van.

'You don't see this developing into a war, do you?'

'I'd know the answer to that if I'd more idea about who's behind it.' He shook his head bemusedly. 'There's something not right here,' he said. 'A wee independent outfit can't possibly imagine they can take over my territory off their own bat.'

'No,' she said drily. 'That wouldn't be cricket.'

Piggy totally missed the irony. 'Damn right it wouldn't,' he said.

Ruby snapped her fingers as an idea occurred to her. 'Why don't I stop by the Royal India for a wee chicken korma on my way home? I could make a few discreet enquiries of Saeed.'

Saeed Ajmal was the proprietor of the Royal India as well as being a city councillor. There was little that went on in his ethnic community that he didn't know about.

Piggy's pink eyes glinted at the prospect of a solution to his problem. 'Ruby,' he said. 'You're a gem.'

'Of course... there is just a slight problem there...' Ruby left the problem unspoken.

Piggy sighed and dug two £10 notes from his wallet and threw them on the desk. 'Here. Don't say I'm not good to you.'

She smiled complicitly at him. 'Just keep in mind,' she said, 'us gems don't come cheap.'

'You can say that again,' he said gruffly. With more than a hint of grudging admiration in his face he watched her close the door behind her. 'Bloody women,' he said. 'Bloody kids!'

He picked up the phone and punched in a set of numbers he knew by heart. He managed to curse twice more before the receiver was picked up at the other end of the line.

'Hullo. Who is it?' The voice had a breathless edge to it.

'It's Piggy. I didn't wake you, did I, big man? I know you sometimes work nights.'

'Naw. Ah'm awake, all right.'

'Is this a bad time?'

'Ah wouldnae say that – just so long as you're quick.'

Piggy thought he heard the sound of a hand slapping bare flesh, followed by a high-pitched squeal. 'Are you alone?' he asked suspiciously. 'This is a business call.'

' 'Course I'm alone.'

'I thought I heard a female voice.'

'Probably just the telly, Piggy. Whit do you take me for?'

'How about a rutting stag and a damned liar, not necessarily in that order?'

Rob Roy made a vain attempt to sound hurt. 'Nae need tae get personal.'

Piggy cut to the chase. 'I'm in need of your services again, eight-hour shift from lunchtime... maybe for the next few days, but I'd need you to start tomorrow.'

'Ah'm sure ah could fit that in.' A stifled giggle in the background. 'Whit's the problem?'

'Some bastard is threatening to beat up customers and chase away business. I need you to replace Vince Henderson for a spell.'

'Nae problem.' There was a brief silence and then Rob Roy asked, 'Does that wee dark-haired lassie still work wi' Vince?'

'Sadie. Yes; what the hell difference does that make?'

'Absolutely none. Ah jist thought Sadie could show me the ropes, know whit ah mean?'

Piggy opted to ignore the question. 'Right,' he said. 'I'll expect you at the depot just before noon.'

'Ah'll be there. See you, Piggy.'

This time Piggy could have sworn he heard female laughter followed by a positive squeal before the line went dead.

CHAPTER SIXTEEN

The Royal India was busy when Ruby entered the lobby where the takeaway counter was situated. She placed her order and asked to speak to the manager. Seeing the waiter hesitate, she added, 'I think he'd like to hear what I have to say before the media gets hold of it.'

He turned on his heel at once.

Saeed Ajmal was a tall man with thinning hair and a welcoming smile. That smile was still in place when he emerged a few minutes later. 'Always nice to see you, Ruby,' he said. 'I hope this isn't a complaint about my restaurant?'

Ruby shook her head. 'Nothing could be further from my mind, Mr Ajmal,' she said. 'It's more in the nature of a community concern.'

The smile wavered. 'How so?'

Ruby drew closer and lowered her voice. 'One of my boss's trailers and some of his customers in the Drumchapel area were attacked last night by two thugs in motorcycle leathers. They claimed to represent a rival outfit known as the Chapatti Tatti. The idea was to attack the staff, scare off any customers and take over the site.'

Ajmal frowned. 'Does Piggy think this van is connected to me?'

'Absolutely not,' Ruby said. 'He'd never heard of the outfit, but I thought you might know them. It looks like someone is out to make trouble, maybe even trying to start a race war.'

Ajmal nodded slowly, digesting Ruby's words.

'For what it's worth,' Ruby said, 'the girl with our driver wasn't sure the attackers were of ethnic origins, but you know what the media can make of this kind of incident.'

Ajmal eyed her grimly. 'Tell your boss I'll contact him the minute I learn anything. This sort of thing has to be nipped in the bud.'

'Couldn't agree more,' Ruby said. The waiter arrived with her order but, as she took out her purse to pay, Ajmal stayed her hand.

'You did the right thing alerting me to this,' he said. 'This is on me. One good turn deserves another.'

Ruby beamed in delight and put her purse containing the £20 back in her bag. One good turn indeed, she thought. It wasn't every day you got one over Piggy.

The CID room was in uproar. Most of the task force were crowded round the television set perched high on a swivel bracket in the corner of the room. Emotions ran from cynical amusement to downright annoyance. The 'chip van war', as it was already being labelled, had clearly grabbed the media's attention. While it did deflect some unwelcome attention from the yet-unsolved Vinnie McGrath murder, the news programme's anchor had already made some unflattering remarks about the police force as a whole.

'Earlier in the programme,' she announced, 'we brought you an exclusive interview with the victims of an unprovoked attack on the Fat Friar, a mobile outlet for fast foods in the city's outskirts. They described in graphic detail how two youths, clad in motorcycle gear and wielding baseball bats, indiscriminately attacked staff and customers alike and claimed to represent a rival outlet with ethnic origins known as the Chapatti Tatti.' Here a photograph showing the colourful van flashed up on the screen. 'The attackers warned that further action would be taken if the van was not withdrawn from that site.

'In a curious twist this channel can exclusively reveal that a similar threat was first visited upon the Chapatti Tatti van. The two boys, Vijay and Sachin Kumar, described their attackers in terms matching the descriptions of those who carried out the later attack on the Fat Friar.'

The woman earnestly looked straight to camera. 'The real question here is: do these grave but still relatively minor skirmishes represent the opening salvos in an all-out turf war, or is something even more sinister going on, unnoticed by the public and law enforcement agencies alike? We will of course update you on this story as it unfolds.'

Chief Superintendent Douglas fumed as he zapped off the television set with the remote. 'Jesus H. Christ,' he said. 'Who's jerking the strings of that uppity bitch?'

DS Lennox was sitting at her desk fielding a phone call as her superintendent spoke. Covering the mouthpiece of the phone, she said *sotto voce* to Munro, 'At least he can't blame this on Buerk.'

Munro grimaced. 'I suppose we should be thankful for small mercies,' she said. In truth she still had not totally forgiven Angus Buerk for disappearing into the wilds without a personal word of apology or explanation to her.

Apart from the personal affront to her dignity, the Black Douglas had not been slow to point out that allowing Buerk to slide under her radar was tantamount to a dereliction of duty.

Out of the corner of her eye she noticed the duty officer hovering in the doorway. He held a slip of paper and was obviously waiting for the right moment to interrupt Douglas. Chance would be a fine thing.

Lennox chose that moment to beat him to it. 'Excuse me, sir,' she said. 'There seems to be a delegation downstairs asking to speak to whoever is in charge of the "chip van war". They represent both outlets in question and they've brought their solicitors with them. It appears both parties wish to present a united front.'

'That must be a first in this city,' Douglas said. 'What's your problem, Sergeant Lennox?'

'I don't think we have an officer assigned to that case yet, sir,' she said.

Douglas's face darkened as he cast around for a victim and the entire room went silent. His eyes were hovering over Munro when the duty officer, brandishing the paper, moved swiftly to interrupt him.

'I think you ought to know about this, chief superintendent,' he said. 'Just came in through the computer network.'

'What is it now, sergeant?' Douglas snapped. 'Can't you see we're in the middle of something?'

'There's been a murder up in the Orkneys,' the officer persisted.

Munro shot Lennox an anxious look as Douglas turned his vitriol on the duty officer. 'Well, what the dickens has that to do with us?' he demanded. 'That's well outside our jurisdiction.'

The duty officer stood his ground. 'I understand it's the same MO as the Vinnie McGrath case,' he said.

Douglas glared at him with a sudden suspicion. 'Coppers are a bit thin on the ground up there,' he reasoned warily. 'Who called this in?'

The sergeant consulted the slip of paper in his hand. 'Chap by the name of Buerk,' he said. 'Apparently he works at the New Metropolitan Uni—'

Douglas roared, as if in pain. 'I know where he works,' he said. Furiously, he snatched the piece of paper from the duty officer's hand. 'Inspector Munro!' he bellowed.

'Sir.'

Douglas made an effort to compose himself. 'I want you on the first plane up there,' he said. 'I don't care how you do it, but I don't want that fellow Buerk out of your sight again until he sets foot in this station to give us some convincing explanation about his activities. Do I make myself clear?'

Munro gazed coolly into his eyes. The Black Douglas, she thought, was an intolerant, sexist bastard, but at that precise moment she could have happily planted a kiss on his miserable, chauvinistic chops. 'As crystal, sir.'

She turned quickly on her heel before he could see the delight in her face and almost lost it when Lennox winked at her.

Of course, there wasn't a flight until the morning and there was still the chip van delegation to deal with. Once he had calmed down, she suggested to Douglas that Lennox and DC Danny Traynor, a relative newcomer to the squad, could be trusted to deal with the situation in her absence. Then again, there was still the outstanding matter of Spider to deal with. She sighed heavily. She was going to have to rely on Mary Lennox a great deal in her absence.

Saeed Ajmal had persuaded Piggy to attend the police meeting along with Henderson (sporting a plaster over his eyebrow) and Sadie. Vijay and Sachin were also present, along with the respective solicitors of both parties.

Although she had decided to sit in on the discussion, Munro wanted it to be clear from the outset that Lennox was in charge of the case. In a conference room, over a cup of tea, she and her colleagues listened to the accounts and descriptions from the staff of the two vans. It was clear from what they said that they had each been visited by the same two perpetrators.

After listening to them and comparing the statements taken by uniformed officers when Henderson had reported his attack, Lennox tried to sum up. 'This pair of tearaways have clearly taken it into their heads to stir things up by pitting one outlet against the other,' she said. 'It's clearly in the interests of the entire community that these perpetrators be brought to book at the earliest opportunity.'

There were some satisfied nods from around the table. 'That's what we want to hear,' Vijay said. 'British justice at work.'

Munro glanced at him sharply but could detect no hint of irony.

'A dose of their own medicine is what they need,' Henderson said.

He was immediately hushed to silence by Piggy. 'Let's just leave this to the police,' he said. His eyes glinted mischievously under the fluorescent lighting as he added, 'That's what we pay our rates for.'

'It's only fair to warn you,' Lennox said, 'there's a fair chance they will strike again.'

'In that case,' Ajmal said, 'might we ask, detective sergeant, how you propose to protect the staff involved?'

Lennox glanced at Munro before answering. 'I'm sure your clients would be the first to recognise what the presence of uniforms around your trailers would do to business,' she said.

'In which case we must reserve the right for our employees to be prepared,' Piggy said.

'No harm in that,' Lennox said. 'So far this has proved to be a local affair. DC Traynor, here, and I will each be responsible for surveillance on one van. I'll liaise with Mr Halbert's outfit and DC Traynor with Vijay and Sachin. We will each be in radio contact with a squad car. I also propose installing small surveillance cameras inside the hatchway of each van. They'll be discreetly positioned so that your customers are unaware of their presence, but they will record anyone or anything approaching the counter. Your staff can operate them at the press of a switch whenever you are open for business.'

'Brilliant,' Vijay said. 'An undercover operation.'

'That sounds very satisfactory,' Piggy said. The others swiftly agreed to the proposals and they departed in better spirits than they had arrived.

'Don't have a big breakfast in the morning,' Munro said to her two colleagues.

'Why not?' Traynor asked.

'Because,' she said, 'you might be eating lots of fish and chips before this is over.'

It was dark by the time Buerk got back to the cottage to report that they had acquired the services of Lachie and his boat the following morning. It would be a final attempt to locate the auk on the cliffs at Fowl Craig. Hornblower had given them a little over two days to acquire the necessary footage of the scientific discovery of the age. After that, the principal would have returned to steal his thunder or expose the empty boast.

'Oh, Angus,' Lucretia simpered in admiration. 'Aren't you a dark horse?' The look on her face should have warned him that there was something more than horses on her mind, but he was too tired to take any notice. It didn't even bother him that the sleeping arrangements had already been sorted out in his absence; he was simply too tired to care.

In her brother's continued absence Lucretia had taken the spare bedroom in the main house, leaving the four men to occupy the bunk beds in the annexe, a recent extension for visitors and house guests of the warden. Crawley, with surprising alacrity for someone nursing a badly damaged ankle, had shown a clear preference for the lower bunk nearest the door, while Cant and Dick had opted for the upper berths. Since Cant had elected to haul his massive bulk above Crawley to be next to the open window, Buerk had to settle for the remaining lower bunk below Dick.

A few minutes after they had all settled into bed, there was a soft knock at the door. 'Everyone decent?' Lucretia called. Failing to get a reply, she entered the room bearing a tray. 'I've made some cocoa,' she said. 'It'll help us all get a good night's sleep after the upsets of the day.'

'Brilliant!' Dick said, sitting up eagerly and reaching for one of the mugs. Before he could get his hands on it, however, Lucretia deftly removed it from the tray and handed it to Buerk. She then offered round the remainder.

'I'll wish you all good night, then,' she said. She paused briefly at the door as if checking that everyone was comfortable, then, with a smile of satisfaction on her face, she left.

'Argh! There's no sugar in this,' Dick said after an impulsive gulp at the contents.

'I'll swop you mine,' Buerk said, pulling a face. 'This one's way too sweet for my taste.'

'Bit out of character, her making us cocoa,' Crawley said sourly. He tried to sit up too quickly and bumped his head on the underside of Cant's bunk.

'No sense in looking a gift horse in the mouth,' Dick said. With a flourish he cheerfully dispatched the remainder of Buerk's over-sweetened cocoa.

Buerk sipped reflectively from the half-empty mug he'd taken from Dick. 'Her heart's in the right place,' he said.

'I think she's taken a bit of a shine to you, boss,' Cant said, yawning.

'Thanks for sharing that with me, Genghis,' Buerk said. Stifling a yawn of his own, he finished his cocoa, slid under the duvet and was soon asleep.

Dick's lanky frame stretched over the end of the bed, which had an awkward wooden strap across the bottom. The only way he could make himself comfortable was to tuck the spare pillow under his feet and lie flat on his back. Unfortunately, in that position he snored a great deal. This was no particular handicap to Dick himself, since he was blissfully unaware of the racket he was creating. Aided by the whisky he had earlier consumed and the exertions of the day, he had slipped fairly rapidly into a frequently recurring dream of his which involved a blonde called Angel. This caused the odd bit of shivering and moaning to underscore the snoring.

The snoring alone was, however, a good deal more than Cant could put up with, and he attempted to stop it in ways which employed increasing degrees of violence. He growled threateningly at Dick to no avail and then yelled more loudly, still with no effect. He threw his pillow next, which fell short of the mark, and then his boots; in his near-comatose state he had forgotten to take them off before climbing into bed. The first missile sailed narrowly past Dick's ear, the slipstream causing a hopeful, but alas momentary, change in rhythm. The second one slipped from Cant's grasp at the vital point of lift-off and fell harmlessly to the floor – harmlessly, at least so far as Dick was concerned. Unfortunately, on the way down it struck Crawley a glancing blow on the head just as he stuck it out to see what the commotion was all about.

As Dick's stertorous breathing continued unabated, Cant decided enough was enough, slid resignedly from his bunk and waddled out of the bedroom, hauling his duvet after him. Swathed in the duvet, he passed through the linking corridor, where he safely negotiated his way round the bicycle propped against the wall, and ended up in the sitting room. There, after throwing a couple of peat blocks to bank up the still-glowing fire, he made himself comfortable on an old sofa. Within a few minutes he was blissfully asleep.

Crawley waited for things to settle down again. He found Dick's snoring almost therapeutic, as it helped to take his mind off the pain in both head and ankle. He strained his ears for any other untoward sound. Nothing! Even that clumsy elephant Cant appeared to have settled somewhere. So far, so good. Now, it was high time he sent his report, already half-composed in his head, to his 'controller at HQ'.

Slowly and painfully he inched his way out of bed. Somehow he found it difficult to keep his eyes open, and there was an awkward moment when he tripped over Cant's other boot and stumbled against the door that had been left ajar. Fortunately his elbow took the brunt of the blow, saving his head from further punishment. For an agonised moment he held his breath, but no one stirred in the room. He crept into the passageway, grimacing in stoic silence as he headed for the sitting room.

Wakened from his slumber by all the activity around him, Buerk listened to Crawley's stumbling progress with initial annoyance and then increasing interest. He assumed at first that he was paying a visit to the toilet, but Crawley's muffled expletives when he collided with the bicycle clearly telegraphed his passage into the sitting room beyond. There was no doubt in Buerk's mind that Crawley had been acting suspiciously all day. Now, Buerk resolved, he would discover exactly what his rival was up to. Stifling a yawn, he slipped out of bed and padded after his accident-prone colleague.

For his part, Dick remained content to act out his dream with Angel. At one point, perhaps subconsciously triggered by the ebb and flow of humanity around him, he felt the call of nature and, in a somnambulant daze, drifted to the toilet, blissfully unaware of the earlier departures. Returning in the same dreamlike trance, he made several futile attempts to scramble into his upper bunk but, perhaps fearful of losing the image of Angel still vivid in his mind, he gave up and collapsed into the bed vacated by Buerk.

Lucretia was also unable to sleep that night, although, in her case, it had nothing to do with Dick's snoring. Rather, she found herself in the grip of a romantic fever concerning Buerk. It had been incubating for some time and had come to a head as she had watched the dramatic rescue of Crawley from his near-fatal fall over the cliff. It was clear to her that Angus believed in her while other doubters fell by the wayside. Equally clearly, such devotion merited some tangible reward. Now, alone in her bed, she could no longer deny her aroused passion. When she had planted a chaste kiss on his brow to acknowledge his bravery, modesty had prevented her from showing her true feelings. Now, in the darkness of the night, no such inhibition presented itself and her fertile imagination conjured up more fitting ways to reward a hero.

Never for a moment did it cross her mind that such thoughts might not be reciprocated. Had she not witnessed at first hand the troubled glances he constantly directed towards her whenever they were alone together? Had she not felt the tension in his voice when he spoke to her? Tormented by all manner of disturbing but pleasurable images of her body and Buerk's entwined in loving embraces, she knew there would be no sleep for her that night until her passion had been assuaged.

The tricky part was meeting with the object of her desire without waking the others. The sleeping tablets, she thought, had been a stroke of genius. Mentally she reviewed the sleeping arrangements she had carefully memorised earlier in the evening when she had delivered the cocoa: three mugs containing two crushed sleeping tablets and one with extra sugar for energy. Now, it was time to take matters into her own hands.

Once or twice she had screwed up her courage and tiptoed to the door, only to be forced to duck quickly inside again as someone walked past. Quite unexpectedly and with no place in her carefully rehearsed scenario, the corridor appeared to have become a major thoroughfare.

First, Cant's ursine figure shambled past clutching a duvet around him. Then, as she eased her door open a second time, it was only to witness Crawley limping painfully past. She was becoming desperate by the time she almost collided with Dick on his way to the toilet. Fortunately he appeared to be sleepwalking. Frustrated, she threw herself on her bed and chewed the pillow until all movement eventually ceased. Finally, she could endure the torment no longer and, clutching her nightdress to her, stepped boldly into the corridor, determined that nothing further would keep her from her heart's desire.

The sleeping tablets had done their work. The room was as silent as the grave save for the sound of restless moaning emerging from Buerk's bed. That was final confirmation that he, too, was tormented by unresolved passion. Unhesitatingly she snuggled in beside the sleeping occupant.

'At last, my darling,' she breathed into his ear.

'Mmm,' Dick moaned reflexively against her warmth, his voice muffled by her ample bosom.

'No need to say anything,' she whispered, her breath suddenly becoming ragged as she reached under the covers.

Dick responded by pulling her into a passionate embrace, as his normally quiescent dream was suddenly transformed into aroused reality. 'Angel,' he murmured hoarsely.

'Darling,' she said, both astounded and delighted by the immediacy and ferocity of the passion she had unleashed, 'I can deny you nothing...'

CHAPTER SEVENTEEN

Ned Goldfiever appeared understandably guarded when St Clair telephoned to broach the subject of the missing video cassette.

'It was discovered quite by chance on top of the hand dryer in the gents' toilet,' St Clair explained. He added casually that the employee making the discovery had recalled Vinnie McGrath having recently requested viewing facilities on his premises. He could only assume McGrath had left the tape by mistake. Having heard the tragic news of Vinnie's demise (no mention of the *Loch Tredwell*) and learning from the newspaper report that Vinnie was a recent employee of Goldfiever's, he wondered if Goldfiever might be the rightful owner.

Even as St Clair gave his tortured reasoning for the call, he wondered if the recipient would swallow it. Nevertheless, he felt Goldfiever gradually came round and perhaps sounded relieved, even genuinely grateful. Over the gravelly tones, however, he could hear the creaking of an expensive leather chair rocking gently back and forth. It somehow conveyed the impression of enormous latent power: a power that could raise a man up to a dizzying position of wealth, but which could just as easily crush him without a moment's hesitation.

'Naturally, Mr St Clair,' the entrepreneur said, 'I have no personal knowledge of the tape of which you speak. We at Southern Line International, however, have a general policy of rewarding the return of stolen property – always with the proviso, of course, that everything is dinky-di and the goods are in bonzer condition. Our Media Edutainment division would be happy to view the tape to verify its ownership and, if they were convinced that no one was coming the raw prawn, a reward would be paid to the finder. I hope I've made myself clear?'

St Clair almost rubbed his hands with glee and winked across at Spider, who had come up with the goods at the second time of asking. 'Absolutely,' St Clair said before adding, a trifle rashly, 'I'll personally see that the goods are delivered.'

The chair creaked smoothly. 'Call at the head of the gangway. I'll alert Byron to expect your visit. If everything appears to be apples you'll be rewarded in due course. Now, if you'll excuse me, I have some rather pressing business to attend to.'

'Of course, the takeover bid... I understand,' St Clair replied ingratiatingly. 'Naturally if there's any other little service I can do...' He stopped talking as he realised the line had already gone dead. One step at a time, he told himself consolingly.

'Whit did he say?' Spider asked. 'A breeze' was how he had described to his employer his second visit to the *Loch Tredwell*. Truth to tell, he was less than happy with the way things were going. He had been asked to put his head in a noose in exchange for having any charges against him dropped: charges of which he was wholly innocent. He had a sneaking admiration for DI Munro and as she had outlined what she wanted him to do, it had all sounded so plausible. Now, the more he thought about it, the more he realised what could go wrong. It was enough to do your head in.

'Goldfiever seemed distracted by his bid to take over TMG,' St Clair said. 'Bloody man barely speaks English. I got the bit about rewarding the return of stolen property, then he started to bang on about *apples* and the goods being *bonzer*, whatever the hell that means. Then he said we'd be met at the gangway by his minder, Byron.'

Spider eyed St Clair warily. 'Maybe he's the guy that topped Vinnie.'

St Clair was only half-listening. 'Wasn't Byron a numpty poet or something? Only a bloody head case would contemplate employing a numpty as a minder.'

At the gangway of the *Brisbane Queen*, Byron's greeting was less poetic, more simian grunt, although his body language hinted that he might be well-versed in more violent forms of self-expression. Following him up the gangway, they were ushered into comfortable chairs in a plush stateroom aboard the floating casino.

St Clair gleefully rubbed his hands in anticipation of his reward, while a nervous Spider asked for a glass of water, which a faintly amused Byron provided from a carafe on the table. Accepting the glass, Spider held it awkwardly as though afraid of spilling its contents on the deep pile carpet.

They were kept waiting for a full ten minutes before Goldfiever made an appearance. To St Clair's surprise, Goldfiever was short – he guessed no more than five six – and was carrying excess poundage. Nevertheless, he had a pugnacious presence which more than compensated for his lack of inches and his excess pounds. He sat down in his chair, which began to creak ominously, and glanced coldly at St Clair. 'I have to tell you, sport,' he said in a broad Australian drawl, 'I'm disappointed with this stunt you tried to pull.'

St Clair shot Spider a questioning look and ran a finger round the inside of his collar. 'I assure you, Mr Goldfiever, this was no stunt. If it wasn't McGrath, then some other customer must have left the tape behind by mistake. I got in touch with you the minute Spider brought it to my attention.'

Goldfiever glanced at his minder. 'What did I tell you, Byron? There's a perfectly rational explanation for the tape being there: it was left by mistake. Danny boy here really doesn't have the brains for duplicity.'

'Or da balls.' The bodyguard's amusement at his attempted joke took the form of a series of small body tremors that seemed to travel from the soles of his Doc Martens all the way to his bald head. To St Clair, his laugh only served to make him more unnerving.

'You must think I came from beyond the black stump,' Goldfiever scoffed. 'Maybe you're just off your bleedin' kadoova. Either way, we figured out what you were up to right from the off. Your man here very obligingly rewound the tape to the beginning, so we knew someone had viewed it. Seemed only logical you'd make a copy. Thinking of cutting yourself in for a slice of the action, eh?'

St Clair grabbed the arms of his chair in rising panic. 'Look, this had nothing to do with me,' he said. 'McGrath showed the video to Spider.'

Spider gulped nervously at the water in his glass.

Goldfiever's lip curled in a sneer. 'I had my man, Goren, take care of McGrath for that act of disloyalty.' He gave a hoarse cackle as he winked at Byron. 'I've sent him off on a cruise now as a reward for services rendered. You see how generous I can be?'

Spider leaned forward in his seat. 'Vinnie was stabbed before being burnt tae a crisp is whit ah heard.'

St Clair glared at Spider, his forehead covered in a sheen of perspiration. 'Spider used to be a boxer,' he wailed. 'He's not right in the head.'

Goldfiever chuckled coldly, like water in a deep well. 'Your sidekick may be a few snags short of a barbie, but you're the one that's been acting as silly as a cut snake, Danny boy. I had McGrath silenced as a deterrent to others. You don't seem to have learned that lesson.'

St Clair pulled a handkerchief from his pocket and mopped his brow, the atmosphere in the stateroom becoming claustrophobic. 'Don't you think you're being just a little ungrateful?' he said. 'I mean, I could just have kept the video and said nothing. Naturally, under the circumstances I won't be looking for any reward.'

'No, you're right,' Goldfiever said, 'I should be grateful for the return of that tape. It's going to make life a little easier for me.' He rocked in his chair, causing it to creak again. 'You deserve something to remember me by; Byron will arrange it now.' He turned dismissively to Spider. 'If you'll excuse us, sport, I've got some private business to discuss with your employer. Byron will see you out.'

Spider seemed so eager to escape, he quite forgot to leave his glass behind. Up on deck the chill wind coming off the river made him shiver, but he gulped gratefully at the cold air, scarcely able to believe his narrow escape. As Byron nudged him none-too-gently down the gangway he became suddenly aware of the sledgehammer clutched in the bodyguard's fist.

St Clair's brand new sports car gleamed under the sulphurous glow of the street lamps along the deserted quayside. Spider eyed Byron warily as he produced a set of keys from his pocket. 'Whit's the score?' he asked. 'Those are the boss's car keys.'

With a sinister smile, Byron sprang the boot lid. 'You wanna bellyache?' he said. 'I'll give ya bellyache.'

Spider never saw the elbow that caught him in the solar plexus. It folded him like a Swiss army knife. In almost the same movement Byron bundled him into the boot and slammed the lid shut.

The next ten minutes felt like a living hell to Spider as the sledgehammer went to work on glass, body panels, radiator. As the car rocked on its springs, Spider could do nothing but curl into a foetal ball. The tumbler, still in his grasp, remained intact.

The din stopped as suddenly as it had begun.

A long time later the lid was again sprung open with a tortured squeal of warped metal. He saw the look of shock on his boss's face. St Clair was also sporting a cut lip and a nasty-looking bruise over his right eye.

'Ah thought ah was a goner,' Spider said in a hoarse whisper.

St Clair's mouth puckered. 'You were closer than you'll ever bloody know,' he said.

Painfully, Spider climbed out. 'How so?'

'I need to claim on the insurance,' St Clair said flatly. 'I was just about to shove this heap into the river.'

'But ah was inside,' Spider protested.

St Clair's eyes glittered with malice. 'They say every cloud has a silver lining. Now, come on, man, give us a hand before I change my mind and stuff you back inside.'

Before Spider could respond, a police van, klaxon blaring, roared along the quayside and screeched to a halt. It was quickly joined by an unmarked Volvo. A male detective led a squad of uniforms out of the van and up the gangway at the double, while a lone female emerged from the car. Showing her warrant card to St Clair, Munro said, 'I expect you remember me?'

'Of course.' St Clair nodded his head in Spider's direction. 'This is my assistant, Mr McVey.'

She gave St Clair a cold smile. 'We've already met,' she said. 'You could say Spider and I have an understanding.'

St Clair looked astounded. 'You do?'

Ignoring him, Munro carefully took the glass Spider offered and dropped it into an evidence bag. 'Good work, Spider,' she said. 'The wire worked a treat. Goldfiever has at least implicated himself in Vinnie's death and given us a name for Vinnie's killer.'

St Clair looked from Munro to Spider and back again. 'You mean to say you've been recording all this time?'

She arched an eyebrow. 'Is that a problem for you?'

St Clair glared at her. 'You could at least have stopped them trashing my car.'

She seemed to notice the wrecked sports car for the first time and shook her head gravely. 'They just don't make them like they used to,' she said.

Distracted by the sight of her colleagues bundling Goldfiever and Byron down the gangway and into the waiting van, Munro heaved a sigh. 'You'll have to excuse me; no rest for the wicked.' As an afterthought, she called over her shoulder, 'Want a lift, Spider? Might as well relieve you of that wire and eliminate your prints from the glass. Maybe Byron has some previous form.'

'Sure,' Spider said. He shrugged apologetically at St Clair before sidling after her.

'What about me?' St Clair demanded furiously.

Munro turned, her smile wintry. 'The good news is we won't be pressing charges against you for receiving stolen goods and sanctioning the electronic duplication of material likely to constitute attempted blackmail. Always provided, of course, you hand in the copy at the station. We'll be alerting the intended victims of what has transpired and warning them about their future conduct.'

In the car, Munro heaved a contented sigh and glanced at Spider. 'That was certainly worth the wait.'

Spider turned to wave regally to his employer before his forlorn figure was lost to view. 'Ye can say that again,' he said.

Retrieving his laptop from the bookshelf, Crawley decided not to risk switching on the light. He reflected darkly that the flickering flames from the fire and the illumination from the laptop itself would be adequate for his purpose. During this ill-conceived search for an extinct species, he had suffered air sickness, been insulted by a deranged twitcher, been mobbed by a flock of demented terns (even now the thought caused an involuntary shudder to run through his tormented body) and almost plummeted to his death over a cliff.

That final episode on North Hill had been the last straw. He no longer cared if the great auk existed or not. Apart from that ambitious Golightly harridan, no one else did either. Buerk was quite obviously covering his back, and Hilary was too drunk to care, while even Cant and Dick were behaving themselves for once in their lives. He was utterly resolved to let Hornblower know what he had been through... if only he could stop yawning.

With the last of his resolve he switched on his laptop and stifled another yawn as the instrument sprang into life. Hooking into his e-mail server, he began composing feverishly:

You wouldn't believe the breeding birds on this island. Nesting sites everywhere make life intolerable. Buerk filming willy-nilly.

Lucretia's brother gone on a celebratory drinking spree.

Unidentified woman killed in sanctuary. Almost died myself after being chased over a cliff.

Returning home soonest.

Crawley

His head slumped to his chest and he had to shake himself awake, staring bleary-eyed at the screen. In his current state of mind he wasn't at all sure that his report made much sense. He yawned again. Perhaps it might be wiser to get some sleep and try again in the morning.

At that precise moment, Cant sat up and began to stretch his massive frame with a loud yawn. The flickering light from the fire cast his magnified shadow on the wall, making him appear like a giant phoenix. It caused Crawley to leap to his feet in fright and inadvertently click the send key. Then the adrenaline kicked in as all the spectres from the day's experiences came flooding back to haunt a mind already tried to the limit of endurance. Emitting a low moan of terror, he fled from the room. He might even have made it, had he not run smack into the bicycle. This time, perhaps mercifully, he knocked himself unconscious on the stone floor.

The noise stirred Lucretia from a light sleep. Pleasurable memories flooded back into her brain. Clearly, she was to be denied her wish of spending the whole night with her lover.

As she reluctantly eased herself from his slumbering embrace, she reflected warmly that that was the only pleasure she had been denied. It was odd, she mused dreamily as she crept back to her own bed: her lover had proved to be taller and more angular than she had envisaged.

Oblivious of all the hubbub around him, Dick simply sank into exhausted release. Never before had his dream appeared so vivid, or so satisfyingly complete.

It was left to Buerk and a bleary-eyed Cant to carry Crawley's unconscious body to the sofa. Having checked his pulse to ensure that he was still in the land of the living, they turned their attention to the glowing computer screen.

Buerk recovered the message from the 'sent' folder and read it through. 'Interesting column,' he said.

Cant rubbed a hand through his tousled hair in annoyance. 'Fifth column, more like,' he growled. 'D'ye see who it's addressed to?'

Buerk shrugged. 'We always knew Creepy came here as Hornblower's stooge.'

'Would have served him right if you'd left him at the bottom of that cliff,' Cant growled.

Buerk exited from the server and shut down the computer. 'He's certainly set the cat among the pigeons now.'

'Let's hope they come home to roost.'

Buerk eyed him sleepily. 'That's chickens, surely?'

'Whatever,' Cant said through a yawn. 'I've just about had enough of birds.'

As Cant waddled sleepily back to his bunk, Buerk was drawn towards the window that faced the small island known as the Holm of Papay. Off its southern tip the tiny yacht still rode at anchor, its sails trimly furled. Bathed in moonlight, the hull gleamed silvery white against the dark velvet of the sea. He sighed heavily. It was a night for making love, he thought, and a vision of Rowena Munro crept unbidden into his mind.

He smiled, in her absence conjuring up little memories of her. To him, she was as mystifying as the phases of the moon, at moments waxing towards him and at others seemingly waning beyond reach. Stifling a yawn, he turned on his heel and padded back to bed.

WEDNESDAY

Chapter Eighteen

Henry Thessinger Hornblower gripped the edge of his desk in a state of high excitement, his breathing all but suspended, as he read for the third time the e-mail message from Crawley. He had come into the office early looking expressly for this communication from his field operative and, wonder of wonders, the agonising wait was finally over. Unbelievably, that bumbling incompetent reported they had pulled it off!

Even then, after a lifetime spent rushing headlong to meet disappointments, both horticultural and educational, an element of caution forced him to carefully reread the message. Why wouldn't Crawley return home 'soonest'? Didn't he know the whole world, let alone his deputy principal, was waiting for the return of such evidence? He comforted himself with the knowledge that that was why people like Crawley would always be minions to more astute men like himself.

One sentence did make him feel a trifle uneasy. Who on earth was this unidentified woman who had been killed? A host of supplementary questions crowded into his fevered imagination. Was there something sinister going on up there? Was someone else on to their story? Again, who would stoop to such dastardly tactics as chasing Crawley over a cliff? Another educational institution? These days that was more than a distinct possibility.

Whatever the whys and wherefores, one thing was abundantly clear. They now had confirmation of Lucretia's claim. He would not have liked to rely on one dubious source alone. There was something unstable about that Golightly woman, and that sort of thing could easily run in families; the fact that Hilary was off getting drunk in celebration merely underlined the point. At least there should be no difficulty in getting the necessary video proof. They would have that by now since Crawley had reported they were already filming. Trust Buerk to knuckle down when there was something in it for him. If Crawley wasn't careful, that blighter could steal a march on him. Not just a lone auk survivor, either, but a positive abundance of birds by the sound of it; and breeding, too. It was almost too good to be true.

Hornblower took only a moment longer to think about his next move. If there were indeed others in hot pursuit of this hottest of stories, he reasoned, he could ill afford to sit on it a moment longer. Certainly not until the crew returned from the wilds of Orkney with all the potential delays that that might entail, otherwise what would have been the point of having a field operative in the actual locale? No, he decided, a man of action would strike now. With a trembling hand, he reached for the telephone. Now he would show that upstart Truelove, and the entire board of governors, who really had what it took to catapult the university into the headlines and shake the rest of the academic community to its very foundations. Maybe now they would finally recognise who really ought to have been made principal.

Buerk woke with sunlight streaming in the window of the annexe and stumbled out of bed to check if its early promise would hold. It looked like a perfect day. Out in the South Wick the aquamarine sea was a picture of tranquility. In the blue sky a few torn pieces of cloud hung motionless over the skerry, and over the trim little yacht.

As he rubbed the sleep from his eyes, thoughts began to crowd into his mind, demanding his attention. For one thing, how was he ever going to live down this auk fiasco? At a pinch he could live with the ribbing of academic colleagues since his arch-rival would be held equally guilty, perhaps even more so since he was Hornblower's toady. No, it was the thought of having to face Rowena Munro, whom he had stood up for a bird that had been extinct for getting on for two hundred years. Then there was the small matter of her commanding officer, Chief Superintendent Douglas, who thought he was implicated in a murder. Now there had been another one. Even to Buerk's untrained mind it looked like a similar method of dispatch. However that had come about, he was yet again in the thick of it. That thought made him groan aloud.

Immediately on sitting down to breakfast, he was confronted with yet another problem. He found himself the unwilling object of Lucretia's attention. Humming cheerfully off-key, she had arisen early to cook for the whole crew the sausage, bacon and eggs she had gone out to buy from the nearby cooperative shop. While exuding bonhomie to all, she was clearly reserving special treatment for him, dancing attendance on his every whim, not even allowing him to pour his own coffee.

Judging from the number of nudges passing between Cant and Dick, her eccentric behaviour was also becoming embarrassingly obvious to the others. Fortunately, Cant provided a welcome distraction by drawing attention to some curious red blotches on Dick's neck.

'What happened to you, Moby?' he asked. 'Scratch yourself with your medallion while you were asleep?'

Dick bestowed an indulgent smile on his colleague. 'Noticed them while I was shaving this morning,' he said dreamily. 'Must have been the midges.'

Cant was not so easily deterred. Putting down his coffee cup, he pulled back the collar of Dick's shirt to examine the love bites more closely and gave a snort of disbelief. 'Damn funny midges they have up here,' he said.

'How d'you mean?' Dick asked, only half-listening as he helped himself to another piece of toast.

Buerk noticed that Lucretia, in the act of refilling the coffee pot over the stove, had suddenly stopped, as if frozen to the spot, clearly quite intent on hearing Cant's reply.

'These ones have apparently got teeth.'

With a half-stifled yelp Lucretia let the coffee pot slip from her grasp and clatter noisily onto the stove, its contents spilling on the hot surface with an angry hiss.

'Clumsy,' Dick scolded her gently, his smile unabated.

Cant waved his cup optimistically in Lucretia's direction. 'I hope that doesn't mean I don't get a refill,' he said.

Lucretia rounded on the grinning miscreants. 'You bunch of idle layabouts,' she snarled. 'Why don't you try fending for yourself for a change?' It seemed as if all trace of her bonhomie had been sloughed from her persona. In a single instant, she had morphed into something more akin to a raging werewolf. Even her canine teeth, Buerk thought, as she now displayed them to the full, clearly resembled lupine fangs. 'As for you, Angus' – she rounded on him with a lycanthropic wail – 'you've proved to be a serious disappointment to me.'

With that she turned abruptly on her heel and stormed from the kitchen before anyone could say 'silver bullet'.

A hush descended over the kitchen, finally broken by Cant saying to no one in particular, 'Aren't some women temperamental? Things have clearly been getting on top of her.'

Buerk vaguely recalled a sound he had registered while he and Cant had been lifting Crawley from the floor the night before. Now that he thought about it, it could have come from Lucretia. 'There was a full moon last night?' he offered helpfully.

'That's just it,' Dick said, emerging from his dreamlike trance. 'It's sheer lunacy trying to suss women out. They never seem to know their own minds.' His eye suddenly alighted on Crawley's untouched plate – odd how ravenous he felt this morning. 'Not eating your breakfast, Fred?' he asked.

'Huh?' Crawley scarcely stirred from the catatonic stupor in which he had come to the table. He had been like that all night, lying awake troubled by the thought that the message he had sent Hornblower might not indeed have been the message he had intended to send.

206

'It's no use talking to him.' Cant winked in Buerk's direction. 'He's just not computing this morning.'

'Looks like he's not eating either,' Dick said. He wasted no further time in sliding the food from the plate of an unprotesting Crawley onto his own and making immediate inroads into the plundered spoils. His mind was already drifting back to the amazing dreams of the previous night. What made it even more puzzling for him was that the idealised vision he had long preserved of the imaginary Angel had been replaced at a stroke by an altogether more rapacious figure bearing a remarkable and rather disturbing resemblance to – dare one say it? – Lucretia.

He smiled at such a far-fetched fantasy. There was far too much aggression in that woman. Even when she smiled, as she had been doing at the boss quite a lot lately (until now), she still appeared threatening. It reminded him of a great white shark going in for the kill, the way she flashed her teeth. His thought processes stopped dead in their tracks as his fingers slid up to the marks on his neck.

Tooth marks!

Cant had been most insistent about them. Surely not Lucretia's? She hadn't so much as given him the time of day since they had set foot on Papa Westray. Nevertheless, there had been something strangely familiar about her perfume as she had leaned over him to pour his coffee this morning. His dreamy smile broadened into a grin. There it goes again, he thought. One day that vivid imagination of his was going to land him in serious trouble.

Confident of the range of defensive measures now in place, Piggy had insisted his number-one trailer be on its usual pitch by the bus terminus in time for the lunchtime peak. Not that it was much of a terminus – a bus-stop signpost with a Plexiglas shelter was as far as it went. Inevitably, some of the indigenous population had attempted to customise it using a sledgehammer or whatever tool could be improvised (someone's head, for example). One local artist had created a starburst effect while others had embellished it with splatter paint interwoven with some explicit graffiti, the most recent of which carried some racial overtones.

In Vincent Henderson's absence, Sadie had been left to manage the business side on her own. Not that she had any complaints; at least, not after Rob Roy McGregor showed up at the depot. One look at his handsome features and impressive physique and her legs had turned to jelly. What he had to offer, she thought, was a great deal more than protection.

Once on the road she soon recovered from her initial awe. 'Ah suppose,' she said, 'you've done this sort of thing before?' She turned in her seat to get a better look at him as he drove the van towards their destination.

Rob Roy grinned at her. 'You mean selling hamburgers?'

She nudged him on the biceps that bulged from the sleeve of his T-shirt. 'You know what ah mean.'

Rob Roy was busy with an appraisal of his own. He was certain she was wearing nothing under her tank-top. 'You mean offering protection to gorgeous bundles of mischief like yourself?'

Sadie clutched at her throat. This promised to be a change from the constant machine-gun slanging match in which she was normally involved with Vince. 'You worked with Piggy for a while?' she asked.

'A good few years now.' He gave a soft chuckle.

'What?'

'Piggy's movin' up the social ladder.'

'That so? What about you?'

He grinned at her. 'Ah aim tae be movin' up wi' him. Becomin' legit, like.'

'I'll bet.' She tilted her head to one side. 'Has anyone ever told you you've got a body like Arnold Schwarzenegger?'

He smirked. 'That whit you think?'

'Better looking, but.'

His eyes roamed over her body for a moment. 'You're a bit of all right yourself, Sadie. You're wasted behind the counter of a chip van.'

'That right?' She met his eyes challengingly. 'Where do you think ah should be?'

Rob Roy thought for a moment. 'Piggy's lookin' for someone tae manage his new disco. Wi' your head for figures, tae say nothin' of your own figure, you could be just whit he's lookin' for.'

'Oh, aye. Pigs might fly.' Despite her dismissive tone, she did not entirely shrug the idea from her mind.

As they arrived at their destination she pointed out where she wanted him to park. Later, as she set up the trailer for business, she returned to his suggestion.

'I didn't know Piggy was thinking of opening a disco,' she said.

He nodded as he opened up the counter at her direction. 'Had it in mind for some time,' he said. 'Somebody making a bid for Customs House brought things to a head.'

'What's he going to call it?'

'Fun Guys.'

She wrinkled her nose. 'Sounds a bit like toadstools.'

He had caught the scintilla of interest in her eyes. 'If you like, ah could put in a word wi' Piggy?'

'That'd be great, thanks.' She looked at him archly. 'What's in it for you, big man?'

He shook his head. 'Ah wasn't thinkin' of takin' any liberties, Sadie,' he said. 'No' wi' a class act like you.'

'Don't get me wrong,' she said quickly. 'Ah don't mind a fellow taking an interest. That's only natural.' She brushed past him in the confined space and started feeding pre-chipped potatoes into the two fat fryers. As she did so she felt his hand make lingering contact with her body. The touch was light but it sent a shiver of excitement through her.

She gave a nervous laugh. 'No room to swing a cat,' she said.

'Doesn't bother me.'

'Me neither.'

He shifted his position awkwardly. This time, to gain access to a cupboard, she dropped on one knee, then had to reach out a hand to steady herself. It found a well-muscled thigh.

'Won't be two ticks,' she said.

'Take as long as you like, darlin',' he said. 'Ah'm no' complaining.'

Out of sight, below the counter, she murmured something incomprehensible to him. Next moment his head snapped back and struck a switch behind him. Then his body arched and they were both making noises. As Rob Roy's eyes rolled in his head, a bus swung round the corner and drew to a halt at the terminus. Had they been paying any attention they might have noticed a motorbike pull up a little further away, but by then they were each totally preoccupied with what was happening inside the van.

'Where's the fire?' Immediately after Watt had posed the question he realised it was not the most sensitive one he could have chosen to ask Vera.

'You'll see,' she said.

The moment he had climbed onto the narrow pillion seat, she had let out the clutch and they had roared out of the library car park, narrowly missing two pedestrians, one using a Zimmer frame.

It had not been a good day for Vera. First, her committee had turned down her request for more money to buy Customs House. That had put her in a foul mood. Then she had had trouble pushing through approval for the new Self-evaluation and Accountability Programme. She had hoped that it would go through on the nod since it was nothing more than an endorsement of an already-agreed process. However, they had nit-picked endlessly over a few extra targets and milestones in line with the draconian cuts the council were being forced to introduce.

The campaign the city council had endorsed was based on five principles which Vera considered acceptable and worthwhile:

Transparency to those for whom the service was provided;

Responsibility and accountability through the setting of personal and departmental targets;

Implicit ownership by enhancing democratic participation through citizens' juries;

Personal development of staff, and

Evaluation of outcomes leading to continuous improvement.

There were two major drawbacks to the scheme's implementation in Vera's eyes. The first was the acronym, TRIPE, which even the dimmest members had eventually twigged. The second was the idea of citizens' juries. This proposal had come from the very top, but that had not stopped some of those in the room from referring to Vera (only in whispers, of course) as Madame Defarge, and the whole scheme as *A Tale of Two Titties*.

Well, fuck the lot of them, she thought. They had had their fun. Now it was time for her to let off a little steam.

CHAPTER NINETEEN

After their eventful breakfast, Lucretia remained resolutely incommunicado, while the others appeared strangely subdued and preoccupied with the minutiae of life. Seeing how things were, Buerk thought now was the moment to slip out quietly and head across the island to the Knap of Howar. There had been something bothering him ever since they'd found the message at the hide the day before and he wanted to see the place for himself, without the distractions of others.

The prehistoric ruins comprised two adjoining rooms which had been partially excavated from a grassy mound near the shoreline facing the neighbouring island of Westray. The house had long since lost its roof and upper works but, protected by the earthen embankments, the thick walls of the buildings were still in a remarkable state of preservation.

He ducked under the stone lintel capping the doorway of one room and immediately picked up the faint scent of perfume, or was it an aftershave? He began to examine the interior, unsure of what exactly he was looking for. The entry in the log at the bird hide had mentioned the place quite specifically and in the context of the great auk being in danger. It didn't really make much sense, he thought, and although it might be nothing more than a hunch he could not quite rid himself of the notion that the mystery woman reportedly seen with Hilary (if Crawley's twitcher acquaintance was to be believed) held the key to the deepening puzzle. He fervently hoped she was not the one Crawley had found dead in the middle of the sanctuary. Then he remembered the blond hairs on Hilary's hairbrush. The dead woman had been dark-haired. So where did the blonde fit in?

The two rooms in the house were divided by a partition of huge upright slabs quarried from the local stratified rock; 'knapped' was how Lucretia had explained it to him, hence the name 'Knap of Howar'. Elsewhere the slabs had been used to form cupboards, hearths and even bench seating.

As he scrambled between the rooms he stubbed his toe on something solid and metallic. Cursing, he bent down to discover a foot pump of the type used to inflate the inner tube of a tyre. On examination, he discovered it still functioned smoothly and showed no trace of rust. It seemed hardly likely that it would have been discarded by any local inhabitant in such surroundings. He wondered how else it could have got there.

He had almost finished his search of the second room when he found two empty beer bottles at the back of a stone recess. Recalling his meeting with Lachie Patterson and his friends, the discovery of alcohol could hardly be construed as a surprise, but the Dogbolter label certainly was. Another coincidence? To Buerk it spelled outsiders. Any beer would be imported to the island at some expense; foreign beer even more so. He was willing to bet it was not the brand consumed by any locals. On the other hand, it had found its way to Hilary's cottage and he was, according to Lucretia, teetotal.

Around him, an area of grass had been flattened and he caught another faint whiff of the scent he had detected earlier. It seemed oddly familiar to him, although he could not place it. He frowned. It might be no more significant than a lovers' tryst or a sheltered spot for a few youths to share a drink, but, thinking of the dead woman, it could also mean something much more sinister; the term 'killing ground' leapt into his mind.

He sat down on a stone bench, his back against the wall, to ponder the significance of his finds. Allowing the morning sunshine to bathe his face, he gradually became conscious of the view framed by the outer doorway of the ancient dwelling. It afforded him a perspective across the sound to the neighbouring island of Westray exactly where the harbour was located. Without moving from his seat he could watch the movement of boats entering or leaving the harbour. The distance almost looked short enough to swim across; he suspected the currents might be treacherous, but it certainly could not be a difficult journey in reasonably calm weather in a small boat... or an inflatable.

On impulse he again glanced around the walls, seeking further clues. He was on the point of giving up when he caught the rainbow sparkle of refracted sunlight low down on the opposite wall. Again the grass here had been partially flattened, but this time in a narrow strip as though perhaps a single person had trodden on it. Here, too, that scent was a little stronger. Reaching into a small crevice in the rock, he found a roll of film protected by a plastic container with a watertight lid. He smiled as he realised that a dewdrop suspended from the container and reflecting the sun's early rays was what had caught his eye. Then it came to him. It was the scent he had noticed on the clothing of the dead woman Crawley had discovered. Could this film belong to her?

His mind immediately went back to the camera complete with telephoto lens Cant had spotted in the hide. It had been missing a film. If they were all linked, what particular set of circumstances could have led to the separate components being abandoned such distances apart?

He glanced at his watch. Time he was getting back. Pocketing the roll of film, he left the empty beer bottles untouched on the ledge and began to cut across country towards Hilary's cottage on the South Wick.

As he reached the dunes that lay behind the cottage he spotted a man sitting far out on the flat rocks of the narrow promontory that separated the north and south bays. His immediate thought was that the man might be spying on the cottage, except that he sat at the water's edge clearly facing out to sea. So what the hell was he doing there: fishing?

Buerk caught a flash of sunlight and then another and eventually realised the man had a mirror and appeared to be signalling to something out on the water, except there was no sign of any boat. Alternatively he might be signalling to someone on the skerry where the small yacht was moored, but there was no sign of any movement on the tiny island either.

Deciding he should investigate, he made his way down to the beach and started to edge out onto the rocks. Now that he was close enough to make out the stranger's dark hair and squat crouching figure, the hairs began to stand up on the back of Buerk's neck. He bore a remarkable resemblance to the man he had seen crouching over the tiller of the inflatable racing from the *Loch Tredwell*. Buerk hesitated, beginning to feel a bit exposed, yet the man seemed completely oblivious of his presence.

The rocks here were festooned with slippery clumps of sea wrack that made the surface treacherous. Some of the weed had air bladders and he had to be careful about where he placed his feet in case he 'popped' them. He still couldn't make out what the man was doing. He decided he would risk another step.

It almost landed him straight into an inflatable dinghy tucked under an overhang in a large slab of rock, the bow attached to it by its painter. It was so well hidden he had not seen it until the last second. A powerful-looking four-stroke outboard motor fixed to its fibreglass transom was tilted back to protect the propeller from damage against the rocks. Detachable aluminium floorboards gave the hull a more stable look. Two plastic paddles were neatly tucked against the sides. He estimated it was about twelve feet in length, with bench seating capable of carrying up to four adults. It looked seaworthy and had to be the tender of something bigger than a small yacht.

As he hesitated over his next move, he heard a heavy footfall and the squish of bursting air bladders behind him. Two things happened simultaneously. As he turned towards the sound his foot slipped on the seaweed and he lost his balance, arms thrown out in a vain attempt to regain equilibrium. In the same instant something very hard caught him a glancing blow on the side of his head. But for the slip at the vital moment, the blow would have caught him full-force behind the ear and he would have been a goner. Nevertheless, he still hit the water with a resounding splash and was immediately dragged under by the fierce current.

The cold sea water revived him but he still had the current to contend with. Being an experienced swimmer, he made no attempt to fight it but rather swam with it. Eventually he surfaced and found he had already been swept well away from his point of entry and some distance around the promontory. It took him a few moments to locate his attacker further out to sea, only there were now two of them standing on the rocks. The second man, the one who had whacked him, completely dwarfed his companion. Buerk recognised the buzz-cut hair and the flash of the gold earring. The two men were still searching the area where he had gone into the water and had clearly made no allowance for the current.

He cursed his own stupidity. He had been so engrossed in looking for clues to the existence of intruders, it had never occurred to him that he and his crew might themselves be objects of interest. The two men must have spotted him at some point on his traversal of the island and he had fallen all too easily into the trap they had set for him. The man crouching at the edge of the sea had been the decoy, watching his every move with the mirror while the other one, probably hiding among the dunes, had followed him out onto the rocks. Curiosity had been his undoing – that and crass stupidity. Taking a deep breath, he ducked his head under again and allowed the current to carry him into the bay.

He stayed underwater until, with his lungs protesting and a roaring noise in his ears, he again surfaced. He found himself being nudged by the slackening current into a sandy beach close to Hilary's cottage. Attempting to stand up, he began to feel dizzy from the aftereffects of the blow and sank gratefully down onto the sand.

CHAPTER TWENTY

On a whim, DS Lennox decided to pick up the bus heading out to the council estate, knowing that a car parked there for very long would draw unwelcome attention. Dressed in jeans and T-shirt, she sat downstairs to keep an eye on anyone entering the bus. As they approached the housing estate one man indeed attracted her attention. He was smartly but casually dressed in a black leather jacket and jeans and wore a distinctive ponytail. More disturbingly, he seemed to have taken an interest in her. Several times during the journey she caught him glancing in her direction. Her concern was that he might be a known criminal – perhaps a drug pusher. While not a flash dresser, he was certainly more prosperous-looking than most of his fellow passengers.

When the bus pulled into the terminus, he made straight for the Fat Friar, and a new scenario flashed into her mind. Could he be one of the phantom attackers? Then reason prevailed; he did not fit the description of either assailant. Besides, it would be hard to hide that ponytail under a crash helmet (nor indeed was he carrying a crash helmet). With only a vague idea of what her next move should be, she joined the queue behind Ponytail.

She was soon aware of stirrings of disquiet in the line ahead of her over its slow progress. Someone ahead uttered an expletive and stomped off without his supper. Ponytail turned towards her. 'A bit much, isn't it?' he said. 'Guy must be dreaming up there.'

'Maybe waiting for a new batch of chips,' she said. Disappointed that she could not come up with anything more original, she noted that Ponytail was not bad-looking. Startling blue eyes fixed on hers. No question of drug-taking there.

'Care for a mint?' As he proffered a packet of extra-strong mints, she noticed his hands. They looked extra-strong too: tool worker's hands. Not a drug pusher, then.

'Thanks.' As she accepted the mint she knew for certain they had never met. Why, then, was he vaguely familiar?

'You're not worried the baseball thugs might come back?' he said.

'I heard about that,' she said. 'Don't they say lightning never strikes twice?'

'We could do with a bolt of lightning to wake up that dozy git.' He motioned towards the serving hatch, where the tall man serving appeared to have at last got his act together.

As she stood on tiptoe to make out what was happening, she could see that a dark-haired girl was now assisting him. The girl held a tissue to her face. Maybe she had a cold? At least the queue was moving now, not that its slowness had really bothered her. There was sufficient distraction closer at hand. She was conscious Ponytail was talking again.

'I was there, you know.'

'Sorry?'

'The last attack,' he said. 'I was one of the victims.'

'No kidding?' Then the thought hit her. 'Did I see you on telly?' She recalled vaguely there had been a brief interview with a public victim before the director had opted to concentrate on Vince and Sadie. She had been on the phone at the time but had caught a subliminal glimpse of the ponytail.

He winced as if in pain. 'Only if you were quick. Big-time embarrassment.' He eyed her curiously. 'Got an eye for that sort of thing, have you?' The challenge was softened by a smile playing at the corners of his mouth.

'Maybe.'

'You're not from around here, though.' It was a statement, not a question.

She glanced at him warily. 'Just visiting.'

'Fancy that.' The smile broadened. 'I'm just here to visit my mum. She likes a fish sup—'

He stopped abruptly in mid-sentence, pupils dilating, and made a sudden lunge for her.

She realised afterwards it was over in a matter of seconds, but at the time it seemed to play out in slow motion. As he moved towards her, she instinctively adopted a defensive posture, spreading her legs to maintain balance as she had been trained to do. Out of the corner of her eye, she caught the blue blur of someone rushing past her towards the van. Next second she felt a sickening crack on the back of her head. She remembered crying out at the force of the blow and thinking that Ponytail could not possibly have delivered it from that angle; he had been trying to protect her. Then everything went dark.

Vera had decided this time to lead a frontal attack on the Fat Friar trailer, leaving Watt to attack the tail of the queue, which had now dwindled to two people. As she rushed

222

headlong for the serving hatch she could see only one person inside. It was a different person from yesterday. Although he looked formidable in size, he seemed quite overawed by the speed and suddenness of her attack and stood mouth agape, as though transfixed.

As she closed on the counter, however, the picture altered with alarming rapidity. In the act of Vera's bringing the baseball bat down on the seemingly paralysed vendor's head, the dark-haired girl (instantly recognisable from her previous attack) rose from under the counter. The surprise put Vera off her aim and the giant let out a roar as the bat struck him a glancing blow on the chest. Before Vera could make a second attempt, the big man recovered dramatically from his earlier catatonic state. Leaning over the counter, he snatched the bat from Vera's grasp in a giant fist. The force pulled her hard against the counter, winding her. Before she knew what was happening, the girl stretched over to whack her with a bottle of dandelion and burdock she had pulled from a stacked crate behind her. The force of the blow smashed the visor of Vera's helmet and sent her reeling back from the serving hatch. That probably saved her. She wheeled away from the van and lurched off towards her motorbike.

Feeling a curious bloodlust course through her veins Sadie bellowed, 'Stop the bastard! He's getting away!'

Watt's fate was already sealed. Having felled Lennox he found himself subjected to a ferocious counterattack from her ponytailed companion. Even as he doubled over, the name 'McManus' flashed through his head. Why did he always appear to plague his existence?

Enraged by the unprovoked attack on the attractive woman he had been chatting up, to say nothing of his previous humiliation, McManus was in no mood to give quarter. A kick to the testicles, followed by a knee to the exposed chin, sent Watt to the ground. There McManus fell on him, using Watt's stomach as a cushion.

'Ya wee midden.' McManus spat the words at Watt. 'Like to hit defenceless lassies and folk wi' their backs turned. Well, if you so much as move a muscle' – he grabbed Watt by his already aching, vulnerable organs – 'I'll turn you off lassies for good, know what ah mean?'

Winded and dazed, Watt nodded his head.

'Ah didn't hear you,' McManus said.

'Yeah,' Watt croaked. 'I get the idea.'

'Oh, it's more than an idea, pal. It's a promise.'

Belatedly, Rob Roy leapt over the counter like a man possessed, but Vera was already well on the way towards her motorcycle. He opted instead for the target McManus had already collared. 'Thanks, pal,' he said. 'I'll take care of this pile of shite until the cops come. They were supposed to be here already.'

McManus readily agreed to release his captive into the big man's tender care. He knelt beside Lennox's prone form and lifted her from the ground. Cradling her in his arms, he melted through the gathering crowd, heading for his mother's house.

Sadie joined Rob Roy and leaned over to tear the crash helmet from Watt. 'Let's have a look at him,' she said.

'He's nothin' much,' Rob Roy said.

She put a hand on Roy's shoulder. 'No' compared to you, big man.'

Badly shaken by her narrow escape, Vera leapt astride her bike. Throwing a last despairing glance at Watt over her shoulder, she started the engine. It was clear that her exciting and cathartic little enterprise had run its course. She had lost her partner in crime. Reluctantly she let in the clutch and abandoned him to his fate, confident that he would not betray her. The ghost of a smile played on her face as the thought occurred to her that even if he did, they might not believe him.

Lennox came round to find herself staring into the anxious face of the man with the pony tail. She tried to sit up and felt the room spin. He held her gently by the shoulders. 'Take it easy,' he said. 'You'll be fine in a jiffy. The name's John McManus by the way.'

She slowly digested the fact that she was lying on a couch, still fully dressed, in someone's chintzy living room. Then she noticed a number of carved wooden figurines seemingly occupying every available surface.

An older woman bent down to peer at her over McManus's shoulder, her face full of concern. 'That wee bastard certainly gave you a nasty bang,' she said. 'If it hadn't been for oor John, he might have kilt you.'

Offering a sympathetic smile, McManus helped Lennox sit up. 'I might have saved you from the blow if you hadn't been so damn suspicious of my motives.'

She tried to shake her head in apology and felt another wave of nausea, less severe this time. 'Sorry' she said. 'I stupidly thought that you were going for me.'

He plumped a cushion at her back; it surprised her that hands like his could be so gentle. 'Now, what put that daft notion in your head?'

She moved her head more carefully this time. 'I was expecting an attack from somewhere, and you weren't to know I'm a police officer.'

Mother and son turned to each other and laughed.

'Don't be daft, lass,' he said. 'I knew you were a cop the minute I got on the bus. Speaking of which, I called for reinforcements. Your assailant is already in custody. I'm afraid his accomplice got away.'

By the time Lennox had eased her feet onto the floor, his mother had returned with a cup of tea, a knowing smile on her face. 'People around here don't miss much,' she said. 'And oor John is more observant than most.'

CHAPTER TWENTY-ONE

Someone seemed to be bellowing in Buerk's ear, except they seemed to be doing it from very far away, or under water. He turned his head towards the sound and sea water ran out of his other ear with a gurgle.

'There you are, boss.' Cant's dulcet tones registered in his waterlogged brain. 'Wondered where the hell you had disappeared to. Water too cold to take your clothes off or what?'

Dick's reproach was equally flippant. 'You might have said you were going for a swim,' he said. 'We'd have been only too glad to escape from the poisonous atmosphere inside the cottage. The way Lucretia is acting, you'd think one of us had done something to upset her.'

Buerk struggled into a sitting position and nodded blankly. Not trusting himself to speak, he let them ramble on. The part of his brain still functioning gathered that a surprisingly subdued Lucretia had finally emerged from behind her closed door. Pleading poor seamanship, she had intimated she intended to remain in the cottage to hold the fort and await Hilary's return. None of the others had thought for a moment to question her decision.

'Crawley?' he asked. His voice still sounded as if it came from inside a conch shell.

Cant shrugged. 'Still hors de combat. Keeps staring at his computer as if maybe it's been hexed.'

'What time is it?' Buerk asked. Their expectant looks made him wonder if he'd forgotten something.

Cant grinned at his perplexed look. 'You've got about twenty minutes before the prearranged rendezvous with your man and his boat,' he said.

Of course! The assignation at the old pier with Lachie Patterson.

Buerk pulled the roll of film, still in its protective tube, from his sodden pocket and slowly struggled to his feet. 'Found this little baby at the Knap of Howar,' he croaked. 'I'll give you odds this came from the camera Genghis found at the bird hide.'

'What's the score here, boss?' Cant asked. 'I know you didn't really opt to go swimming with your clothes on.'

Buerk rubbed the side of his head ruefully. 'On the way back I came across two bruisers who seemed keen to end my interest in whatever the hell is going on here.'

Dick peered curiously at his head. 'So that's where that lump came from,' he said.

'Hence the early morning dip,' Cant said grimly.

'It's what saved my life,' Buerk said. 'The current swept me away before they could finish me off.' He brandished the roll of film. 'In any event, I think I've finally found something I can trust Crawley to deal with.'

By the time they arrived at the old pier the sun was shining brightly on a sea whose surface was ruffled by a slight breeze. A few cumulus wisps were shepherded towards the far horizon. Buerk had changed his clothes and delegated to a still-dazed Crawley the task of developing the roll of film he'd found at the Knap of Howar, using the facilities in

Hilary's darkroom. Still photography was the one practical area within the department's range of activities that Buerk was confident his rival could manage without the risk of ruining it.

They found Lachie hosing down the afterdeck of the *Mallimack*. At his invitation they started ferrying equipment aboard. After Cant and Dick rigged the camera on a gimbal device fastened to the port-side gunwale by the wheelhouse, Lachie got the *Mallimack* under way.

A small clinker-built dinghy, attached to a stern cleat, danced in the *Mallimack*'s wake. Buerk stared at it thoughtfully for a few moments. It occurred to him that, over the past few days, he had seen quite a few dinghies of one kind or another. He pushed such thoughts to the back of his mind and moved inside to join Lachie in the wheelhouse. The islander gave him a friendly grin and motioned towards a worn seat over which a scuba diver's wetsuit lay draped.

'Sorry, Angus,' he said. 'Just throw that stuff into the locker in the corner.'

Buerk picked up the wetsuit and folded it neatly into the locker. As he did so, he noticed more scuba gear stowed inside. Two air tanks were strapped to a rack beside the locker, their gauges indicating they were almost full. Curious, he asked, 'You do much diving?'

'Sometimes go down after scallops or to look over the odd wreck for the hell of it.' He shrugged. 'Don't have so much time for it since my old man retired. You interested?'

Buerk settled on the bench seat. 'I'm a member of the university sub-aqua club,' he said. 'I try to keep my hand in.

The way things are going back there, it's a case of sink or swim for all of us.'

As Lachie negotiated the channel between the pier and the outlying skerry known as the Holm, Buerk caught himself feeling uneasy. For a moment he could not figure out what was bothering him; something was missing. Then it hit him. The yacht that had triggered all kinds of sentimental thoughts the previous night was no longer resting at anchor. It had gone.

He rubbed his eyes and scanned the horizon. There was no sign of the small craft. He frowned at the apparent suddenness of her departure. Hadn't she still been there just before his attack? At first, he'd thought the man with the mirror was signalling to her.

'I noticed a trim little yacht nestling in the inlet at the southern tip when we arrived,' he said. 'She was still there an hour or so ago.'

Lachie shot him a curious look. 'Odd you should say that,' he said, peering intently through the windscreen as he brought the boat round onto a new course. 'I saw her sometime on Monday passing by Fowl Craig in a freshening breeze. She made a run for it past the North Wick, heading for the shelter the Holm affords the South Wick where you boys are staying. I reckon from the erratic course she was taking that her steering gear had been damaged. The next time I saw her she had moved to anchor off the Holm. Sounds as if they managed to make the repairs she was needing.'

Buerk pursed his lips. 'Know anything about her? Where she came from, who was sailing her?'

Lachie shook his head. 'She's not a local boat, but the two men aboard didn't look any great shakes at sailing her. It took them all their time to round the promontory without running aground on the rocks, and I thought that was odd at the time.'

'How so?'

'Well, I reckon that yacht was rigged for single-handed sailing.'

Buerk pursed his lips again. 'Don't suppose there was any sign of a woman on board?'

Again the emphatic head shake. 'I only saw the two men,' he said. 'They were towing an ugly inflatable astern that didn't seem to belong with that yacht.'

Buerk was suddenly alert. 'How do you mean?'

Lachie shrugged. 'It just clashed with her clean lines and the rest of the neat fittings on board. I'd have expected a much smaller dinghy for that yacht.'

Buerk digested the information in silence as they closed in on Fowl Craig. The cliffs looked even more impressive looking up at them from sea level. Under Lachie's expert seamanship the *Mallimack* inched closer. The sheer, brooding bulk of Fowl Craig loomed over the small fishing boat until the sky began to darken. Buerk and his crew gazed in awe at the spectacle before them as their senses were assailed by the massed inhabitants of the cliffs.

The sea air was pungent with the ammoniacal stench of guano. The ceaseless pounding of the surf against the base of the cliff and the combined cries of the seabirds echoing from the rock wall made conversation difficult. They had to shout or make do with hand gestures. All around them, on the cliff face, in the sea and in the sky, they were faced with a bewildering number and variety of species aggressively squabbling over territory and endlessly foraging for food.

Using what shelter from the wind the wheelhouse offered, Cant began recording, concentrating mainly on the tightly packed cliff ledges. He combed them systematically, using the powerful zoom facility to get big close-ups of any bird remotely resembling their elusive quarry. Most of them were nearer the base of the crag. Braced against the wheelhouse, a coolly sceptical Buerk scanned the cliffs with binoculars he had borrowed from Lachie. Having lashed the effects mike to the gunwale, Dick was crouched beside Cant, poring over an illustrated spotter's guidebook he had picked up from the cottage. He struggled to keep pace with the birds his colleagues described as they appeared in their respective viewfinders.

At first the game of trying to spot a great auk proved amusing for Cant and Dick, but as the number of false alarms and disappointments steadily grew, the repetitive nature of the work soon began to pall. The final disappointment came after a particularly convincing shout from Cant.

'There's a great auk for sure, boss,' he called, focusing on a large black bird with a white patch on its breast and a thick, black, blunt-ended beak.

This time Lachie broke the tension with a quiet chuckle. He had leaned out of the wheelhouse window to peer at the close-up on the viewfinder. 'Och, that's jist a cooterneb,' he said disparagingly.

'Come again?' Cant said in disbelief.

Dick checked the reference book and gave a knowing smirk. 'I think he's using the local term for a razorbill.'

'Aye, that's the chiel,' Lachie said. 'There'd be a big white patch between the beak and eyes if it was to be an auk.' He chuckled softly and turned back to the helm, throwing over his shoulder, 'But you'll no' be seeing any of these beasties outside a museum.'

Deciding he had as much footage as he needed for his alternative scenario, Buerk gave his two men instructions to pack up. Neither appeared unhappy about the prospect of returning to base. Buerk stuck his head into the wheelhouse to let Lachie know they were ready to return to the old pier. Lachie gave a brief nod, brought the *Mallimack* onto her new heading and began to whistle. It appeared that it was a relief to all of them to be able to draw back from the oppressive atmosphere under the menacing shadow of the cliff.

As they forged steadily through the gentle swell in brilliant sunshine, Buerk studied the changing shoreline through Lachie's binoculars. Some seals lay basking on the partially submerged rocks of the promontory where he had earlier spotted the troll-like figure and almost met his end. A solitary cormorant now stood sentinel on the spot at its seaward end. Soon, they had rounded the promontory, heading for the gap separating it from the Holm, and then into the South Wick where the white shell sand on the beach acted as a foil to the aquamarine sparkle of the waters in the bay. He smiled as he focused on a well-drilled formation of sanderlings darting in comic unison in and out of the tidal surge in haphazard forays for food.

The smile faded as he recalled that it had been somewhere among their footprints that the last recorded sighting of Hilary had allegedly been made before he had vanished completely from the island. According to Crawley's twitcher informant, Hilary had not been alone when he had staggered off. With his own recent encounter with the troll and his companion fresh in his mind, the question uppermost in Buerk's thoughts was whether Hilary had gone voluntarily. The melancholy cry of a curlew pierced the air as it quartered its solitary beat high above the dunes as if to underscore the grim alternative.

A change in the rhythm of the diesel engine heralded their approach towards the old pier. Buerk became aware of a deeper roar coming from overhead. Squinting up into the sun, he could just make out the police markings on the fuselage of a helicopter.

A mischievous grin on his face, Lachie leaned his upper body out the window of the wheelhouse. Gesturing with his thumb, he yelled above the roar, 'Must be the top brass from the mainland. More than likely they've come to arrest you for trying to film the great auk without a permit.'

Buerk returned his grin.

The helicopter hovered overhead for a few minutes before settling on some level ground behind the old pier. As the noise subsided and the giant rotor blades slowly came to a halt, three figures ducked from the passenger section and headed towards the pier in time to greet the *Mallimack*. While Lachie berthed his vessel, Buerk noticed that one of the helicopter passengers was a woman. She was accompanied by a uniformed police officer and a man in civilian clothes. The woman detached herself from the others and moved forward to the edge of the pier. As she did so, Buerk felt a sudden surge of excitement run through his body.

By the time Lennox had made it back to the CID room, only Danny Traynor showed any concern for her well-being. 'I've set up the video replay,' he said. 'You sure you're okay to sit through it?'

'I'm fine, Danny, nothing a couple of paracetamols couldn't fix. Let's look at the tape.'

She followed him slowly towards the viewing room.

'You know,' he said, 'that should have been me instead of you on the receiving end.'

'Don't talk soft,' she said. 'The attack could just as easily have been against the other van.'

'But it wasn't, was it?'

As she sat down to watch, she glanced thoughtfully at Traynor. It had probably just been an instinctive reaction of envy on his part rather than from any genuine concern for her welfare – she had been in the wars and he had not. The more she thought about his words, however, the more she realised there had been something skewed about the attacks. DC Traynor never had been under any real threat. There had been two attacks against the same Fat Friar outlet and really nothing but a verbal skirmish at the Chapatti Tatti trailer. Could the race card simply be a red herring?

While McManus had been taking her to the casualty department of the local hospital for a quick check-up, Chief Superintendent Douglas had apparently made it clear to Traynor that he regarded Watt as the ringleader in the chip van war. In his opinion it was only a question of time before Watt gave up the name of his accomplice. However, despite being threatened with two charges of aggravated assault and one of incitement to start a race war, Watt steadfastly remained mute on the subject of his accomplice.

To begin with it looked as if the video experiment was going to be useless. It juddered and flickered as if the camera had been given a series of jolts. Eventually, the picture settled and Lennox and Traynor could only watch in an awkward silence as they had an unequivocal view of what Sadie was doing on her knees. The camera had obviously been inadvertently moved by one of the van's occupants.

'Bloody hell,' Traynor said.

'Quite,' Lennox agreed.

Mercifully the camera received yet another jolt and the view switched back to an over-the-counter shot, revealing a file of disgruntled customers waiting impatiently for an understandably clumsy server to get on with it.

The first customer's voice was loud enough for the remote microphone to pick up. 'Whit happened tae Vince and Sadie?' he asked. 'This guy disnae know whether he's comin' or goin'.'

'Needs a bomb under him,' his companion said. Then, out of nowhere, Sadie appeared on the scene and the queue began to dwindle speedily.

'Look.' Traynor pointed. 'There you are with some bloke who's trying to chat you up.'

Did more than just try, Lennox thought, but instead she said, 'It just looks that way.' She felt herself colour, but fortunately Traynor was distracted by events on the screen.

'Here come the tearaways,' he said.

What happened to Lennox was mercifully unclear as the screen filled with the sturdy frame of Watt's alleged accomplice. The menacing figure, face hidden by the helmet's visor, brought the baseball bat swinging down towards Rob Roy. Traynor gave a whoop of triumph as they watched first Roy grab the bat and tug the assailant against the counter and then Sadie smash the visor on the attacker's helmet with a bottle. 'We've got the bastard,' he said.

'Not yet we haven't,' Lennox cautioned him. 'All we've got is a brief glimpse of smouldering eyes and a snub nose before the assailant turns away.'

Traynor slumped in his seat. 'Accounts for a fair percentage of the population.'

'Wait a minute,' Lennox said. 'Run that last bit again in slo-mo.'

Traynor replayed attack and counterattack.

'That's a woman's face,' she said calmly.

'What?' This time he ran it forward frame by frame as the visor came off.

'There,' Lennox said.

Traynor froze the screen the moment before the figure turned away. He frowned. 'How can you tell?'

'How many guys do you know who wear eye shadow and lipstick?'

Traynor grinned. 'Well, none, apart from Adrian in accounts. I take your point.'

'Right,' she said. 'Give this to the media. Get them to enlarge it and pose the question "do you recognise this woman?" That ought to get some response. Hopefully, the right sort.'

Traynor's grin broadened. 'You're a genius, serge. That bump on the head must have done you some good.'

'Gee, thanks,' she said. 'I'll take that as a compliment.'

CHAPTER TWENTY-TWO

Buerk could scarcely believe his luck. Before Lachie had made the lines fast, he had already leapt ashore to greet DI Rowena Munro. The baseball cap worn at a jaunty angle failed to contain the ponytail of flaming red hair. Judging from the amount of braid on his uniform she was accompanied by a senior police officer, although Buerk's attention did not linger on him or on their companion, a smiling, bespectacled civilian.

'What a wonderful surprise,' Buerk said. 'What on earth brings you all the way here?'

The green eyes flashed challengingly. 'Some unfinished business,' she said curtly. 'Nor have I forgotten that you stood me up, even if you try to pretend it never happened.'

He gave her a look which he hoped conveyed abject apology. 'How could I ever forget?' he said. 'Surely Sergeant Lennox explained the circumstances?'

'Not wholly to my satisfaction,' she said, 'and on top of that I gather you've found another body.' She made it sound like an accusation. 'You know, Angus, you'll really have to do something about the company you're keeping.'

He shot her a rueful smile. 'What can I say? Trouble seems to follow me wherever I go.'

She gave him a long, hard stare. 'I have to ask myself, are you the innocent party you claim to be or are you somehow the catalyst for the mayhem that constantly surrounds you?'

'Just because I'm paranoid doesn't mean someone's not out to get me,' he protested. 'Only this morning I was ambushed by two guys, whacked on the head and knocked into the sea.' He waved a hand in the general direction of the promontory that divided the North and South Wicks. 'The only reason I survived was because they thought I'd drowned.'

He bent his head, inviting her to examine the wound behind his ear. For the first time she seemed to show an element of concern for his welfare.

'You need to get that attended to.' She beckoned to her colleagues and added in a whisper, 'Lucky you're so thick-skinned or you might not have been around to stand up anyone else.'

'All right,' he said. 'No need to rub it in.'

As the two men came forward she made the introductions.

'Chief Inspector Howie from Kirkwall and Dr Mackie, our chief medical examiner who flew up with me this morning.' She turned to her companions. 'This is the man I was telling you about: Angus Buerk of New Metropolitan University.'

Buerk shook hands with the two men, wondering exactly what she had told them. Howie was a stern-looking man with blond hair under his braided cap, a military bearing and a handshake that made Buerk's eyes water. His penetrating gaze seemed to bore into Buerk as if he might discern some sign of guilt there. It looked odds on that he'd been having a word with the man Munro called the Black Douglas.

Mackie was a short, rather podgy man who wore an amused expression on his face. Buerk vaguely remembered seeing him on the deck of the *Loch Tredwell* at the Vinnie McGrath crime scene. He briefly examined Buerk's scalp wound and decided it needed no further treatment. 'Lucky you did fall into the sea,' he said with a twinkle in his eye. 'The salt water has cleaned the wound. It's healing nicely.'

'It's done nothing for my hairstyle,' Buerk said.

'Did you know either of your attackers?' Munro asked.

Buerk shrugged. 'I'm fairly certain they were the same ones from the inflatable that shot off from the *Loch Tredwell*, but what would they be doing here? Lachie, the skipper of the *Mallimack*, tells me he'd never set eyes on either of them until a couple of days ago.'

Munro looked at him curiously, as though she might question him further, but then decided not to pursue it for the moment. 'We'd like you to show us where the body you reported is located,' she said. 'The chief inspector would also like to have a word with the rest of your party.'

'Fine by me,' Buerk said. 'I just hope you're not squeamish around birds.'

She looked at him with a puzzled frown. 'Birds?'

He nodded. 'Crawley stumbled upon the body when he rather unwisely took a short-cut through an Arctic tern sanctuary. I'm afraid there's hordes of them.'

'We'll manage,' she said a trifle brusquely. Buerk was amused to see that she tucked her hair more firmly under her cap. 'Crawley is Buerk's colleague at the university,'

241

she explained to Howie. 'What's he doing here?' she asked Buerk. 'I thought you and he...'

Buerk made a vague gesture implying a situation well beyond his control. 'It certainly wasn't my idea. To be fair it wasn't Crawley's either.'

'Care to elaborate on that?'

'Frankly, he's here to keep an eye on the rest of us for the deputy principal. Hornblower doesn't altogether trust us on our own.'

Her eyebrows shot up. 'I can't say I blame him. The rate at which you turn up bodies hardly makes you a person who inspires confidence. Not that Crawley appears any better.'

'Where is this Crawley individual now?' Howie asked impatiently.

'Resting back at Hilary's cottage.' Buerk grimaced. 'I'm afraid he had a bit of an accident.'

Howie frowned and waited for him to elaborate.

'He fell over a cliff.'

The frown darkened.

'Who's Hilary?' Munro asked.

Buerk swallowed hard. 'Lucretia's brother and the warden of the bird sanctuary,' he said. 'She's a colleague. Between them they started this crazy excursion by reporting the sighting of a great auk. Hornblower then thought it would be a great wheeze – to say nothing of a boost to his ego – if we could capture it on film.'

'Did you say a great auk?' Howie looked as though he had just had an attack of indigestion.

'Afraid so.' Buerk looked pleadingly at Munro and added, 'I couldn't bring myself to explain that over the phone. I knew you'd think I was making it up.'

'You'd have been right,' she said, shaking her head in disbelief.

'A great wheeze, indeed,' Mackie said, his eyes twinkling in amusement. 'I'm bound to say universities have changed a bit since my day.'

'That's one way of putting it,' Howie said, clearly unimpressed. 'I presume this Hilary person is back at the cottage too?'

Buerk shifted uneasily. 'There's evidence he may have had recent visitors, only...'

'Only what, Buerk?' Hands on hips, Munro shot him a dark look.

'He's... um, nowhere to be found.'

Howie stared at him in disbelief. 'Good grief, Buerk,' he said. 'What the hell kind of operation are you running here?'

Buerk turned his eyes towards the heavens. 'I'm not altogether sure you want to know, sir,' he said.

'Oh, but we do,' Munro assured him grimly. 'We want to know absolutely everything...'

Cant and Dick were dispatched back to the cottage with the equipment and to alert Lucretia and Crawley to expect the new arrivals. Meanwhile, Buerk led the police delegation across the maritime heath to the boggy site marked by Cant's improvised flagpole. Lachie was 'invited' by Howie to accompany them since, as Howie put it, he wanted someone uncontaminated by this 'auk madness' to help him sort out the shambles.

Dr Mackie shrugged into his Tyvek coveralls, perched a pair of half-moon spectacles on the end of his nose and slipped on a pair of gloves before setting to work, unhurriedly examining the knife and its wound around the hilt of the blade. Buerk quietly retrieved the tripod and handkerchief.

As time passed, Howie grew restive. He had been standing a few paces back from the body as if he found it distasteful to get too close. 'How does it look, Mackie?' he asked.

Kneeling by the side of the body, the medical examiner was peering into the victim's mouth. Turning, with just a hint of irritation in his voice, he said, 'Of course I won't know for certain until I do a proper post-mortem. The knife is wedged between the first and second vertebrae in an apparent match of the McGrath case. The haft is interesting though: possibly hand-carved from an unusual hardwood – maybe ironwood. There's a small inset of silver in the shape of some kind of hawk.'

'Wouldn't be an eaglehawk, by any chance?' Munro asked.

Mackie eyed her sharply. 'Can't imagine that was a total shot in the dark,' he said. 'Won't know the answer for sure until I can get it under a microscope. There also had to be a reason why the killer didn't remove the knife this time. Maybe he was disturbed. It's certainly valuable but, more to the point, he would have been attached to it, pardon the pun.

Maybe he was in too big a hurry. I certainly don't intend to take it out here.'

Turning his attention back to the body, he continued, 'On the other hand, the bruising to the ankles and lacerations to the head and face, to say nothing of the state of her clothes, would suggest she was killed elsewhere and dragged by the feet into this boggy area, probably with the idea of avoiding immediate discovery.' An amused glance at Buerk. 'After all, they could hardly have expected someone to barge into the middle of a bird sanctuary during the breeding season. Now, where was I?'

He reached out with a pair of tweezers to remove a tight wad of plant debris from inside her mouth. Teasing out an almost-intact flower from the bolus of mud, he transferred it to a plastic evidence bag. Straightening up, he held the bag under their noses. 'Do you see this little fellow?'

Buerk and Munro peered at a flower head the size of a thumbnail. It had dark purple petals surrounding a pale yellow eye at its centre.

'Looks like a tiny primrose,' Buerk said.

'Very good,' Dr Mackie said, eyes twinkling approvingly at him over his spectacles. Buerk was starting to wish he would stop twinkling. '*Primula scotica*, to be exact, better known as the Scottish primrose. This little fellow's ancestors probably survived the Ice Age. It's quite rare and it certainly doesn't grow in this bog.'

'I'm impressed,' Howie said. 'Didn't know you dabbled in botany.'

Mackie shot him a self-deprecating smile. 'Come up here on holiday most years,' he explained.

'So, if you knew where it does grow,' Munro mused aloud, 'you might have a good indication of where the victim was originally killed.'

The medical examiner beamed broadly at her. 'An excellent deduction, Inspector Munro.'

She frowned. 'Are you able to estimate the time of death and is it possible to tighten the connection with the McGrath killing on the *Loch Tredwell*?' she asked.

Dr Mackie gave a long-suffering sigh and massaged his lower back. 'I don't approve of guesswork,' he said. 'Judging from the amount of attention the birds have paid to her, I'd say she's been dead for at least three days, maybe more. It bears enough comparison with the MO in the McGrath case to state it's likely to be the same killer. A clean strike between the first and second cervical vertebrae requires a fair degree of skill. It's certainly a professional hit and one requiring some strength.'

'The sort of strength a troll might have?' Munro said.

'What?' Howie said.

She smiled apologetically. 'The word "troll" has been used by more than one witness in these cases.'

Buerk glanced at her curiously. 'Matter of fact, I'd say that description fits the bill perfectly for the taller of the two men I ran into.'

Munro nodded with satisfaction and again turned to Howie. 'It was also Buerk who discovered McGrath's body on board the *Loch Tredwell*.'

'I remember you telling me that.' Howie shot Buerk another suspicious look, as if that confirmed his involvement in both murders.

For his part Buerk's gaze was still on Munro until Mackie interrupted his thought processes.

'According to my best estimate you're off the hook for this one, young man, since Inspector Munro assures me you were definitely in the city on Monday night and the body has certainly been here beyond that timescale.'

Buerk shot Munro another sidelong glance. 'I'm heartened to learn that the inspector remembers where I was on Monday night.' He had the satisfaction of seeing her turn her head away.

Finishing his examination, Mackie moved clear of the victim just as Chief Inspector Howie finally seemed to pluck up the nerve to take a closer look.

'Hang on a minute,' he said. He bent down to take a closer look at the victim's face, in which a gold-tipped incisor tooth was prominent after the removal of the plant debris from her mouth. 'I think I know this woman. I'm sure her name's Mavis something-or-other.'

He glanced round at the others as if seeking support. 'There was an incident just before I was transferred here from another island, much further south. She was taking part in a demo against the proposed reforestation of an area that had been on the migration route of flocks of barnacle geese for aeons. Some thirty-five thousand of the blighters overwinter there from the end of October to the middle of April. Some of the farmers had even applied for licences to shoot them. Meadows, that's it... Mavis Meadows. Tough old bird herself. She used to wear one of those surgical collars.'

Mackie nodded. 'If there was prior damage to her vertebrae, that might account for the killer being unable to withdraw the blade this time. Cervical osteoarthritis, for example, can sometimes cause bone spurs to grow on the stabilising joints between the vertebrae. I'll look into it.'

Munro shot Howie a quizzical look. 'I know the tooth seems unusual, sir,' she said, 'but how is it you remember her so well?'

For the first time Howie's stern features relaxed into a smile. 'She gave me rather a nasty bite on the finger,' he said. 'Happened while I was trying to persuade her not to stick her camera in people's faces – one of those professional jobs with a bloody great telephoto lens. The finger turned septic and I might have lost it altogether despite wearing gloves at the time. Less fortunately for her, she broke her tooth on my wedding ring... even tried to sue me for its replacement.'

Buerk was suddenly extremely curious. 'Any special reason for the camera, chief inspector?'

Howie nodded. 'Mavis Meadows was a freelance naturalist photographer – damn good at it too,' he admitted grudgingly. 'Her problem was she could never quite resist stepping over the line to take sides in environmental disputes. Got involved in quite a few punch-ups.'

'That's interesting,' Buerk said. 'We found a rather expensive camera complete with telephoto lens abandoned in the hide at Hyndgreenie Loch.'

Mackie eyed him curiously. 'That's another coincidence right there,' he said. 'There's a few colonies of the Scottish primrose on North Hill around the hide. I've taken a few

248

snaps of it there as well as on the links at the southern end of the island.'

'This might be the time to tell you I found a roll of film among the ruins at the Knap of Howar.'

Munro looked at him sharply. 'You have been a busy boy, haven't you? Don't you ever just get on with your job without trying to play detective all the time?'

'I try to, believe me,' Buerk protested. 'Things just seem to happen to me. It was after that I was attacked by the two men.'

Howie glanced irritably at Buerk and said in his most authoritative voice, 'I think we'd better take a look at those sites after we wrap up here. It does strike me, however, that our chances of finding any forensic evidence after your lot have been tramping around in their hobnail boots are fairly slender.'

'At least he found the film,' Munro said, with a sidelong glance at Buerk that gave him renewed hope. 'It might tell us what Mavis Meadows found that led to her death.'

'It doesn't follow that the film was in any way connected to her or her death,' Howie said.

'Except I have a hunch that DI Munro is perfectly correct,' Buerk said, a little more forcefully than he had intended. He was rewarded by a fleeting smile from Munro before the chief inspector put him in his place again.

'Police work isn't based on hunches, Buerk. We try to stick with hard evidence.'

'I've already taken the liberty of asking my colleague to develop the film,' Buerk said. 'Let's hope he comes up with some of that hard evidence you're talking about.'

Howie stared at him hard but elected to say nothing more.

After the body had been bagged and its position marked to await removal, Buerk led the trio to the bird hide and then to the ruins at the Knap of Howar, where he showed them where he had found the film. There was no sign of the bottles or of the foot pump.

Buerk ran a hand through his hair. 'I don't get it,' he said. 'The things were here this morning.' Then it dawned on him. 'Of course,' he said. 'They doubled back here to tidy up. They must have spotted me here and decided to set a trap for me.'

Hands on hips, Howie glared at him. 'Sure you didn't drink the two bottles and imagine the rest?'

Buerk looked evenly at the chief inspector. 'Don't think I've ever tasted Dogbolter.'

Mackie suddenly exploded with laughter. 'Goodness me,' he said. 'The last time I came across that brand of beer, I was on holiday in Perth.'

Munro looked at him sharply. 'You mean Perth in Scotland?'

Mackie chuckled again. 'No, Perth, Australia – I was visiting my daughter at the time. To be exact, we were having a bar lunch in Fremantle.'

Munro smiled grimly at Buerk. 'Chief Superintendent Douglas has got one thing right,' she said. 'This has Goldfiever written all over it.'

CHAPTER TWENTY-THREE

After watching the video footage of the second attack on the Fat Friar and making her startling discovery, Lennox began to feel woozy again, perhaps brought on by the flickering images. Traynor had a quick word with Douglas, mentioning something about health and safety in the workplace. In a rare moment of concern, Douglas promptly dispatched her homewards.

She was scarcely settled in her armchair, hoping to catch a news bulletin on television, when the doorbell rang. Reluctantly getting back on her feet, she muted the TV and discovered John McManus on the doorstep with a large bunch of flowers.

He shot her a hesitant smile. 'DC Traynor told me you'd be here,' he said. 'Maybe, though, my timing isn't too great?'

'No, you're all right,' she said. So far as she was concerned, his timing was impeccable. McManus had waited at the accident and emergency station until she was given the all-clear and then dropped her off at the police station. At that point neither of them had seemed able to decide on their next move. 'These for me?'

'Yeah. Thought you could do with cheering up.' He handed over the flowers and half-turned to go.

'Look,' she said hastily, 'I was just going to put the kettle on. Care to join me in a cuppa?'

'That'd be grand, thanks.' As he stepped inside she had to reach out a hand to steady herself. 'Look,' he said, 'why don't you sit down and let me make the tea?'

'Best offer I've had all day,' she said. 'Kitchen's that way.'

She slumped back in her chair and listened to him whistle as he filled the kettle and started rummaging in her biscuit tin. God, she thought, he's going to see the state of my fridge.

A few minutes later he came in with a tray. She watched him as he poured the tea. The ponytail would take a bit of getting used to, but she liked his hands. Expressive hands.

He offered her a plate with three chocolate digestives on it. 'Couldn't help noticing you're a bit short on a few basics,' he said. 'I'll nip out and get you a few things after tea.'

'I'm not crippled altogether,' she protested. 'I've only had a bang on the head.'

He grinned. 'Then let's just hope it's knocked some sense into you.'

'If I'd any sense I would be asking you what you do for a living.' It was out before she could stop herself, but he threw back his head and laughed.

'I'm a sculptor.'

'You're kidding.'

He wagged a finger at her. 'Don't you start.'

'Sorry. Do you get commissions or what?'

'These days I do. I started off as a shipwright in the yards and used to make bits and pieces out of spare wood.' He shrugged. 'When I got laid off, I used the redundancy money to put me through art school. The bits and pieces just grew from there.'

'Of course,' she said. 'All those statues and carvings I saw at your mother's house. You made those?'

He nodded. 'She's still my greatest fan. I've got a show coming up at a gallery in town, but my biggest piece to date is the figurehead on the *Loch Tredwell*.'

'No kidding?' she said. 'I noticed it when we attended the scene after the fire. It's brilliant, but where on earth do you get a model that big?' She used her hands to indicate a generous figure.

He grinned. 'Mostly scaled-up drawings from books I get in the library,' he said. 'I used an agency model as well.' His shoulders came up in an apologetic shrug. 'Had to be sure I was getting the proportions right, didn't I?'

'Of course.' Feeling somewhat inadequate where 'proportions' were concerned, she quickly moved on. 'You must have been relieved that the figurehead didn't get destroyed in the fire.'

'Yeah. Lucky that film crew were there.'

'Right,' she said. She refrained from adding that the Black Douglas thought it had not been entirely down to luck.

When they had finished, he gathered up the tea things and washed them in the sink.

'I'll just pop out to the supermarket now,' he said. At the door, he hesitated. 'The business with the model,' he said. 'It was a strictly professional relationship... there was nothing funny going on there.'

'You mean she was just a figurehead?'

His smile carried more than a hint of relief. 'Exactly.'

'Thanks for telling me, John.' When the door closed behind him, there was a smile of quiet satisfaction on her face.

Crawley beamed smugly, waving a hand over the first grouping of photographs he had laid out on the kitchen table. 'These shots were taken, judging from the position of the shadows, somewhere in the afternoon. The date on the film indicates they were taken on the Saturday before we arrived.'

'The day before Lucretia received Hilary's e-mail,' Buerk said.

Crawley shivered as though he felt a sudden draught.

The prints were still damp from the developing tank and had been arranged in chronological order. As the new arrivals crowded round the table, the photographs revealed a busy little harbour scene. The first two were general shots, taken at a distance with a powerful lens.

'That's Pierowall Harbour over in Westray,' Howie said at once.

Crawley shot him a sidelong scowl. Why did someone always have to muscle in?

It had been late afternoon by the time Buerk had trooped into the cottage at the head of Munro's party. At their arrival, a cynical smile had crept into Lucretia's face. She was only too aware that what had brought them to Hilary's cottage had been a gruesome murder rather than any concern for Hilary's present whereabouts. As for Crawley, he was now showing his true colours. In his eagerness to make a contribution to the police investigation he had forgotten all about her tender ministrations and her anxiety for her brother's welfare. In that respect he was unlike Dick, who stood close by her side.

The next two shots showed more detail of the same harbour. In the first one, a mid close-up, a sleek white power boat partially blocked the view of a small white yacht, but in the other shot a petite, blonde-haired girl could be seen on the yacht's deck, smiling at two teenagers with a camera, one hand on hip and the other clutching the rigging in a posed shot. This print produced an immediate chain reaction.

'That's Janet Maltby,' Munro said. 'Her picture has been on the telly and some of the newspapers because of this drawn-out takeover battle between TMG and Goldfiever.'

'And that's the yacht that was standing off the skerry when we arrived at the cottage,' Buerk added. 'It was still there around midnight on Tuesday, but disappeared this morning.'

'Aye, that's the yacht all right,' Lachie agreed. 'Except in this picture there's no sign of the inflatable they were trailing. I saw her rounding Mull Head with two men crewing her. One of them looked like a trow, for sure.'

'A trow?' Munro said.

'Local term for a troll,' Howie explained. 'Up here they're considered to be quite human-like, only twice as devious.'

Buerk ruefully rubbed his head. 'I think we've already met.'

'There are plenty of shots of an inflatable here,' Crawley said, banging more snapshots quickly down on the table for fear of losing his audience.

Howie cleared his throat gruffly. 'All in good time, Crawley, all in good time.' It was clear he was trying to regain some control over the proceedings. 'Before we go any further, can someone please enlighten me on who this Janet Maltby is?'

'She's the daughter of Sir Rankin Maltby, chairperson of the Thistle Media Group...' Munro began to explain.

'Who just happens to be at the centre of a hostile takeover battle with Ned Goldfiever.' As Buerk completed Munro's sentence, his tone had Howie again glaring at him.

Munro was quick to make the connection. 'You'll recall, sir, I mentioned my governor is convinced that Goldfiever, who has attracted our interest over a number of his activities, is somehow involved in the death of Vinnie McGrath.' She glanced complicitly at Buerk. 'He's currently helping us with another matter, but we probably don't have enough hard evidence to convict him in court. I should think one of his fancy lawyers will have him out sharpish.'

Buerk was still preoccupied with another puzzle. 'When Lachie saw the yacht rounding the head,' he said, 'there was no sign of the girl on board.'

Lachie nodded in agreement. 'That's right,' he said. 'The two guys I saw crewing the yacht were running for the shelter of the South Wick with what looked like their steering gear damaged.'

Buerk again picked up the thread. 'It's no more than a stone's throw from this cottage to the beach there,' he said. 'Hilary's cottage is the first house anyone would come across if they were making a landfall in the South Wick. Now, according to that female twitcher, it was also from the South Wick that Hilary was last seen boarding a yacht from a dinghy in the company of a blonde-haired girl and two men. According to her, they all looked to be under the influence of alcohol.'

'Where are you going with this, Buerk?' Howie asked impatiently.

'Supposing...' Buerk raised a hand to quell a few groans of protest. 'Just supposing they were not under the influence of drink as Crawley's twitcher friend supposed, but instead had been bashed about a bit by the two guys I met and manhandled to the dinghy against their will? It would look much the same to someone happening on the scene.'

'Yes, well, that's all very fanciful, but we're all in danger of running ahead of ourselves again.' Chief Inspector Howie glared around the room as if defying anyone to dispute his authority. He reserved particularly severe glances for Buerk and Crawley. 'Let's just stick with what the photographs actually show us, shall we?'

Crawley did not need a second invitation. 'In the final set of photographs,' he said, 'the finish is grainy and the definition poor. They have obviously been taken at night without a flash, relying solely on moonlight.'

The first snapshot had been taken at too great a distance to reveal much detail beyond the fact that an inflatable was silhouetted in the water against a white background and with a faint iridescent glow trailing from the paddles. In it were two shadowy occupants paddling for the shore.

'That could be our two friends coming ashore,' Buerk said, 'and that might just be the hull of a white launch or power boat in the background. You can just make out a bit of brightwork at the edge of the shot.'

The room was silent as everyone craned closer to study the snapshots.

The second snapshot was a close-up of the two occupants as they came ashore, one a dark-haired man with a solid build and the other one taller by far. They could just make out the buzz-cut hair, the shadow of a scar on the left side of his face and an earring glinting in the moonlight.

'That's definitely the two charmers I had the dubious pleasure of meeting this morning,' Buerk said ruefully. 'The big guy with the drastic haircut is Lachie's trow – the one that whacked me.'

'Hang on a minute,' Munro said, jabbing a finger at the troll. 'I recognise him.' She pulled from a pocket the crumpled EvoFIT picture that Jackie Lynch had helped Lennox piece together with the help of a computer artist. 'This is the bruiser that was hanging around Vinnie McGrath's gym locker shortly after his death. Goren something-or-other.' She smoothed out the paper and consulted the name she had scribbled on the photofit print-out. 'Goren Nordmann is his name: a compatriot of Goldfiever's and handy with a knife, according to Interpol.'

'I'm fairly sure they're the same men I saw aboard the yacht,' Lachie said, pointing to another shot of the two men sitting inside a walled enclosure, one of them drinking from a beer bottle. The image was too faint to make out the label. What might have been part of a rubber inflatable craft connected to a foot pump showed less distinctly at the edge of the picture.

'This last photograph was taken at the Knap of Howar,' Buerk said, recognising the grassy area beside the ruins he had visited. 'It's from the spot where I found the roll of film. This area was mentioned in the log entry at the Hyndgreenie bird hide where we found the camera.'

Howie pursed his lips dubiously. 'I must say it would be a lot better if we could positively link the film with the camera.'

'We'll certainly be able to lift some latent prints off the bottles, if not the film tube,' Dr Mackie said. Until this point he had been content to stay in the background, but now his own particular expertise was needed. 'Naturally, I'll have to eliminate those of you who subsequently handled the objects in question. I think tracing the serial number on the camera is probably our best shot, since by all accounts it's been passed around willy-nilly.'

Cant gave Dick a sharp nudge. 'Who's he calling silly, Moby?'

Dick, for once, appeared strangely unresponsive to his colleague's usual line of banter. It seemed to Cant that his colleague had been standing unnecessarily close to Lucretia throughout the period they had spent examining the photographs. It might account for her also having said very little until now: a highly unusual state of affairs.

Buerk shifted restlessly. 'The forensic stuff is important back-up,' he said, 'but it's going to take too long to get anything positive from it. My gut feeling is there's something going on right under our noses and if we don't act soon we may be too late to do anything about it.'

Howie raised his eyebrows to the heavens. 'I'm sorry, but this is pure speculation,' he said.

'Maybe!' Buerk said the word quietly, but his mind was already racing.

Munro turned to look at him, a curious smile playing at the corners of her mouth. 'Not thinking like a detective again, Angus?' she asked. 'I thought I warned you about that.'

He grinned. 'Just a hunch, that's all, but I think it ties in with the facts well enough.'

Howie heaved a long-suffering sigh. 'All right. Let's hear it.'

Buerk surveyed the expectant faces around him. 'Just suppose our two mystery men rumbled the fact that they were being photographed by the late Mavis Meadows as they came ashore and for some reason didn't want this to become public knowledge.'

Munro nodded encouragingly, picking up the thread. 'So they decide they'd better silence her.'

Buerk nodded. 'Exactly as they tried to do to me. Realising what's about to happen, she takes the film from her camera, stashes it in the ruins and makes a run for it in the dark, heading instinctively towards the hide, where she hopes she might be able to give them the slip.'

Munro picked up the thread. 'Unfortunately she can't, and they catch up with her at the hide and snatch the camera. When they don't find what they're looking for...' She shrugged and left the rest to their imagination.

'That theory, fanciful as it may be, certainly fits with the available evidence,' Mackie conceded.

'Which is way too circumstantial for my liking,' Chief Inspector Howie said, shaking his head. 'Maybe Buerk has a theory about why these photographs are important enough to warrant Meadows' murder?'

'I may have a theory about that, sir,' Munro said evenly.

Buerk grinned at her, folding his arms challengingly. 'Well, don't keep us in suspense,' he said.

'Suppose for the moment these two villains were working for Goldfiever,' she said.

This time the police chief threw his hands in the air. 'More speculation,' he said. 'You can't possibly know that, Inspector Munro, far less prove it.'

'Let's hear her out anyway,' Buerk said.

With a nod to Buerk, Munro started again. 'From what Angus has already told us, they were perfectly willing to dispose of him for doing a bit of snooping on his own account. There had to be a strong reason for them being prepared to dispatch everyone who crossed their path. I think our two friends, or whoever put them up to it, were interested in Janet Maltby from the outset. The earlier photographs suggest Mavis Meadows had also spotted the Maltby girl in Westray. The takeover story would have aroused her interest. Perhaps she suspected even then that the girl was in danger.'

Howie was clearly far from convinced. 'What on earth are you suggesting, Inspector Munro: some sort of kidnapping?'

'Why not?' Buerk demanded. 'If Lachie's right and her yacht was forced to land at the South Wick to get assistance of some kind, Hilary's cottage is the first place they'd reach. Since they didn't want anyone to know about their activities, they'd be obliged to take him with them. That also fits with what Crawley was told by his twitcher friend.'

'She's no friend of mine,' Crawley said, giving another shudder at the recollection of what had ensued from their meeting.

Lucretia made a sudden grab at Dick's arm for support. 'You don't think Hilary has suffered the same fate as this Meadows woman?' she wailed.

Chief Inspector Howie glared at her, his patience clearly beginning to wear thin. 'This is all very well,' he said. 'But, rather inconveniently for your theory, the yacht itself seems to have sailed off into the sunset.'

Buerk held up his hands in a gesture of submission. 'Well, there I have to admit I'm stumped.'

The chief inspector again shook his head at Munro. 'I'm sorry, detective inspector,' he said. 'I'd like to believe this theory of yours. We don't often get much excitement up here, but I think rather than rushing to make any judgement, I'd prefer to wait for Mackie's report in the fullness of time. Speaking of which' – he glanced at his watch – 'we should be getting back to Kirkwall ourselves. I have to deal with a budget review meeting at five.'

Munro glanced at Buerk before addressing Howie. 'I've orders to remain here, sir,' she said. 'Chief Superintendent Douglas was most insistent I stay behind and do a little more digging. He wants to see if I can turn up anything that might add substance to our theory that Goldfiever might somehow be behind these murders.'

Buerk was ecstatic at the news, but the police chief merely gave Munro a dyspeptic look which suggested she was wasting her time. 'Very well, inspector,' he said. 'Superintendent Douglas made it perfectly clear to me on the telephone that this was your case because of a possible link with this man McGrath in his patch. Personally I can't stand Douglas myself; there's too much of the dark side about him. Just don't expect me to give you any additional personnel; we're stretched pretty thin in this corner of the world. The Westminster government appear to have all but forgotten we exist.'

Within the hour, the whole group came out to watch the police chief and Dr Mackie lift off from the island to a deafening roar and a miniature sandstorm. By this time the remains of Mavis Meadows, with her secrets now sealed in a body bag, were also safely stowed aboard.

'So you're going to do a little digging around, are you?' Buerk teased Munro when they could make themselves heard above the receding chatter of the rotors. 'I hope it's not my grave you've got in mind.'

She gave a casual shrug of the shoulders. 'Now, what gave you that idea, Angus? Doc Mackie's confirmed the murders have been committed by the same person. Like the man said, you're in the clear.'

He eyed her tentatively for a moment. 'You want to know what I think?' he said.

'Sure,' she said quietly. 'Now that I know you can think, I'm interested.'

'I think the Black Douglas still has me in the frame as a suspect and he sent you hotfooting it up here to get the proof.'

She put her hand on his arm as they slowly strode back to Hilary's cottage, allowing the others to get ahead of them. It was the lightest of touches but it sent a little frisson of pleasure coursing through him. 'The super won't like it, but he'll have to accept Jed Mackie's evidence. You're right about another thing, too; what my governor would dearly love is to pin these two murders on Goldfiever. By putting our heads together we've already come up with a possible motive, except we aren't yet able to prove anything. You were really quite incidental to Douglas's game plan; you were just a tenuous lead to Goldfiever. If you ask me, he simply let his prejudices colour his judgement. But then' – she gave him a complicit smile – 'he totally lacks a woman's intuition.'

He looked pointedly at the hand on his arm. 'So, what exactly does that intuition tell you about us?'

She smiled mysteriously. 'It says you're entitled to harbour some expectations, but they're not yet infinite.'

He raised a quizzical eyebrow. 'I sincerely hope the odds are a little better than those of finding the great auk.'

Her smile broadened. 'I should hope so. After all, there's absolutely no substance to your great auk story. It's just a myth, so you can't reasonably harbour any expectations at all there.'

'You are a bit of a tease,' he scolded her softly.

'Comes with the job, I'm afraid.'

They paused near the doorway, turning towards each other. They might even have kissed had Cant not chosen that moment to double back, clearly deciding he'd had enough of kicking his heels while his boss engaged in dalliance.

'What's the score then, boss?' he asked brusquely. 'I take it the great auk hunt is up the spout?'

Buerk glanced at Munro and had to fight to restrain a smile.

With one hand ever-so-casually draped around Lucretia's shoulder, Dick decided now was the right moment to put his oar in too. 'Well, Genghis,' he said, 'I'd say that idea is well and truly sunk.'

Buerk froze for a second, then reached out to grab Dick by the shoulders. 'Moby,' he said, 'you're an absolute bloody genius.'

'I am?' Dick turned to smirk at Lucretia. 'Of course, I knew that already. Lucretia is just after telling me I'm—'

'Stop right there, Moby,' Buerk said, putting a hand up to Dick's mouth. 'That stuff's on a need-to-know basis and I for one don't need to know.'

He swung round to catch Lachie's attention. 'When you go diving for sunken wrecks,' he said, his mind in overdrive, 'how exactly do you go about the task of locating them?'

CHAPTER TWENTY-FOUR

The press conference got off to a better start than Hornblower could ever have anticipated in his wildest dreams. More than thirty journalists, including a gentleman from the *Times Educational Supplement*, had filed into the assembly hall at the university. It was a splendid setting. The magnificent hammer-beam ceiling carved from native oak was held together by twenty thousand wooden dowels. Through the stained-glass windows the sun cast a rainbow blessing on the occasion as though it were given by heaven itself. A local radio station jostled with lead persons from the main television channels for microphone space, while their electronic news-gathering crews sorted out lighting and camera positions in their usual stimulating spirit of rivalry and skulduggery.

For the sake of authenticity and convenience, the deputy principal had been obliged to call the conference at the university. He would have much preferred to hold court at home in his rose garden, even if some of his prize bushes were not quite at their best. A bout of mildew flourishing in the unseasonably damp weather had rather put a blight on things. Not even the wizard botanists at the university seemed to be able to put their collective green fingers on the problem. The answer, they mumbled in knowing unison, probably lay in the soil.

Nothing, however, could dampen Hornblower's spirits as he prepared to announce the scientific discovery of the century – at least, that was the carrot he had somewhat modestly dangled before the media. He told himself that it was the hand of fate, aided of course by his own foresight, courage and initiative, that had decreed that this would take place during the absence from campus of his detested rival, Nathaniel Truelove. He could not resist a quiet chuckle at the thought of how the principal would react to the sensational news on his return the following day. Now, as he stepped boldly forward onto the podium, Hornblower felt he had every right to feel pleased with himself.

Still wondering what kind of breakthrough was about to be announced, the assembled representatives of the fourth estate had begun to show signs of restlessness. The betting among them was evenly divided between the medical faculty (a cure for the common cold was nothing to be sniffed at), and the veterinary department (although a failed attempt to clone Charlie the camel had got a few people's backs up).

Hornblower finally strode to the centre of the stage and raised a commanding hand for silence. Standing before the array of microphones and subjected to a battery of floodlights and camera flashes, Henry Thessinger Hornblower began to hold court to the fourth estate as if to the manner born, conscious he held his audience in the palm of his hand.

'Ladies and gentlemen,' he began confidently. 'It is with a great deal of pride and enormous pleasure that I am able to share with you a startling piece of news of scientific discovery and academic achievement.'

Inside the lecture hall Hornblower was conscious of the fact he might have heard a pin drop, had it not been for some shuffling of feet and squeaking of restless bums on seats.

'In the early hours of this morning I received dramatic news from the remote island of Papa Westray, which, as you all undoubtedly know' – a brief smile of shared worldly knowledge – 'lies amidst the, um, islands of the most northern outpost of our ancient realm.' In truth, he had never quite got round to locating exactly where Papa Westray was on a map.

From the audience, he might just have imagined that someone, doubtless from a tabloid rag, muttered in not-so-*sotto voce*, 'Get on wiv it!'

Hornblower cleared his throat. 'A small research team from this university, under my guidance, having received a prior and exclusive tip-off, have now obtained irrefutable proof of the existence of the great auk. As you know, this species was universally regarded by the scientific community as being extinct...'

His final sentence was all but drowned out amid a general hubbub from the media people who sat in front of him. He again held up a hand for silence. The noise level subsided more slowly this time.

'In the next day or so,' Hornblower continued, 'documentary evidence in video format of this remarkable achievement will be available to the world. In the meantime, I am more than happy to answer any immediate questions you might have.'

One or two members of the press quietly slipped from the lecture theatre to telephone their editors. One local journalist, with more than a passing acquaintance with New Metropolitan University, rose to his feet. Hornblower recalled that, post-merger, he had written of Truelove's appointment in what could only be considered, by the neutral observer, hagiographic terms. Now, Hornblower saw an opportunity for revenge.

'Mr Prior of the *Mercury*,' he said in a disparaging tone. 'Haven't you come a long way? You must have had wings.' He was merely letting his hard-bitten audience know that the questioner might be from the local rag but he, H. T. Hornblower, was a man of the world, educated in the classical tradition.

Prior smiled tolerantly and waited for a few sporadic guffaws to die down before asking his question. 'Why is such an important announcement being made by the deputy principal rather than the actual head of the university?'

Hornblower beamed affably at his audience. He had been expecting just such a question from some doubting scribe. He slowly removed his spectacles, in the way of experienced media handlers, thus demonstrating that he was a man of vision (in reality, without his glasses he could no longer focus clearly even on his questioner in the front row). He chewed pensively on one leg of the spectacles to assure his audience that he was a deep thinker. Finally, he sent a tolerant smile of his own in the general direction of his questioner to show he was a man of compassion, not readily given to harbouring grudges.

'There's no mystery about that, Mr Prior,' he said confidently. 'The incumbent principal has elected to spend this particular week flying off to distant outposts in pursuit of matters which some might consider could have been delegated to less senior personnel. I have no wish to pass judgement on his decision.' His tone managed to convey that the principal's tenure might be somewhat precarious and that whatever those matters might have been that Truelove was engaged in, they were in no way comparable to the importance of this present announcement.

'Suffice it to say,' Hornblower continued pompously, 'this discovery required someone to act decisively. What you must know above all else, Mr Prior, is that I was formerly principal at Queen's College before the... um, unfortunate coalition was forced upon us by a government minister blind to the irreparable harm to *esprit de corps* that such actions may cause. The expedition team, of which I will happily say more, is led by a former head of department at Queen's, Mr Fred Crawley, while the exclusive revelation was made to another Queen, Ms Lucretia Golightly.' Hornblower was already savouring his moment of triumph. 'Since virtually the whole operation was a Queen's affair, I felt it only natural to proclaim the achievement to you all. I will, of course, continue to monitor the progress of colleagues who have demonstrated an understandable loyalty to me, personally.'

Sensing a possible human interest angle, to say nothing of a conflict of interest, a young female reporter from the

BBC current affairs programme stood up quickly and caught his attention.

'Does your team contain an acknowledged ornithological expert, who could positively confirm this alleged sighting?' she asked.

Hornblower directed a confident smile at the questioner, whom he had already noted approvingly was smartly dressed, her skirt not quite covering her rather becoming knees as she crossed her legs (which she seemed to be doing rather a lot), and obviously highly intelligent. He did not altogether consider her use of the word 'alleged' to have been strictly necessary, but he was prepared to forgive her. The BBC, he knew, was renowned for its fairness, and he was the first to admit that the news he had just delivered had to appear startling to such an attractive young thing. Already, he could see himself being the subject of an in-depth interview on her programme and perhaps having a cosy chat over a glass of sherry afterwards.

'Yes,' he said. 'The team has the benefit of the services of the aforementioned Ms Golightly, formerly head of biological sciences at Queen's—'

'Isn't it true that her actual qualification is in horticulture?'

Hornblower noted with some irritation that the interruption had again come from Prior. The ignoramus hadn't even had the good grace to wait for recognition from the chair. This blighter needed to be put firmly in his place.

'I rather think we might be splitting hairs here,' he countered with a disdainful smile.

Prior, however, was not to be so easily brushed aside. 'It hardly qualifies her as an ornithological expert,' he said. He sat down again, apparently satisfied at getting his own back.

Unabashed, Hornblower played his trump card. 'I was about to add, before the winged messenger interrupted me,' shooting Prior a pitying smile, 'that Ms Golightly was instrumental in taking the team to Papay in response to an initial sighting by the warden in residence. He, of course, was appointed by the Royal Society for the Protection of Birds and has appeared regularly on wildlife television programmes broadcast by the BBC – qualification enough, I should have thought, Mr Prior?'

Hornblower was so confident now he risked a complicit glance at the young woman from the BBC to indicate that they were practically on the same team. He may even have cast a lingering glance at her knees again.

This time a bearded reporter from the *Herald* got in ahead of the irrepressible Prior, who had also shot to his feet. 'Why did the warden elect to offer your institution an exclusive,' the *Herald* man asked, 'rather than contact the RSPB or the media directly?'

'Because he has... um, over time, maintained a positive relationship with our university and Ms Golightly in particular,' Hornblower replied, congratulating himself on his adroit handling of a potentially tricky situation.

'Who just happens to be his sister,' Prior interjected. This caused a ripple of laughter and muttered comments among the audience that completely wiped the smile off Hornblower's face.

'How soon can we expect to see the video evidence?' a reporter for an independent channel demanded.

'When the board of governors agree to release it,' Hornblower said, thinking of the possible revenue that would accrue to the university and the personal kudos which would inevitably come his way. He was suddenly conscious that the independent man wanted to ask a supplementary question.

'Was the video equipment broadcast-standard?'

'Um... I don't want to go into that kind of detail now,' Hornblower said, shifting uncomfortably from one foot to the other. 'Suffice it to say that the quality will be adequate to document our claim.'

The young woman from the BBC, smiling sweetly, again caught his attention (as did her knees). 'Obviously you'll be hoping the news of your discovery will help the university to secure greater funding to support such activities as educational television?' she said.

Hornblower shot her a look of gratitude. This was more familiar ground. What a pleasure it was to deal with people of integrity. The thought suddenly occurred to him that he would probably offer the BBC an exclusive on the video material (he hadn't liked the cut of the independent reporter's jib from the outset).

'Of course I am,' he said, his beaming smile paternal (the glance at her knees less so), 'but not just for the television department.' He wagged a friendly finger of admonishment at her. 'Other areas of the university need to be fostered too – horticultural research, for example.'

'Surely your whole case rests on the video evidence your team brings back?' The question was again from the BBC woman, who this time tugged firmly at the hem of her skirt. 'Evidence it must surely have been difficult, not to say hazardous, to obtain.'

'I... ah, don't think it helps to get things out of perspective.' Hornblower felt a little miffed and began to have second thoughts about the quality of female BBC employees, despite their other... um, attributes.

'Isn't it true that even as we speak you are trying to reduce staffing levels in your television department?'

Hornblower glared at his *bête noire*, Prior, who of course had put the question. Damn and blast the man. 'Um... I don't think that kind of question is relevant in this context,' Hornblower said. He stood on one leg in sheer vexation at the questioner while a battery of flash photography all but blinded him. 'The entire university is suffering from a lack of funds, Mr Prior, and there are other people waiting to put their questions.'

'Does this mean you believe the role of television to be unimportant?' The BBC again. Damn her knees... um, eyes. She seemed to think she had some God-given right to use this occasion as a platform to start some one-woman crusade for television. Just when everything seemed to be looking like a bed of roses, some pest had to come along and take the bloom off things. She was still at it, too, while again tugging at the hem of her skirt as if under the impression his eye might have been improperly straying in that direction. The very idea!

'You are aware that your principal has recently been elected to the BBC's educational committee?' She asked her question as if she might have inside knowledge of how annoyed he had been when Truelove had told him of the appointment. 'Perhaps you would care to comment on his possible reaction to your idea that educational television is unimportant?'

Hornblower ran a finger round his collar; it was beginning to feel uncomfortably hot inside the hall. All these damn lights. 'I... um, didn't actually say that educational television was unimportant...'

'Just not as important as horticulture?' Yet another sneering jibe from Prior. This time an outbreak of sniggering blossomed around the audience like a Mexican wave.

Hornblower sensed that matters were beginning to slip out of his control. He had to do something drastic if he was to swing the fickle pendulum of media sympathy back his way.

'I don't think you fully appreciate how dangerous the circumstances in which my team have all been working are,' he blurted out. 'It's quite possible that someone committed murder to prevent our team being first with this story.'

The growing restlessness was abruptly stilled. Scenting a story in which his readers might finally take an interest, the reporter from one of the tabloids leapt to his feet and demanded, 'What evidence do you have for making such a claim?'

'One of my colleagues was hounded over a cliff.'

Pandemonium broke out in the room.

'By whom?' several reporters asked simultaneously.

Hornblower bit his lip, startled at the reaction his careless remark had prompted. He suddenly found himself swaying on the edge of a precipice. Trying to bluff his way out of trouble, he said, 'We... um, don't yet know the answer to that.'

The questions, however, now positively rained down on him.

'Who was pushed over the cliff?'

'One of my trusted members of staff.'

'Not Crawley?' Prior asked. The manner of his asking suggested it was an educated guess.

'Yes.'

'What happened to him?'

'Was he killed?'

'I believe he might just have survived.' Somewhere at the back of his mind Hornblower thought that if things here were to blow up in his face, then Crawley would assuredly not survive for long.

'Did someone rescue him?'

'We, um, don't have any details about that either.'

'Who's responsible for making the film?'

'Um... Buerk.' The single word came out as a strangled whisper, almost choking him.

'Could you repeat that?'

He was almost certain the questioner had been Prior again, damn his eyes. He had to clear his throat and take a sip of water before he could get the name out. 'Angus Buerk, but Fred Crawley is—'

'Did Buerk confirm the sighting of the great auk?'

'Of course not,' Hornblower said hotly.

There was a sudden hush in the room.

'You mean he doesn't believe this great auk story?' Prior asked.

'No, no. I mean that it was Crawley's job to liaise with me.'

But the damage had been done. Inevitably someone made the connection.

'Wasn't Buerk the guy who found Vinnie McGrath's body on the *Loch Tredwell*?'

'You'll have to, um, consult with the police regarding that incident.'

'Didn't Buerk single-handedly tackle a police suspect, an ex-boxer, while trying to make a citizen's arrest?' It was the tabloid stringer who wanted this confirmed.

'Are these incidents in any way related to what's happening up there in Papa Westray?'

'Yes... no! I mean, how the blue blazes would I know that?'

'You said you were masterminding the operation.'

'Hasn't Buerk just reported another death in Orkney?' Prior asked. He already knew the answer to that too, having heard it from a police contact.

'What?' Beads of perspiration stood out on Hornblower's head.

The irked tabloid stringer, who'd had the retainer he paid the police for titbits cut off by his editor, made a bolt for the exit, swiftly followed by a number of others. Hornblower's head began to spin. This was most definitely not how it was supposed to have gone; some of it was even news to him. It appeared that his mole had been economical with the truth. As a result, his carefully orchestrated media triumph had all-too-swiftly turned into something of a personal disaster, raising many more questions than he had answers and leaving no one any longer showing the slightest interest in him.

Suddenly, all the attention had switched to that blackguard Buerk and the distant happenings on Papa Westray. In time-honoured fashion the media representatives had abandoned the anodyne press release Hornblower had belatedly tried to issue, to go in search of the truth at source. Should the truth prove elusive, well, they could always put their own spin on the murky waters that lay between that and a downright lie. In the twinkling of an eye, Hornblower found himself alone, bewildered and more than a little apprehensive about the consequences of his impetuous actions.

CHAPTER TWENTY-FIVE

When John McManus returned laden with provisions, DS Lennox called out to him urgently. 'Quick,' she said, 'we're on the telly.'

Intrigued, he dropped the shopping and slipped onto the arm of her chair.

'We can exclusively reveal,' the news reporter was saying, 'that the so-called "chip van wars" were nothing more than a cynical ploy by two thugs to stoke racist fires through rapidly escalating acts of violence – a violence, we might add, against which the police have adopted a strategy that is rather more miss than hit. While they allowed one cowardly thug to slip through their fingers,' – the picture switched to a shot from the remote camera inside the trailer showing a close-up of one helmeted assailant being struck by a bottle-wielding Sadie, while Rob Roy fiercely fought for the baseball bat with which he had been attacked – 'the two gallant employees were more than ready to defend themselves. Indeed, they subsequently apprehended the ringleader, librarian Harvey Watt.' A grainy shot of Watt lying prone with Rob Roy standing over him briefly flashed on the screen.

Lennox groaned aloud. 'The Black Douglas isn't going to like this,' she said. 'They're using our own footage to show us in a bad light. The media knew I was there but effectively useless.'

McManus put a consoling arm around her shoulders (something to which she did not object). 'They've given the big man the credit for felling Watt, too,' he said. 'And no way was that wimp the ringleader.'

The report cut to the two employees who were now being interviewed. 'With me are the heroes of the hour, Sadie McPherson and Roy McGregor,' the reporter said. He turned first to the dark-haired girl. 'Sadie, how long have you worked for Mr Halbert, the owner of the Fat Friar?'

Sadie smiled demurely. 'Since ah left school two years ago, but ah'm hoping Mr Halbert might consider me for a senior position in his new disco, Fun Guys.'

The reporter nodded encouragingly. 'I think our viewers would agree you deserve some reward for your heroics today,' he said. 'What did you think of Roy's performance?'

Sadie darted a simpering smile at Rob Roy. 'I thought his performance was outstanding,' she said. 'It brought a lump to ma throat, so it did.'

The reporter turned to her colleague. 'You've obviously got a fan there, Roy. What was going through your mind as the attack took place?'

Rob Roy grinned at the camera. 'Well, at first ah was kinda rooted to the spot, know whit ah mean?' He turned to glance at his partner. 'But, see, the minute that nutter went fur Sadie, ah pure exploded, so ah did.'

'And what's your opinion of the way the police handled it?'

Rob Roy smirked. 'Obviously, on this one they fell flat on their face, big time.'

Lennox let out another groan and slumped in her chair. 'I'm never going to hear the end of this,' she said.

The reporter rounded off his piece. 'Teamwork appears to be the answer here,' he said. 'Perhaps that's a lesson for the police. We can also exclusively reveal that while the identity of the second assailant remains a mystery, her gender does not. Previously assumed by the police to be a man, we now have evidence from a surveillance camera that the second attacker was a woman. We leave you with a picture taken from a remote camera. Perhaps one of our viewers may recognise her and contribute to her capture. That would be in keeping for the new spirit abroad in this part of the city.'

Lennox groaned a third time for good measure. 'They haven't even given us the credit for the on-board camera,' she said.

McManus leaned forward to stare at the picture of the partially unmasked face. 'There's something about that face,' he said. 'I'm sure I've come across her recently.'

Lennox sat up sharply as she saw the possibility of redeeming herself. 'Can you remember where?'

He shook his head. 'It'll come to me,' he said. 'My memory is usually reliable.' Reluctantly he got to his feet. 'In the meantime I have to go. I have some books to return to the library, Watt or no Watt.' Seeing the disappointed look on her face, he added, 'Of course, I'll want to check up on you again. I could always bring you a wee crime novel if you like?'

She pulled a face at him. 'Don't you dare.'

'Then again, how about *Know the Rules of Baseball*?'

This time she threw a cushion at him. 'Get out, traitor,' she yelled.

She was in bed when McManus telephoned.

'The female assailant,' he said. 'I've remembered where I saw her.'

'Where?'

'The library.'

'Not another member of staff?'

'Not in the branch; maybe at headquarters. She barged in at closing time as though she owned the place.'

'Get a look at her?'

'That's just it; she was wearing those motorcycle leathers and the helmet with the visor down most of the time. I only got a glimpse.'

'Damn,' she said. 'To be this close. It does narrow the field, though.'

'Tell you who knows her for sure, apart from Watt, of course.'

'Who?'

'Watt's assistant librarian. She was looking daggers at the latecomer when she breezed in. I think she had a thing for Watt herself.'

'Thanks, John. I owe you double.'

'I'll remember that. Speak to you soon.'

Lennox laid her head back on the pillow and thought through what she had to do.

The least scintilla of wind had gone. Beneath them the sea moved sluggishly in long compact waves, which slid foamlessly over the rocks. Lachie turned the *Mallimack* towards the southern tip of the skerry known as the Holm of Papay. Some distance above the western horizon, the sun appeared like a giant orange disc screened by a diaphanous veil as tendrils of mist seeped through the narrows and spilled out across the surface of the water, conferring a surreal atmosphere to their surroundings. Astern, the barnacle-clad supports of the old pier faded ghostlike from sight. High above their heads and hidden from view, a curlew gave a mournful cry as though it might be lost in the mist.

Thoroughly enjoying the break from his fishing routine, Lachie kept one eye on his instruments, his face taking on an eerie appearance from the glow of the sonar screen. Buerk leaned over his shoulder as the screen was constantly refreshed by the sweeping arm of the needle. Lachie explained he was looking for a darker blotch on the uniform green. There had already been two false alarms, one from a sluggish shoal of sand eels, quickly dismissed, and another from an ancient wreck broken up long ago. Struggling to cram his legs into the wetsuit the skipper had provided, Buerk had shot a questioning eye at Lachie. Each incident brought the same emphatic shake of the head from Lachie.

'Too scattered for our purpose,' he said. 'We're looking for something a bit more compact.'

They pressed on, edging steadily nearer the skerry. Buerk finally shrugged his upper torso into the neoprene rubber wetsuit.

A few minutes later Lachie became animated. 'This is more like the thing,' he said, gesturing at the screen. 'Off our starboard bow and about the right dimensions.'

Buerk broke off from checking the gauge on the air tank, feeling his pulse rate surge. 'Might as well take a look,' he said, heading for the door of the wheelhouse.

Munro, who had insisted on accompanying them, put a hand on his shoulder as the engine note died and a tense stillness filled the air. 'You're sure you know what you're doing, Angus?'

He smiled at her, affecting a nonchalance he didn't entirely feel. 'Do I ever?' he asked. 'On the other hand, I could get used to all this sudden concern for my well-being.'

'Just see that you live that long.' Her face was stern as she carried his air tank to the starboard bulwark. Walking awkwardly with flippers on his feet, he joined her there.

They dropped anchor less than a hundred metres from the southern tip of the skerry, the shorebreak visible despite the mist. Lachie joined them to offer some advice. 'When you locate the wreck,' he said, 'take care to avoid snagging the tank on anything and don't take all day about it. I don't like the look of this mist; we haven't seen the worst of it yet.'

Perched on the gunwale, Buerk nodded, slipped on the harness, opened the valve to his air supply and made a nervous final adjustment to his visor.

'Here,' Lachie said, handing him an underwater torch encased in a tough rubber coating. 'You might just find this useful in a dark corner, though I don't want you in too many of those, mind. Good luck, Angus laddie.'

'Thanks,' Buerk said, taking the proffered lamp and looping the thong attachment around his wrist.

A moment later he tumbled backwards over the side and into the water. Following Lachie's instructions, he kicked slowly with his flippers to conserve energy, staying just a few feet below the surface. The water was incredibly clear; he could see the sandy bottom between scattered rocks which became more frequent in places until they joined to form a solid mass. Long strands of kelp rose yellow and brown from jagged lumps of it and fish sprayed in all directions at his approach. He knew he was heading towards the Holm from the way the sea bed, some twenty feet below him, was already starting to shelve upwards.

He was almost on top of the wreck before he realised it was there, although the term 'wreck' seemed hardly appropriate. From stem to stern the yacht looked in pristine condition. It was certainly the same one as in the photographs Crawley had developed from Mavis Meadows' roll of film; the same one he had seen standing off the Holm the previous night bathed in moonlight and which had so mysteriously vanished during the morning. It was resting at a slight angle in just enough water to cover the truck of the mast, its keel wedged in a fissured outcrop of rock on the bottom.

Turning sharply around the sleek lines of the bow, he almost lost his mouthpiece as he caught sight of the elegant scrolling on the nameplate. Kicking on around the hull, he sent a shoal of sand eels scattering in a silver starburst only for them to vanish before his eyes as they burrowed into the sand. After completing a full circuit he had still found no obvious sign that the trim yacht had been holed. Nor was there any evidence, as he slid across the deck, of any serious calamity having befallen her mast or superstructure.

He wondered about the crew. Crawley's twitcher friend had reported two men getting into a dinghy with Hilary and a girl who Buerk believed had to be Janet Maltby. Where were they now? Judging from the size of the yacht it would be a tight squeeze to accommodate four people, never mind that one of them was the troll-like Goren Nordmann.

His curiosity aroused, Buerk funnelled down a narrow companionway, switching on the torch in the sudden gloom. A solid-looking door led off either side of a narrow passageway with a third one facing him at the far end.

The first door on the right stood open, secured back on its hinges. It gave onto a tiny galley with just enough room for one person to work. The door of a stowage locker appeared to have been wrenched from its hinges and the locker's contents, mainly tins, had spilled out and rolled into one corner of the sloping floor. A few lighter items, including the locker door itself, had floated upwards to become trapped in the angle between the bulkhead and the roof. There was evidence, too, that a fire extinguisher had been removed from its bulkhead mounting, but no sign of it in the galley. On one side of the food locker was a wall-mounted, brass ship's oil lantern, Buerk guessed for emergency use should the generator fail. There had been a pair of lanterns at one time, for he could see the marks where the other one had also been forcibly removed from the bulkhead, perhaps during the sinking. The overall impression he gleaned was that the galley had been trashed by a clumsy or angry intruder.

On the other side of the passageway from the galley he found a small cabin equipped with two bunk beds. This room also seemed to have suffered some upheaval, but this time he saw clear signs of coercion. Short lengths of nylon rope had been tied to the corner posts of both bunks, suggesting to him that two people might have been forcibly restrained there. The idea was further reinforced by some broken furnishings and fittings in the cabin as though a struggle had taken place.

As he continued his search into the passageway again, he noticed a recess in which a small, square hatch set into the flooring had been lifted and not quite fully replaced. Directing the torch towards the disrupted section, he discovered a small red-painted seacock housed immediately below the hatch. From the signs over the direction arrows he gathered it was designed to enable bilge water to be pumped from the yacht. Pulling himself down to take a closer look, he saw that the valve had been turned in the other direction and the pump disconnected. In that position, he realised, the seacock would simply have allowed sea water to come flooding into the vessel. He had found the reason for the yacht's disappearance. She had been scuttled.

It had been Dick's offhand remark about being 'sunk' that had first put the idea into his head. Now, his gut feeling was that it had been done by someone who knew the layout of the yacht and had known exactly what to do, quickly and efficiently. The hatch cover had probably been pushed aside by the force of the incoming water. He was willing to stake money on the possibility that the yacht had been scuttled by its owner, Janet Maltby. She must have been desperate before taking such drastic action to so beautiful a possession.

Conscious of Lachie's warning about tardiness, he checked his watch and was about to make his escape when he realised he had not investigated what lay behind the third door at the forward end of the passageway. Deciding he might as well be thorough, he examined the door and saw that it opened outwards. He decided this had to be the heads; probably not worth bothering about. He tried the door anyway.

The handle turned all right, but as he tugged at the door it refused to move. Swimming closer, he noticed two heavy sliding bolts had been secured on his side of the door. The bolts were presumably designed to secure the door in a storm. He tried to slide them back, but the lower one wouldn't budge. Peering closer, he noticed the door had partially splintered in several places as though someone inside had tried desperately to kick it open while the bolts were still in place. As a result the lower bolt was jammed tight against its housing.

His curiosity aroused, he cast around for something to prise it open. It was then he spotted the fire extinguisher lying in a corner of the corridor. He was surprised to find that it had been discharged although there was no sign of any fire. There was also a sizeable dent at its base. Bracing himself against the galley bulkhead, he used the extinguisher as a hammer to knock the sliding bolt loose. In the confined space under water he found it difficult to gain much leverage, but after some perseverance both bolt and its restraining sheath gave way with a sudden rush and the door burst open.

This time he did lose his mouthpiece as the corpse of a giant of a man was catapulted into his startled embrace. Recovering, he had a close-up view of an ugly gash behind the left ear. The jaw on that side was also clearly broken: recent injuries to add to an older scar running across his face. There was a look of horror and astonishment in the staring sightless eyes and the skin had turned a mottled, blue colour. Buerk gave a shudder of revulsion as he registered the single earring and the buzz-cut hairstyle.

He recognised the corpse from man in the photograph Crawley had earlier developed, the one Munro had identified from the EvoFIT interpretation. Goren Nordmann had been one of the two shadowy figures who had landed at the Knap of Howar in the inflatable dinghy and later had almost lured Buerk to his own death on the promontory between the North and South Wicks. Whatever Nordmann's role had been in this continuing mystery, it was now at an end.

Unsure what to do with the corpse, Buerk tried to stuff it back where he had found it, but the corpse, grotesquely distended with waste gases which didn't help its appearance any, refused to oblige. Deciding to give up and leave the corpse floating in the passageway, he discovered another problem, potentially more serious. A buckle on Nordmann's belt had somehow become entangled with the straps of his air tank. Try as he might he couldn't pull himself loose. Even from beyond the grave, it seemed Nordmann was having one last try at doing him in. He checked his pressure gauge; he was running low on air.

There was only one thing he could do. Unhooking the harness belt, he shrugged the tank from his back. With one last gulp of air from the mouthpiece, he abandoned the air tank and struck out for the top of the companionway and the surface. His last sight of Goren Nordmann revealed him floating at the top of the passageway, a thin stream of air bubbles still trailing from the attached tank.

Buerk surfaced close to the hull of the *Mallimack*, where Munro and Lachie were on hand to help him over the side. All around the fishing boat he could see that the mist had thickened while he had been submerged.

Munro's face was anxious. 'What happened to your air tank?'

'I'll get to that in a moment,' he said breathlessly. 'The yacht's down there, all right, and it looks like she's been deliberately scuttled by opening a seacock.' He shot Munro an apologetic glance. 'I'm sorry to have to tell you I also found another dead body trapped inside – Goren Nordmann's dead body, to be exact.'

'Damn,' Munro said. 'I knew I shouldn't have let you go down on your own.'

Buerk glared at her sharply. 'If you'd seen the state of him down there you'd know it had nothing to do with me. My guess is someone bashed him rather hard about the head and locked him in the heads.' He gave a helpless shrug. 'If he wasn't already dead, he would have drowned when the boat was scuttled.'

'Nasty way to meet your end,' Munro said. 'It must have taken quite some effort to incapacitate Nordmann.'

Buerk nodded. 'I think a fire extinguisher may have played a part.' He turned to smile apologetically at Lachie. 'Sorry about the air tank, big man. Nordmann seemed to have formed such an attachment to it, I felt obliged to leave it with him for the time being.'

'No problem,' Lachie said. 'I always carry a spare. I've dropped a buoy over the side and we'll get it back eventually. The main thing is you made it back in one piece.'

'You're not the only one to have made a discovery,' Munro said. 'While you've been down there we've made one of our own.'

'What is it?'

He followed her pointing finger. Through the mist and less than five hundred metres away, he could just make out the sleek outline of a white power boat, the deep burbling note from its throttled-back diesel engines resonating eerily over the water. A moment later they heard the rattle of its anchor chain and its engines were cut.

Back inside the vaporous gloom of the wheelhouse, a steaming mug of tea at his elbow, Buerk filled Munro in about his various discoveries. He was also thinking about hers. 'Do you remember the power boat in the photographs Crawley developed?'

She nodded, still digesting the information they had acquired. Absently, she took a towel from Lachie to start rubbing at Buerk's hair. 'It could be just a mighty big coincidence,' she said.

'I seem to remember your governor, for one, doesn't believe in coincidences.'

As he unzipped the top half of his wetsuit, she helped him extricate his upper body and started rubbing his back vigorously with the towel. 'You got that one right,' she said.

'I expect you'll be wanting to have a word with whoever is on that boat?' His voice had begun to sound a little strange.

'You bet.' She broke off from her towelling efforts. 'For a start, it might be interesting to see if they have any crew missing. I've got a feeling the late Goren Nordmann will turn out to be an acquaintance of theirs.'

He turned to put his hands around her hips and draw her towards him. 'We'll need to stick close to each other.'

The green eyes narrowed and, for a brief moment, he saw something behind them he had not seen before, something unsettling and unpredictable. 'Why?'

'They might be armed and dangerous.'

Her expression changed again. As she slowly disengaged herself from his grasp, it took on an exasperated look. 'Then aren't you lucky you've got me to protect you?' she said. With that she threw the towel at him and turned to walk out of the wheelhouse.

Buerk pulled the towel from his face, broke into a grin and reached for the mug of tea.

CHAPTER TWENTY-SIX

Buerk and Munro transferred to the *Mallimack*'s own dinghy to make the short trip across to the power boat lying off the Holm. Long white tendrils of vapour clung to the oars as Buerk pulled away. The chafe and creak of the rowlocks, the muffled rataplan of water against the hull and the poor visibility somehow all conspired to heighten the eerie atmosphere surrounding their mission. Peering intently into the gloom, Munro navigated from her seat in the stern. Nevertheless, they collided with an inflatable attached to the stern of the sleek vessel before they could make out her name.

Buerk peaked the oars and took a moment to catch his breath. 'Blasted thing seems to turn up everywhere I go,' he whispered.

'Let's see what this one's owners have to say for themselves,' she said.

'Ahoy there, *Sundance*,' he called up to the boat. 'Permission to come aboard?'

'What the...' They heard a muttered expletive before a dark-haired man with a well-muscled body leaned over the burnished rail to glare at him. Buerk and Munro exchanged a quick glance with each other, aware from the photographs that they had found Nordmann's companion. This was the man, Buerk realised, who had lured him out to the promontory. The man had not seen his face, but there had to be a possibility that he in turn would be recognised. Despite the damp chill in the air, the man was dressed in shorts and T-shirt revealing his impressive physique.

'What's your business, sport?' he said. The strong antipodean accent bristled with suspicion and hostility.

Buerk straightened in his seat, a forced smile on his face. 'Angus Buerk,' he announced. 'I'm in charge of a video unit trying to make a documentary about the local seabirds. We saw you drop anchor and wondered if you could help.'

'Don't see how,' the man said.

'We're looking for some rare specimens,' Munro improvised. 'Thought you might have spotted some on your travels and could point us in the right direction.'

The man half-turned away and called out what might have been a muffled warning before again leaning over the rail. 'You from that fishing boat anchored offshore?'

'That's right,' Buerk said. 'The *Mallimack*'s a crab boat; we're just hitching a ride to do some offshore filming.'

The man pondered this for a moment and seemed to come to a decision. 'Name's Moss. Come on up.'

Buerk secured the dinghy's painter to the foot of a short ladder bolted to the stern and helped Munro to scramble aboard.

'We're not really into birds,' Moss explained. 'Hoping to do a spot of shark fishing is all.'

'That so?' Buerk took in the spacious cockpit equipped with four fishing chairs, each bolted to the afterdeck and fitted with a padded harness to hold its occupant secure against any sudden or excessive strain while wrestling with big game fish. They could equally double up, he thought, as a means of restraining anyone who didn't want to be there. He noticed also that the decks were spotless and the brightwork burnished to satisfy the most zealous seafaring martinet. In addition, there was a marked absence of fishing gear or bait, let alone any evidence of shark.

A slim young man, in white sweater with horizontal navy stripes and white trousers, suddenly appeared at the head of a steep companionway leading from the fly bridge and began to descend a little too precipitately. A white cap with navy skip sat slightly askew on his head and completed an outfit that might have been more at home in a fashion magazine than on a shark-catching trip.

As he stepped onto the deck he appeared to stumble and had to clutch at his companion for support. It could have been a slip of the foot, but his whole demeanour suggested a man who either had been drinking or was in a highly nervous state; perhaps even both.

'Whassup, Moss?' the newcomer demanded, swaying slightly as he peered intently at Buerk. 'Who're theesh people?'

Buerk thought he detected a warning frown on Moss's face as he took hold of his companion's arm.

'This is Wally, the skipper of the *Sundance*,' Moss said. He turned to his shipmate. 'Our visitors here are part of a television crew, Wally.' Moss spaced each word as if he were talking to a child.

Wally suddenly turned pale, his reaction surprising Buerk. 'Struth, Moss, you off your bleeding kadoova? Why didya let the bloody media come aboard – ouch! Bloody hell, Moss, you're breaking my arm!'

Moss maintained his grip on his companion's arm, a fixed smile, directed at Buerk, never leaving his face. 'You didn't say whether you were BBC or one of the independent lot.'

Buerk shook his head with a self-effacing smile. 'Oh, we're hardly in that league, I'm afraid. Just a university video unit.'

Moss visibly relaxed, releasing his hold on Wally. 'There you are, Wally,' he said in a soothing tone. 'They're just an *amateur* outfit.' He stressed the word 'amateur' before adding, 'They want our help in their search for some rare birds. Don't you think we should try to help... find out what they're looking for?'

'Know nothing about birdsh.' Wally's tone was defiant as he rubbed his arm.

'No, but where are our manners?' Moss said. 'We can at least offer our visitors a drink before they leave.'

Wally visibly brightened. 'Bonzer idea, Moss.' He turned first to Buerk. 'Whash your poison, mate? Drop of the amber nectar or a glass of cab-sauv? We got the whole kit an' caboodle here.'

Buerk exchanged a look with Munro before replying. 'Won't say no to a heavy beer if you have any.'

'No worries.'

Turning to Buerk with a smile that didn't get anywhere near his eyes, Moss spoke in a confidential undertone. 'Don't mind Wally. He's inclined to ship a little more snake oil than is good for him. Doesn't help when he starts the day with a beer and a dingo's breakfast.'

Buerk looked at him quizzically. 'A bit like the hair of the dog, you mean?'

'That's the ticket,' Moss said. 'What about the Sheila? What's your poison, miss?'

'Thanks all the same, but if you don't mind, I'll pass.' Munro had drifted closer to Wally to get a better look at the open hatchway. Instinctively, she engaged Wally in conversation. 'It's a beautiful boat. Yours?'

Wally spluttered. 'Not bally likely. I just crew it for Mr... the owner.'

Not their boat, then, and not a charter either, which had been her first guess. In the mist it was hard to be accurate about the size of the craft, but she estimated at least twelve metres in length and about a third of that in the beam. There was someone with money behind this pair. 'Bet she can go at a fair lick.'

Wally shot her a lopsided grin, a note of pride creeping into his voice. 'You betcha. Thirty-three knots on full throttle. We got two Volvo engines generating four hundred and eighty horsepower.'

Munro looked suitably impressed. 'Puts my Volvo car in the shade. Mind if I use your loo? Accommodation aboard a fishing boat is a bit on the primitive side.'

'Sure, help yourself,' Wally said. His hand shot out towards the companionway, narrowly missing Munro. 'Heads are off to the right just beyond the day saloon. Don't mind the mess; I wasn't expecting visitors.'

Smart move, Buerk thought, watching Munro negotiate the short mahogany-panelled companionway leading down to what looked like a spacious day cabin, with sleeping accommodation probably forward of that. Plenty of room for at least four or five people, although, so far, he'd seen no obvious evidence of anyone else on board. If they were to find any evidence of Hilary or Janet, it was likely to be below decks.

Moss motioned Buerk to sit in one of the swivel chairs. Buerk noted that the Australian chose a seat with his back to the companionway. Was it confidence that Munro would find nothing amiss? Then again, perhaps he was more concerned with keeping an eye on Wally. The deck area where they sat was covered by a sun canopy, screening it from the fly bridge above where the controls and navigation equipment would be housed. Everything about the demeanour of his erstwhile attacker suggested he was the one really in charge here.

'Might as well fetch me a stubby while you're at it, Wally.' Moss threw the order over his shoulder to his nominal skipper and winked at Buerk. 'Only hospitable to join a guest.'

Buerk kept one eye on Wally at the drinks table set against the bulkhead under the awning. Still rubbing his arm, Wally appeared to be muttering to himself as he took two bottles of dark beer from a small cool-box. With elaborate care, he put them on a tray. Even from where he sat, Buerk recognised the Dogbolter labels. All of a sudden, it seemed the island was awash with the stuff; or could it be that they had finally tracked down the source? Wally had meanwhile topped up his own glass from a half-full bottle of whisky on the table.

Buerk was well into what he would have called stout rather than beer when Munro emerged at the top of the companionway. Moss's expression had never changed throughout Munro's prolonged visit below deck. For her part, Munro appeared to pause at the top of the stairway and give Buerk an almost imperceptible shake of her head.

'Won't you join us, Miss...' Moss paused to eye Munro warily. 'I'm sorry, I didn't catch your name.'

'My fault,' Buerk said, leaping up from his chair. 'Very remiss of me. Detective Inspector Munro, Glasgow CID.'

There was a clatter from the direction of the drinks table as Wally dropped the ice bucket, sending its contents skittering across the deck.

'Butterfingers.' Buerk felt Moss's rebuke was as much a warning as a weak attempt to laugh off the incident.

'Your friend seems a trifle overwrought,' Munro said, opting to remain standing. 'Something must have upset him. Anything we can do to help?'

'Don't trouble yourself on Wally's account,' Moss said coldly. 'Probably just laddered his tights. Comes from shipping too much neck oil.'

'It's a big boat for just the two of you,' Munro said. She addressed herself pointedly to Wally as he swayed unsteadily, trying to put some rescued ice into his glass.

'There was someone else...' Wally began guiltily before he caught the look in Moss's eye.

'Yeah, unfortunately he had to drop out.' Moss hastily completed the sentence for Wally and made a vague gesture. 'Ya know how it is. Last-minute change of plans.'

'These things happen,' Buerk said, calmly acknowledging Munro's pointing finger at her watch. 'It can leave you with a sinking feeling.'

This time Wally managed to knock over the whisky bottle on the table and took two attempts to right it.

'You simply can't get the right kind of hired help these days,' Moss growled, shaking his head. He turned away from his so-called skipper towards Munro to distract her from his companion's behaviour. 'Anyway, what's a detective doing mixed up with a film crew?'

Munro gave a forced chuckle. 'Slightly ironic, really,' she said. 'You could say I've been helping them with their enquiries.'

'I don't get it,' Moss said, jabbing a thumb in Buerk's direction. 'He said he was looking for rare birds. Where does a cop fit in there?'

Munro shrugged apologetically. 'Bit of a long shot really,' she said. 'We're after a protected species.'

'That right?' Moss said, glancing at Buerk as if seeking confirmation. 'Must be a special species to warrant a personal police escort.'

Buerk smiled amiably. 'You could say that,' he said, glancing across at Wally. 'We were hoping for a glimpse of the great auk.'

This time Wally gave a shriek, let his glass fall from his trembling hands and fled from the scene.

Moss turned an unsmiling gaze on Buerk. 'I really must apologise for Wally,' he said. 'A weak stomach, you understand – maybe something he ate didn't agree with him.' He climbed to his feet, his voice hardening. 'I think maybe we should call a halt here. To be honest, I really don't think we can help you. We're really not into bird watching.'

'Like we said, it was a bit of a long shot,' Buerk said, rising from his chair and pointedly examining the label on his bottle. 'Thanks for the beer; looks like the dog has bolted yet again.'

'I hope your friend gets back on an even keel soon,' Munro added before starting to descend into the dinghy. 'We wouldn't like to think of him going overboard altogether.'

Moss gave a forced laugh. 'That'd be just beaut,' he said. 'I suppose we could always use him as bait when we go shark fishing.' There was no mistaking the threat to his companion.

As Buerk made to reply, Munro gave a warning shake of her head. He obediently joined her in the dinghy, pushed off from the *Sundance* and took up the oars.

'You two take care now,' Moss called after them. 'It can be mighty dangerous moving around in this mist.' This time the menace in his voice was directed at them.

As he began to make headway back towards the *Mallimack*, Buerk could see Moss standing by the rail, glowering thoughtfully after them, until he was swallowed up by the mist. Once they were out of earshot of the *Sundance*, he sounded Munro out. 'What did you think of Captain Courageous back there?'

She shook her head. 'I think I rattled his cage more than a bit,' she said. 'Looked to me as if Wally was scared stiff.'

Buerk nodded grimly. 'I didn't buy that shark fishing story either. There wasn't the slightest whiff of fish, let alone shark, aboard the *Sundance*.'

'Depends what kind of shark you had in mind,' she said. 'Beyond the saloon there's a fully equipped galley and dinette, then three master bedrooms, two with en-suite. We're talking megabucks here. These two are just hired hands, and it's obvious that Moss and Nordmann were the muscle and poor old Wally was just the navigator – skipper in name only. If we could get him away from his minder, I don't think it would take much to get him to talk.'

'You might be right,' he said. 'I thought you were just beginning to make some progress there when you decided it was time for us to leave. What was that all about?'

'Sorry about that,' she said. She produced a small square of material from her pocket. 'Found this on one of the bunks. I doubt if even Wally owns an embroidered silk handkerchief. On the other hand, I just didn't like the look of the automatic pistol Moss had behind his back.'

Buerk stopped rowing to stare at her. 'He was packing a gun?'

She nodded. 'Tucked into his belt. When he leaned forward his T-shirt rode up his back. I noticed it as I came up the stairway.'

Buerk frowned. 'He's already had one go at getting rid of me,' he said. 'I guess you prevented a second. It had to be your presence that made him think twice about bumping me off aboard the *Sundance*.'

She nodded. 'I think Moss just wanted us gone, one way or the other,' she said. 'By the way, what's a dingo's breakfast?'

He tried and failed to suppress a smile. 'Consensus has it that it's a yawn, a leak and a good look round.'

CHAPTER TWENTY-SEVEN

Back on board the *Mallimack*, Lachie set course for the sanctuary of the old pier, the poor visibility obliging him to maintain a slow headway, only the instruments offering any clue to their exact position. Sheltering inside the wheelhouse, Buerk gave voice to something that had been bothering him since he and Munro had left the *Sundance*.

'I just can't understand why those two villains would risk being seen hanging around the Holm,' he said. 'If they killed Mavis Meadows and were also involved in kidnapping Janet Maltby and Hilary, which I'm convinced they were, I should've thought the last thing they'd want to do was draw attention to themselves.'

Munro gave a pensive nod. 'I know what you mean, Angus. They're obviously counting on the mist to hide their current movements. From what I saw of that boat they'd have every navigational aid they could possibly need, but none of that explains why they're still hanging around. It's not their boat, so someone else might be calling the shots. From the profusion of aerials aloft they obviously have a top-notch radio communication system. Maybe they're awaiting orders from a third party.'

Buerk nodded in return. 'You're thinking that third party could very well be Goldfiever.' His brow furrowed as he turned towards Lachie. 'We have to be missing something here. Is there anything over there on the Holm that could possibly offer a reason for them hanging around?'

The big fisherman shook his head. 'There's not much over on yon skerry, unless you count a few sheep and some storm petrels and fulmars nesting among the rocks.'

'There has to be something else,' Munro said, disappointment etched on her face. 'They weren't interested in birds any more than they were in sharks. Like you, Angus, I'm convinced that they're here for a reason.'

Buerk's mind flashed back to the ropes tied to the bunk beds. 'Or for a person,' he said. 'To be honest I'd half-expected to find both Janet Maltby and Hilary at the bottom of the sea along with the yacht, but things turned out a little differently. That gives us some hope. I think we have to assume they had something to do with scuttling the yacht and with Nordmann's demise. For those considerable indiscretions they've obviously been taken somewhere other than the *Sundance* for safekeeping.'

'But where?' she asked with a mystified shake of her head. 'Moss didn't seem bothered about me nosing around. I'm fairly certain Hilary and Janet weren't aboard the *Sundance*, although the handkerchief I found suggests they may have been temporary guests. Logically, they have to be somewhere that would explain the need for that pair of villains to return to the Holm.'

Lachie looked up from his instruments, a frown on his weatherbeaten features. 'I suppose there's the chambered cairn.'

They both looked at him sharply.

'What's a chambered cairn?' Buerk asked.

Lachie stroked his chin. 'I should have thought of it before now,' he said. 'Some experts claim it was the communal burial ground of the original inhabitants of the Knap of Howar.'

Munro gave an involuntary shiver. 'Not exactly what we had in mind,' she said. 'Could there be any artifacts inside worth stealing?'

Lachie gave a scornful laugh. 'Och, the place would've been cleared out years ago and anything valuable taken to museums elsewhere. There's nothing there now but the empty underground burial chambers themselves.'

'Chambers!' Buerk exchanged a look with Munro. 'Are they, by any chance, big enough to accommodate two adults inside?'

'Och, you can do that all right,' Lachie said. 'I've taken the odd visitor over there myself, but they don't usually stay long. It's a bit gloomy inside the old burial chambers.'

Buerk became more animated. 'What if they had no option?'

'Don't get your hopes up too soon,' Munro cautioned him.

'I know,' he said. His eyes twinkled mischievously. 'It could be another dead end.'

Munro groaned at his feeble joke. 'Still,' she said, 'it might be worth a try.'

'Then it'll have to be tonight,' Buerk said resolutely. 'Mist or no mist. I have a hunch these boys will be gone by the morning – or have a reception committee waiting, since we've tipped our hand somewhat.'

'You're on,' she said, turning eagerly to the skipper of the *Mallimack*. 'You'll help us out one last time, Lachie, won't you?'

Lachie grinned. 'Aye, I suppose I might as well see this thing through,' he said. He began gesticulating towards the pier which had finally loomed out of the mist. 'If you two are quite finished talking about reception committees, I think you'll find there's another sort waiting for you ashore.'

Peering through the mist, Buerk could just make out a group of people milling around on the pier. As they approached he was able to pick out the familiar forms of Crawley, Cant and Dick, who all seemed to be fending off the attentions of some half-dozen East Asian gentlemen all laden with filming equipment and all babbling excitedly at the same time.

Lachie gave a chortle of amusement. 'Looks like the Japanese have invaded Papay,' he said.

As he brought the *Mallimack* alongside the old pier, Buerk jumped ashore and, at once, the gathering started to regroup around him.

A red-faced Cant pushed his way through the throng. 'Better have a word, boss,' he said. 'If you can't calm them down, we could have another Pearl Harbour on our hands.'

'And, in case you haven't noticed,' Dick added, 'we're heavily outgunned in camera power.' He cast an envious eye over the impressive array of equipment on display. 'That's state-of-the-art gear these boys are packing. They've even got an underwater camera, would you believe?'

'Have they, by golly?' Buerk's interest level suddenly shot sky-high.

'You'll have to deal with this nonsense, Buerk.' Crawley's bluster came from a position directly behind him. 'I simply can't reason with them.'

Resisting the temptation to reply to Crawley, Buerk turned instead to address the melee. 'Angus Buerk, New Metropolitan University,' he announced in his most authoritative voice. 'May I be of any assistance?'

As if by magic the rumpus died down. One bespectacled Japanese man stepped forward, clutching a map. He bowed stiffly in Buerk's direction and introduced himself. 'Ken Yamadori, Tokyo Broadcasting System, TV news.' Another bow elicited a reciprocal gesture from Buerk. 'We wish to make film for Japanese people about great auk.'

Buerk stared at him for a moment, wondering if he had heard correctly. 'Come again?'

Gradually, with much bowing back and forth, he pieced together the story. It transpired that Yamadori was a film producer who, together with his crew, had been filming on the shores of Loch Ness. They had been in search of evidence of the existence of the legendary monster, when the news had been flashed to Yamadori that the equally implausible discovery of the great auk had been announced at a press conference called by Hornblower at the university. In response to instructions faxed to him by his sponsors, he had immediately chartered a plane to fly them directly to Papa Westray.

Buerk excused himself to confer briefly with Munro. He said, 'It seems a safe bet that Hornblower has jumped the gun about the great auk's existence, because of a rather ambiguous e-mail Crawley has sent him. Given their location, the Japanese contingent had a head start, having made straight for Inverness airport. It is equally certain that the whole media circus will be close on their heels.'

'Not a happy prospect,' she said. 'What can we do about it now?'

Having no wish to be hounded by a pack of news hounds, Buerk suggested it was about time they brought their own expedition to a swift conclusion. First, they had some unfinished business to complete. As Buerk now explained, the very presence of his Japanese counterpart offered them the solution. The plan required a degree of cooperation with the newcomers. They had no way of knowing if it would be willingly given, but they had to try.

Buerk beckoned the producer to join them. 'Mr Yamadori, may I present Detective Inspector Munro of the Criminal Investigation Department?'

Yamadori frowned. 'You are investigating a crime?'

Munro nodded. 'Murder, to be exact.'

Yamadori's eyebrows shot up. 'Ah, so! This is... connected to great auk discovery?'

'In a way, yes,' Buerk said quickly. 'We need your help to bring the criminals to justice.'

The Japanese producer looked at him sharply. 'You know who they are?'

Buerk nodded and pointed through the mist in the direction of the *Sundance* riding at anchor. 'They're in that white power boat moored off the Holm.'

'The Holm?'

Buerk pointed to its position on the map in Yamadori's hand. 'That small island over there.'

The producer nodded, then shot him a puzzled look. 'What about great auk?'

'Believe me,' Buerk said flatly, 'you'll see as much of the auk as we have.'

Yamadori eyed him thoughtfully for a moment, then came to a decision. 'What do you wish me to do?'

Buerk glanced at Munro and took a deep breath. 'I'd like to borrow your underwater camera for about an hour, and then Inspector Munro would like you to create a diversion.'

In the end, after making a rapid translation of what was required of his excitable colleagues, Yamadori provided a camera-operator to go with the underwater camera: a compact unit equipped with a powerful lamp on either side of the waterproof housing. Having briefed his own crew about his intentions, Buerk then managed to persuade Lachie to venture out yet again, the *Mallimack* now laden with additional passengers and their equipment.

Soon after Lachie had relocated the marker buoy over the sunken yacht, Buerk made a second dive, this time accompanied by a Japanese camera-operator. He pointed out to the startled man exactly what he wanted recorded. With that task successfully completed, it was now time to put the second phase of his plan into operation.

CHAPTER TWENTY-EIGHT

From his seat in the stern of the *Mallimack*'s dinghy, Buerk did a rapid mental checklist of the readiness of his assembled task force. Munro, her face lit by the mist-shrouded red ball of the setting sun, sat beside him. He felt the reassuring pressure of her arm against his.

Cant and Dick sat on opposite sides of the two main thwarts, each leaning into an oar, their joint enthusiasm making up for a lack of cohesion and skill. Buerk had impressed on them the need for silence, and miraculously they seemed to be heeding the warning. With the need for secrecy, the enveloping mist was finally working in their favour.

Earlier, Dick had clambered aboard clutching a large Thermos and a packet of sandwiches which, Cant had only too readily explained with an air of grievance, had been a present from Lucretia. She had insisted he needed the coffee to fend off the night chill and the food to keep up his strength. Catching Buerk's eye on him as he tucked away such unexpected reserves in an inside pocket of his anorak, Dick had merely given a helpless shrug. It seemed to imply that attempting to fathom the idiosyncrasies of the female mind was a futile exercise, and it was best to go with the flow.

Only Crawley had failed to demonstrate any real enthusiasm for the current expedition. Though his injured ankle still appeared to trouble him (he affected a pronounced limp if he noticed anyone looking in his direction), perversely, he had insisted on coming along. Sitting morosely in the bow of the dinghy, he was clearly at war with himself as he tried desperately to reconcile the opposing forces within him. On the one hand he wished to be safe in bed; on the other, he did not want to miss out on any of the action which might still redeem his possibly tarnished reputation back at the university. As Cant had colourfully put it, he was now inside their tent, pissing out, rather than vice versa, even if his aim was still a little haphazard.

From time to time Crawley would take a sip from a small bottle of brandy he had discovered in Hilary's medicine chest and which, since his accident, he had found he required to steady his nerves. Having now burned his boats so far as his pact with Hornblower was concerned, he was aware that unless he could salvage something from this ill-fated expedition, he was likely to find his professional prospects as empty and adrift as the *Mary Celeste*.

As he watched his rowing dinghy drift off into the mist under Buerk's command, Lachie tuned the radio in the *Mallimack*'s wheelhouse to pick up the latest news and weather reports. A south-westerly wind was forecast by morning, with rain to follow. One other item briefly caught his attention. The hostile takeover bid for the Thistle Media Group apparently still hung in the balance, the chairperson of the beleaguered company, Sir Rankin Maltby, refusing to add anything to his earlier statement and insisting he was still considering his position.

Cant and Dick were proving proficient enough with the oars and although for a time they could only hear the waves lapping tantalisingly on the shoreline of the Holm, eventually, to everyone's relief, they made a landfall on the rocky shore towards the northern end of the islet. Having manoeuvred the dinghy out of the water and anchored the painter securely above the high-water mark, the group now squatted down around Buerk for a final briefing.

'Might be an idea if we split up here,' he said. 'Moby and Genghis, I want you two to make your way down the west side of the island to the southern tip. All you have to do is keep the sea on your right-hand side and you'll be fine. Fred and I will accompany DI Munro across to the eastern side of the island before heading south. If there is any skulduggery going on in or around the chambered cairn at the southern end, maybe at least one group will discover it.'

'I get it,' Dick whispered eagerly. 'You're aiming for the classic pincer movement of a Panzer tank division?'

Buerk put an encouraging hand on his shoulder. 'That's the general idea, Moby, except I'd prefer you made a lot less noise than a tank.' He checked the luminous dial on his watch. 'It's just gone nine fifteen. Let's aim to meet up at the cairn by ten sharp; that should give us plenty of time to contend with any unforeseen eventualities. Any questions?'

As Dick adjusted his watch, Cant tapped Buerk on the shoulder. 'Let me get this absolutely clear, boss,' he said. 'You want us to arrive bang on the stroke of ten. Is that right?'

Buerk searched for any hidden pitfalls in the question before nodding encouragingly. 'Absolutely spot-on, Genghis.'

Cant climbed ponderously to his feet. 'Okay, Moby,' he whispered, 'I've left my watch back at the cottage, so I'm relying on you. We don't want anyone saying we let the side down.'

Buerk watched the pair disappear into the mist with some misgivings. He wondered if perhaps he ought to have gone with them, but then that would have left Munro to play nursemaid to Crawley. He sighed heavily. Shrugging personal feelings to the back of his mind, he gestured to the others to follow him.

They travelled as quietly as they could over the uneven ground. Before they had taken more than a dozen steps, it became obvious it was going to prove difficult to keep together. Instinctively he reached out towards Munro and felt her hand close around his.

The rough terrain was strewn with loose rocks which caused frequent stumbles, and more than once they startled a fulmar nesting in a scrape among the rocks. The birds invariably spat angrily at them and held their ground. On each successive occasion that they projected the noxious contents of their gut in his direction, Crawley became less enthusiastic about continuing, his recent experience with nesting birds all too vivid in his mind. He began to lag behind.

Some sixth sense warned Buerk just in time to avert a major disaster. He had been aware for some time that the ground to their left had been rising steadily. Yet the roar of the waves pounding on the rocks below, which he would have expected to recede in volume, paradoxically now seemed somehow louder. Without warning, he felt a sharp uprush of moist air, the mist seeming to part before his eyes. It was then he saw the chasm that had opened up almost under his feet. Having seen only the low, sandy inlets to the west side of the island, he had not appreciated that the exposed eastern coastline was raised into jagged cliffs for much of its length. The skerry was apparently wedge-shaped, presenting its lowest side to Papa Westray, and it appeared they had struck the far side just where the sea had carved a deep gash into the rising cliffs. In that single heart-stopping moment he instinctively pulled Munro towards him and suddenly she was in his arms, her mouth seeking his.

Eons later she broke free, her breathing ragged. 'You pick the darnedest moments, Angus,' she said.

'Needs must,' he said, feeling the warmth of her body against him. He tried to kiss her again, but this time she reluctantly resisted.

'Call me an unfeeling killjoy if you must,' she said, struggling to regain control of her own emotions, 'but your friend Crawley has gone awfully quiet. I haven't heard even a whimper for some time.'

Before Buerk could recover his senses the night air was pierced by a howl of fear punctuated by numerous shrill bird calls. He cursed softly. 'Good grief. Not again!'

He felt his way gingerly along the edge of the chasm in the direction of the sounds, dreading what he might find. To his relief it transpired that on this occasion the birds had saved Crawley from disaster. Having strayed into a small nesting colony of storm petrels just a yard from the chasm, he had sent them shooting skywards in a chorus of angry protest.

That had been the last straw. Crawley had simply thrown himself to the ground, where he remained, head buried in his arms, until Buerk fell over him, Less than half the size of the terns, the petrels whirled about the traumatised figure, almost invisible in the gloom save for the occasional flash of a white rump. The vaporous night and Crawley's own fevered imagination had lent credence to a nonexistent threat.

Cant and Dick had made good progress down the west side of the island, the night air loud with the penny-whistle piping of oyster catchers and the yowling of other seabirds as though someone might have disturbed them. They felt excited to be out in the dark, the sea surging and sloshing beside them. Its sounds reinforced their strict obedience to Buerk's orders to stick close to the coast on their right. The ground here was less boulder-strewn than elsewhere on the Holm and, apart from Dick becoming temporarily entangled in a barbed-wire fence (a brief threat to the family jewels), their passage was unremarkable. Some time after that incident Cant planted himself resolutely on a boulder and pulled out a handkerchief to mop his perspiring brow.

'What time do you make it, Moby?' he asked. 'We must be more than halfway there by now. Reckon we're due a rest.'

Dick peered at the luminous dial of his watch. 'I make it dead on half-nine,' he said, nudging Cant over to make room for himself on the boulder.

'Great. That gives us bags of time.' Cant resettled his bulky frame on the rock and glanced expectantly at his companion. 'I could fair go a bite to eat. This sea air is making me hungry.'

Dick's hand automatically reached into his inside pocket to retrieve his sandwiches. 'Lucky Lucretia gave me these,' he said. 'She must have had a premonition we'd get peckish.'

Cant turned to glare at his colleague suspiciously. 'She certainly had something on her mind, but if you ask me it had more to do with your pecker than your stomach.'

Sensing the edge in Cant's voice, Dick hastily offered him a sandwich. 'Here, Genghis. According to Napoleon, an army marches on its stomach.'

Somewhat mollified, Cant beamed at his companion. 'Thanks, Moby, you're a pal. Eh, what's in that flask she gave you, by the way?'

'Coffee, I think. Want some?'

'You bet.'

Suitably refreshed and rested, they moved on and soon detected a change in the contours of the land as they approached the southern end of the island.

'We need to hang a left here to keep the coastline on our right,' Cant announced. 'The cairn can't be too far away; we'd probably see it by now if it wasn't for this bloody mist.'

317

This time Dick opted to take a seat. 'Might as well take the weight off our feet while we have the chance,' he whispered. 'The boss said ten. No sense getting there too soon.'

As Dick shared out the remaining sandwiches, Cant pulled a hip flask from his pocket and topped up the Thermos. They sat eating and drinking like two midnight picnickers without a care in the world.

Eventually Cant passed the half-empty Thermos back to Dick and struggled to his feet. 'Best keep a wee bit in reserve,' he said. 'Must be about time we were making the final push. Remember the boss wanted us there bang on time.'

Dick again consulted his watch. 'No need to panic,' he said nonchalantly. 'We've still got a good half-hour yet.'

Cant had taken a mere two steps when he ground to a sudden halt. 'Hang on a minute,' he said. 'It was half-past at the last stop. It's ten we're supposed to rendezvous with the boss.'

'I know that,' Dick said, sounding peeved at this fresh assault on his integrity. 'My memory's still functioning.'

'Well, your bloody watch isn't,' Cant growled.

Dick held the watch to his ear to confirm the worst. 'My God, you're right,' he said in sudden alarm. 'The boss will kill us.'

'Less of the "us".' Cant jabbed a stubby finger into Dick's chest to reinforce his point. 'It's your bloody watch. Come on, we'd best get a move on. Better late than never.'

Munro checked her watch as they came within sight of the cairn, an eerie shadow looming low out of the mist. 'Bang on schedule,' she whispered.

'Good,' Buerk said. He strained his ears but could hear nothing but the rhythmic breaking of the waves against the rocky shore. They waited for Crawley to catch up with them. There was still no sign of Cant and Dick.

'Damn spooky place, this,' Crawley muttered nervously.

Buerk glanced about himself, vainly searching for his two crew members. Nothing stirred in the swirling mist, the damp clammy air redolent of the tang of sea wrack. The only extraneous sound came from a distant foghorn.

'You don't suppose anything's happened to them?' Crawley said. His hand instinctively shot out to grab Buerk's arm.

'Something's always happening to that pair,' Buerk muttered irritably. 'Anyway, no point in hanging around here. We might as well go ahead and investigate the cairn.'

Shrugging off Crawley's hand he led the way across the open ground to a metal hatch that covered the entrance to the underground chamber. Munro followed closely behind with Crawley now attaching himself to her like a leech.

Buerk noticed that the rectangular hatch was not quite set into its housing, but lay at a slight angle to it as if someone had replaced it carelessly or hurriedly. Alongside the hatch, some glass tiles had been more recently inlaid into a concrete roof to accommodate the occasional intrepid tourist who might venture here. He slid the cover clear of its housing. 'Keep a weather eye open while I check this place out,' he whispered.

Crawley darted furtive glances over his shoulder. 'Just don't take all night about it,' he said. 'This place gives me the bloody creeps.'

Buerk shone Lachie's powerful lamp down the shaft. A metal ladder set into the side led from the hatch opening to a gravel-covered floor about twelve feet below. As he began to descend he found evidence of occupation. A supply of candles and matches lay on a ledge while, at the bottom, he discovered the remains of a recent meal of bread and cheese in a plastic box.

The chamber in which he now stood was no more than a narrow vestibule a few feet broad. As he shone the torch into the total darkness at either end, the initial feeling of euphoria began to evaporate. They appeared to be too late. Again, the birds appeared to have flown.

Munro's voice echoed down the shaft to him, her head thrust into the opening at the top of the ladder. 'See anything?'

'Somebody's been down here, all right,' he said, 'but there's no sign of life now.' Dejectedly he switched off the lamp and thrust it inside his jacket to facilitate the climb back to the surface.

'Wait,' Munro commanded as he started up towards her. 'Look down again, without switching on your torch this time.'

Puzzled, Buerk did as he was told. As his eye grew accustomed to the darkness, he caught the faint flickering light low down on the side wall of the vestibule. Turning back to investigate, he saw the light came through a gap along part of the side wall at ground level. It had been too weak to register against the powerful beam from his torch. As he descended to the bottom of the shaft again, he shone his lamp around the gap and saw that it was high enough to allow him to crawl through. Kneeling down, he again tucked the torch into his jacket and thrust his head through.

The flickering light came from a brass ship's lantern standing on the gravel floor. As tendrils of mist curled around it, he recalled seeing its partner aboard the sunken yacht. He switched on his torch again and picked out two figures sitting on a tarpaulin, their backs propped against the far wall. They were bound and gagged and, while neither looked seriously injured, both looked somewhat dazed. He was in no doubt about their identity.

CHAPTER TWENTY-NINE

The slim girl with cropped blonde hair was Janet Maltby. Buerk recognised her from the photographs and from her frequent appearances as a television presenter. Some of this began to make sense to him now. The yacht was of course hers. The man beside her with the unkempt beard had to be Hilary Golightly, Lucretia's brother. He couldn't see much resemblance, but then the light level was poor and although Lucretia might occasionally threaten to sprout fur it had not, so far, stretched to a beard. He stuck his head back out into the vestibule to yell at Munro: 'Get the brandy off Crawley, tell him to keep his eyes peeled and get down here fast!'

He heard Munro relaying his orders to Crawley and then the clatter of her feet on the ladder. He ducked back under the lintel ahead of her. There was room to stand up inside but the air smelled stale and dank. He had removed both gags and had Janet Maltby untied by the time Munro arrived to offer her the brandy. The first mouthful prompted an immediate coughing fit.

Recovering, Janet gasped, 'Am I glad to see you, whoever you are. I thought no one was ever going to find us down here.'

Munro smiled. 'Detective Inspector Munro,' she said. 'You'll have to ask Angus Buerk, here, to explain the full story, but we don't have time for that right now. The main thing is you're going to be fine. Just take the next mouthful a little more steadily.'

Munro checked her over as Janet took another sip. Apart from a nasty bruise on the side of her jaw already showing purple, she seemed unharmed. Buerk had meanwhile untied Hilary, who also sported a few cuts and bruises. As they took turns to explain, the final pieces of the jigsaw fell into place.

Janet had been on a sailing holiday around the Northern Isles. She had sailed from Westray in late evening, taking advantage of the tides and the long summer evenings. She had intended to round the north end of Papa Westray and drop anchor off the Holm when she spotted a dinghy with the two thugs aboard. They had fired a distress flare over her bows, so she assumed they were in trouble and felt bound to offer help. The moment they were alongside, they boarded her like common pirates, declaring they intended to hold her to force her father to agree to Goldfiever's takeover bid.

In desperation, she decided to sabotage the steering gear to thwart their plan. She waited until they were well clear of Fowl Craig and had rounded the promontory between the North and South Wicks. The attempt succeeded, forcing them to run for shelter in the bay of the South Wick just as Lachie had guessed. They needed help to repair the damage and, approaching the nearest cottage, managed to coerce Hilary into helping effect some running repairs. Naturally the two villains then felt they had no choice but to take him captive.

'That'd be the point at which someone spotted you being frogmarched to the inflatable,' Buerk said. 'Except they got the wrong end of the stick and thought you were on a drunken bender. What happened to your face?'

Hilary took up the story, obviously still irked at the injustice. 'One of them – a foul-mouthed great oaf called Nordmann – slapped Janet on the jaw when she tried to escape.' He shrugged. 'Naturally I protested at the outrage.' His shoulders heaved in a gesture of defeat. 'I'm afraid I was no match for that brute.'

Janet rubbed her jaw ruefully. 'Lucky it wasn't a punch or he'd have broken my jaw,' she said. 'I suspect it's going to need plenty of make-up to disguise the bruise before my next TV appearance. At any rate, after my break for freedom, they kept us tied to our bunks. Later, when we lay anchored off the Holm, the one called Moss released me so that I could speak to my father on the telephone. After the call, our captors grew complacent, perhaps thinking their job was almost over. They even demanded I cook a meal for all of us in the galley. While Moss was up on deck, trying to get a signal, Nordmann decided to get fresh with me. When I resisted, he tried to hit me again.'

Buerk saw where this was going. 'Sounds like that was the last straw?'

Janet brushed the hair back from her face and gave a bleak smile. 'I'm afraid I turned the fire extinguisher on him,' she said. 'While he was blinded, I used the other end to whack him over the head – I thought I might even have killed him. Having committed myself, I untied Hilary and together we crammed the unconscious brute into the heads and slid the bolts home. We knew all the commotion would bring Moss down. That's when I had the idea to scuttle the boat.' She gave a helpless shrug. 'I was desperate.'

Hilary took up the story. 'Once the valve was opened, she just sank like a stone. By the time Moss realised what was happening we were already waist-deep in water below deck. He splashed about a bit, calling for Nordmann, but didn't spot the bolted door to the heads.'

'In the confusion we made the mistake of jumping overboard and trying to swim for the shore,' Janet continued, 'but Moss was too quick for us. Having the inflatable and a gun, he had the whip hand. He merely waited until we swam ashore before recapturing us. By then we were too exhausted to offer further resistance. He was quite cut up about his mate's disappearance.' She paused to heave something between a sob and a sigh before continuing. 'In any event, I'm afraid he rather took it out on Hilary. After trussing us down here, I'm guessing he called up another party on his radio telephone – there's no signal down here. They have an accomplice aboard a white power boat, so I expect they were planning to make some rendezvous.'

'That'd be the *Sundance*,' Buerk said. He had been listening with a mixture of admiration for their actions and anger at their treatment. 'We've already met your friends,' he said grimly. 'I take it you've already worked out that Nordmann didn't make it out of the heads?'

Janet gave an involuntary shudder as Munro helped her to her feet. 'Am I in some kind of trouble? I mean... I suppose I killed him one way or the other.'

Munro shook her head. 'I'm sure a good lawyer would have no trouble making out a case of self-defence,' she said reassuringly. 'Goren Nordmann was already a suspect for premeditated murder in two separate cases, never mind the kidnapping charges we'll be laying at the door of his friends.'

Buerk smiled grimly. 'It seemed a no-brainer that they were holding you hostage to force your father into accepting Goldfiever's hostile takeover bid on the Thistle Media Group.'

'Angus here is a big fan of your father's firm,' Munro said. She darted a teasing smile at Buerk. 'He was really keen for TMG to remain independent.'

Janet smiled at Buerk. 'They had my father over a barrel,' she said. 'We were beginning to think they had probably succeeded until you appeared on the scene. How on earth did you manage to track us down?'

Buerk grinned. 'Let's say it was a stroke of genius recording the sighting of the great auk.'

Janet gave a wry smile. 'That was down to Hilary,' she said.

They were both on their feet now. Hilary was busy trying to rub the circulation back into his wrists and ankles. 'I'd been completing my monthly returns to the RSPB when I saw the yacht drop anchor in the South Wick,' he said. 'I had a quick squint at the new arrivals through my telescope, which, by the way, they stole from me. Next thing I see is this big hulk and his surly accomplice frogmarching Janet up the beach. It was obvious that they were up to no good. While they were banging on my door I hit on the idea of adding the auk to my list. It was a long shot, of course, but I thought it might just arouse enough suspicion in my sister's mind if I sent the return to her.'

'I noticed the strands of blonde hair where you'd run Hilary's hairbrush through your hair,' Buerk said. 'DI Munro also found your handkerchief aboard the *Sundance*. You left plenty of clues which started us thinking this was more than a wild auk chase.'

Janet brushed a lock of hair back from her brow. 'They suspected we were up to something at the cottage and smashed the computer in a fit of pique, but, to be honest, Hilary's idea seemed a little too far-fetched for me to have any hope of it succeeding.'

Buerk gave a quiet chuckle. 'I'm glad to say Hilary's sister took the bait. She even managed to persuade our deputy principal to send us up here in the hope of capturing a resurrected great auk live on video.'

In spite of everything that had happened to her, Janet started to laugh. Even Hilary could not resist a grudging smile. 'Common sense was never Lucretia's strong suit,' he conceded.

'I'm just grateful you came to look for us, whatever the reason,' Janet said, suddenly forced to lean against Munro for support.

'I think we need to get out into the fresh air,' Munro said, flashing a warning look at Buerk.

'Agreed.' He removed his jacket and draped it around Janet's shoulders. 'High time we were out of here,' he said.

As they started towards the low doorway, a bloodcurdling howl echoed around the walls of the empty vestibule next to the chamber. It reached a crescendo, then abruptly halted with the unmistakeable thump of a body landing heavily on the gravel floor.

'What in God's name was that?' Hilary asked in alarm.

Munro darted a despairing look towards Buerk. 'I could hazard a guess.'

Buerk immediately scrabbled through the low gap between the chamber and the vestibule. Crawley lay sprawled on the gravel floor. A low moan escaped from his lips as Buerk dropped to his knees beside his stricken colleague. 'Fred, are you all right?'

'That's far enough, sport.' A familiar drawl echoed down from the top of the ladder.

'Moss!' Buerk found himself looking up into the muzzle of an automatic pistol. The next instant he was blinded by a torch shining into his eyes.

'Back into your hole,' Moss ordered, 'and take your drongo of a buddy with you. Struth! What a pathetic bunch of amateur snoops you are. Did you really imagine I wouldn't see through your little charade this afternoon?'

Buerk glared at Moss in a helpless fury, partly at the treatment meted out to Crawley, but mainly at his own stupidity. He had taken far too long to get the captives out of such a natural trap. 'This man's badly hurt,' he protested. 'He shouldn't be moved any more than is absolutely necessary.'

'Don't come the raw prawn with me,' Moss growled threateningly. Cautiously, he put a foot on the top rung of the ladder. Still pointing the gun at Buerk, he started to descend. 'I'm the one calling the shots here and I say it's necessary. Now, unless you want to join your limp dick of a mate on the injured list, move him inside.'

Buerk saw it was useless to argue, but moving Crawley in the confined space was no easy matter. Eventually, with Munro's assistance he managed to half-push, half-drag his hapless colleague back into the chamber from which he had just emerged.

'Now, I'd be obliged if you'd send out little Miss Maltby,' the disembodied voice called from the vestibule. 'It seems Daddy would like one final piece of personal assurance she is well before he signs on the dotted line.'

'Stay right where you are,' Buerk said to Janet. 'If he wants you, he can come and get you.'

'No,' she said resolutely, shaking her head. 'It'll be better for your friend if I do what he says. Besides, I'm in no danger. He needs me alive.'

'Only until your father has signed his company over to Goldfiever,' Munro warned, clutching Janet's arm to restrain her.

'My decision,' Janet said, breaking free. She ducked under the low opening into the vestibule. Buerk poked his head out in time to see Moss, by now at the foot of the ladder, threaten her with the gun.

'Up you go, miss, and no tricks,' Moss warned. 'Remember what happened to you the last time. Besides, Wally is waiting for you. He's all agog at the thought of having you back aboard the *Sundance*.'

Janet glared defiantly at him and started shakily to climb the ladder. Moss followed at a safe distance.

'You won't get away with this,' Buerk called, feeling like a bad actor in an even worse movie.

'Don't count on it, sport,' Moss crowed. 'I've got a rather heavy stone to put on top of the hatch. Whether you ever get past it makes no odds to me. Sir Rankin needs to hear a few more words from his little baby to be convinced he should sign away his rights. Finally, Ned Goldfiever will have his company, and me and Wally will be long gone.'

By now Janet had cleared the top of the ladder, Moss close behind her. When his head was level with the hatch cover he flashed his torch down the shaft. 'So long, you bunch of useless snoops.'

Buerk steeled himself for the clang of the metal hatch cover slamming into place, but instead he heard a surprised yelp of pain and then Moss plummeted from the ladder in a reprise of Crawley's earlier dive. This one was a back somersault with half-twist, and somehow, at close quarters, his fall was even more awesome. The vestibule was plunged into darkness as his torch hit the gravel, flickered briefly, then went out.

Buerk crawled out of the side chamber yet again, closely followed by Munro.

'What happened?' she asked.

Buerk scrabbled about in the gravel until he found the torch and was surprised to find it still worked. He shone it on Moss's inert form. 'Somebody put his lights out.' His voice carried a note of quiet satisfaction.

The tension was finally broken by a familiar voice from the top of the shaft. 'You okay down there, boss?'

Buerk stood up, shock and astonishment turning to anger. 'You're late, Genghis,' he bellowed up the shaft. 'What the hell kept you?'

His face gleaming with perspiration and wreathed in a massive grin, Cant said, 'You could say that for us time stood still.'

As he caught Munro's eye, Buerk struggled to keep his composure. 'What's that supposed to mean, you great ninny?'

'It means my watch stopped.' Dick's detached and apologetic voice echoed from the hatchway.

Buerk felt his legs give from under him. As his back slid down the wall, he saw that Munro had started to laugh uncontrollably. There was nothing he could do but join her.

CHAPTER THIRTY

At nightfall, the *Mallimack* again slid away from the old pier. A light breeze had got up, slowly dispersing the blanket of mist until only small pockets lingered over the water and eddied round the wheelhouse. For this trip Buerk had asked that Lachie take a few new passengers on board; the afterdeck was now crowded with five volunteers from the Japanese film crew.

Some ten minutes later, engine revs cut to a minimum, the skipper brought the *Mallimack* abaft the *Sundance*. In the low swell the fishing boat's beam end nudged against the low stern platform (the inflatable being absent) with just sufficient force to upset the team of boarders already poised waiting to scramble over the rail. Lachie chuckled as the film crew, laden with what seemed like bulky camera cases and equipment, landed awkwardly on the stern quarters of the power boat in the full glare of the spotlight fixed to his wheelhouse roof.

From somewhere below decks on the *Sundance* came the sound of breaking crockery. Wally had been standing at the gas cooker about to make himself some coffee when the jolt had thrown him across the galley. 'M-Moss? Is that you, Moss?' he enquired in a tremulous voice.

Adhering to the plan he and Buerk had rehearsed earlier, Yamadori called out politely, 'Excuse please, we wish to speak with those on board.'

A moment later, capless and pale-faced, Wally poked his head anxiously out from the foot of the companionway. Almost in the same instant there was a loud crash from somewhere behind Yamadori followed by a muttered curse in Japanese as one of the camera crew stumbled on the slowly shifting deck.

'Wh-whassat? Who's out there?' Already dazzled by the glare from the *Mallimack*'s spotlight, Wally had to shade his eyes as twin lights on either side of a camera flared into life on board the *Sundance*, casting Yamadori into a sudden spectral silhouette.

Taking a few tentative steps to the top of the companionway, Wally swayed nervously, like an actor with stage fright, trying to catch a glimpse of an audience rendered invisible by the lights. 'L-look,' he stammered. 'If this is someone's idea of a joke, I'm not amused. G-go away... whoever you are.'

'Where is accomplice, please?' Yamadori demanded. His voice remained polite but grew a little more insistent and, this time, was much nearer.

Accomplice? In his present state of anxiety, exacerbated by drink, the stage-effect lighting and unexplained noises made it easy for Wally to imagine that an invading army was closing in on him. Nervously licking his lips, he took one step away from the unseen horde and reached for the flare gun tucked into his belt. The small, plastic-coated Very pistol was the only object approaching a weapon he could lay his hands on.

'Moss ain't here,' Wally flung out defiantly, only to instantly regret his rashness. Now they knew he was alone.

Trust Moss never to be around when he was needed, he thought bitterly. Bloody typical of him, too, to take the automatic pistol, leaving him alone on watch with this toy. There had been a time when Moss would have shown him more consideration, but ever since that bloody Nordmann had been dispatched by Goldfiever to 'stiffen their resolve', Moss had been acting as silly as a cut snake. When Wally had asked Moss what had happened to Nordmann after the yacht sank, he'd just said, 'Never mind that. I'm in charge now.'

Wally kicked at a step in frustration. The truth was he was fast becoming totally ticked off with the brainless drongo. All Moss was good for these days was acting tough and slapping people around. Nordmann was the one who had encouraged it, treating Wally like a dog right from the off. Then having to play nursemaid to that Maltby girl seemed to have knocked Moss off his kadoova. Finally, that bunch of amateur filmmakers had sent him over the edge completely; he'd been dishing out orders left, right and centre. Who the hell did Moss think he was, anyway – Captain bloody Bligh?

Venting his burgeoning spleen at his unseen oppressors, he yelled out at the top of his lungs, 'I dunno what the hell you people want, but you've no business being here. So why don't you just shove off?'

'We know you speak untruths,' the stranger insisted calmly. 'This will not look seemly on Japanese television.'

As if to underline the point, what seemed like a video camera clicked into record mode and a rifle microphone was thrust out of the gloom almost under Wally's nose. His heart leapt as he took another involuntary step backwards. Christ! Another television crew! Japanese, if he wasn't mistaken. Where the hell did they spring from? Moss wouldn't be able to shrug a second lot aside so easily. Wally was also vaguely aware of a whiff of something worrying coming from the galley. Had he forgotten to do something important in there?

'No worries,' Moss had said. 'Everything'll be apples,' he had assured him. Well, with all this media attention, it was as plain as the nose on Moss's ugly kisser that they'd been rumbled. What the hell could be keeping him anyway? He'd promised it'd only take a jiffy to bring the Maltby girl back on board, and it was already well over two hours since he'd taken the inflatable ashore.

'I don't give a monkey's about Japanese television,' he blustered. 'Far as I'm concerned, you fellas are trespassing and I'm warning you for the last time to clear off. I-I've got a gun here and... I-I'm not afraid to use it.'

He was suddenly aware of a chorus of angry, jabbering voices raised against him. They sounded uncomfortably close. He took another step backwards and lost his footing, a definite smell of gas in his nostrils. In an involuntary reflex action his finger tightened on the trigger and the Very pistol went off in his hand.

'Aaa... gh.'

The incandescent glow of the flare momentarily blinded him as it dementedly ricocheted back and forth off the mahogany walls of the companionway. In the same moment he felt several pairs of hands grab him, haul him up the companionway and bundle him over the side of the vessel

335

into freezing cold sea water. The buggers were going to drown him, he thought. A moment later there was a deafening, whooshing roar in his ear, before night was turned into day as the magnesium flare found its way into the galley and ignited the escaping gas.

It had taken Buerk and his party some time to make their way from the chambered cairn back to the beached rowing boat. Only wisps of mist now clung to the weed-covered rocks along the shoreline, the exposed stipes of sea-tangle revealed by the ebbing tide. Away to the north, a solitary fog bank, lit by moonlight, still hugged the sea like a ghostly glacier, but the light breeze that had stirred into life was steadily repulsing and dispersing it.

Save for a pronounced limp, Moss had emerged relatively unscathed from his fall and, to prevent any attempted escape, his hands had been tied behind his back. Awkwardly, he and Buerk now held the front corners of an improvised gurney made from the tarpaulin they had found inside the cairn. On this makeshift stretcher lay a semi-conscious Crawley, with Cant and Dick bearing his weight at the rear. Munro led the way, accompanied by Janet and Hilary, who, fortified with the remainder of Dick's flask, both appeared to have made a speedy recovery.

As they picked their way along the shore by moonlight there was a sudden blaze of light from the *Sundance* offshore. Buerk had been expecting some kind of show, but even he was totally unprepared for what happened next. It brought the whole party to a jolting halt. Under the bright light of what seemed like a firework display, they saw a figure dragged unceremoniously to the rail of the *Sundance* and dispatched overboard before other figures leapt to join it in the water.

'That's Wally,' Moss called out, rounding on his startled captors. 'Those buggers are trying to drown him.'

The next second the *Sundance* erupted in a huge explosion punctuated by a jet of flame shooting skywards. The entire craft seemed to disintegrate before their eyes. In an instantaneous knee-jerk reaction they threw themselves to the ground, unceremoniously pitching Crawley from his makeshift stretcher and causing him to yelp in pain. Dick appeared to have time to heroically fling himself over Janet Maltby.

Buerk gazed in awe at the spectacle. 'When you ask these Japanese boys to create a diversion,' he said, 'they really take you at your word.'

'You can say that again,' Dick said. He was still clinging protectively to Janet Maltby. Something about Dick's demeanour left Cant nursing a suspicion that his apparent heroism had not been entirely motivated by altruism.

Moss glared accusingly at Buerk as they each struggled to their feet with varying degrees of ease. 'They're trying to drown Wally,' he said. 'Are you lot just going to stand there and do nothing?'

'You've certainly changed your tune,' Buerk said, 'but you've got it wrong. Those guys have probably just saved your pal's life.' Out of the corner of his eye he saw that Dick was helping Janet to her feet, the look of gratitude she shot his sound man doing nothing to improve his temper.

Wally broke the surface gasping from the sudden shock of immersion in cold sea water. Coughing up saltwater, he struck out blindly at the two Japanese camera crew on either side of him, convinced that they were about to drag him down again. He did not at first understand why they kept yelling at him and gesticulating for him to move away from the *Sundance* so urgently.

It was not until the explosion threatened to burst his eardrums and he felt the breath of a fiery dragon that he realised how close he had come to oblivion. Not that he was entirely safe yet, for a blazing film of diesel oil had suddenly transformed a swathe of the sea into a new hazard for swimmers. Finally grasping the seriousness of his position, he allowed himself to be dragged towards the safety of the *Mallimack*.

A few minutes later he felt a boathook dig into his colourful sweater, ruining it beyond redemption, as Lachie hauled him unceremoniously onto the fishing boat's gently heaving deck. Wally lay there for some time, gasping for breath and retching miserably from the acrid smoke in his lungs, before helping hands half-carried, half-dragged him into the wheelhouse. 'This is the last bloody straw,' he said. 'I need to talk to that copper.'

Lachie's first concern was to pick up the men in the water. He had taken his boat closer to the *Sundance*, now reduced to isolated islands of smouldering flotsam, than sanity alone would allow. Mercifully none of the film crew had been injured and other losses were reduced to a minimum. Most of the hardware had been mock-ups of the real thing; only the underwater camera had been real, and that had made it back safely. Wally and his two rescuers had been the last men to be hauled on board.

Holding the boat against the ebbing tide, Lachie had to wait another ten minutes for Buerk and his party to climb aboard from their dinghy before he could head for the old pier and a good stiff drink. His daily routine of twenty crab pots up and twenty pots down, repeated at numerous offshore locations, had been enlivened over the last twenty-four hours. With a wry smile, he thought he was ready to slip back into that familiar routine. He'd had more than enough excitement to last him for a while.

CHAPTER THIRTY-ONE

A fine drizzle cast a pall over the airport terminal buildings which the orange glow from the distant city skyline failed to disperse. Dr Nathaniel Truelove, Principal of New Metropolitan University, strode out of the international arrivals door of the airport's terminal building and headed towards the waiting taxi rank, his mood in keeping with the weather. Before the return flight he had completed an exhausting schedule of meetings aimed at recruiting potential students to the university and attracting donations from former students who had made it big in the world of commerce and industry, and holding talks about setting up some outreach courses for local students.

He was aware that his modest success would attract welcome dollars to offset the dwindling grants allotted by decision makers (a misnomer if ever there was one) at the Department of Education. They had themselves never known what it was like to provide adequate higher education from substantially reduced resources. As well as those recruited from overseas, Truelove wanted to do more for the disadvantaged at home, but he realised there was only so much one man could do.

He frowned as a vaguely familiar figure detached itself from the deep shadows and walked towards him, proffering a share of the umbrella he held aloft. 'Dr Truelove?'

340

Caught a little off-guard, the principal hesitated uncertainly. 'Ye... s?'

'Frank Prior of the *Mercury*.' As the shadowy figure moved into the light, Truelove recognised the journalist both as a trustworthy and insightful reporter of the facts and as a fellow member of the amateur dramatic society where Prior had the part of Banquo in 'the Scottish Play'.

'Of course,' he said. 'Sorry, Frank. I was miles away. For a moment there I thought I'd seen a real ghost.'

Prior smiled. 'Spotted you emerging from the doorway and thought you were a little ahead of schedule,' he said. 'Look, I've got my car here. Can I offer you a lift home?'

Truelove shot an appraising glance at the taxi queue and then at his would-be Good Samaritan. 'That's very civil of you, Frank,' he said, accepting with a weary smile. 'Managed to catch an earlier flight, but I take it you didn't drive all the way out here just on the off-chance of giving me a lift.'

Prior acknowledged the implied question with a faint smile. 'I was seeing my niece off to a package holiday in the sun.' As he steered Truelove towards the car park, his smile broadened. 'To be absolutely truthful there are some issues I'd like to discuss with you: off the record, of course. First, though, how was the trip? I trust it proved profitable?'

Truelove sighed wearily. 'On a balance sheet, I dare say it'll look profitable enough,' he said. 'Off the record, I can't help thinking this sort of thing's wasted time and effort. We're fiddling while the country burns. We need to gear our whole society to social need, not personal greed. We...'

He sighed again. 'Sorry. The answer to your question was, I suppose, "needs must".'

Prior nodded sympathetically, choosing his moment as he halted at his car and unlocked the door for Truelove. 'I know and applaud where you stand on a perceived alienation in society, but I confess I was hoping to have a quiet word with you about quite another matter.' He got into the driving seat before adding, 'I rather think perhaps it's also symptomatic of our present ills.'

Once the ticket barrier had released them onto the motorway Truelove glanced curiously at the journalist. 'All right, Frank,' he said. 'Enough of this cryptic stuff. What's on your mind?'

Prior cleared his throat. 'I don't suppose you could possibly have heard on the ether that your deputy principal, Hornblower, called a press conference this afternoon?'

'No, I slept most of the way back. What was it about?'

'According to Hornblower, your university television unit has not only sighted, but filmed the supposedly extinct great auk in Papa Westray.'

For a split second Truelove hesitated, then his theatrical training came to his rescue. A less perceptive observer than Prior might have noticed nothing amiss. 'Did Hornblower offer any proof of this discovery?' he asked with studied calmness.

Prior shook his head. 'Not as such. There was the promise of video evidence to come, but no one, and I mean no one, is able to confirm the great auk's existence. I talked to a contact in nearby Westray who expressed complete disbelief at the possibility; ventured to suggest it was likely to be either another hoax – they apparently had one a number of years back – or downright idiocy from whoever was in charge.'

'The television unit, you say?' Truelove took a moment to mentally run through the personnel that might be involved and weighed up the two possibilities. 'Was young Angus Buerk involved?'

'With the filming, yes, but Hornblower made it clear that Fred Crawley and the Golightly woman were the principals in this cast.'

Truelove decided that the alternatives Prior's contact had laid out were equally viable. 'Hornblower is a damn fool,' he said finally.

Prior eyed him shrewdly. 'You knew nothing about it – the trip to the Orkneys or the press conference?'

Truelove shook his head as his eyes rolled heavenwards. *'There's no art to find the mind's construction in the face.'*

Prior grinned. 'Can I quote you on that?'

Truelove shook his head again. 'This conversation was off the record, remember?'

Prior smiled ruefully. 'Right.'

'However,' Truelove added with a bleak smile, 'just then I was quoting the Bard. I couldn't possibly stop you doing likewise.'

For Buerk and Munro it was to be a long and busy night. They had thanked Yamadori and his crew for their help and obtained a copy of the underwater video footage. They struggled back to the overcrowded cottage in the early hours. There was, however, much work still to do. Munro at once set up an interview with the remaining two kidnappers.

Seeing the game was up, Moss reluctantly admitted his part in Goldfiever's schemes. Over a mug of soup (made by Lucretia), Wally sat huddled with a blanket around his shoulders and started to plead a more passive role in the proceedings. To avoid any later retractions, Buerk had arranged to have the entire interview captured on camera. Prompted by Munro, it soon became clear that Goldfiever was indeed the mastermind behind it all. Both men were downright condemnatory of the increasingly ruthless methods of his hired assassin, Nordmann.

It had gone bad right from the start with Nordmann's heavy-handed approach. He and Moss had been dispatched by Goldfiever to recover the video McGrath had stolen. They had approached the *Loch Tredwell* unseen in the inflatable, but Vinnie had refused to reveal the video's hiding place. They had resorted to violence. The blowtorch had been Nordmann's idea. He poured paraffin on the deck around McGrath and threatened to light it. The plan backfired dramatically when he failed to control the blowtorch and managed to set fire to the cabin. Realising that McGrath would point the finger at them, Nordmann impetuously killed him using his favoured method. Moss had been furious with him but realised there was nothing he could do but flee the scene.

Goldfiever had also come up with the idea of kidnapping Janet Maltby to force through his takeover bid with TMG. He sent Nordmann along with Moss and Wally, mainly to get Nordmann out of town, but also to stiffen their resolve. The assassin proved more hindrance than help. He took exception to the naturalist photographer, Mavis Meadows, taking photographs of the *Sundance* moored alongside Janet Maltby's yacht over on Westray. Her actions might well have been innocent enough but he resented anyone encroaching on his space. When she then took the ferry ahead of them across to Papa Westray, he was already looking out for her.

Wally dropped the other two off in their inflatable to make landfall on the beach at the Knap of Howar. He remained on board the *Sundance*, keeping in touch by radio. Meadows was there to snap their landing but, alas, not discreetly enough. Nordmann and Moss rumbled her and pursued her to the hide at Hyndgreenie. Instead of simply holding her prisoner with the other intended captives, Nordmann reacted to some insult and a carefully aimed kick by sticking his knife into her. He then became further enraged when unable to recover his prized possession. When Wally alerted them by radio to the fact Janet Maltby had set sail from Westray for Papay, they could not completely cover their tracks before they had to launch the dinghy and play out the distress flare ruse to get on board.

Becoming aware of Buerk's interest, Moss had planned to add him to the list of captives. Again, Nordmann had overplayed his hand by trying to kill him. He then demonstrated another regrettable talent: this time for harbouring lecherous intentions towards their target hostage, Janet Maltby. After that, one disaster seemed to follow another until it was almost a relief to be through with the whole business.

After taping the confessions, mobile phones fairly hummed with communications to people who might reasonably have been expected to be abed. Janet Maltby spoke briefly but emotionally to her father, who was most definitely not asleep. Her news gladdened his heart and immediately set in motion a chain of events that would abruptly end any further talks of merger with Ned Goldfiever's SLIME outfit.

Munro spoke briefly to Lennox and subsequently suffered no compunction in waking up the Black Douglas to tell him the good news that his long-held dream of charging Goldfiever with fostering and abetting murder was again back on the agenda. Despite the late hour, that seemed to please him, but it took her considerably longer to win him round to the idea that Buerk not only was off the hook but had played a significant part in enabling the villains to be brought to book. From the smile on her face as she replaced the receiver, there was no doubting the satisfaction that the opportunity to put her senior officer straight had personally afforded her.

Next, Buerk risked calling his principal who had only just arrived home, beset with problems that were not of his own making. Already, forewarned by Prior, he had been obliged to hold the press at bay while considering his own position. He had promised a news statement the following day. Buerk went into meticulous detail with him, not only about what had taken place in reality, but about how it might best be presented to press and academic colleagues alike. The relief and gratitude in Truelove's voice was almost palpable.

Then Munro contacted Chief Inspector Howie, who promised a helicopter at first light bearing himself, Dr

Mackie, who was carrying out the post-mortem on Meadows at Kirkwall, and a uniformed escort for the prisoners. Conveniently, there happened to be a team of Royal Navy divers on a courtesy visit to Scapa to facilitate the underwater recovery of Nordmann's body (and Lachie's oxygen tank). The chief inspector decided that this time he would personally supervise proceedings, relieving Munro of such tedious chores. He also offered to organise the secure return of Wally and Moss to Chief Superintendent Douglas.

Finally there was the small matter of arranging for an air ambulance to ferry the hapless Crawley directly to hospital in Inverness.

THURSDAY

CHAPTER THIRTY-TWO

Lennox and Traynor watched from her Polo as Watt's assistant librarian arrived punctually to enter the library. A skittish breeze plucked at the hem of Jacqueline's skirt and sent the previous night's accumulated debris from the nearby Chinese takeaway eddying into shadowed corners. A low window ledge and an overhanging roof made it an attractive corner for teenagers to gather.

Lennox shifted in her seat behind the wheel to study Jacqueline. 'It certainly wasn't her face we saw on the TV,' she said.

Traynor shook his head in agreement. 'Much too skinny, that one. Anyway, I'm still having a hard time believing that the guy who's been knocking eight bells out of his fellow citizens is our local librarian. Now you're telling me the other perp might be one as well?'

She felt the back of her head gingerly and gave a rueful smile. 'No need to remind me how delicate the situation is,' she said. 'It still hurts, and in places a dose of aspirin can't reach.'

Traynor grimaced. 'The Black Douglas is not one for sympathy.'

Her mouth tightened into a thin line. 'He's nothing if not predictable,' she said. 'We need to try to rectify the situation for our own sakes. It's a matter of professional pride, Danny.'

'Right.' Across the road the lights came on inside the library and the big door was opened. 'Time to go to work,' he said.

As he made to leap from the car, Lennox caught him by the arm. 'Take it easy, Danny,' she said. 'No need to go through the window now the door's open. Some cooperation from this girl could be really handy.'

He shot her an apologetic grin. 'I hear you, boss,' he said.

Jacqueline was shelving the previous night's returns and almost leapt in the air when Lennox tapped her on the shoulder and held out her warrant card. 'Miss Jacqueline Smith?'

For just a moment Lennox thought she caught a flicker of colour spreading across the pale cheeks. Her eyes were red too, as though she had been crying.

'Yes,' she said.

'Detective Sergeant Lennox. This is my colleague, Detective Constable Traynor. We'd like to ask you a few questions.'

Jacqueline seemed to recover herself. 'This is about Harv... I mean, Mr Watt?'

Lennox glanced around her. A down-and-out had shuffled in from the street and picked up a newspaper, but he seemed more interested in what was going on between them. Meeting her steely gaze, he hastily ducked his head behind the newspaper. Out the corner of her eye she saw McManus drift in and begin to browse the unsorted returns shelf. He glanced briefly in her direction and winked. She shot him a warning glare and, with an eloquent shrug, he ambled into the reference room.

'Is there somewhere we can talk?' Lennox asked.

Jacqueline frowned. 'We can go into the staffroom, but this is hardly a convenient time. I'm on my own until noon.'

'What happens then?'

Jacqueline shrugged. 'If they're to be believed, headquarters say they'll send someone to cover.'

Traynor leaned threateningly towards her. 'If it's more convenient,' he said, 'we could always close the library and have our little chat at the station.'

Jacqueline looked from one to the other and sniffed. 'Let's get this over with.' She led the way into the staffroom.

Lennox took in the worn table and chairs and the battered saucepan on the small cooker. A dark red substance had congealed around one of the burners and a faint smell of cabbage hung in the air. 'Cosy,' she said.

'Life in the fast lane,' Traynor added.

Jacqueline sniffed again. 'Tell me about it,' she said.

Lennox took the proffered seat and came straight to the point. 'We're trying to identify Mr Watt's accomplice.'

'Accomplice!' Jacqueline's mouth puckered. 'That's bloody rich.'

Lennox eyed her sharply. 'That's not how it struck you?'

'You lot have so got the wrong end of the stick,' she said. '*She* led him by the nose.'

'Come on,' Traynor said. 'That's not how everyone else appears to see it.'

Jacqueline sniffed yet again. Lennox was beginning to wonder whether she had a cold. 'They don't know what I've seen and heard.'

Lennox exchanged a brief look with Traynor. 'We believe this lady has a habit of visiting the library around closing time.'

Jacqueline gave a bitter laugh. 'Took you long enough to work that out,' she said. 'She's destroyed Harvey, that's for sure. Not that it doesn't serve him right for allowing her to work out her depraved fantasies on him like that. It's... it's disgusting.'

'Oh, yes?' Traynor said. 'What sort of fantasies might they be?'

Jacqueline spat the words at him as though they were infectious. 'Sexual fantasies, of course.'

'You mean to say they had sex in the library?'

'In this very room. She led him by the nose, whipped him like a dog.' The floodgates had opened now and they could not have stopped Jacqueline if they had tried. 'I saw some of the marks on him,' she said. 'He could hardly walk afterwards. I don't know how he had the strength to hit these people.'

So that was it, Lennox thought. The eternal triangle. 'Who was she, Jacqueline?'

The assistant librarian bit her lip. 'You won't ask me to testify in court, will you? I'd never get another job in a library if I did.'

'It may not come to that,' Lennox said. Despite the visceral surge of excitement inside her, she forced herself to

352

stay calm. 'With corroborating evidence we might persuade her to own up.'

'It's still a civilised society,' Traynor said. 'Give or take the odd pockets of violence around fast-food outlets.'

Jacqueline hesitated a moment further, as if savouring the moment. 'It's Vera Goodnight,' she said. 'She's the one who led Harvey astray. This was her idea from beginning to end.'

Lennox glanced at Traynor, whose look of astonishment mirrored her own. 'Let me be absolutely clear about this,' she said. 'You're talking about Vera Goodnight, the director of cultural and recreational services?'

Jacqueline made a small grimace of satisfaction. 'The very same.'

'Do you happen to have her photograph anywhere?' Lennox asked.

'There's one in the last issue of the library review,' Jacqueline said. 'We've got copies on the counter.'

When she was gone, Traynor whispered in Lennox's ear. 'You do know Vera Goodnight has some powerful friends?' he said. 'One of whom happens to be Chief Superintendent Douglas.'

Lennox looked at him calmly and said, 'I know, Danny, but he won't go against hard evidence. Now, there's a man with a ponytail in the reference room. Ask him to come in here, will you?'

Traynor looked at her, opened his mouth to speak, then decided against it and left.

Jacqueline returned with the magazine, closely followed by Traynor and McManus. On the inside of the cover there was a full-page photograph of Vera Goodnight in a smart business suit. Lennox presented it to McManus.

'Is this the woman you saw enter the library at closing time?'

McManus studied the picture, then placed two fingers to block out the hair and chin. 'I'd recognise those eyes and cheekbones anywhere,' he said. 'They're the same as those in the TV mugshot as well.'

Lennox turned to Jacqueline. 'Mind if I keep this copy?'

'Be my guest.'

'Thanks,' Lennox said. 'You've been most helpful.'

There were beads of moisture in the corners of Jacqueline's eyes. 'My pleasure.'

They had reached the front door when Jacqueline called, 'Sergeant Lennox.'

Lennox turned to see the assistant librarian come towards her with a baseball bat held gingerly by the middle.

'I found this in the cupboard earlier,' Jacqueline said. 'I hope I haven't destroyed any fingerprints.'

Lennox carefully took the bat from her. 'Now that's what I call hard evidence,' she said. 'That was very public-spirited of you, miss. Thank you.'

'Yeah, right,' Jacqueline said.

When Lennox looked back, Jacqueline was already at the stacks shelving books.

McManus caught up with her at the door and spoke softly in her ear:

'*Heav'n has no rage, like love to hatred turn'd,*
'*Nor hell a fury, like a woman scorn'd.*'

She turned to stare at him. 'Very poetic, Mr McManus,' she said.

He shrugged. 'Not me. Congreve.'

CHAPTER THIRTY-THREE

A brisk south-westerly wind herded skeins of cumulonimbus into towering folds that promised rain before the morning was out. The windsock strained at its mast as the small group of people huddled together, seeking what shelter they could against the solitary building. They watched the small private aircraft wobble slightly as it dropped down through the cloud ceiling, level out and land on the tiny and surprisingly busy airfield.

A tall man with an erect bearing emerged and came smartly down the steps of the aircraft.

'That's Sir Rankin Maltby,' Buerk said to Munro standing beside him. She was awaiting the arrival of the Royal Navy chopper which would bring Chief Inspector Howie, Dr Mackie and the navy diving team. The air ambulance had already arrived and departed to Inverness with Crawley aboard.

Together they watched Janet run towards her father and embrace him before she turned to point in their direction. One arm still around his daughter, Sir Rankin approached with a purposeful stride. There were dark circles around his eyes from lack of sleep, but they shone with gratitude as he beamed at each in turn.

'Detective Inspector Munro... Angus, I owe both of you a considerable debt of gratitude. You saved both my daughter's life and my company. There must be something I can do for you in return.'

'There's no need for that, sir,' Munro said modestly. 'All in the line of duty, as my governor might say.'

'Some of us wouldn't say no to a lift home, though,' Buerk added with a winning smile.

Sir Rankin's laugh was that of a man from whom a heavy burden had been lifted, but Janet turned to her father, her face now more serious. 'There is another reason for giving Angus a lift, Dad,' she said. 'His crew have collected some interesting video footage. I think it could be edited into a rather eye-catching programme – better still if we can put it together in time for tonight's edition of *Today in Action.*'

Sir Rankin's eyebrows shot up as he looked at his daughter. 'Well, if you think it's up to snuff for our top current affairs programme, we'd better have a look at it.' He glanced quizzically at Buerk. 'I take it Angus would like to be in on the act?'

'I wouldn't dream of excluding him,' Janet said.

Buerk beamed at the pair of them. 'It'd be my pleasure.'

As Cant and Dick filed on board Sir Rankin's plane, Lucretia, who had come out to the airfield with her brother, announced in an uncharacteristically subdued tone that she had decided to stay on for a few days with Hilary. 'I think I need some private time for meditation,' she announced. 'I feel lately things have rather got on top of me.'

Buerk nodded gravely. 'I'll let Truelove know,' he said. 'I'm sure he'll understand.'

357

As they watched Hilary and Lucretia walk off arm in arm, Munro leaned towards Buerk. 'I'd like you to meet my boss when we're both back in town,' she said.

He smiled. 'Is that a personal wish or merely a polite way of saying I'm required to accompany you to the station to help with your enquiries?'

She leaned closer. 'I want to see the look on his face when you explain to him exactly what persuaded your deputy principal to send you to Papa Westray.'

'You do realise it's only going to confirm his worst opinion about us academics?'

'I have a nasty suspicion you're every bit as devious as he is,' she said. 'Matter of fact, I'm counting on it.'

'Anything else you're counting on?' he asked.

'Let's just say I'm not counting any chickens,' she said. 'When the dust settles over this case and Goldfiever is behind bars, I'm going to take some time off. I know Sir Rankin has already made you an offer you simply can't refuse. What I don't know is how you're going to contend with all this media attention. Let's just wait and see how it all pans out.'

CHAPTER THIRTY-FOUR

The inaugural meeting of the new board of governors, comprising heads of the various faculties of New Metropolitan University and invited captains of industry from the city and its environs, was going on satisfactorily under Principal Truelove's chairmanship. There had been a few sticky moments at the beginning, as some members shifted uncomfortably in their seats at what he had to say, which was no more than he had intended.

'Like a few others before me,' he had said, 'I hold the view that the major problem in society today is alienation. People feel alienated because they find themselves the victims of forces beyond their control in our society. They feel frustrated by having little say in determining their own destinies.

'There is, however, a particular form of alienation. I mean alienation *from humanity*. The prevailing sense of values in our society dehumanises some people, making them insensitive, even ruthless in their dealings with fellow humans. They become self-centred and grasping. The irony is that these people are often considered the leaders of society. Yet, all the while, they are scrambling for position, trampling roughshod on some, viciously backstabbing others, all in pursuit of personal glory and success.'

At this point some members took this personally and became involved in a heated exchange over the deputy principal's ill-considered press conference. There was even a determined attempt to call for Hornblower's immediate resignation, but Nathaniel Truelove managed to persuade his board that such a move would not be in the best interests of the university as a whole – at least, not in the immediate future. He rather stressed his last two words.

Truelove surveyed the room with a gaze that brooked no further interruption. He continued, 'I am glad to report, however, that not everyone in our university has been acting purely out of self-interest. There are individuals who have taken on board the issue of corporate responsibility, setting aside self-interest for the good of our institution. Man is a social being, these individuals would maintain. Real fulfilment for such a person lies in serving his fellow citizen. A great university such as ours ought to foster such fulfilment. It has always been my earnest desire that we should be in the vanguard, setting the example for others to follow. A small beginning has been made.'

Nathaniel Truelove paused to make a theatrical gesture towards the television monitor already in place in the corner of the boardroom.

'I am pleased,' he continued, 'indeed, thrilled to tell you this evening that one young man has shown himself more than willing to adopt these ideals. That young man is Angus Buerk.'

Truelove paused to take a sip of water, conscious of the buzz of expectation in the room.

'I'm proud to announce that the Thistle Media Group have endowed a chair in educational television to this university in perpetuity and *Professor* Angus Buerk is to be installed as its first recipient. This appointment is in recognition of the role he has played not only in thwarting a hostile takeover bid, enabling the company to remain proudly and nationally independent, but also in helping our own police force to solve some heinous crimes. Finally, it is in recognition of his personal acceptance of corporate responsibility for this university.'

There was a general outbreak of applause from the board, even from the most grudging of the ex-Queen's faction, which only subsided as Truelove held up his hand for silence to allow him to continue. 'I am also delighted to tell you I have just received word from the Education Office that, in recognition of the new spirit of enterprise abroad in our university, they will be increasing our research grant for the first time in a decade.'

This time the applause went on unabated for a full three minutes, allowing Ms Dewdrop, Truelove's secretary, ample time to come in and remind him that the scheduled television programme was due to begin.

'Members of the board,' Truelove resumed, 'I propose a short interlude in the proceedings to allow us to view the screening of a television documentary by the Thistle Media Group's still-independent channel, highlighting the kind of enterprise to which I earlier referred.'

He leaned forward to switch on the monitor with a triumphant flourish. The board collectively relaxed and allowed itself to be transported to a seemingly idyllic island where seabirds wheeled and soared above sea-washed cliffs to opening titles and soothing introductory music.

Feeling anything but soothed and wishing that she could be transported far from her present position, Vera Goodnight was wearing out the carpet in front of her TV screen and could scarcely concentrate on the early-evening news programme. She was aware, however, of some blonde bimbo of a presenter, introducing TMG's *Today in Action* in front of a scenic backdrop portraying the massive rock slabs of Mull Head. Vera was only too aware that her own life was very much on the rocks.

'Many of you may have felt that the age of romance and chivalry has been left behind by a materialistic society,' Janet Maltby began. 'A society which is full of "I'm all right, Jack"s.'

Vera glared bitterly at the screen and said with some feeling, 'You can say that again.' To clarify her precarious legal position, she had tried to get in touch with Victor Parkes, QC, but had been told by his secretary that he was out (though Vera knew damn well that Parkes was skulking in his office) and going to be busy for some time prosecuting a case against Ned Goldfiever. Trust a lawyer to weasel out of commitment.

She had learned that Harvey Watt had decided to come clean about his 'reluctant association with his domineering partner' in their recent premeditated attacks on a Fat Friar fast-food outlet. This after a visit from the mousey Jacqueline, who had apparently persuaded him that it was in his own interests to do so. Vera also clutched in her hand a note from the council's chief executive informing her of her immediate suspension from duty following 'yet unspecified allegations concerning the corruption of a subordinate colleague'. The nerve of the wimp. He needed a good whipping!

Just as the presenter smiled knowingly at her in a big close-up, Vera caught sight of DS Lennox and DC Traynor walking up the drive to her house. Angrily she switched off the television, knowing she would simply have to take the rap. Who knows, she thought, some jail time might even prove interesting. Her body gave a little shiver at the thought just as there was a loud knock at the door.

Following his own share of knocks, Crawley lay in a hospital bed unable to move. With his left leg in traction and a protective collar around his neck, he was in considerable physical discomfort. All that, however, was nothing compared to the mental anguish he was being forced to endure while viewing the TMG news programme on the television set. His primary care nurse had obligingly wheeled the TV into place in front of his bed in an attempt to cheer him up.

He lay helplessly as the attractive female lead, whom he recognised as Janet Maltby, continued:

'You may also have felt that academic research was the dry and dusty preserve of timid, aloof eggheads with little grasp of the real world. You could have been excused for thinking this only if you had never met Angus Buerk.'

As the screen portrayed Buerk on the end of a long cable, dramatically scaling a sea cliff with a limp Crawley over his shoulder, Miss Maltby continued in voiceover:

'While some of his colleagues were quite literally falling down on the job, the charismatic television director's daring rescue of his "fellow citizen" in peril was merely his way of limbering up for a tilt at organised crime.'

Crawley groaned inwardly. To his pain-wracked mind the voiceover came across as a sickening hagiography at his expense. It was typical of the unfeeling arrogance of Cant and Dick to have filmed the entire incident without ever cracking a light that they had done so. The thought made him shake his head in dismay, only to instantly regret his action as he winced in sudden agony at the excruciating pain in his neck.

Some considerable distance away from Crawley, Hornblower also regarded Buerk as a major pain in the neck, which no amount of rose-hip wine could eradicate. In his case, he scowled at a portable television set as he sat in his rose arbour, his favourite corner of the whole garden. Somehow, he ought to have known that viewing the programme would be the final indignity, but some hypnotic influence that Buerk seemed to hold over him had compelled him to do so. Unable to forsake his beloved ramblers threading through the trelliswork at such a critical time, he had run out an extension cable to the small set at the appointed hour.

Hornblower had been 'grounded' by Truelove to await his fate, which even now was being debated by the university's board of governors. He was under strict instructions to say absolutely nothing to anyone, least of all the press.

Moving gently to and fro on the swing seat in the sanctuary of his arbour, Hornblower would from time to time turn away from the screen to snip at the dead heads of a few blown roses with a pair of secateurs. At first his actions were fitful, but with every passing second they became more frequent and forceful as his anger mounted. The seat began to move more rapidly as he reached on the back swing to snip viciously at a mildewed flower stalk. 'Damn you, Buerk,' he said aloud. 'Trust you to come up smelling of roses.'

Snip. Swing.

'And damn you, Crawley,' he snarled. This time he brandished the secateurs above his head with only half an eye on the small screen. 'A few feathers flutter in your face and you end up throwing yourself over the edge of a cliff and landing us all in the soup – bird's nest, of course.'

Snip. Snip. Swing. Swing. It never occurred to Hornblower that he might himself be getting dangerously near the edge.

Lucretia appeared on-screen in the act of planting a grateful kiss on Buerk's cheek.

Snip. Snip. Snip. The seat was rocking on its base.

'And damn you... you treacherous harridan. You and your lunatic brother are both off your rockers.'

On-screen, the camera had now zoomed into a close-up of the presenter confidentially addressing her public:

'There has been considerable public speculation, and even more private debate in the groves of academe, on why this expedition was originally conceived, let alone sanctioned. A small but strident minority of academics – mainly from rival institutions, it has to be said – claim that it was an *ingenuous* blunder by one academic...'

The film briefly cut to a clip of Hornblower holding forth at his ill-fated press conference.

'...who suspended rational belief to dispatch a TV crew to capture on film a bird known to have been extinct for almost two centuries.'

Hornblower glowered at the screen, then turned to make a ferocious lunge at a low-growing branch covered in black spot.

SNIP. The swing had just reached its apogee.

Suddenly there was a blinding flash of blue light, accompanied by a violent jolt and a searing pain running up his arm. In the same instant he felt himself being propelled out of his seat at a rate accelerated by the downswing and unceremoniously dumped in a dense thicket of thorn-covered roses.

When he came to, he felt nothing. He was lying on his back, a curious scorching smell hanging in the air. This eventually gave him the clue to what had happened. In an excess of zeal with the secateurs he had inadvertently cut through the cable snaking through the garden, which had in turn given him a shock and set fire to the trellis. By the time he began to regain his senses, a pall of sooty smoke hanging over blackened briar stumps was all that remained of his beloved rose arbour.

Buerk lay back on the sofa, watching the programme unfold towards its denouement, hands clasped behind his head, feet propped up on a cushion. When Sir Rankin had seen the raw material that had been gathered, he had immediately decided they should devote the entire programme to it. The invitation to work alongside the programme's director on the material had been a no-brainer for Buerk, once he had obtained permission from his principal. TMG's legal team had already cleared the item with the police. Buerk had found the cooperative experience to be a rewarding one. The possibility of further commissions boded well for the future of the department.

On-screen, Janet Maltby was winding up her programme:

'The principal of Metropolitan University insists that the real reason for the expedition was an *ingenious* tip-off to a kidnapping that ultimately led to the solving of two brutal murders and the exposure of attempted commercial blackmail, both clearly linked to the same man.'

At this point an unflattering insert of Ned Goldfiever was flashed up on the screen before Janet gave a shrug of her attractive shoulders.

'We may never know which of these two disparate claims is the absolute truth, but let it be recorded that thanks to the ingenuity and initiative of Angus Buerk and his crew, in close collaboration with Detective Inspector Rowena Munro...'

An insert of Munro and Buerk standing very close together appeared on screen (when had that been taken?).

'...their principal's claim has been upheld.'

The presenter bestowed a knowing parting smile on her audience.

'Let it also be stated for the record that the enterprising Angus Buerk did achieve the seemingly impossible goal set for him by his deputy principal – even if you, the viewer, feel our conclusion is strictly for the birds.'

The screen cut from a small offshore skerry to an underwater shot of a sunken yacht. The camera began to zoom in on the bow. Gradually the letters of the nameplate filled the screens of viewers all over the land. *THE GREAT AUK* was revealed before the final credits began to scroll over it.

Buerk waited for his name and that of the university to appear among the credits, then switched off, yawned and stretched his body on the sofa. The downside of all this, he thought, was that now he had been appointed professor, he would have to attend subsequent board meetings which would almost certainly prove to be duller than the one going on at that moment.

He was jolted out of his musings by the ringing telephone. A familiar voice brought him fully awake when he answered.

'You are a clever one, Angus,' Rowena Munro said. 'I really enjoyed the programme.'

'It made us look damn good,' he conceded.

'We *are* damn good,' she insisted.

'How did the Black Douglas react after I left?'

'He's cock-a-hoop. It's even possible he's finally got you out of his system. On the downside, this is going to make him impossible to work with.'

'Some things never change,' he said. 'It can't have done your own promotion chances any harm either.'

'One step at a time. Remember, fulfilment lies in service to one's fellow citizen.'

'How could I ever forget?'

'At least I've been confirmed as DI.'

'No more acting?'

'You should know, Angus, I was never acting.'

'I knew you were for real right from the start.'

'That's good to hear.'

'You'll also be pleased to know, according to Elvira, my planet is no longer retrograde.'

'About time, too. Say, I'm not disturbing any wild celebration party, am I?'

'No party. Matter of fact, I'm all on my lonesome.'

'That can't be right.'

'Now that you mention it, I have to agree.'

'I was wondering if you'd like to join me for a celebratory glass of champagne?'

'Sounds good. Where?'

'My place. I've got a bottle of Mount Ida Shiraz dusted off and some venison defrosting should the need arise later.'

'I like the sound of *later*,' he said. 'Give me ten minutes – no, five.'

'Angus.'

'Yeah?'

'Just get here in one piece.'

He was already reaching for his jacket.

www.ingramcontent.com/pod-product-compliance
Lightning Source LLC
Chambersburg PA
CBHW072340020726
47506CB00004B/949